消失的地平线

LOST HORIZON

英国文学卷

中英对照全译本

[英] 詹姆斯·希尔顿 著
James Hilton

盛世教育西方名著翻译委员会 译

盛世教育西方名著翻译委员会
主　任：杜　毅　尚慧诗
本册委员：孙　怡　郝佳庆　周思敏
　　　　　帅君枚　宁雪扬

世界图书出版公司
上海·西安·北京·广州

图书在版编目（CIP）数据

消失的地平线：英汉对照 /(英) 希尔顿 (Hilton,J.) 著；盛世教育西方名著翻译委员会译. ——上海：上海世界图书出版公司，2012.7

ISBN 978-7-5100-4601-8

Ⅰ.①消… Ⅱ.①希… ②盛… Ⅲ.①英语－汉语－对照读物②长篇小说－英国－现代 Ⅳ.①H319.4：I

中国版本图书馆 CIP 数据核字(2012)第 100418 号

消失的地平线

[英] 詹姆斯·希尔顿 著

盛世教育西方名著翻译委员会 译

上海世界图书出版公司 出版发行

上海市广中路 88 号

邮政编码 200083

北京兴鹏印刷有限公司印刷

如发现印刷质量问题，请与印刷厂联系

（质检科电话：010-84897777）

各地新华书店经销

开本：880×1230 1/32 印张：9 字数：270 000

2012 年 7 月第 1 版第 1 次印刷

ISBN 978-7-5100-4601-8/H·1192

定价：18.80 元

http://www.wpcsh.com.cn

http://www.wpcsh.com

前　言

　　通过阅读文学名著学语言，是掌握英语的绝佳方法。既可接触原汁原味的英语，又能享受文学之美，一举两得，何乐不为？

　　对于喜欢阅读名著的读者，这是一个最好的时代，因为有成千上万的书可以选择；这又是一个不好的时代，因为在浩繁的卷帙中，很难找到适合自己的好书。

　　然而，你手中的这套丛书，值得你来信赖。

　　这套精选的中英对照名著全译丛书，未改编改写、未删节削减，且配有权威注释、部分书中还添加了精美插图。

　　要学语言、读好书，当读名著原文。如习武者切磋交流，同高手过招方能渐明其间奥妙，若一味在低端徘徊，终难登堂入室。积年流传的名著，就是书中"高手"。然而这个"高手"，却有真假之分。初读书时，常遇到一些挂了名著名家之名改写改编的版本，虽有助于了解基本情节，然而所得只是皮毛，你何曾真的就读过了那名著呢？一边是窖藏了50年的女儿红，一边是贴了女儿红标签的薄酒，那滋味，怎能一样？"朝闻道，夕死可矣。"人生短如朝露，当努力追求真正的美。

　　本套丛书的英文版本，是根据外文原版书精心挑选而来；对应的中文译文以直译为主，以方便中英文对照学习，译文经反复推敲，对忠实理解原著极有助益；在涉及到重要文化习俗之处，添加了精当的注释，以解疑惑。

　　读过本套丛书的原文全译，相信你会得书之真意、语言之精髓。

　　送君"开卷有益"之书，愿成文采斐然之人。

CONTENTS

目 录

PROLOGUE

引子

CIGARS had burned low, and we were beginning to sample the disillusionment that usually afflicts old school friends who have met again as men and found themselves with less in common than they had believed they had. Rutherford wrote novels; Wyland was one of the Embassy secretaries; he had just given us dinner at Tempelhof – not very cheerfully, I fancied, but with the equanimity which a diplomat must always keep on tap for such occasions. It seemed likely that nothing but the fact of being three celibate Englishmen in a foreign capital could have brought us together, and I had already reached the conclusion that the slight touch of priggishness which I remembered in Wyland Tertius had not diminished with years and an M.V.O. Rutherford I liked more; he had ripened well out of the skinny, precocious infant whom I had once alternately bullied and patronized. The probability that he was making much more money and having a more interesting life than either of us, gave Wyland and me our one mutual emotion – a touch of envy.

The evening, however, was far from dull. We had a good view of the big

雪茄微弱地燃烧着。我们也开始感觉到一丝幻灭的气息，这种感觉经常使再次碰面的老同学感到难过，因为他们发现彼此的共同之处比他们原本确信的还要更少一些。卢瑟福在写小说，而维兰德是大使馆的一位秘书，他刚在特贝霍夫饭店请我们吃饭，可我认为这并不令人兴高采烈，他带有身为一个外交官在某些场合必须随时保持的镇静。这似乎不算什么，只是 3 个未婚的英国男子在一个外国首都碰到了一起而已。而且，我已经得出了一个结论，那就是我所记得的维兰德身上那种微弱的自命不凡并没有随岁月而消失；我更喜欢卢瑟福，他已经从一个皮包骨头、像个小大人似的孩子蜕变得非常成熟，当年我可是交替着欺负他和保护他呢！他比我们当中的任何一个人都挣得多，并过着更有意思的日子，这种可能性带给我和维兰德一种同样的妒忌。

但那晚绝不单调。当来自中欧各个地方的飞机降落时，我们好好

Luft-Hansa machines as they arrived at the aerodrome from all parts of Central Europe, and towards dusk, when arc-flares were lighted, the scene took on a rich, theatrical brilliance. One of the planes was English, and its pilot, in full flying-kit, strolled past our table and saluted Wyland, who did not at first recognize him. When he did so there were introductions all around, and the stranger was invited to join us. He was a pleasant, jolly youth named Sanders. Wyland made some apologetic remark about the difficulty of identifying people when they were all dressed up in Sibleys and flying-helmets; at which Sanders laughed and answered: "Oh, rather, I know that well enough. Don't forget I was at Baskul." Wyland laughed also, but less spontaneously, and the conversation then took other directions.

Sanders made an attractive addition to our small company, and we all drank a great deal of beer together. About ten o'clock Wyland left us for a moment to speak to someone at a table nearby, and Rutherford, into the sudden hiatus of talk, remarked: "Oh, by the way, you mentioned Baskul just now. I know the place slightly. What was it you were referring to that happened there?"

Sanders smiled rather shyly. "Oh, just a bit of excitement we had once when I was

地欣赏了这些汉莎航空公司的巨大飞行器。临近黄昏，当机场的弧光灯都点亮时，一种丰富的、充满戏剧性的光辉景象呈现出来。其中一架飞机是英国的。身着全套航空服的飞行员溜达着经过我们的桌子，并和维兰德致意。最初维兰德没有认出他来，当他想起时，便向周围所有人引荐，这位陌生人被邀请加入我们。他是个讨人喜欢的年轻人，名叫桑达斯。维兰德向他致歉，表示当他们这些人穿着航空服、戴着飞行帽时很难辨认出来。对这些，桑达斯哈哈大笑，回答道："哦，的确，我非常了解，不要忘了我在巴斯库待过。"维兰德也哈哈大笑起来，但不大自然，随即我们的交谈便转到了其他话题上。

桑达斯的加入使我们这个小群体变得更吸引人，我们所有人一起喝了许多啤酒。大约10点钟，维兰德离开了我们一会儿，到旁边的一张桌子去找某人说话。然后卢瑟福突然在谈话的间隙插进来说道："哦，顺便说一句，你刚才提到了巴斯库，我稍稍了解这个地方，你是不是指那里发生了什么事？"

桑达斯相当害羞地笑了笑："哦，仅仅是我在那里服役时发生

in the Service." But he was a youth who could not long refrain from being confidential. "Fact is, an Afghan or an Afridi or somebody ran off with one of our buses, and there was the very devil to pay afterwards, as you can imagine. Most impudent thing I ever heard of. The blighter waylaid the pilot, knocked him out, pinched his kit, and climbed into the cockpit without a soul spotting him. Gave the mechanics the proper signals, too, and was up and away in fine style. The trouble was, he never came back."

Rutherford looked interested. "When did this happen?"

"Oh – must have been about a year ago. May, 'thirty-one. We were evacuating civilians from Baskul to Peshawar owing to the revolution – perhaps you remember the business. The place was in a bit of an upset, or I don't suppose the thing could have happened. Still, it *did* happen – and it goes some way to show that clothes make the man, doesn't it?"

Rutherford was still interested. "I should have thought you'd have had more than one fellow in charge of a plane on an occasion like that?"

"We did, on all the ordinary troop-carriers, but this machine was a special one, built for some maharajah originally – quite a stunt kind of outfit. The Indian Survey people had been using

的令人兴奋的小事而已。"但他毕竟是个年轻人，无法保守机密太长的时间，"事情是这样的，一个阿富汗人，要么就是别的什么人劫持了我们的一架客机逃跑了，然后就是你所能想象出来的那些非常棘手的事了，这是我曾经听到的最厚颜无耻的事。那家伙截住了飞行员，将他一拳击倒，然后脱掉他的航空服，神不知鬼不觉地爬进了驾驶舱，给了地面机械师以恰当的信号，再以很棒的架势起飞，之后便顺利飞走了。问题是，他再也没有飞回来。"

卢瑟福看起来非常感兴趣，"这是什么时候发生的？"

"哦，那肯定是一年前了，大约是 1931 年的 5 月，因为革命的爆发，我们正从巴斯库向白沙瓦疏散平民，也许你还记得这桩事，那个地方处于有点混乱的状态，否则我无法设想这种事能够发生，但它的确发生了。它以某种方式表明人们看衣识人，难道不是吗？"

卢瑟福依旧很感兴趣，"我还觉得在那种类似的情况下，你们应该会让不止一个人来负责一架飞机呢。"

"我们是这样，所有普通的军用运输机都如此，但这架飞机是一个特例，起初它是为一些印度邦主建造的、一种相当小型的设备，印度勘探人员在克什米尔做高海拔

it for high-altitude flights in Kashmir."

"And you say it never reached Peshawar?"

"Never reached there, and never came down anywhere else, so far as we could discover. That was the queer part about it. Of course, if the fellow was a tribesman he might have made for the hills, thinking to hold the passengers for ransom. I suppose they all got killed, somehow. There are heaps of places on the frontier where you might crash and not be heard of afterwards."

"Yes, I know the sort of country. How many passengers were there?"

"Four, I think. Three men and some woman missionary."

"Was one of the men, by any chance, named Conway?"

Sanders looked surprised. "Why, yes, as a matter of fact. 'Glory' Conway – did you know him?"

"He and I were at the same school," said Rutherford a little self-consciously, for it was true enough, yet a remark which he was aware did not suit him.

"He was a jolly fine chap, by all accounts of what he did at Baskul," went on Sanders.

Rutherford nodded. "Yes, undoubtedly…but how extraordinary… extraordinary…" He appeared to collect himself after a spell of mind-wandering.

飞行时一直使用它。"

"那你是说这飞机从来没有抵达过白沙瓦了？"

"据我们目前所能发现到的，它从来没有到达过那里，也没有在其他任何地方降落，这架飞机有相当可疑的问题，当然如果那个家伙是个土著，他可能把飞机开进山里，考虑把那些乘客当做人质以便敲诈。我推测他们不知什么原因全部死了。前线有很多区域，可能是在那里坠落了，然后就再也听不到什么消息了。"

"没错，我知道这类地方，飞机上有多少乘客？"

"我认为有四位，三位男士和一位修女。"

"其中的一位男士是不是碰巧叫康维？"

桑达斯看起来非常吃惊，"哦，是的，事实上，'荣耀'的康维——你知道他吗？"

"我和他在同一所学校。"卢瑟福略微不自然地说，虽然绝对是真的，但他意识到他说这句话并不合适。

"通过他在巴斯库全部的所作所为来看，他是一个非常棒的小伙子。"桑达斯继续说。

卢瑟福点点头，说："没错，毋庸置疑……但多么不同寻常……不同寻常……"他似乎在一阵着魔般的冥想之后回过神来，然后他

Then he said: "It was never in the papers, or I think I should have read about it. How was that?"

Sanders looked suddenly rather uncomfortable, and even, I imagined, was on the point of blushing. "To tell you the truth," he replied, "I seem to have let out more than I should have. Or perhaps it doesn't matter now – it must be stale news in every mess, let alone in the bazaars. It was hushed up, you see – I mean, about the way the thing happened. Wouldn't have sounded well. The Government people merely gave out that one of their machines was missing, and mentioned the names. Sort of thing that didn't attract an awful lot of attention among outsiders."

At this point Wyland rejoined us, and Sanders turned to him half-apologetically. "I say, Wyland, these chaps have been talking about 'Glory' Conway. I'm afraid I spilled the Baskul yarn – I hope you don't think it matters?"

Wyland was severely silent for a moment. It was plain that he was reconciling the claims of compatriot courtesy and official rectitude. "I can't help feeling," he said at length, "that it's a pity to make a mere anecdote of it. I always thought you air fellows were put on your honor not to tell tales out of school." Having thus snubbed the youth, he turned, rather more graciously, to

说，"这件事从来没有出现在报纸上，否则我觉得人们应该已经读过有关它的报道，这是怎么回事？"

突然，桑达斯看起来相当不安，我觉得他甚至脸都有些红了，"告诉你们实情吧，"他回应道，"我似乎已经说出了我不应该说的东西，但可能现在也没有什么关系了，毕竟那算是陈年旧事了，我把它重新公布出来吧；你看，它曾经被隐瞒过，我的意思是关于这件事发生的情况，听起来不算特别好。政府方面的人也仅仅是宣布他们的一架飞机失踪了，然后提了一下飞机的名称而已，这类事不会吸引局外人非常大的注意力。"

就在这时，维兰德再次加入我们当中，桑达斯半带歉意地转向他，"哎，维兰德，这些家伙刚才一直讨论'荣耀'的康维，恐怕我泄露了巴斯库事件，我希望你不要介意这件事。"

维兰德严肃地沉默了一会儿，非常明显，他要对同胞彬彬有礼，还要与官员的严正形象协调一致。"我忍不住觉得，"他详细说，"只将这事作为一件奇闻轶事是一种遗憾，我总觉得你们这些空军家伙是依靠荣誉维持生命的，不会将这件事说出去。"如此斥责过这个年轻人之后，他便和蔼地转向卢瑟福，"当然，你的心情可以理解，

Rutherford. "Of course, it's all right in your case, but I'm sure you realize that it's sometimes necessary for events up on the Frontier to be shrouded in a little mystery."

"On the other hand," replied Rutherford dryly, "one has a curious itch to know the truth."

"It was never concealed from anyone who had any real reason for wanting to know it. I was at Peshawar at the time, and I can assure you of that. Did you know Conway well – since school days, I mean?"

"Just a little at Oxford, and a few chance meetings since. Did *you* come across him much?"

"At Angora, when I was stationed there, we met once or twice."

"Did you like him?"

"I thought he was clever, but rather slack."

Rutherford smiled. "He was certainly clever. He had a most exciting university career – until war broke out. Rowing Blue and a leading light at the Union and prizeman for this, that, and the other – also I reckon him the best amateur pianist I ever heard. Amazingly many-sided fellow, the kind, one feels, that Jowett would have tipped for a future premier. Yet, in point of fact, one never heard much about him after those Oxford days. Of course the War

"另一方面，"卢瑟福索然无味地回应道，"人类具有一种好奇心，渴望去了解真相。"

"对于任何一个真正想要了解它缘由的人，这事从未被遮掩过，我当时就在白沙瓦，对此我能够向你保证。你非常了解康维吗？我是说，从学生时代开始。"

"在牛津时只是有一点了解，从那以后，我们有一些机会碰面，你和他常见面吗？"

"在安哥拉，我在那里驻扎期间见过一两次。"

"你喜欢他吗？"

"我觉得他很聪明，可相当懒散。"

卢瑟福微微一笑，"他当然很聪明，他具有最令人兴奋的大学生涯，直到战争爆发。他获得过划船蓝色奖章，在学生会里是位重要人物，他是这两方面奖励的获得者。我也认为他是我曾经听过的最出色的业余钢琴家，是一位令人惊叹的多面手，会让人觉得这类人将像乔伊特那样，成为未来首相候选人的顶尖人物。但其实，牛津时代以后，我就再也没听到过他的消息，

cut into his career. He was very young and I gather he went through most of it."

"He was blown up or something," responded Wyland, "but nothing very serious. Didn't do at all badly, got a D.S.O. in France. Then I believe he went back to Oxford for a spell as a sort of don. I know he went East in 'twenty-one. His Oriental languages got him the job without any of the usual preliminaries. He had several posts."

Rutherford smiled more broadly. "Then of course, that accounts for everything. History will never disclose the amount of sheer brilliance wasted in the routine decoding F.O. chits and handing round tea at legation bun-fights."

"He was in the Consular Service, not the Diplomatic," said Wyland loftily. It was evident that he did not care for the chaff, and he made no protest when, after a little more badinage of a similar kind, Rutherford rose to go. In any case it was getting late, and I said I would go, too. Wyland's attitude as we made our farewells was still one of official propriety suffering in silence, but Sanders was very cordial and he said he hoped to meet us again sometime.

I was catching a transcontinental train at a very dismal hour of the early morning, and, as we waited for a taxi, Rutherford asked me if I would care to spend the

当然，是战争打断了他的事业。他非常年轻，我推测他多半是去参加战争了。"

"他被炸伤了，要不就是发生了什么事。"维兰德回答，"可没什么非常严重的事，他混得不算糟糕，在法国还获得了个"区参谋"的军衔，然后，我确信他回牛津大学从事了一段时间的指导教师的工作，他在 1921 年去了东方，他掌握的那几种东方语言令他不用任何常规的准备便获得了工作，他有好几种职务。"

卢瑟福更加爽朗地笑了起来，"那么说，这就是一切的理由！历史永远不会揭露荒废在解码野战指令情报这种例行公事中，以及公使馆茶会中分发茶水时那些纯粹的光彩。"

"他当时是在领事馆的服务部门，并非外交部。"维兰德傲慢地说道，很明显，他不愿意开玩笑，而且，当听到类似这些更有揶揄味道的话之后，他也不作抗议。卢瑟福站起身来准备走，不管怎么说，天色已晚，我说我也应该走了。当我们告辞时，维兰德的态度依然是一种官方的得体的冷静和彬彬有礼，但桑达斯却非常热情，他说他希望以后能再次见到我们。

天还没亮，我就去赶横贯大陆的火车。当我们等出租车时，卢瑟福问我是否愿意到他下榻的旅店

interval at his hotel. He had a sitting room, he said, and we could talk. I said it would suit me excellently, and he answered: "Good. We can talk about Conway, if you like, unless you're completely bored with his affairs."

I said that I wasn't at all, though I had scarcely known him. "He left at the end of my first term, and I never met him afterwards. But he was extraordinarily kind to me on one occasion. I was a new boy and there was no earthly reason why he should have done what he did. It was only a trivial thing, but I've always remembered it."

Rutherford assented. "Yes, I liked him a good deal too, though I also saw surprisingly little of him, if you measure it in time."

And then there was a somewhat odd silence, during which it was evident that we were both thinking of someone who had mattered to us far more than might have been judged from such casual contacts. I have often found since then that others who met Conway, even quite formally and for a moment, remembered him afterwards with great vividness. He was certainly remarkable as a youth, and to me, who had known him at the hero-worshipping age, his memory is still quite romantically distinct. He was tall and extremely good looking, and not only

来消磨这小段时光。他说他有一个起居室，我们能够聊聊天，我说这对我来说再合适不过了，于是他回答道："那太好了，我们可以聊聊关于康维的事，如果你愿意的话，除非你对他的事已经彻底厌烦了。"

我说虽然我对康维几乎不了解，可我对他的事根本谈不到厌烦。"在我大学第一学期的期末，他便离开了，之后我再也没有见过他。但曾经有段时期，他对我格外好，我是个新生，这世上不存在什么理由会让他这么做。虽然这仅仅是些毫无价值的琐事，但我一直铭记着。"

卢瑟福表示同意："是的，我也非常喜欢他，尽管如果用时间来衡量的话我很少能见到他。"

然后是一段有点令人难堪的冷场。在这期间，显而易见，我们两个人都在回想一位对彼此来说都很重要的人，这不是可以通过两三次的交谈就能说得出的。从那会儿开始，我经常发现，其他碰到康维的人，甚至是在相当正式的场合仅有一面之缘的人，也会对他记得非常清楚。作为一位青年人，他当然是不同凡响，而对我来说，在崇拜英雄的年纪认识了他，对他的记忆还停留在相当独特的浪漫色彩的阶段。他身材修长，模样俊好，不仅对各种体育运动都很精通，而

excelled at games but walked off with every conceivable kind of school prize. A rather sentimental headmaster once referred to his exploits as "glorious", and from that arose his nickname. Perhaps only he could have survived it. He gave a Speech Day oration in Greek, I recollect, and was outstandingly first-rate in school theatricals. There was something rather Elizabethan about him – his casual versatility, his good looks, that effervescent combination of mental with physical activities. Something a bit Philip-Sidneyish. Our civilization doesn't often breed people like that nowadays. I made a remark of this kind to Rutherford, and he replied: "Yes, that's true, and we have a special word of disparagement for them – we call them dilettanti. I suppose some people must have called Conway that, people like Wyland, for instance. I don't much care for Wyland. I can't stand his type – all that primness and mountainous self-importance. And the complete head-prefectorial mind, did you notice it? Little phrases about 'putting people on their honor' and 'telling tales out of school' – as though the bally Empire were the fifth form at St. Dominic's! But, then, I always fall foul of these sahib diplomats."

We drove a few blocks in silence, and then he continued: "Still, I wouldn't have

且可以拿走学校中可以想象出来的每一类奖项。曾经有一次，一位相当易动感情的校长引用了"荣耀"一词来评价他的成绩，然后由此便产生了他的绰号。可能只有他才能够配得上这个绰号。我回忆起他曾在一年一度的授奖演讲日上用希腊语演讲，他也是学校戏剧表演中最杰出的一流演员；他身上那不经意的多才多艺，他那英俊的外表，他那精神与身体活力的兴奋结合令他相当像伊丽莎白女王一世时代的杰出人物，还有一点儿像菲利普·西德尼，在当今，我们的文明却很少能培养出类似他这样的人才。我用这种想法给卢瑟福做了评论，他回应道："没错，千真万确。对他们这样的人有一个特殊的贬义词，我们称他们为'浅薄的涉猎者'。我认为比如像维兰德那样的人一定会这样称呼康维。我不怎么喜欢维兰德，我不能容忍他的风格，完全一副循规蹈矩和自视过高的样子。他头脑里完全是长官的意志，你注意到了吗？他那关于'将人们置身于他们应得的荣誉中'和'将事情泄露出来'的一小段评论，仿佛可恶的皇帝是来自圣多美尼克教堂的第五种类型，我总是与这类外交官先生犯冲突。"

我们在沉默中驶过了几个街区。然后他继续说道："但是我并

missed this evening. It was a peculiar experience for me, hearing Sanders tell that story about the affair at Baskul. You see, I'd heard it before, and hadn't properly believed it. It was part of a much more fantastic story, which I saw no reason to believe at all, or well, only one very slight reason, anyway. *Now* there *are* two very slight reasons. I daresay you can guess that I'm not a particularly gullible person. I've spent a good deal of my life traveling about, and I know there are queer things in the world – if you see them yourself, that is, but not so often if you hear of them second-hand. And yet…"

He seemed suddenly to realize that what he was saying could not mean very much to me, and broke off with a laugh. "Well, there's one thing certain – I'm not likely to take Wyland into my confidence. It would be like trying to sell an epic poem to *Tit-Bits*. I'd rather try my luck with you."

"Perhaps you flatter me," I suggested.

"Your book doesn't lead me to think so."

I had not mentioned my authorship of that rather technical work (after all, a neurologist's is not everybody's "shop"), and I was agreeably surprised that Rutherford had even heard of it. I said as much, and he answered: "Well, you see, I was interested, because amnesia was Conway's trouble at one time."

没有错过这个晚上。对我而言，这是个特别的经历，桑达斯讲了那个关于在巴斯库的事情，你知道，我曾经听说过，可不太相信，这仅仅是一个更加稀奇古怪的故事的一部分，我根本找不到什么理由去相信这事，或者，仅有一个非常微不足道的理由。而现在有两个非常微不足道的理由了。我敢说，你能够猜出来我并非一个易上当受骗的人。我花了我生命的一大部分时间四处旅行，而且我知道世界上存在稀奇之事——倘若你自己亲眼所见，那就是真的，可倘若你只是道听途说，则不太会相信，但是……"

他似乎突然意识到他所说的话对我来说没有特别大的意义，就停了下来，哈哈大笑，"那么，有件事是肯定的——我不喜欢让维兰德知道我的私房话，那就像试着推销一部史诗给《珍闻》杂志。我更愿意和你说说。"

"也许你太恭维我了。"我说。

"你的书并未让我如此认为。"

我并未提及过我那些有点技术性工作的作者身份（毕竟一个精神病诊所并非人人需要的"商店"），而且我非常惊奇卢瑟福甚至听到过这些事。我同样将想法都告诉他。卢瑟福回答道，"没错，你看。我很感兴趣，因为丧失记忆曾一度是康维的困扰。"

We had reached the hotel and he had to get his key at the bureau. As we went up to the fifth floor he said: "All this is mere beating about the bush. The fact is, Conway isn't dead. At least he wasn't a few months ago."

This seemed beyond comment in the narrow space and time of an elevator ascent. In the corridor a few seconds later I responded: "Are you sure of that? How do you know?"

And he answered, unlocking his door: "Because I traveled with him from Shanghai to Honolulu in a Jap liner last November." He did not speak again till we were settled in armchairs and had fixed ourselves with drinks and cigars. "You see, I was in China in the autumn on a holiday. I'm always wandering about. I hadn't seen Conway for years. We never corresponded, and I can't say he was often in my thoughts, though his was one of the few faces that have always come to me quite effortlessly if I tried to picture it.

I had been visiting a friend in Hankow and was returning by the Pekin express. On the train I chanced to get into conversation with a very charming Mother Superior of some French sisters of charity. She was traveling to Chung-Kiang, where her convent was, and, because I knew a little French, she seemed to enjoy chattering to me about her work and

我们抵达旅店后，他得去办公室拿钥匙。当我们上到第五层楼时，他说："所有这些仅仅是些拐弯抹角的东拉西扯罢了，事实是康维并没有死，至少他几个月前还没有死。"

在电梯上升的短暂时间和狭窄空间里似乎不适合聊这些。进入走廊的几秒钟之后，我回应道："你肯定吗？你怎么知道的？"

他回答着，同时将门打开，"因为去年11月，我曾和他一起乘一架日本客机从上海前往檀香山旅行。"他没有再讲话，直到我们在椅子上安坐好，倒上酒，点好雪茄。"你知道，秋季我一般在中国度假，我总是四处闲游。而我已经很多年没见过康维了，我们从不联系，我不能说他经常出现在我的思绪里，但如果我试着想象一下的话，他是为数不多的总是能毫不费力地跃入我脑海的几张脸孔之一。

我当时在汉口拜访一个朋友，然后乘北京的快车返回，在火车上碰巧和一位非常迷人的法国慈善姐妹会的女修道院院长交谈甚欢。她要前往重庆，她的修道院在那里，因为我知道一点法语，她似乎非常愿意和我喋喋不休地讨论她的工作以及日常事宜。其实，我对普通的教会机构没有多少同情心，

affairs in general. As a matter of fact, I haven't much sympathy with ordinary missionary enterprise, but I'm prepared to admit, as many people are nowadays, that the Romans stand in a class by themselves, since at least they work hard and don't pose as commissioned officers in a world full of other ranks. Still, that's by the by. The point is that this lady, talking to me about the mission hospital at Chung-Kiang, mentioned a fever case that had been brought in some weeks back, a man who they thought must be a European, though he could give no account of himself and had no papers. His clothes were native, and of the poorest kind, and when taken in by the nuns he had been very ill indeed. He spoke fluent Chinese, as well as pretty good French, and my train companion assured me that before he realized the nationality of the nuns, he had also addressed them in English with a refined accent. I said I couldn't imagine such a phenomenon, and chaffed her gently about being able to detect a refined accent in a language she didn't know. We joked about these and other matters, and it ended by her inviting me to visit the mission if ever I happened to be thereabouts. This, of course, seemed then as unlikely as that I should climb Everest, and when the train reached Chung-Kiang I shook hands with genuine

可就像现在的很多人一样，我准备承认它们，就像罗马人独自站在自己的阶层中，因为他们至少工作努力，而不是在充满其他阶级的世界里装腔作势，就像被任命的长官一样。还有，顺便说一下，那位女士在对我谈论重庆的那所教会医院时，提及了一位几周前被送进医院的感冒患者，她们都觉得他一定是个欧洲人。尽管他无法说明自己的情况，也没有什么证件，他穿的是当地人的衣服，而且是最贫穷的那类人的衣服。当被修女们带进来时，他的确病得非常严重。他会讲一口流利的汉语，法语讲得也相当不错，火车上的这位同伴对我保证在他辨认出修女们的国籍之前，他也会与她们用纯正口音的英语沟通。我说我不能想象如此的场景，我含蓄地对于她能够判断她完全不理解的一门语言的口音是否纯正和她开玩笑，我们对于这件事还有其他的事开玩笑，最终以她邀请我去游览修道院而结束，如果我正好要去附近的话。若我去爬珠穆朗玛峰，这当然不太可能。当火车抵达重庆时，我怀着诚挚遗憾的心情与她握手道别，我们偶然的接触就此结束了。但我恰好在几小时之内又回到了重庆。火车在向前一两英里远的地方抛了锚，然后又非常困难地将我们退回车站，在那里我们得知替代的引擎不可能在 12 小时

regret that our chance contact had come to an end. As it happened, though, I was back in Chung-Kiang within a few hours. The train broke down a mile or two further on, and with much difficulty pushed us back to the station, where we learned that a relief engine could not possibly arrive for twelve hours. That's the sort of thing that often happens on Chinese railways. So there was half a day to be lived through in Chung-Kiang – which made me decide to take the good lady at her word and call at the mission.

"I did so, and received a cordial, though naturally a somewhat astonished, welcome. I suppose one of the hardest things for a non-Catholic to realize is how easily a Catholic can combine official rigidity with non-official broad-mindedness. Is that too complicated? Anyhow, never mind, those mission people made quite delightful company. Before I'd been there an hour I found that a meal had been prepared, and a young Chinese Christian doctor sat down with me to it and kept up a conversation in a jolly mixture of French and English. Afterwards, he and the Mother Superior took me to see the hospital, of which they were very proud. I had told them I was a writer, and they were simple-minded enough to be a-flutter at the thought that I might put them all

之内到达，这类事情在中国的铁路上经常发生。所以我这半天将会在重庆逗留——这让我决定应邀去修道院拜访那位很不错的女士。

"我真的去了，而且得到了热忱的欢迎，很自然地，她对我的到来感到些许讶异。我猜对一个非天主教徒来说，最难理解的事情之一就是一个天主教徒怎么能够将十足正式的刻板和非正式的随心所欲结合在一起，这太过复杂了吧？总之，这也没关系，那些修道的人们组成了相当快乐的群体。我到那里还不到一个小时，我就发现饭菜已经准备好了，一位年轻的中国基督教医生在我旁边坐下来。他一直用法语还有英语的混合体和我愉快地交谈，随后，他和女修道院长带我参观那所他们觉得非常自豪的医院。我告诉他们我是一位作家，他们太单纯了，以至于涌现出的第一个念头就是我会将他们全部写到书里。我们从病床旁边经过，那位医生逐一解释病例。那个

into a book. We walked past the beds while the doctor explained the cases. The place was spotlessly clean and looked to be very competently run. I had forgotten all about the mysterious patient with the refined English accent till the Mother Superior reminded me that we were just coming to him. All I could see was the back of the man's head; he was apparently asleep. It was suggested that I should address him in English, so I said 'Good afternoon,' which was the first and not very original thing I could think of. The man looked up suddenly and said 'Good afternoon' in answer. It was true; his accent was educated. But I hadn't time to be surprised at that, for I had already recognized him, despite his beard and altogether changed appearance and the fact that we hadn't met for so long. He was Conway. I was certain he was, and yet, if I'd paused to think about it, I might well have come to the conclusion that he couldn't possibly be. Fortunately I acted on the impulse of the moment. I called out his name and my own, and though he looked at me without any definite sign of recognition, I was positive I hadn't made any mistake. There was an odd little twitching of the facial muscles that I had noticed in him before, and he had the same eyes that at Balliol we used to say were so much more of a Cambridge blue

地方一尘不染，非常干净，看起来管理得非常完善。我已经将那个带有纯正英语口音的神秘病人遗忘得一干二净了，直到修道院院长提醒我，我们就要走近他了。我能够看见的全部就是这个人的后脑勺，显而易见，他睡着了，似乎有什么东西在提示我应该用英语与他交谈，于是我说："Good afternoon。"这是我最先说出但并非原本想说的一个词。那个人突然抬头回答道："Good afternoon。"千真万确，他的口音是受过教育的。但我都没有时间对此感到惊奇，因为我已经将他认出来了，尽管他留了胡须，容貌整个变了，并且我们已经很长时间没有见过面了。他是康维，我肯定。但如果我停下来思考片刻，我很可能得出他不可能是康维的结论，幸运的是，我依靠着一时冲动而行动。我喊出了他的名字以及我自己的名字，尽管他抬眼看着我，没有任何认出我来的迹象，可我绝对确定我没有犯任何错误。他面部肌肉有轻微的古怪抽搐，之前我已经在他脸上注意到过，他还拥有那双与以前一样的双眼，在巴里欧时我们总是说在那其中剑桥蓝的成分比牛津蓝多一些。但除了这一切之外，他是一个不容易被弄错的人——让人见一次就会永远记住的人。当然，医生和修道院院长都格外兴奋。我告诉他们我认识这个

than an Oxford. But besides all that, he was a man one simply didn't make mistakes about – to see him once was to know him always. Of course the doctor and the Mother Superior were greatly excited. I told them that I knew the man, that he was English, and a friend of mine, and that if he didn't recognize me, it could only be because he had completely lost his memory. They agreed, in a rather amazed way, and we had a long consultation about the case. They weren't able to make any suggestions as to how Conway could possibly have arrived at Chung-Kiang in his condition.

"To make the story brief, I stayed there over a fortnight, hoping that somehow or other I might induce him to remember things. I didn't succeed, but he regained his physical health, and we talked a good deal. When I told him quite frankly who I was and who he was, he was docile enough not to argue about it. He was quite cheerful, even, in a vague sort of way, and seemed glad enough to have my company. To my suggestion that I should take him home, he simply said that he didn't mind. It was a little unnerving, that apparent lack of any personal desire. As soon as I could I arranged for our departure. I made a confidant of an acquaintance in the consular office at Hankow, and thus the necessary passport and so on were made

人，他是个英国人，是我的一位朋友，如果他认不出我，只可能是因为他完全丧失了记忆，他们相当震惊地表示同意我的观点，然后我们对他的病情进行了长时间的讨论。他们对于康维如何在这种条件下来到重庆无法作出任何提示。

"简而言之，我在那里待了两周，希望以某种或其他方法诱导他恢复记忆。我没有成功，可他又重获健康，我们聊了很多。当我相当坦率地告诉他我是谁、他又是谁时，他非常温顺，没有对此争辩。他的精神相当振奋，甚至以一种相当含糊的方式，表示很高兴有我陪伴。对于我应该带他回家的建议，他简单地说他不介意。这确有点失常，他很明显地缺乏任何一种个人欲望。我尽快安排好我们的离开。在汉口的领事办公室，我有个心腹知己。因此护照等随后的手续没有什么麻烦就弄好了。的确，对我而言，看在康维的分上，整件事似乎最好对公众加以隐瞒，不要成为报刊的头条，我很高兴我成功地做到

out without the fuss there might otherwise have been. Indeed, it seemed to me that for Conway's sake the whole business had better be kept free from publicity and newspaper headlines, and I'm glad to say I succeeded in that. It could have been jam, of course, for the press.

"Well, we made our exit from China in quite a normal way. We sailed down the Yangtse to Nanking, and then took a train for Shanghai. There was a Jap liner leaving for 'Frisco that same night, so we made a great rush and got on board."

"You did a tremendous lot for him," I said.

Rutherford did not deny it. "I don't think I should have done quite as much for anyone else," he answered. "But there was something about the fellow, and always had been – it's hard to explain, but it made one enjoy doing what one could."

"Yes," I agreed. "He had a peculiar charm, a sort of winsomeness that's pleasant to remember even now when I picture it, though, of course, I think of him still as a schoolboy in cricket flannels."

"A pity you didn't know him at Oxford. He was just brilliant – there's no other word. After the War people said he was different. I, myself, think he was. But I can't help feeling that with all his gifts he ought to have been doing bigger work. All that Britannic Majesty stuff isn't my idea

了这一点。否则这就会造成拥堵，当然，是指新闻媒体的。

"然后，我们以一种正常的方式离开了中国。我们乘船沿着长江前往南京，然后再乘火车到上海，当晚正好有一艘日本客轮要到圣弗朗西斯科，所以我们便急匆匆地上了船。"

"你为他做了相当多的事。"我说。

卢瑟福没有回绝，"如果为其他任何人，我认为我不会做这么多，"他回答道，"可这家伙身上有某些东西，某些难以解释的东西，但它令你乐于尽力帮助他。"

"没错，"我表示同意，"他具有一种独特的吸引力，一种令人愉悦的迷人气质。这种感觉我现在描绘起来都能记得，当然，尽管我还把他当成那个身着法兰绒板球衫的学生。"

"你在牛津不认识他是一种遗憾，他光彩夺目——没有其他的词汇了，战后人们说他不同了，我自己也认为他是变了，但我忍不住感觉以他全部的天赋，他应该从事更伟大的工作。所有大不列颠君主

of a great man's career. And Conway was – or should have been – *great*. You and I have both known him, and I don't think I'm exaggerating when I say it's an experience we shan't ever forget. And even when he and I met in the middle of China, with his mind a blank and his past a mystery, there was still that queer core of attractiveness in him."

Rutherford paused reminiscently and then continued: "As you can imagine, we renewed our old friendship on the ship. I told him as much as I knew about himself, and he listened with an attention that might almost have seemed a little absurd. He remembered everything quite clearly since his arrival at Chung-Kiang, and another point that may interest you is that he hadn't forgotten languages. He told me, for instance, that he knew he must have had something to do with India, because he could speak Hindostani.

"At Yokohama the ship filled up, and among the new passengers was Sieveking, the pianist, *en route* for a concert tour in the States. He was at our dining table and sometimes talked with Conway in German. That will show you how outwardly normal Conway was. Apart from his loss of memory, which didn't show in ordinary intercourse, there couldn't have seemed much wrong with him.

的职员，在我的想法里，都并非一个伟人应有的事业，而康维是一个伟人，或者说应该是一个伟人。你我二人都了解他，我并不觉得当我在说我们都不该忘记的那段经历时我在夸张。甚至当我和他在中国的中部地区碰面时，即使他的思维一片空白，他的过往是个谜团，但他身上仍具有那种吸引力的奇异精髓。"

卢瑟福怀旧地停顿了一下，然后继续说道："你能够想象，我们在客轮上重新找回了我们旧日的友情吗？我将我对他的了解尽可能多地告诉他，他全神贯注地聆听，可能有点荒谬。自从他抵达重庆之后，他对每一件事都记得相当清楚，另一点可能让你感兴趣的是，他并没有忘记那几门语言，比如，他告诉我说，他清楚他与印度一定有一些联系，因为他能说印度斯坦语。

"在横滨，船已经满了，在新来的乘客当中有一位叫清上近素的钢琴家，途经这里去美国做巡回演出，他在我们的餐桌上吃饭，偶尔用德语与康维聊天，这就能看出正常的康维是多么外向，除去他丧失了记忆之外，普通的交流无法表现出来他有什么异常。

"A few nights after leaving Japan, Sieveking was prevailed upon to give a piano recital on board, and Conway and I went to hear him. He played well, of course, some Brahms and Scarlatti, and a lot of Chopin. Once or twice I glanced at Conway and judged that he was enjoying it all, which appeared very natural, in view of his own musical past. At the end of the program the show lengthened out into an informal series of encores which Sieveking bestowed, very amiably, I thought, upon a few enthusiasts grouped round the piano. Again he played mostly Chopin; he rather specializes in it, you know. At last he left the piano and moved towards the door, still followed by admirers, but evidently feeling that he had done enough for them. In the meantime a rather odd thing was beginning to happen. Conway had sat down at the keyboard and was playing some rapid, lively piece that I didn't recognize, but which drew Sieveking back in great excitement to ask what it was. Conway, after a long and rather strange silence, could only reply that he didn't know. Sieveking exclaimed that it was incredible, and grew more excited still. Conway then made what appeared to be a tremendous physical and mental effort to remember, and said at last that the thing was a Chopin study. I didn't think myself it could be, and I wasn't

"在离开日本之后的几个晚上,清上近素被邀请到甲板上进行钢琴独奏会,康维和我都去聆听他演奏。当然,他弹得非常出色,有几首勃拉姆斯和史卡拉第的作品,还有很多肖邦的作品。我有一两次瞥了瞥康维,发现他对所有的音乐都很享受,他之前的音乐修养非常自然地牵引着他。在演出节目的最后,音乐会在一系列非正式的加演要求中延长着,清上近素对此非常和蔼地满足着,我认为会有一些狂热的乐迷在钢琴周围聚集着。他再次弹奏了肖邦的作品,他极其擅长肖邦的作品。最后他离开钢琴向后门走去,仍然被一群崇拜者尾随着,但很明显,他感觉已经为乐迷奉献了足够多了。与此同时,一件相当古怪的事发生了,康维坐到钢琴键盘前,弹奏了一段快速活泼的章节。我辨认不出来是谁的作品,可这却吸引清上近素以巨大的激动之情返回来,问这是什么曲子,在一段长长的且相当古怪的沉默之后,康维只回应了他不清楚。清上近素大喊着这简直难以置信,他越来越激动。然后,康维似乎在做体力和精神的巨大努力去回忆着,最终说那是一首肖邦的练习曲。我自己也觉得这首曲子不是肖邦的,因此当清上近素完全加以否认时,我一点都不惊奇。但康维对此突然变得异常恼怒,这令我非常吃惊,

surprised when Sieveking denied it absolutely. Conway, however, grew suddenly quite indignant about the matter – which startled me, because up to then he had shown so little emotion about anything. 'My dear fellow,' Sieveking remonstrated, 'I know everything of Chopin's that exists, and I can assure you that he never wrote what you have just played. He might well have done so, because it's utterly his style, but he just didn't. I challenge you to show me the score in any of the editions.' To which Conway replied at length: 'Oh, yes, I remember now, it was never printed. I only know it myself from meeting a man who used to be one of Chopin's pupils… Here's another unpublished thing I learned from him.'"

Rutherford studied me with his eyes as he went on: "I don't know if you're a musician, but even if you're not, I daresay you'll be able to imagine something of Sieveking's excitement, and mine, too, as Conway continued to play. To me, of course, it was a sudden and quite mystifying glimpse into his past, the first clew of any kind that had escaped. Sieveking was naturally engrossed in the musical problem, which was perplexing enough, as you'll realize when I remind you that Chopin died in 1849.

"The whole incident was so

因为直到那时，他对任何事情都不曾显现出一丝情绪。'我亲爱的伙计，'清上近素抗议道，'我清楚肖邦存世的每一件作品，我能向你保证他从来没有写过你刚刚弹奏的那首曲子。他极有可能写出这样的曲子，因为这完全是他的风格，可他就是没有写过，我要求你给我看看这个乐谱的任何一个版本。'对此，康维最终回应道：'哦，没错，我现在想起来了，这曲子从来没被印刷过，我仅仅是通过遇到过的一个人……他曾经是肖邦的学生……才知道这首曲子……这里还有另外一首我从他那里学来的未曾发表过的曲子呢。'"

卢瑟福用他的双眼打量我，然后继续说："我不清楚你是否是一个音乐家，可即使你不是，我也敢说你可以想象到清上近素的兴奋之情，还有当康维继续弹奏这首曲子时我的兴奋之情。当然，对我而言，那是对他过往的突然而又相当神秘的一瞥，是已经消失的东西的第一线索，清上近素自然全神贯注在这个音乐问题上，这问题足够令人困惑，当我提醒你肖邦早在1849年就去世了时，你就会意识到。

"整件事情如此深奥，在某种

unfathomable, in a sense, that perhaps I should add that there were at least a dozen witnesses of it, including a California university professor of some repute. Of course, it was easy to say that Conway's explanation was chronologically impossible, or almost so; but there was still the music itself to be explained. If it wasn't what Conway said it was, then what *was* it? Sieveking assured me that if those two pieces were published, they would be in every virtuoso's repertoire within six months. Even if this is an exaggeration, it shows Sieveking's opinion of them. After much argument at the time, we weren't able to settle anything, for Conway stuck to his story, and as he was beginning to look fatigued, I was anxious to get him away from the crowd and off to bed. The last episode was about making some phonograph records. Sieveking said he would fix up all arrangements as soon as he reached America, and Conway gave his promise to play before the microphone. I often feel it was a great pity, from every point of view, that he wasn't able to keep his word."

Rutherford glanced at his watch and impressed on me that I should have plenty of time to catch my train, since his story was practically finished. "Because that night – the night after the recital – he got back his memory. We had both gone to

意义上我也许应该加上至少十来个见证人，包括一位有些名望的加利佛尼亚大学的教授。当然，人们可以轻易地说康维的解释在年代学里完全不可能，或者几乎不可能；而且还有音乐本身也需要被解释。倘若情况不是康维所说的那样，那么又是什么情况呢？清上近素向我保证，倘若这两首曲子被发表了的话，6 个月之内它们便会成为每一个艺术大师的保留曲目，即使这是一种夸张的话，也表达了清上近素对这些曲子的观点。在争论了很长时间之后，我们不能解决什么问题，因为康维坚持他的看法，而且他开始看起来很疲乏了，我很焦急地带他从人群里出来，让他上床休息。最后的一件事大概就是做一些留声机录音。清上近素说他一抵达美国便会将全部的安排弄妥当；康维也作出他的承诺：在麦克风前演奏几首。我经常感觉，无论从哪方面来说，这都是一个巨大的遗憾，因为他没能遵守他的承诺。"

卢瑟福瞥了一眼手表，提醒我还有很充裕的时间去赶火车，因为他的故事实际上几乎结束了。"因为那天晚上——就在钢琴独奏会的当晚——他重拾了记忆。我们俩都躺在床上，我一直清醒着，他来

bed and I was lying awake, when he came into my cabin and told me. His face had stiffened into what I can only describe as an expression of overwhelming sadness – a sort of universal sadness, if you know what I mean – something remote or impersonal, a *Wehmut* or *Weltschmerz,* or whatever the Germans call it. He said he could call to mind everything, that it had begun to come back to him during Sieveking's playing, though only in patches at first. He sat for a long while on the edge of my bed, and I let him take his own time and make his own method of telling me. I said that I was glad his memory had returned, but sorry if he already wished that it hadn't. He looked up then and paid me what I shall always regard as a marvelously high compliment. 'Thank God, Rutherford,' he said, 'you are capable of imagining things.' After a while I dressed and persuaded him to do the same, and we walked up and down the boat deck. It was a calm night, starry and very warm, and the sea had a pale, sticky look, like condensed milk. Except for the vibration of the engines, we might have been pacing an esplanade. I let Conway go on in his own way, without questions at first. Somewhere about dawn he began to talk consecutively, and it was breakfast-time and hot sunshine when he had finished. When I say 'finished' I don't

到我的舱室将一切都告诉我。他的脸紧绷着，我只能用一种非常忧伤的表情来描述，一种普通的忧伤，如果你清楚我的意思的话——某种冷淡或是和个人无关的表情，一种无奈或是失意，或者是德国人称呼的什么东西。他说他能够记起每一样东西了，就在清上近素弹奏期间，记忆开始回到他脑海，尽管最后仅仅是以片段的形式。他在我床边坐了很长时间，我没有打搅他，让他用自己的方式告诉我。我说我非常高兴他恢复了记忆，倘若他不希望回忆起这些往事，我也会觉得很难过。他抬起头看了看，然后给了我一句我将一直视为不可思议的高度赞扬，'谢天谢地，卢瑟福，'他说，'你真具有想象力啊。'过一会儿，我穿好衣服，劝他也去穿好衣服，然后我们在甲板上散步。这是个宁静的夜晚，星光灿烂，非常温暖，大海是一幅苍白而粘腻的模样，就像浓缩的牛奶。如果不是引擎的震动，我们就像在广场上散步。我让康维以他自己的方式继续，最开始没有提问题。在接近黎明时，他开始滔滔不绝地讲。当他讲完时，已经是早餐时间，太阳也很炙热了。当我说'结束了'时，我的意思并非是在第一次交谈之后，他没有告诉我更多的事情，在接下来的 24 小时中，他又给了我很多非常重要的情况补充。他非常

mean that there was nothing more to tell me after that first confession. He filled in a good many important gaps during the next twenty-four hours. He was very unhappy, and couldn't have slept, so we talked almost constantly. About the middle of the following night the ship was due to reach Honolulu. We had drinks in my cabin the evening before; he left me about ten o'clock, and I never saw him again."

"You don't mean –" I had a picture in mind of a very calm, deliberate suicide I once saw on the mail boat from Holyhead to Kingstown.

Rutherford laughed. "Oh, Lord, no – he wasn't that sort. He just gave me the slip. It was easy enough to get ashore, but he must have found it hard to avoid being traced when I set people searching for him, as of course I did. Afterwards I learned that he'd managed to join the crew of a *banana-boat* going south to Fiji."

"How did you get to know that?"

"Quite straightforwardly. He wrote to me, three months later, from Bangkok, enclosing a draft to pay the expenses I'd been put to on his account. He thanked me and said he was very fit. He also said he was about to set out on a long journey – to the northwest. That was all."

"Where did he mean?"

"Yes, it's pretty vague, isn't it? A good many places lie to the northwest of

不高兴，无法入睡，所以我们几乎持续交谈。大约第二天半夜时分，客轮按时抵达旧金山，前一天的晚上我们在我的客舱里喝酒；大约10点钟他离开了，从此我再没见过他。"

"你的意思该不是……"我在头脑里勾画了一幅非常镇静、从容不迫的自杀画面。我曾经在从圣头港前往金斯敦的邮轮上见过。

卢瑟福哈哈大笑，"哦，我的上帝，不，他不是那类人。他仅仅是趁我不注意溜掉罢了，抵达岸边很容易，可如果我派人找他，他肯定会发现要避免被追踪是非常困难的。当然，我确实派人找了他，后来我获悉他加入一艘向南前往斐济的香蕉货船上成了船工。"

"你如何知道的呢？"

"相当直接，3个月之后他从曼谷给我写了一封信，附有一张汇票以便偿还我为他的开销，他很感谢我，还说他非常好，他也说了他准备启程前往西北进行一次长途旅行，就这些。"

"他说哪里了吗？"

"说了，非常模糊，不是吗？有很多地方位于曼谷西北方向，甚

Bangkok. Even Berlin does, for that matter."

Rutherford paused and filled up my glass and his own. It had been a queer story – or else he had made it seem so; I hardly knew which. The music part of it, though puzzling, did not interest me so much as the mystery of Conway's arrival at that Chinese mission hospital; and I made this comment. Rutherford answered that in point of fact they were both parts of the same problem. "Well, how *did* he get to Chung-Kiang?" I asked. "I suppose he told you all about it that night on the ship?"

"He told me something about it, and it would be absurd for me, after letting you know so much, to be secretive about the rest. Only, to begin with, it's a longish sort of tale, and there wouldn't be time even to outline it before you'd have to be off for your train. And besides, as it happens, there's a more convenient way. I'm a little diffident about revealing the tricks of my dishonorable calling, but the truth is, Conway's story, as I pondered over it afterwards, appealed to me enormously. I had begun by making simple notes after our various conversations on the ship, so that I shouldn't forget details; later, as certain aspects of the thing began to grip me, I had the urge to do more, to fashion the written and recollected fragments into

至柏林也是嘛。"

卢瑟福停顿一下，将我和他自己的杯子斟满。"这是个诡异的故事，或者是他令故事看起来如此，我无从获知。其中音乐的部分虽然令人迷惑，但并不像康维去那家中国教会医院的神秘事件令我如此感兴趣。"我说了这种观点。卢瑟福回答道："其实，这是同一问题的两个方面。""那么，他是如何前往重庆的呢？"我问道，"我觉得那晚在轮船上他一定将所有事情告诉你了。"

"他告诉了我一些情况，但对我而言，非常荒谬，在告诉你这么多之后，剩下的部分，我必须保密了。只能说那是一个相当长的故事，在你必须去赶火车以前，时间甚至都不够描述一个大概了。此外，还有个更方便的方法；虽然我对于展现我那并不怎么样的文学创作技巧有一些小困难，但事实是，康维的故事引人入胜，令我反复思考。我已经开始在我们那些各种各样的交谈之后记录简单的笔记，因此我就不会忘记一些细节。后来，当这个故事的某些方面开始紧紧抓住我时，我有了一种强烈欲望，想要做更多的事，想要将记录和收集的片断塑造为一个单一的叙述性故事。这个，我的意思并非

a single narrative. By that I don't mean that I invented or altered anything. There was quite enough material in what he told me: he was a fluent talker and had a natural gift for communicating an atmosphere. Also, I suppose, I felt I was beginning to understand the man himself." He went to an attaché case, and took out a bundle of typed manuscript. "Well, here it is, anyhow, and you can make what you like of it."

"By which I suppose you mean that I'm not expected to believe it?"

"Oh, hardly so definite a warning as that. But mind, if you *do* believe, it will be for Tertullian's famous reason – you remember? *quia impossible est.* Not a bad argument, maybe. Let me know what you think, at all events."

I took the manuscript away with me and read most of it on the Ostend express. I intended returning it with a long letter when I reached England, but there were delays, and before I could post it I got a short note from Rutherford to say that he was off on his wanderings again and would have no settled address for some months. He was going to Kashmir, he wrote, and thence "east." I was not surprised.

是我臆造或者更改了任何东西，在他告诉我的东西中，已经有了足够的素材，他是个口齿伶俐的谈话者，具有一种传达气氛的天赋，我也认为我开始理解他这个人了。"他拿过来一个公文包，掏出一捆打印的手稿，"那么，拿去吧，总之你随意处置吧！"

"通过你的话，我觉得你的意思是，不期待我相信这些？"

"哦，不要这么早确定，但请记住，如果你确实相信，那它将符合特图利尔的著名理由——你记得吗——天下没有不可能之事。这可能不是个很糟糕的论据，告诉我你对整个事件的想法。"

我带上这些书稿离开了，在去奥斯登的快车上阅读了其中的大部分。我本打算回到英国后将书稿还回去，并写封长信。但耽误了几天，我还没将信寄出去就收到了卢瑟福的一封短信，说他准备再次漫游了，几个月内都不会有固定的地址，信里写他准备前往克什米尔，也就是"东方"。我并不惊奇。

CHAPTER 1

第一章

DURING that third week of May the situation in Baskul had become much worse and, on the 20th, Air Force machines arrived by arrangement from Peshawar to evacuate the white residents. These numbered about eighty, and most were safely transported across the mountains in *troop-carriers*. A few miscellaneous aircraft were also employed, among them being a cabin machine lent by the maharajah of Chandrapore. In this, about 10 A.M., four passengers embarked: Miss Roberta Brinklow, of the Eastern Mission; Henry D. Barnard, an American; Hugh Conway, H.M. Consul; and Captain Charles Mallinson, H.M. Vice-Consul.

These names are as they appeared later in Indian and British newspapers.

Conway was thirty-seven. He had been at Baskul for two years, in a job which now, in the light of events, could be regarded as a persistent backing of the wrong horse. A stage of his life was finished; in a few weeks' time, or perhaps after a few months' leave in England, he would be sent somewhere else. Tokyo or Teheran, Manila or Muscat; people in his profession never knew what was coming.

5 月的第三周，巴斯库地区的局势变得更糟。20 号时，空军飞机按照安排，从白沙瓦抵达巴斯库以便疏散白人居民。疏散人数大约有 80 个，大多数人都被军用运输机安全转移，跨越了群山。有几架不同样式的飞机也加入进来，在它们当中有一架小型客机，是由印度禅达坡邦主借予使用的。大约上午 10 时，有 4 名乘客登上这架飞机：东方布道团的罗伯特·布琳克罗小姐，美国人亨利·巴纳德，领事赫夫·康维和副领事查尔斯·马林逊上尉。

这些名字随后出现在了印度和英国的报纸上。

康维，时年 37 岁，曾经在巴斯库待了两年，就目前为人所知的情况来看，他的工作可以被视为在赛马中压错了马匹，欲罢不能，而他生命中的一个阶段也应该结束了。几周以后，或者也许在英国休假几月以后，本来他会被派往其他的某个地方，东京或者德黑兰，马尼拉或是马斯喀特。从事他这种职业的人永远不清楚什么将会降临。

He had been ten years in the Consular Service, long enough to assess his own chances as shrewdly as he was apt to do those of others. He knew that the plums were not for him; but it was genuinely consoling, and not merely sour grapes, to reflect that he had no taste for plums. He preferred the less formal and more picturesque jobs that were on offer, and as these were often not good ones, it had doubtless seemed to others that he was playing his cards rather badly. Actually, he felt he had played them rather well; he had had a varied and moderately enjoyable decade.

He was tall, deeply bronzed, with brown short-cropped hair and slate-blue eyes. He was inclined to look severe and brooding until he laughed, and then (but it happened not so very often) he looked boyish. There was a slight nervous twitch near the left eye which was usually noticeable when he worked too hard or drank too much, and as he had been packing and destroying documents throughout the whole of the day and night preceding the evacuation, the twitch was very conspicuous when he climbed into the aeroplane. He was tired out, and overwhelmingly glad that he had contrived to be sent in the maharajah's luxurious airliner instead of in one of the crowded troop-carriers. He spread himself indulgently in the basket seat as the plane

他在领事馆工作已经有十来年了，这么长的时间，足以让他对自己所面对的机遇做出自我评估。他知道那些美差事并不属于他，这是一种诚挚的安慰，而不仅仅是用"吃不到葡萄说葡萄酸"来安慰自己根本不喜欢那些美差事。他更喜欢不怎么正式但更为独特的工作，即使这些工作并不是常人眼中比较好的工作。毫无疑问，似乎对别人而言，他自己混得相当糟糕，但其实他觉得他干得很不错，因为他拥有一个富于变化、充实愉快的 10 年时光。

他身材修长，古铜色肌肤，有一头修剪得很短的棕色头发和蓝灰色的双眼。他看起来似乎一脸严肃而且郁郁寡欢，笑起来时（但这种情况不怎么频繁发生）显得很孩子气。当他工作太辛苦或者喝了太多酒时，左眼附近会出现轻微的神经抽搐，通常非常明显。在撤离前的一天一夜，他一直在捆扎和销毁文件，因此当他爬进飞机时，这种抽搐显而易见，他已经精疲力竭了。但让他特别高兴的是，他设法乘坐了这架邦主的豪华座机，而并非一架拥挤不堪的军用运输机。当飞机向上翱翔时，他在篮式座椅上肆意伸展着，他是那种可以习惯于巨大艰苦的人，会期待一些微小的舒适来作为补偿。他的精神为之一振，虽然可能要忍受前往撒马尔罕

soared aloft. He was the sort of man who, being used to major hardships, expected minor comforts by way of compensation. Cheerfully he might endure the rigors of the road to Samarkand, but from London to Paris he would spend his last tenner on the Golden Arrow.

It was after the flight had lasted more than an hour that Mallinson said he thought the pilot wasn't keeping a straight course. Mallinson sat immediately in front. He was a youngster in his middle twenties, pink-cheeked, intelligent without being intellectual, beset with public school limitations, but also with their excellences. Failure to pass an examination was the chief cause of his being sent to Baskul, where Conway had had six months of his company and had grown to like him.

But Conway did not want to make the effort that an aeroplane conversation demands. He opened his eyes drowsily and replied that whatever the course taken, the pilot presumably knew best.

Half an hour later, when weariness and the drone of the engine had lulled him nearly to sleep, Mallinson disturbed him again. "I say, Conway, I thought Fenner was piloting us?"

"Well, isn't he?"

"The chap turned his head just now and I'll swear it wasn't he."

"It's hard to tell, through that glass panel."

的严酷旅程，但是从伦敦到巴黎，他将会在飞机上安逸地度过。

飞行持续了一个多小时之后，马林逊说，他认为飞行员并未保持直线航行，随后他立即坐到了前面的座位上。他是个二十五六岁的年轻人，粉红色的脸颊，非常聪明却没有受到很好的教育，这是公立学校的局限导致的，但他们也有自身的优势。一次考试的失败成为他被派往巴斯库的主要原因，在那里康维与他共处了 6 个月，并逐渐喜欢上了他。

但康维不想对一个飞机上的谈话多费力气，他懒洋洋地睁开了眼，回应道："飞机选择什么航线，飞行员大概最清楚。"

半小时以后，当疲倦以及引擎的嗡嗡声让他差不多要睡着时，马林逊再次打扰他说："我说，康维，我在想，是费纳在驾驶飞机吗？"

"哦，他没在驾驶吗？"

"刚才那家伙扭过头来，我发誓他不是费纳。"

"通过玻璃板很难说。"

"我在任何地方都能认出费

"I'd know Fenner's face anywhere."

"Well, then, it must be someone else. I don't see that it matters."

"But Fenner told me definitely that he was taking this machine."

"They must have changed their minds and given him one of the others."

"Well, who is this man, then?"

"My dear boy, how should I know? You don't suppose I've memorized the face of every flight-lieutenant in the Air Force, do you?"

"I know a good many of them, anyway, but I don't recognize this fellow."

"Then he must belong to the minority whom you don't know." Conway smiled and added: "When we arrive in Peshawar very soon you can make his acquaintance and ask him all about himself."

"At this rate we shan't get to Peshawar at all. The man's right off his course. And I'm not surprised, either – flying so damned high he can't see where he is."

Conway was not bothering. He was used to air travel, and took things for granted. Besides, there was nothing particular he was eager to do when he got to Peshawar, and no one particular he was eager to see; so it was a matter of complete indifference to him whether the journey took four hours or six. He was unmarried; there would be no tender greetings on arrival. He had friends, and a few of them would probably take him to

纳的脸。"

"哦，那么一定是其他的某个人，我没发现这有什么关系啊。"

"但费纳肯定地告诉过我，他会驾驶这架飞机啊。"

"他们肯定改变了主意，给了他其他的一架飞机吧。"

"哦，那么这个人是谁呢？"

"我亲爱的孩子，我怎么会清楚啊！你不要认为我已经记住了每个空军飞行上尉的脸。"

"我知道他们当中的很多人，但无论如何，我不认识这个家伙。"

"那么他肯定就属于你不清楚的少数人里了。"康维微微一笑，接着说道，"当我们非常快地抵达白沙瓦时，你可以去认识他，亲自向他询问所有的事情吧。"

"这样我们根本抵达不了白沙瓦，飞机完全偏离了航线，还有，我不能不奇怪，飞得如此之高，他是不是根本无法辨认飞到了什么地方。"

康维并不担心，他已经习惯于空中旅行，将所有事情视为理所应当。此外，在他抵达白沙瓦以后，没什么他急着要去做的特殊事情，也没什么他急着要去见的特别之人，因此航程将花 6 个小时还是 4 个小时对他而言根本没有任何区别，他还没有结婚，抵达之后也没有温柔的问候，他有些朋友，其中一些可能会带他去夜总会，请他喝

the club and stand him drinks; it was a pleasant prospect, but not one to sigh for in anticipation.

Nor did he sigh retrospectively, when he viewed the equally pleasant, but not wholly satisfying vista of the past decade. Changeable, fair intervals, becoming rather unsettled; it had been his own meteorological summary during that time, as well as the world's. He thought of Baskul, Pekin, Macao, and other places – he had moved about pretty often. Remotest of all was Oxford, where he had had a couple of years of donhood after the War, lecturing on Oriental History, breathing dust in sunny libraries, cruising down the High on a push-bicycle. The vision attracted, but did not stir him; there was a sense in which he felt that he was still a part of all that he might have been.

A familiar gastric lurch informed him that the plane was beginning to descend. He felt tempted to rag Mallinson about his fidgets, and would perhaps have done so had not the youth risen abruptly, bumping his head against the roof and waking Barnard, the American, who had been dozing in his seat at the other side of the narrow gangway. "My God!" Mallinson cried, peering through the window. "Look down there!"

Conway looked. The view was certainly not what he had expected, if, indeed, he had expected anything. Instead of the trim,

酒，这是一种令人愉悦的盼望，可也不算是期待的渴望。

当他回顾同样愉快但不完全满意的过去 10 年时，他没有那种怀旧式的叹息。变幻无常，难得的空闲间歇变得相当难以确定，这就是他自己对这段时间的分析总结，也是对世界局势的概括。他想到巴斯库、北京、澳门还有其他一些他频繁光顾的地方，所有当中最遥远的就是牛津了，战后他在那里有几年的指导教师生活，讲授东方历史；在充满阳光的图书馆里呼吸尘土；骑脚踏车沿着校园游览风光，这情景很吸引人，可没有令他激动；他有一种感觉，他仍然是他全部过往经历的一部分。

一阵熟悉的倾斜提示他飞机开始准备降落。他非常想对马林逊那烦躁不安的模样打打趣，如果不是那个年轻人突然起身造成自己脑袋"嘭"地撞到舱顶上，这也许真的会发生。当时马林逊要去叫醒美国人巴纳德，他正在狭窄过道的另一侧的座位上打瞌睡。"我的上帝！"马林逊叫道，通过窗户凝视外面，"向下看那里。"

康维看了看，景象肯定并非他预料的，如果他确实已经预料到任何东西的话。他看到的并非是由几

geometrically laid-out cantonments and the larger oblongs of the hangars, nothing was visible but an opaque mist veiling an immense, sun-brown desolation. The plane, though descending rapidly, was still at a height unusual for ordinary flying. Long, corrugated mountain-ridges could be picked out, perhaps a mile or so closer than the cloudier smudge of the valleys. It was typical frontier scenery, though Conway had never viewed it before from such an altitude. It was also, which struck him as odd, nowhere that he could imagine near Peshawar. "I don't recognize this part of the world," he commented. Then, more privately, for he did not wish to alarm the others, he added into Mallinson's ear: "Looks as if you're right. The man's lost his way."

The plane was swooping down at a tremendous speed, and as it did so, the air grew hotter; the scorched earth below was like an oven with the door suddenly opened. One mountaintop after another lifted itself above the horizon in craggy silhouette; now the flight was along a curving valley, the base of which was strewn with rocks and the débris of dried-up watercourses. It looked like a floor littered with nutshells. The plane bumped and tossed in air-pockets as uncomfortably as a row-boat in a swell. All four passengers had to hold onto their seats.

何图形排列整齐的军营还有巨大的长方形飞机库，他什么都看不到，除了在茫茫浓雾笼罩下的一片被太阳烤成红褐色的广袤荒原。虽然飞机在急速降落，可还是在与普通飞行不同的高度之上。他能够看到一些绵延的，呈波状的山脉，也许与云雾缭绕的山谷间不到一英里，虽然康维之前从未在如此的海拔高度观赏过，可这典型的边疆景色也令他感到十分古怪。这里不是什么他能够想象就在白沙瓦附近的地方，"我无法辨认出这是世界上的什么地方。"他评论道，然后，他不希望惊动其他人，便更私密地和马林逊耳语补充道："看起来你像是正确的，这个飞行员迷失了方向。"

飞机以惊人的速度突然降落着，当它这样降落时，空气逐渐变热，下面烧焦般的土地仿佛是突然开了炉门的火炉。一座山顶连着另一座，在地平线上升起崎岖的轮廓；现在飞机正沿着蜿蜒的山谷飞行，谷底散布着岩石还有干枯的河床，仿佛布满乱丢着栗子壳的地板；飞机在气团里使劲颠簸摇晃，就像置身于浪涛里的小船上一样令人难受，全部的4个乘客都不得不紧紧抓住座位。

"Looks like he wants to land!" shouted the American hoarsely.

"He can't!" Mallinson retorted. "He'd be simply mad if he tried to! He'll crash and then – "

But the pilot did land. A small cleared space opened by the side of a gully, and with considerable skill the machine was jolted and heaved to a standstill. What happened after that, however, was more puzzling and less reassuring. A swarm of bearded and turbaned tribesmen came forward from all directions, surrounding the machine and effectively preventing anyone from getting out of it except the pilot. The latter clambered to earth and held excited colloquy with them, during which proceeding it became clear that, so far from being Fenner, he was not an Englishman at all, and possibly not even a European. Meanwhile cans of gasoline were fetched from a dump close by, and emptied into the exceptionally capacious tanks. Grins and disregarding silence met the shouts of the four imprisoned passengers, while the slightest attempt to alight provoked a menacing movement from a score of rifles. Conway, who knew a little Pushtu, harangued the tribesmen as well as he could in that language, but without effect; while the pilot's sole retort to any remarks addressed to him in any language was a significant flourish of his revolver. Midday sunlight, blazing on the

"看起来他想着陆了!"美国人嘶哑地大喊。

"他不能啊,"马林逊反驳道,"如果他试着降落,那他就是疯了,他会坠毁的,然后……"

但飞行员确实着陆了,以相当出众的技术令飞机颠簸并向前滑行后停在了一条溪谷旁边的狭小空地上。但此后发生的事情更令人迷惑不解而且不怎么安心:一大群满脸胡须包着头巾的土著人从各个方向涌现出来围住飞机,有效地阻止任何人离开飞机,除了飞行员。那飞行员爬到地面后与他们激动地交谈,在这个过程进行期间,大家逐渐明朗,他完全不是费纳,也根本不是英国人,甚至不可能是欧洲人。同时,汽油桶从附近的油料堆里被取出来,然后倒进容积格外大的飞机油箱里。看到4位被囚禁的乘客在大声叫喊,他们只是咧开嘴大笑,然后沉默着视而不见。同时乘客们最轻微的企图下飞机的举动,都会引来20条枪的威胁。康维知道一点普什图语,他也能用这种语言和这些土著人大声理论,但没有一点效果,当他用任何一种语言向飞行员作交涉时,那家伙唯一的反应便是意味深长地挥舞他的左轮手枪。正午的太阳照耀在机舱顶部,令里面的空气很炙热,乘客因为炎热以及努力抗争而几乎晕过去。他们完全无能为力,因为在疏散撤离时不能携带武器是一

roof of the cabin, grilled the air inside till the occupants were almost fainting with the heat and with the exertion of their protests. They were quite powerless; it had been a condition of the evacuation that they should carry no arms.

When the tanks were at last screwed up, a gasoline can filled with tepid water was handed through one of the cabin windows. No questions were answered, though it did not appear that the men were personally hostile. After a further parley the pilot climbed back into the cockpit, a Pathan clumsily swung the propeller, and the flight was resumed. The takeoff, in that confined space and with the extra gasoline load, was even more skillful than the landing. The plane rose high into the hazy vapors; then turned east, as if setting a course. It was mid-afternoon.

A most extraordinary and bewildering business! As the cooler air refreshed them, the passengers could hardly believe that it had really happened; it was an outrage to which none could recall any parallel, or suggest any precedent, in all the turbulent records of the Frontier. It would have been incredible, indeed, had they not been victims of it themselves. It was quite natural that high indignation should follow incredulity, and anxious speculation only when indignation had worn itself out. Mallinson then developed the theory

个条件。

当油箱终于被拧上时，一只装满温水的油桶通过一扇机舱窗户被递了过来，虽然这些人似乎不存在什么个人的敌意，但问题也没有被回答。进一步会谈之后，飞行员爬回到机舱里，一个帕坦人笨拙地转动着飞机上的螺旋推进器，飞机又继续飞行了。在有限的空间里，虽然带着过量的汽油负荷，但飞机起飞甚至比降落更为灵巧自如。飞机高高地升入朦朦胧胧的蒸汽中，然后转向东方，好像在调整航线，此时下午已过半。

一件最非同寻常又令人迷惑的事情！当越发凉爽的空气令他们清醒时，乘客几乎不能相信这事真的发生了。在前线地区所有的暴动记录中，没有人能回忆起任何一件类似的事情，或者也无法提出任何先例。确实，如果他们几个没有亲身成为这一暴行的受害者的话，这简直令人无法相信。这是相当自然的事，像高度愤慨应该尾随着怀疑之情，而当愤慨结束以后便只能是焦虑和沉思。然后马林逊提出了一个推测：在没有任何其他推测出现

which, in the absence of any other, they found easiest to accept. They were being kidnaped for ransom. The trick was by no means new in itself, though this particular technique must be regarded as original. It was a little more comforting to feel that they were not making entirely virgin history; after all, there had been kidnapings before, and a good many of them had ended up all right. The tribesmen kept you in some lair in the mountains till the government paid up and you were released. You were treated quite decently, and as the money that had to be paid wasn't your own, the whole business was only unpleasant while it lasted. Afterwards, of course, the Air people sent a bombing squadron, and you were left with one good story to tell for the rest of your life. Mallinson enunciated the proposition a shade nervously; but Barnard, the American, chose to be heavily facetious. "Well, gentlemen, I daresay this is a cute idea on somebody's part, but I can't exactly see that your Air Force has covered itself with glory. You Britishers make jokes about the hold-ups in Chicago and all that, but I don't recollect any instance of a gunman running off with one of Uncle Sam's aeroplanes. And I should like to know, by the way, what this fellow did with the real pilot. Sandbagged him, I bet." He yawned. He was a large, fleshy man, with a

的情况下，他们发现这个最为容易去接受。他们被绑架是为了勒索赎金。这种伎俩本身绝不新鲜，尽管这个特殊的技术肯定被视为原创。他们的情况并非完全是历史的第一次，这样就感觉起来稍微舒坦了一些。毕竟，之前曾经出现过绑架事件，而其中的大部分都以好的结局收场。这些土著人会一直将你关在山中的洞穴里，直到政府付了赎金，然后你就会被释放；你会被相当公平地处置，而且赎金也并非你自己支付，当整件事持续时，只是有点令人不太愉悦而已，然后，当然，空军部队会派一支轰炸中队，你便可以平安离开了，并带着一个精彩的故事以便你的余生可以讲给大家听。马林逊紧张地发表了自己的看法，但巴纳德这个美国人却相当滑稽："好吧，先生们，我敢说就某些人的部分而言，这是个聪明的想法，但我不能确切地看出你们的空军有何辉煌成就。你们英国人总是拿关于芝加哥等地的劫机事件开玩笑，但我却回忆不出来任何一个持枪歹徒劫持一架山姆大叔的飞机逃跑的先例，顺便提一句，我想知道，这家伙对那位真正的飞行员做了什么；我打赌是把他塞进沙袋了。"他打了个哈欠，他高大且肥胖，一张刚毅的脸上满带幽默滑稽的皱纹，完全无法被那悲观主义的眼袋所抵消。在巴斯库，没有人对他有多少了解，除了知道

hard-bitten face in which good-humored wrinkles were not quite offset by pessimistic pouches. Nobody in Baskul had known much about him except that he had arrived from Persia, where it was presumed he had something to do with oil.

Conway meanwhile was busying himself with a very practical task. He had collected every scrap of paper that they all had, and was composing messages in various native languages to be dropped to earth at intervals. It was a slender chance, in such sparsely populated country, but worth taking.

The fourth occupant, Miss Brinklow, sat tight-lipped and straight-backed, with few comments and no complaints. She was a small, rather leathery woman, with an air of having been compelled to attend a party at which there were goings-on that she could not wholly approve.

Conway had talked less than the two other men, for translating SOS messages into dialects was a mental exercise requiring concentration. He had, however, answered questions when asked, and had agreed, tentatively, with Mallinson's kidnaping theory. He had also agreed, to some extent, with Barnard's strictures on the Air Force. "Though one can see, of course, how it may have happened. With the place in commotion as it was, one man in flying-kit would look very much like another. No one would think of doubting

他来自波兰，在那里他的工作被猜测和石油有些关联。

同时，康维自己正忙着完成一件非常实际的任务。他将他们所有人身上的每一小张纸片都收集起来，然后在上面用各种本地的语言写上信息，每隔一段时间便向地面投几片。在如此人迹罕至的荒野，这种机会极其渺茫，但也可值得尝试一下。

第四位坐着的人，也就是布琳克罗小姐，紧闭着双唇，笔直地靠在那里。没有只言片语，也没有抱怨，她瘦小却相当坚韧，仿佛被强迫去参加一个她完全不赞同的聚会一般。

康维说的话比另外两个男士少很多，因为他得将求救信息翻译为方言，这是精神的考验，需要注意力集中。但被询问时，他也得回答问题，还要对马林逊的"绑架"推测暂时同意，在某种程度上，他也赞同巴纳德针对空军的谴责。"当然，尽管大家能够看出来这件事是如何发生的，在那种类似出现骚乱的地方，一个身着航空服的人会看起来非常像另外一个，没有人会考虑去怀疑任何身着合适的服装，看起来像是很了解他的工作的

the *bona fides* of any man in the proper clothes who looked as if he knew his job. And this fellow *must* have known it – the signals, and so forth. Pretty obvious, too, that he knows how to fly… still, I agree with you that it's the sort of thing that someone ought to get into hot water about. And somebody will, you may be sure, though I suspect he won't deserve it."

"Well, sir," responded Barnard, "I certainly do admire the way you manage to see both sides of the question. It's the right spirit to have, no doubt, even when you're being taken for a ride."

Americans, Conway reflected, had the knack of being able to say patronizing things without being offensive. He smiled tolerantly, but did not continue the conversation. His tiredness was of a kind that no amount of possible peril could stave off. Towards late afternoon, when Barnard and Mallinson, who had been arguing, appealed to him on some point, it appeared that he had fallen asleep.

"Dead beat," Mallinson commented. "And I don't wonder at it, after these last few weeks."

"You're his friend?" queried Barnard.

"I've worked with him at the Consulate. I happen to know that he hasn't been in bed for the last four nights. As a matter of fact, we're damned lucky in having him with us in a tight corner like this. Apart from knowing the languages, he's got a

老实人。而且这家伙肯定很清楚一些东西——信号指令以及其他等等，再清楚不过的是，他也知道怎样飞行……还有，我也赞同你的观点，这是一类某些人置身水深火热之中的事，某些人将会有麻烦，虽然你可以确定，但我怀疑不应该会是他。"

"好吧，先生，"巴纳德反应道，"我当然非常崇拜你能够看到问题两面性的方式，毋庸置疑，这是正确的态度，甚至当你一直被欺骗时也该如此。"

美国人，康维细想着，具备一种能够说些傲慢的话、而不会冒犯他人的诀窍，他宽容地微微一笑，却没有继续交谈。他的疲惫是一种无法避开可能的危险的困倦。直到下午很晚的时候，当巴纳德与马林逊一直在争吵，并就某些观点求助于康维时，他已经睡着了。

"他彻底累垮了，"马林逊评论到，"在这样持续的几周过后，我并不奇怪。"

"你是他的朋友？"巴纳德问。

"我们一起在领事馆工作过，我碰巧清楚过去的四天四夜他都没有上床休息过，其实，我们真他妈幸运，有他与我们一起待在这个小小的角落里。除了了解多种语言

sort of way with him in dealing with people. If anyone can get us out of the mess, he'll do it. He's pretty cool about most things."

"Well, let him have his sleep, then," agreed Barnard.

Miss Brinklow made one of her rare remarks. "I think he *looks* like a very brave man," she said.

Conway was far less certain that he *was* a very brave man. He had closed his eyes in sheer physical fatigue, but without actually sleeping. He could hear and feel every movement of the plane, and he heard also, with mixed feelings, Mallinson's eulogy of himself. It was then that he had his doubts, recognizing a tight sensation in his stomach which was his own bodily reaction to a disquieting mental survey. He was not, as he knew well from experience, one of those persons who love danger for its own sake. There was an aspect of it which he sometimes enjoyed, an excitement, a purgative effect upon sluggish emotions, but he was far from fond of risking his life. Twelve years earlier he had grown to hate the perils of trench warfare in France, and had several times avoided death by declining to attempt valorous impossibilities. Even his D.S.O. had been won, not so much by physical courage, as by a certain hardly developed technique of

之外，他自有一套和他人周旋之道，倘若任何人能够帮我们摆脱困境，那么一定是他，可他对大多数事情都相当冷漠。"

"好吧，那让他睡他的觉吧！"巴纳德赞同道。

布琳克罗小姐做出了一句鲜有的评论。"我认为他看起来是个非常勇敢的男人。"她说道。

康维不太确定他是个非常勇敢的人。他紧闭着双眼，身体彻底疲惫不堪了，但实际上并未睡着，他能够听到和感觉到飞机的每一次摆动，他也以一种复杂的感觉听着马林逊对自己的赞扬，那是他对自己的怀疑。他意识到一种紧张之情在他的胃里翻腾，这是他精神焦虑不安时的身体反应。就像他清楚地从过去的经历中知道，他不是那种因为冒险本身而喜爱冒险的人。他有时会享受这种情况并且为之激动，这对于迟钝的情感有净化的作用。可他绝对不喜欢以生命来冒险。12 年前他便逐渐痛恨在法国堑壕战里的危险经历，他好几次都是通过拒绝毫无任何可能的无畏企图才能避免死亡。甚至他那区参谋军衔的获得在很大程度上也不是凭借内在的勇气，而是通过某种艰难开发出来的耐久性技术。自从战争开始以来，他对危险的兴趣越来越缺少，除非它能带来极度胆战心惊之感。

endurance. And since the War, whenever there had been danger ahead, he had faced it with increasing lack of relish unless it promised extravagant dividends in thrills.

He still kept his eyes closed. He was touched, and a little dismayed, by what he had heard Mallinson say. It was his fate in life to have his equanimity always mistaken for pluck, whereas it was actually something much more dispassionate and much less virile. They were all in a damnably awkward situation, it seemed to him, and so far from being full of bravery about it, he felt chiefly an enormous distaste for whatever trouble might be in store. There was Miss Brinklow, for instance. He foresaw that in certain circumstances he would have to act on the supposition that because she was a woman she mattered far more than the rest of them put together, and he shrank from a situation in which such disproportionate behavior might be unavoidable.

Nevertheless, when he showed signs of wakefulness, it was to Miss Brinklow that he spoke first. He realized that she was neither young nor pretty – negative virtues, but immensely helpful ones in such difficulties as those in which they might soon find themselves. He was also rather sorry for her, because he suspected that neither Mallinson nor the American liked missionaries, especially female ones. He himself was unprejudiced, but he was

他依旧双眼紧闭,被马林逊的话所触动,然后有点沮丧。他的命运注定了他的镇定总是和勇气相悖,然而这实际上是某种更冷静更没有男子气概的东西。在他看来,他们似乎全部都置身于一种非常糟糕的尴尬情况,而他对此远远没有充满非凡的勇气,对可能蕴含的什么麻烦,他感到一种极端的厌恶。举个例子,这里有布琳克罗小姐,他预见到在某些情况下他不得不依据推测来行动,因为她是个女性,她比其余所有人都更在意这件事。他害怕一种情况发生,这就是他无法避免不合时宜的行为。

不过,当他表现出一副苏醒过来的样子之后,第一个就和布琳克罗小姐聊起来。他意识到她既不年轻也不漂亮——品德也不怎么样,但在如此的困境中,却是能提供巨大帮助的人,就像他们在这种环境下可以很快地找到自己的位置。他也对她感到相当抱歉,因为他注意到马林逊和那个美国人都不喜欢传教士,特别是女传教士,他本身没有什么偏见,可他却担心她会发

afraid she would find his open mind a less familiar and therefore an even more disconcerting phenomenon. "We seem to be in a queer fix," he said, leaning forward to her ear, "but I'm glad you're taking it calmly. I don't really think anything dreadful is going to happen to us."

"I'm certain it won't if you can prevent it," she answered; which did not console him.

"You must let me know if there is anything we can do to make you more comfortable."

Barnard caught the word. "Comfortable?" he echoed raucously. "Why, of course we're comfortable. We're just enjoying the trip. Pity we haven't a pack of cards – we could play a rubber of bridge."

Conway welcomed the spirit of the remark, though he disliked bridge. "I don't suppose Miss Brinklow plays," he said, smiling.

But the missionary turned round briskly to retort: "Indeed I do, and I could never see any harm in cards at all. There's nothing against them in the Bible."

They all laughed, and seemed obliged to her for providing an excuse. At any rate, Conway thought, she wasn't hysterical.

All afternoon the plane had soared through the thin mists of the upper atmosphere, far too high to give clear sight

现他的直率有点不太自然，甚至会更不安。"我们似乎置身于一种奇怪的进退两难的窘境，"他朝她的耳朵俯下身，"可我很高兴你能镇定地对待，而且我并不真的觉得任何可怕的事情将会发生在我们身上。"

"我敢肯定如果你能够阻止它的话，那它便一定不会发生。"她回答道，但这并未令他感到安慰。

"你必须让我清楚，我们是否能做任何事情可以让你更为舒适一些。"

巴纳德抢过话，"舒适？"他扯着沙哑地回应道，"哎，当然了，我们非常舒适，我们正在享受旅行，真遗憾，我们没有扑克——否则我们就能打桥牌了。"

尽管康维不喜欢桥牌，但他对于这句评论的乐观精神非常喜欢。"我猜布琳克罗小姐不打桥牌。"他笑道。

但传教士活泼地扭过身来反驳道："我确实会打，而且我根本没看出扑克牌里有任何有害的东西，《圣经》也不存在抵制它们的条文。"

所有人都哈哈大笑，似乎感激她提供了一个借口。无论如何，康维觉得她没有歇斯底里。

整个下午，飞机都在高空稀薄的空气里穿梭翱翔，因为飞得太高以至于无法看清下面有些什么。时

of what lay beneath. Sometimes, at longish intervals, the veil was torn for a moment, to display the jagged outline of a peak, or the glint of some unknown stream. The direction could be determined roughly from the sun; it was still east, with occasional twists to the north; but where it had led depended on the speed of travel, which Conway could not judge with any accuracy. It seemed likely, though, that the flight must already have exhausted a good deal of the gasoline; though that again depended on uncertain factors. Conway had no technical knowledge of aircraft, but he was sure that the pilot, whoever he might be, was altogether an expert. That halt in the rock-strewn valley had demonstrated it, and also other incidents since. And Conway could not repress a feeling that was always his in the presence of any superb and indisputable competence. He was so used to being appealed to for help that mere awareness of someone who would neither ask nor need it was slightly tranquilizing, even amidst the greater perplexities of the future. But he did not expect his companions to share such a tenuous emotion. He recognized that they were likely to have far more personal reasons for anxiety than he had himself. Mallinson, for instance, was engaged to a girl in England; Barnard might be married; Miss Brinklow had her work, vocation, or

不时的，在稍长的间隔里，这纱帐般的薄雾消失了片刻，下面便呈现出锯齿状的山峰轮廓，或者是某条不知名的河流闪烁的光芒。通过太阳方向能够粗略地被判断出来，飞行依然向东，偶尔偏向北方；但飞机飞往什么地方还需要依靠飞行的速度，所以康维不能准确地推断出来。尽管飞机似乎已经消耗了大量的汽油；尽管这也取决于一些不确定的因素，康维对于飞行员的技术没有一丝了解，可他肯定这个飞行员，不管他可能是谁，绝对是个专家；在岩石纵横的山谷里着陆便可以证明这点，还有此后的其他事件也能证明。康维不能压制住一种情感，这情感产生于总是伴随着他的任何令他光彩以及无可争议的能力。他是如此习惯被他人寻求帮助，以至于仅仅意识到某个人既不想也不需要他的帮助时，他都会有一丝安宁，甚至在未来更为巨大的困惑混乱里，也是如此。但康维不期待他的同伴们会来分享如此的纤细情感。他意识到比起他自己，他们几个可能具有更多的个人理由而感到焦虑不安。举个例子，马林逊在英国已经和一个姑娘订了婚；巴纳德可能已婚了；而布琳克罗小姐有她的工作、假期或者她认为的其他什么。而很偶然，马林逊碰巧又是最不沉着的一个，当时间一小时一小时地流走时，他自己表现得愈发激动敏感，同时也对康维

however she might regard it. Mallinson, incidentally, was by far the least composed; as the hours passed he showed himself increasingly excitable – apt, also, to resent to Conway's face the very coolness which he had praised behind his back. Once, above the roar of the engine, a sharp storm of argument arose. "Look here," Mallinson shouted angrily, "are we bound to sit here twiddling our thumbs while this maniac does everything he damn well wants? What's to prevent us from smashing that panel and having it out with him?"

"Nothing at all," replied Conway, "except that he's armed and we're not, and that in any case, none of us would know how to bring the machine to earth afterwards."

"It can't be very hard, surely. I daresay you could do it."

"My dear Mallinson, why is it always *me* you expect to perform these miracles?"

"Well, anyway, this business is getting hellishly on my nerves. Can't we *make* the fellow come down?"

"How do you suggest it should be done?"

Mallinson was becoming more and more agitated. "Well, he's *there,* isn't he? About six feet away from us, and we're three men to one! Have we got to stare at his damned back all the time? At least we might force him to tell us what the game

那张非常冷酷的脸庞不满起来——他曾经还在背地里大为赞赏呢。一次，就在引擎的轰鸣声中，一场激烈的争执风暴引发了。"看这里，"马林逊愤怒地大喊，"我们就百无聊赖地坐在这儿，让那个疯子为所欲为吗？有什么办法可以不砸碎隔船板而将那家伙弄出来？"

"我们完全无能为力，"康维回应道，"他有武器但我们没有，而且无论如何，我们当中没有一个人知道如何操纵飞机让它着陆。"

"这肯定不会非常困难的，我敢说你能做到。"

"亲爱的马林逊，为什么你总是期待我去上演这样的奇迹呢？"

"好吧，无论如何，这情况正像恶魔般地扰乱我的神经；难不成我们不能让这家伙将飞机降落吗？"

"你建议我们应该做什么呢？"

马林逊逐渐变得越来越急躁，"哦，他就在那里呢，不是吗？大约距我们6英尺远，况且我们是三对一啊！难不成我们就一直盯着他那该死的后背？至少，我们可以逼迫他告诉我们这到底是怎么回事

is."

"Very well, we'll see." Conway took a few paces forward to the partition between the cabin and the pilot's cockpit, which was situated in front and somewhat above. There was a pane of glass, about six inches square and made to slide open, through which the pilot, by turning his head and stooping slightly, could communicate with his passengers. Conway tapped on this with his knuckles. The response was almost comically as he had expected. The glass panel slid sideways and the barrel of a revolver obtruded. Not a word; just that. Conway retreated without arguing the point, and the panel slid back again.

Mallinson, who had watched the incident, was only partly satisfied. "I don't suppose he'd have dared to shoot," he commented. "It's probably bluff."

"Quite," agreed Conway, "but I'd rather leave you to make sure."

"Well, I do feel we ought to put up some sort of a fight before giving in tamely like this."

Conway was sympathetic. He recognized the convention, with all its associations of red-coated soldiers and school history books, that Englishmen fear nothing, never surrender, and are never defeated. He said: "Putting up a fight without a decent chance of winning is a poor game, and I'm not that sort of hero."

啊。"

"非常好，咱们拭目以待。"康维向客舱和驾驶舱之间的隔板走了好几步。这驾驶舱位于飞机前面稍微高些的地方，有一块大约6英寸长的正方形玻璃窗格，它能够被滑动开，飞行员将头一扭，通过它，轻微俯身便能与乘客沟通。康维用他的指关节轻叩玻璃隔板，里面的反应就像他所预计的那样滑稽可笑。玻璃板被滑到一旁，左轮手枪的枪管伸了出来，没有一句话，就这样，康维没有争辩什么便退回来，玻璃又再次滑回去。

马林逊观望着事态发展，并不满意这样的结果。"我觉得他不敢开枪，"他评论道，"也许是吓人。"

"没错，"康维赞同道，"可我觉得最好让你去确定一下。"

"好吧，我确实感觉咱们在被驯服前应该进行一些斗争。"

康维表示赞成。通过红衣士兵协会的所有社交活动还有学校里面的历史书籍，他认识到这样一种惯例，英国人不害怕任何东西，他们从不投降，从未被击败过。他说："没有合适的获胜机会便斗争，这是不明智的，我并非那类英雄。"

"Good for you, sir," interposed Barnard heartily. "When somebody's got you by the short hairs you may as well give in pleasantly and admit it. For my part I'm going to enjoy life while it lasts and have a cigar. I hope you don't think a little bit of extra danger matters to us?"

"Not so far as I'm concerned, but it might bother Miss Brinklow."

Barnard was quick to make amends. "Pardon me, madam, but do you mind if I smoke?"

"Not at all," she answered graciously. "I don't do so myself, but I just love the smell of a cigar."

Conway felt that of all the women who could possibly have made such a remark, she was easily the most typical. Anyhow, Mallinson's excitement had calmed a little, and to show friendliness he offered him a cigarette, though he did not light one himself. "I know how you feel," he said gently. "It's a bad outlook, and it's all the worse, in some ways, because there isn't much we can do about it."

"And all the better, too, in other ways," he could not help adding to himself. For he was still immensely fatigued. There was also in his nature a trait which some people might have called laziness, though it was not quite that. No one was capable of harder work, when it had to be done, and few could better shoulder responsibility; but the facts remained that

"你说得好，先生，"巴纳德热心地插话道，"当某个人抓住你的小辫子时，你也可能甘之如饴，然后接受。是我的话，我会享受生活，只要生活还继续，抽一支雪茄吧！我希望你们不要觉得一丝额外的危险会影响我们。"

"我并不介意，但这可能会让令布琳克罗小姐困扰。"

巴纳德很快做了修正："对不起，女士，但你不介意我吸烟吧？"

"一点也不，"她通情达理地答道，"我自己并不吸烟，可我就是喜欢雪茄的味道。"

康维感觉所有女人都可能做这样的评论，她自然是最典型的一个，不管怎么说，马林逊的激动情绪稍微镇定了一点。为了显示友好，他递给康维一支烟，但自己却没有点上。"我清楚你的感觉，"康维柔和地说，"前景很糟糕，甚至更糟糕，因为我们对此能做的并不多。"

"换个角度，也有可能会更好。"他忍不住补充道。他仍然觉得非常疲惫。在他的天性里，也有一种被一些人称作"懒散"的特点，虽然并不特别突出。当不得不去做时，没人有能力应对更困难的工作，而且没人能更好地肩负责任；但其实他并不热衷于实践，也完全不喜欢责任。这两者都包括在他的

he was not passionately fond of activity, and did not enjoy responsibility at all. Both were included in his job, and he made the best of them, but he was always ready to give way to anyone else who could function as well or better. It was partly this, no doubt, that had made his success in the Service less striking than it might have been. He was not ambitious enough to shove his way past others, or to make an important parade of doing nothing when there was really nothing doing. His dispatches were sometimes laconic to the point of curtness, and his calm in emergencies, though admired, was often suspected of being too sincere. Authority likes to feel that a man is imposing some effort on himself, and that his apparent nonchalance is only a cloak to disguise an outfit of well-bred emotions. With Conway the dark suspicion had sometimes been current that he really was as unruffled as he looked, and that whatever happened, he did not give a damn. But this, too, like the laziness, was an imperfect interpretation. What most observers failed to perceive in him was something quite bafflingly simple – a love of quietness, contemplation, and being alone.

Now, since he was so inclined and there was nothing else to do, he leaned back in the basket chair and went definitely to sleep. When he woke he noticed that the

工作中，他将它们处理得很好。但他总是准备让位给其他能够胜任或者做得更出色的任何人。毋庸置疑，这种小聪明令他在部队服役中取得成功，而且承担比预想中更少的风险。他没有足够的信念将他的处事方式强加给别人，或者当真在无所事事时，为自己的无事可做当作一次重要的炫耀。他的敏捷偶尔只能被看做是一种简单到鲁莽的举动，而他在危急时刻的镇定，尽管令人佩服，可却经常被怀疑为太过谨慎。官方人士喜欢认为他是一个把种种努力的目标强加于自己的人，他外表的冷淡仅仅是掩盖他良好情感素养的外衣。一种暗暗的怀疑伴随着康维，时不时涌上来，他的确像看起来那般沉着冷静，不管发生了什么，他都不会谴责别人。但这就像懒散一样，也无法完美解释，大多数旁观者在对待他的问题上都有失偏颇，他的个性有种相当不可理解的简单——喜欢宁静、沉思和独处。

现在，自从他屈身侧坐着以来，他没有做任何事，他倚靠在摇篮椅上干脆睡起觉来。当他醒来时，他发现另外几个人——尽管他

others, despite their various anxieties, had likewise succumbed. Miss Brinklow was sitting bolt upright with her eyes closed, like some rather dingy and outmoded idol; Mallinson had lolled forward in his place with his chin in the palm of a hand. The American was even snoring. Very sensible of them all, Conway thought; there was no point in wearying themselves with shouting. But immediately he was aware of certain physical sensations in himself, slight dizziness and heart-thumping and a tendency to inhale sharply and with effort. He remembered similar symptoms once before – in the Swiss Alps.

Then he turned to the window and gazed out. The surrounding sky had cleared completely, and in the light of late afternoon there came to him a vision which, for the instant, snatched the remaining breath out of his lungs. Far away, at the very limit of distance, lay range upon range of snow-peaks, festooned with glaciers, and floating, in appearance, upon vast levels of cloud. They compassed the whole arc of the circle, merging towards the west in a horizon that was fierce, almost garish in coloring, like an impressionist back-drop done by some half-mad genius. And meanwhile, the plane, on that stupendous stage, was droning over an abyss in the face of a sheer white wall that seemed part of the sky itself until the sun caught it.

们有各种各样的焦虑——也同样屈服了。布琳克罗小姐双眼紧闭，直挺挺地坐着，仿佛某个陈旧过时又失去光彩的时装塑模；马林逊懒洋洋地靠在他的位置上前倾坐着，下巴抵在手上，那个美国人甚至在打鼾。康维觉得他们所有人都非常明智，没什么理由让自己大喊大叫以致十分疲倦。但立刻，他意识自己身上出现了某种生理感觉，有点头昏眼花，心脏怦怦直跳，有一种吸引力在猛烈地吸食着自己。他记得之前一次也有类似的症状——那是在瑞士的阿尔卑斯山上。

然后他转向窗户，向外望去。周围的天空异常清澈，在午后的阳光里有一种梦幻般的景象向他飘来，立刻便将他剩余的氧气从他肺里抢夺了出来。在远处，非常遥远的地方，一些冰峰层峦叠嶂装饰着冰河，就像飘浮在辽阔的云层之上。他们围绕着飞了整整一个圆周，然后向西融合进地平线当中，地平线的颜色强烈刺眼，就像被几个半疯癫的印象派天才大师完成的彩画幕布。与此同时，在这巨大的舞台上，飞机嗡嗡着盘旋在一个深渊之上，对面是一道峻峭的白色悬崖，直到阳光投射到它之前，它都似乎是天空的一部分。然后，像从莫林看到的许多层峦叠嶂的少女峰一样，山峦闪烁着令人炫目的灿灿美妙银光。

Then, like a dozen piled-up Jungfraus seen from Mürren, it flamed into superb and dazzling incandescence.

Conway was not apt to be easily impressed, and as a rule he did not care for "views," especially the more famous ones for which thoughtful municipalities provide garden seats. Once, on being taken to Tiger Hill, near Darjeeling, to watch the sunrise upon Everest, he had found the highest mountain in the world a definite disappointment. But this fearsome spectacle beyond the window-pane was of different caliber; it had no air of posing to be admired. There was something raw and monstrous about those uncompromising ice-cliffs, and a certain sublime impertinence in approaching them thus. He pondered, envisioning maps, calculating distances, estimating times and speeds. Then he became aware that Mallinson had wakened also. He touched the youth on the arm.

康维不容易对一般事物留下印象，作为一种惯例，他不怎么在意"风景"，特别是那些更加著名的由颇有创见的市政当局提供的园林座椅的景区。一次，他被带到大吉岭附近的老虎山，观赏埃非尔士峰[1]的日出，他对这世界最高峰完全失望了。但这种窗格玻璃外的恐怖景象却完全不同，它没有那种故作姿态以便被崇拜的气质，那些坚硬的冰山雪峰里饱含某种原生态又荒诞不经的东西，接近它们就会产生某种雄伟崇高但不合时宜之感。他思忖着，研究着地图，计算距离，估计时间和速度。然后他逐渐意识到马林逊也已经清醒了。他碰了碰小伙子的胳膊。

---

[1] 埃非尔士峰：即珠穆朗玛峰。

CHAPTER 2

第二章

IT was typical of Conway that he let the others waken for themselves, and made small response to their exclamations of astonishment; yet later, when Barnard sought his opinion, gave it with something of the detached fluency of a university professor elucidating a problem. He thought it likely, he said, that they were still in India; they had been flying east for several hours, too high to see much, but probably the course had been along some river valley, one stretching roughly east and west. "I wish I hadn't to rely on memory, but my impression is that the valley of the upper Indus fits in well enough. That would have brought us by now to a very spectacular part of the world, and, as you see, so it has."

"You know where we are, then?" Barnard interrupted.

"Well, no – I've never been anywhere near here before, but I wouldn't be surprised if that mountain is Nanga Parbat, the one Mummery lost his life on. In structure and general lay-out it seems in accord with all I've heard about it."

"You are a mountaineer yourself?"

"In my younger days I was keen. Only

这是康维的典型特点，他让其他人兴奋活跃，对于他们惊奇的大喊大嚷，他也没有什么反应；但之后，当巴纳德寻求他的意见时，他就会用一位大学教授阐明问题的方式，不偏不倚而简明扼要地给出了一些观点。他认为很有可能，他说，他们仍然在印度区域里；飞机已经向东飞行了几个小时，因为实在太高了以至于看不到什么东西，但也许航线是沿着某一个向东西方向延伸的河谷。"我希望我可以不仅依靠记忆，但我的印象中这里是印度河上游的河谷。到现在为止，我们可能已经被带到了世界上一个非常引人入胜之处，就像你看到的，就是如此。"

"那么，你清楚我们在什么地方了？"巴纳德打断道。

"哦，不清楚——我之前从没到过这附近的任何地方，但如果那座山就是那位哑剧演员丧命的南迦帕尔巴特峰，我不觉得吃惊；以其结构还有大致形状况来看，它似乎和我曾听到的全部情况非常一致。"

"你是一位登山爱好者吧？"

the usual Swiss climbs, of course."

Mallinson intervened peevishly: "There'd be more point in discussing where we're going to. I wish to God somebody could tell us."

"Well, it looks to me as if we're heading for that range yonder," said Barnard. "Don't you think so, Conway? You'll excuse me calling you that, but if we're all going to have a little adventure together, it's a pity to stand on ceremony."

Conway thought it very natural that anyone should call him by his own name, and found Barnard's apologies for so doing a trifle needless. "Oh, certainly," he agreed, and added: "I think that range must be the Karakorams. There are several passes if our man intends to cross them."

"Our man?" exclaimed Mallinson. "You mean our maniac! I reckon it's time we dropped the kidnaping theory. We're far past the frontier country by now, there aren't any tribes living around here. The only explanation I can think of is that the fellow's a raving lunatic. Would anybody except a lunatic fly into this sort of country?"

"I know that nobody except a damn fine airman *could*," retorted Barnard. "I never was great at geography, but I understand that these are reputed to be the highest mountains in the world, and if that's so, it'll be a pretty first-class performance to

"我年轻时热衷登山，当然，仅仅是在瑞士的一般性登山而已。"

马林逊愠怒地插话道："讨论一下我们将会到什么地方才更有意义，我向上帝祈祷有人能够告诉我们。"

"好吧，对我而言，看起来我们好像正在前往远处的那座山脉，"巴纳德说，"你不这么认为吗，康维？你会原谅我这么称呼你吧。但倘若我们所有人都准备共同冒点小风险的话，总保持礼仪真是遗憾。"

康维觉得任何人直接以他的名字称呼他是非常自然的，认为巴纳德为此事的道歉毫无必要。"哦，当然如此，"他表示赞同并补充道，"我认为那座山脉一定是喀拉昆仑山，如果我们的人打算穿过山脉的话，那里有很多隘口可以通行。"

"我们的人？"马林逊大喊道，"你的意思是我们的那位疯子吗？我以为现在是我们放弃绑架论的时刻了。到现在为止，我们已经远离前线区域了，这附近又不存在任何活动的部落。我能思考出来的唯一解释就是那家伙是个精神错乱的疯子。除了疯子以外，还有谁会飞到这类荒野之地啊？"

"我知道没有人会，除了那个该死的'出色'飞行员以外，"巴纳德反击道，"我在地理上从来不

cross them."

"And also the will of God," put in Miss Brinklow unexpectedly.

Conway did not offer his opinion. The will of God or the lunacy of man – it seemed to him that you could take your choice, if you wanted a good enough reason for most things. Or, alternatively (and he thought of it as he contemplated the small orderliness of the cabin against the window background of such frantic natural scenery), the will of man and the lunacy of God. It must be satisfying to be quite certain which way to look at it. Then, while he watched and pondered, a strange transformation took place. The light turned to bluish over the whole mountain, with the lower slopes darkening to violet. Something deeper than his usual aloofness rose in him – not quite excitement, still less fear, but a sharp intensity of expectation. He said: "You're quite right, Barnard, this affair grows more and more remarkable."

"Remarkable or not, I don't feel inclined to propose a vote of thanks about it," Mallinson persisted. "We didn't ask to be brought here, and heaven knows what we shall do when we get *there,* wherever *there* is. And I don't see that it's any less of an outrage because the fellow happens to be a stunt flyer. Even if he is, he can be just as much a lunatic. I once heard of a

出色，可我清楚这座山被誉为世界上最高的山脉，倘若真是这样，那么越过这些山脉会是一次非常一流的表演。"

"这也是上帝的意志。"布琳克罗小姐出乎意料地插了句话。

康维并未给出意见。是上帝的意志还是那人的疯狂——对他而言，如果你对大多数事情有足够充分的信心，那你可以自行选择，或者在上帝的意志与那人的疯狂之间二选一。这是当他凝视着秩序井然的小机舱和窗外背景那如此狂放的自然景象形成鲜明对比时想到的。如果可以相当肯定以哪种方式看待这个问题，那一定会很令人满意。然后，他凝视着窗外，思考着。这时一种奇异的转变发生了，笼罩着整座山的光线变成了浅蓝色，随着斜坡降低逐渐加深为紫色。一种比他平常的超然态度更深沉的东西油然而生——不完全是兴奋，也非胆怯，而是一种强烈的期望。他说："你相当正确，巴纳德，这件事变得越来越奇特。"

"奇特或不奇特，我都不愿意对此发表看法，"马林逊坚持道，"我们没有要求被带到这里，不管这是什么地方，天晓得我们到了哪儿，应该做些什么。我倒没有看出来会有一丝暴行发生的迹象，因为那家伙碰巧是个特技飞行员，即使他是，他也只能是个精神病患者，

pilot going mad in mid-air. This fellow must have been mad from the beginning. That's my theory, Conway."

Conway was silent. He found it irksome to be continually shouting above the roar of the machine, and after all, there was little point in arguing possibilities. But when Mallinson pressed for an opinion, he said: "Very well-organized lunacy, you know. Don't forget the landing for gasoline, and also that this was the only machine that could climb to such a height."

"That doesn't prove he isn't mad. He may have been mad enough to plan everything."

"Yes, of course, that's possible."

"Well, then, we've got to decide on a plan of action. What are we going to do when he comes to earth? If he doesn't crash and kill us all, that is. What are we going to *do*? Rush forward and congratulate him on his marvelous flight, I suppose."

"Not on your life," answered Barnard. "I'll leave you to do all the rushing forward."

Again Conway was loth to prolong the argument, especially since the American, with his level-headed banter, seemed quite capable of handling it himself. Already Conway found himself reflecting that the party might have been far less fortunately

我曾经听说过一个飞行员在空中变疯了呢。这家伙肯定是从开始就变疯了，这是我的理论，康维。"

康维沉默着。他发现在马达的轰鸣声中连续不断地叫喊很是令人厌恶。毕竟，争论这种可能性没有丝毫的意义。可当马林逊急迫地发表观点时，他说道："真是个非常有条理的疯子，你知道的。不要忘了，他降落以便加油，也仅仅是为了让这种飞机爬上如此的高度。"

"这无法证明他没疯，他可能已经疯狂到足够去计划一切事情。"

"没错，当然，有可能。"

"好，那么，我们该决定一个行动计划。当他着陆时，我们要做些什么？倘若他不让飞机坠毁，没将我们全部杀死，我们该怎么做？我觉得我们应该跑上前去，祝贺他完成了他的绝妙飞行。"

"还不一定来得及让你能活下来庆贺呢，"巴纳德答道，"你就一个人留下来跑去向他道贺吧。"

康维再次对这种拖拖拉拉的争吵表示厌恶，特别是从那个美国人以一种头脑冷静的戏谑方式，似乎认为自己相当有能力来处理问题开始。康维已经发现，这个群体还远远未曾行之有效地组织起来。

constituted. Only Mallinson was inclined to be cantankerous, and that might partly be due to the altitude. Rarefied air had different effects on people; Conway, for instance, derived from it a combination of mental clarity and physical apathy that was not unpleasant. Indeed, he breathed the clear cold air in little spasms of content. The whole situation, no doubt, was appalling, but he had no power at the moment to resent anything that proceeded so purposefully and with such captivating interest.

And there came over him, too, as he stared at that superb mountain, a glow of satisfaction that there were such places still left on earth, distant, inaccessible, as yet unhumanized. The icy rampart of the Karakorams was now more striking than ever against the northern sky, which had become mouse-colored and sinister; the peaks had a chill gleam; utterly majestic and remote, their very namelessness had dignity. Those few thousand feet by which they fell short of the known giants might save them eternally from the climbing expedition; they offered a less tempting lure to the record-breaker. Conway was the antithesis of such a type; he was inclined to see vulgarity in the Western ideal of superlatives, and "the utmost for the highest" seemed to him a less reasonable and perhaps more

只有马林逊脾气烦躁不安，这可能部分是由于海拔，稀薄的空气对人体有不同的影响，比如，康维有一种头脑清醒而身体麻木的复杂感觉，但这种感觉并非令人不愉悦的，的确，他一小阵一小阵地呼吸着清新寒冷的空气。毫无疑问，整个情形是骇人听闻的。但他在此时，却没有能量去怨恨任何事情。事情进行得如此有目的性，又带有如此令人迷惑的兴趣。

当他凝视着这雄伟的山峦时，一阵满足的喜悦也涌上他心头——在这个世界上依然保留着如此遥远，难以亲近的，但又充满风土人情的地方。现在，喀拉昆仑山的冰川垒壁比以前更加醒目地伸向北方那逐渐变成灰褐色的阴暗天空；山峰隐约闪现着令人胆战心惊的寒光，绝对的巍峨、遥远，虽然没有名字，但却具有尊严。它们比那些知名的巨大山峰要矮几百英尺，但却使它们永远免受登山者的探险搅扰；它们给破纪录者提供的是一个不怎么有吸引力的诱惑。康维站在这类人的对立面；他倾向于在西方崇高理想观里看到庸俗。而那"最高的极限"对他而言，似乎是不怎么合理的，但可能与那些"一般的高度"相比更具平凡的主张。其实，他不在乎那些过多的争斗，

commonplace proposition than "the much for the high." He did not, in fact, care for excessive striving, and he was bored by mere exploits.

While he was still contemplating the scene, twilight fell, steeping the depths in a rich, velvet gloom that spread upwards like a dye. Then the whole range, much nearer now, paled into fresh splendor; a full moon rose, touching each peak in succession like some celestial lamp-lighter, until the long horizon glittered against a blue-black sky. The air grew cold and a wind sprang up, tossing the machine uncomfortably. These new distresses lowered the spirits of the passengers; it had not been reckoned that the flight could go on after dusk, and now the last hope lay in the exhaustion of gasoline. That, however, was bound to come soon. Mallinson began to argue about it, and Conway, with some reluctance, for he really did not know, gave as his estimate that the utmost distance might be anything up to a thousand miles, of which they must already have covered most. "Well, where would that bring us?" queried the youth miserably.

"It's not easy to judge, but probably some part of Tibet. If these are the Karakorams, Tibet lies beyond. One of the crests, by the way, must be K₂, which is

他对纯粹的功名已经厌烦了。

当他还在凝视着飞机窗外的景色时，黄昏降临，深深地浸染在那丰厚的，像天鹅绒一样的朦胧中；就像染色一样向上扩展。然后，整座山脉现在离得更近了，在闪现的光辉里渐渐惨白。一轮满月渐渐升起，接连绕过每一座山峰，好像天上的明灯，直到绕过青蓝色天空那闪闪发光的长长地平线。空气逐渐变冷，一阵狂风大作，飞机颠簸令人很不舒服。这些新的痛苦削弱着乘客的精神。乘客们不能推测出飞机在黄昏后还能不能继续飞行。现在，仅剩的希望就在于燃油的耗尽。而这在不久之后就会出现。马林逊开始对此事争论不休，康维却带有几分不情愿，因为他是真的不清楚，所以只给出了他自己的估计：极限距离可能将达到 1000 英里，他们一定已经飞行了其中大部分的航程。"那么，我们将会被带到哪里去呢？"这个年轻人凄惨地询问着。

"不好判断，也许是西藏的某个部分，倘若这些山就是喀拉昆仑山，那么西藏就在这里。顺便说一句，其中的一座山峰肯定是 K₂，通

generally counted the second highest mountain in the world."

"Next on the list after Everest," commented Barnard. "Gee, this is some scenery."

"And from a climber's point of view much stiffer than Everest. The Duke of Abruzzi gave it up as an absolutely impossible peak."

"*Oh, God!*" muttered Mallinson testily, but Barnard laughed. "I guess you must be the official guide on this trip, Conway, and I'll admit that if I only had a flash of café cognac I wouldn't care if it's Tibet or Tennessee."

"But what are we going to do about it?" urged Mallinson again. "Why are we here? What can be the point of it all? I don't see how you can make jokes about it."

"Well, it's as good as making a scene about it, young fellow. Besides, if the man *is* off his nut, as you've suggested, there probably *isn't* any point."

"He *must* be mad. I can't think of any other explanation. Can you, Conway?"

Conway shook his head.

Miss Brinklow turned round as she might have done during the interval of a play. "As you haven't asked my opinion, perhaps I oughtn't to give it," she began, with shrill modesty, "but I should like to say that I agree with Mr. Mallinson. I'm sure the poor man can't be quite right in

常被认为是世界第二高峰。"

"仅随在埃菲尔主峰之后，"巴纳德评说，"哎呀，这真是一种自然风光啊。"

"从一个登山者的观点出发，这山比埃菲尔主峰更要艰险。艾伯路奇公爵把它当成一个绝对不可能攀登的山峰而放弃了。"

"哦，上帝！"马林逊烦躁地嘟囔着。但巴纳德却哈哈大笑："我猜你一定是这次旅行的官方导游，康维，我得承认，如果我只有一瓶科汉克咖啡白兰地，我才不在乎它是西藏的还是田纳西的呢。"

"但我们要怎么处理啊？"马林逊再次催促道，"我们为什么在这里？这到底能够表明什么？我不清楚你们怎能对此事开玩笑。"

"那么，还是将它视为一种自然风景吧，年轻人，此外，如果按照你说的，每个人都摘掉他的面纱，那也许就也不存在任何意义了！"

"他肯定是疯了，我无法想出其他任何解释，你能吗，康维？"

康维摇摇头。

布琳克罗小姐扭过头来，好像她每一次在谈话间隔都这么做。"因为你们并未询问我的观点，也许我不应当说，"她过于谦卑地说道，"但我想说我同意马林逊先生的观点。我可以肯定，这个可怜的

his head. The pilot, I mean, of course. There would be no excuse for him, anyhow, if he were *not* mad." She added, shouting confidentially above the din: "And do you know, this is my first trip by air! My very first! Nothing would ever induce me to do it before, though a friend of mine tried her very best to persuade me to fly from London to Paris."

"And now you're flying from India to Tibet instead," said Barnard. "That's the way things happen."

She went on: "I once knew a missionary who had been to Tibet. He said the Tibetans were very odd people. They believe we are descended from monkeys."

"Real smart of 'em."

"Oh, dear, no, I don't mean in the modern way. They've had the belief for hundreds of years, it's only one of their superstitions. Of course I'm against all of it myself, and I think Darwin was far worse than any Tibetan. I take my stand on the Bible."

"Fundamentalist, I suppose?"

But Miss Brinklow did not appear to understand the term. "I used to belong to the L.M.S.," she shrieked, "but I disagreed with them about infant baptism."

Conway continued to feel that this was a rather comic remark long after it had occurred to him that the initials were those

人的头脑完全不正常，当然，我的意思是那个飞行员。总之倘若他没疯的话，对他而言，这实在没有什么理由，"她补充说，非常自信地喊着，压过了嘈杂的声音，"你们知道吧，这是我第一次坐飞机旅行！真的是第一次！之前没有事情能迫使我坐飞机，尽管我的一个朋友曾尽全力劝说我从伦敦飞往巴黎。"

"而此时，你是从印度飞到西藏，"巴纳德说道，"有时事情就是这样。"

布琳克罗继续说，"我曾认识一个去过西藏的传教士，他说西藏人非常古怪，他们相信我们是猴子的后裔。"

"他们真是聪明。"

"哦，亲爱的，不，我并不是指现代意义的，他们有这种信仰已经好几百年了，这仅仅是他们的众多迷信之一，当然，我自己抵制所有迷信，而且我觉得达尔文远比任何一个藏民还要糟糕，我坚信《圣经》。"

"我猜你是个信奉原教旨主义的人？"

但布琳克罗小姐似乎并没理解这句话的含义。"我过去隶属于L.M.S.[2]，"她尖声喊叫道，"可我对于婴儿洗礼一事并不同意"

康维觉得这是一种相当滑稽

---

2 L.M.S：指伦敦传道协会。

of the London Missionary Society. Still picturing the inconveniences of holding a theological argument at Euston Station, he began to think that there was something slightly fascinating about Miss Brinklow. He even wondered if he could offer her any article of his clothing for the night, but decided at length that her constitution was probably wirier than his. So he huddled up, closed his eyes, and went quite easily and peacefully to sleep.

And the flight proceeded.

Suddenly they were all wakened by a lurch of the machine. Conway's head struck the window, dazing him for the moment; a returning lurch sent him floundering between the two tiers of seats. It was much colder. The first thing he did, automatically, was to glance at his watch; it showed half-past one, he must have been asleep for some time. His ears were full of a loud, flapping sound, which he took to be imaginary until he realized that the engine had been shut off and that the plane was rushing against a gale. Then he stared through the window and could see the earth quite close, vague and snail-gray, scampering underneath. "He's going to land!" Mallinson shouted; and Barnard, who had also been flung out of his seat, responded with a saturnine: "If he's lucky." Miss Brinklow, whom the entire

的讨论，很长时间之前这便在伦敦教会组织中出现。还有，他记起那次在奥斯顿车站进行的关于神学的争执所带来的麻烦场景。他开始觉得布琳克罗小姐身上有某些轻微吸引人的东西。他甚至在想，他是否应当为她拿上一件自己的衣服以便她夜晚不着凉，但最终觉得，她的身体也许比自己的更结实，于是他蜷缩起来，闭上双眼，相当轻松平和地睡着了。

飞机继续飞行着。

突然，他们所有人都被飞机的猛然倾倒所惊醒，康维的头撞上了窗户，这让他眩晕了一会儿；然后飞机的一个回侧令他在两排座位当中的地方跟跟跄跄。这时天更冷了，他做的第一件事便是下意识地瞥了一眼他的表：显示是1点半，他肯定已经睡了挺长一段时间了。他的耳朵里充斥着很大的震动声，他把它当成幻觉，直到他意识到引擎已经关闭，飞机正逆着大风滑翔着。然后他通过窗子向外看，能够看到朦朦胧胧的一片灰色在下面疾驰着，此时地面已经相当接近了。"他准备着陆了！"马林逊大叫道，而刚刚被从座位上抛出来的巴纳德，讥讽地回应道："如果他幸运的话。"布琳克罗小姐似乎完全未被整个骚动干扰，只是镇定地调整了一下她的帽子，仿佛多佛海港

commotion seemed to have disturbed least of all, was adjusting her hat as calmly as if Dover Harbor were just in sight.

Presently the plane touched ground. But it was a bad landing this time – "Oh, my God, damned bad, *damned* bad!" Mallinson groaned as he clutched at his seat during ten seconds of crashing and swaying. Something was heard to strain and snap, and one of the tires exploded. "That's done it," he added in tones of anguished pessimism. "A broken tail-skid, we'll have to stay where we are now, that's certain."

Conway, never talkative at times of crisis, stretched his stiffened legs and felt his head where it had banged against the window. A bruise, nothing much. He must do something to help these people. But he was the last of the four to stand up when the plane came to rest. "Steady," he called out as Mallinson wrenched open the door of the cabin and prepared to make the jump to earth; and eerily, in the comparative silence, the youth's answer came: "No need to be steady – this looks like the end of the world – there's not a soul about, anyhow."

A moment later, chilled and shivering, they were all aware that this was so. With no sound in their ears save the fierce gusts of wind and their own crunching footsteps, they felt themselves at the

就在视野中。

不久，飞机着陆了，但这却是一次糟糕的着陆——"哦，我的上帝！真他妈糟糕，真他妈糟透了！"飞机冲撞和摇摆了10秒钟，马林逊用力抓着座位抱怨道。一声猛烈的撞击声响了起来——其中一个轮胎爆炸了。"完蛋了，"他以痛苦悲观的声调补充道，"一个尾橇破了，我们不得不待在现在的地方了，那是肯定的。"

康维在危急时刻从来不多嘴，他伸展着僵硬的双腿，摸了摸脑袋上碰到窗户的地方。起了个包，没什么事。他必须做点什么去帮助这些人。但当飞机停止移动时，他是4个人里最后一个站起来的。"当心点，"当马林逊扭开舱门然后准备跳到地面上时，他大声喊道。可怕的是，在一阵相对的沉默之后，传来了年轻人的声音："没必要担心——这里看起来是世界的尽头——总之，没有一个人。"

片刻之后，他们全部都意识到这里是如此的寒冷和令人瑟瑟发抖。他们的耳朵里没有其他声音，只有狂风在猛烈撕扯，还有他们自己嘎吱嘎吱的脚步声。他们觉得自

mercy of something dour and savagely melancholy – a mood in which both earth and air were saturated. The moon looked to have disappeared behind clouds, and starlight illumined a tremendous emptiness heaving with wind. Without thought or knowledge, one could have guessed that this bleak world was mountain-high, and that the mountains rising from it were mountains on top of mountains. A range of them gleamed on a far horizon like a row of dog-teeth.

Mallinson, feverishly active, was already making for the cockpit. "I'm not scared of the fellow on land, whoever he is," he cried. "I'm going to tackle him right away…"

The others watched apprehensively, hypnotized by the spectacle of such energy. Conway sprang after him, but too late to prevent the investigation. After a few seconds, however, the youth dropped down again, gripping his arm and muttering in a hoarse, sobered staccato: "I say, Conway, it's queer… I think the fellow's ill or dead or something… I can't get a word out of him. Come up and look… I took his revolver, at any rate."

"Better give it to me," said Conway, and though still rather dazed by the recent blow on his head, he nerved himself for action. Of all times and places and situations on earth, this seemed to him to

己置身于某种严厉、残酷抑郁的怜悯当中，连土壤和空气都饱含了这种情绪，月亮看起来已经消失在云层背后，星光伴着狂风的嘶吼照亮出一种无边的空旷。不需要思考和知识，任何人都能够猜到这凄凉的世界是高山环抱，山峰又从其他的山顶上耸立出来。有一列山脉在遥远的地平线处熠熠生辉，仿佛一排犬牙。

马林逊非常激动地行动起来，已经准备好打开驾驶舱门。"在陆地上，我才不害怕这家伙呢，无论他是谁，"他大叫道，"我打算立刻与他解决这个问题……"

其他几个人担心地四处看，被这如此紧急的场面弄得精神恍惚。康维在他后面冲过去，但太晚了，他没有能够及时地阻拦他的行动。可几秒过后，这个年轻人又跳了下来，紧紧抓住康维的胳膊，用嘶哑的声音喃喃自语，绷着脸断断续续地说："我说，康维，真是古怪……我认为这家伙是病了，要不就是死了或是怎么的；我从他那里得不到一句话，过来看看……不管怎么说，我拿到了他的左轮手枪。"

"最好把枪给我，"康维说，尽管仍然被刚才头上那一撞弄得相当眩晕，可他仍然有勇气来行动。对他而言，现在周遭的环境和

combine the most hideous discomforts. He hoisted himself stiffly into a position from which he could see, not very well, into the enclosed cockpit. There was a strong smell of gasoline, so he did not risk striking a match. He could just discern the pilot, huddled forward, his head sprawling over the controls. He shook him, unfastened his helmet, and loosened the clothes round his neck. A moment later he turned round to report: "Yes, there's something happened to him. We must get him out." But an observer might have added that something had happened to Conway as well. His voice was sharper, more incisive; no longer did he seem to be hovering on the brink of some profound doubtfulness. The time, the place, the cold, his fatigue, were now of less account; there was a job that simply had to be done, and the more conventional part of him was uppermost and preparing to do it.

With Barnard and Mallinson assisting, the pilot was extracted from his seat and lifted to the ground. He was unconscious, not dead. Conway had no particular medical knowledge, but, as to most men who have lived in outlandish places, the phenomena of illness were mostly familiar. "Possibly a heart attack brought on by the high altitude," he diagnosed, stooping over the unknown man. "We can do very little for him out here – there's no

情形都相当恶劣，以至于令人恐惧和不舒服。他僵硬着爬到一个位置上，在那里他能够不很清楚地看到紧闭着的驾驶舱。一股浓重的汽油味扑鼻而来，所以他没有冒险划火柴。他仅仅能够辨认出飞行员，他身体向前缩成一团，脑袋趴在操纵杆上。他摇了摇他，解开他的头盔，然后松开他脖子上的衣服。片刻之后，他扭过头来报告说："是的，他确实出了一些事，我们必须将他弄出去。"每个旁观者感觉康维也可能发生了一些事。他的声音更加刺耳，更加尖锐；他似乎不再在某种深刻且充满疑问的边缘徘徊不前。在这种时刻，这种地点，这种寒冷的天气里，他的精疲力竭现在已经不再是什么理由了。很简单，有一个工作必须去完成。他更加习惯的角色就是眼下准备去做的事。

在巴纳德与马林逊的协助下，飞行员被从座位拉出来，放到地上。他没有意识了，但并没死，康维没有专业的医学常识，但像他这种经常在外国地区生活的人，对疾病的症状大部分都很熟悉。"可能是高海拔造成的心脏病发作。"他诊断道，同时俯下身去审视这个不认识的男子。"在这里我们能够为他做的太少了——在没有什么可以为他遮蔽这恐怖的大风的地方，最

shelter from this infernal wind. Better get him inside the cabin, and ourselves too. We haven't an idea where we are, and it's hopeless to make a move until daylight."

The verdict and the suggestion were both accepted without dispute. Even Mallinson concurred. They carried the man into the cabin and laid him full-length along the gangway between the seats. The interior was no warmer than outside, but offered a screen to the flurries of wind. It was the wind, before much time had passed, that became the central preoccupation of them all – the leit-motif, as it were, of the whole mournful night. It was not an ordinary wind. It was not merely a strong wind or a cold wind. It was somehow a frenzy that lived all around them, a master stamping and ranting over his own domain. It tilted the loaded machine and shook it viciously, and when Conway glanced through the windows it seemed as if the wind were whirling splinters of light out of the stars.

The stranger lay inert, while Conway, with difficulty in the dimness and confined space, made what examination he could by the light of matches. But it did not reveal much. "His heart's faint," he said at last, and then Miss Brinklow, after groping in her handbag, created a small sensation. "I wonder if this would be any use to the poor man," she proffered

好将他抬进机舱里面，我们自己也是。我们弄不清楚我们在什么地方，直到天亮之前都没有希望挪动一步。"

这一定论和建议被大家一致接受，没有争执。甚至马林逊都同意。他们将这人抬进舱内，把他沿着座位当中的过道安置好。里面不比外面暖和多少，但还是提供了阻挡猛烈寒风的屏障。没过多长时间，这风已经成为了所有人的心头之患——成为了整个悲哀之夜的主旋律。它不是普通的风，它不仅仅是强冷风，不知什么原因，它就围绕着他们几个人狂暴的呼啸着：仿佛一位艺术大师在自己的领域中垂胸顿足，肆意咆哮。它令负重的飞机倾斜起来，恶狠狠地摇晃着。当康维通过窗户望出去，这风似乎仿佛是要将星星的光芒旋转着撕成碎片。

这陌生人躺在那里，一动不动，在机舱昏暗局促的空间中，康维凭借着火柴的光亮仔细地检查，但没有发现什么，"他的心脏很脆弱。"他最后说。然后布琳克罗小姐摸索了一阵手提包之后，拿出一个小瓶，"我在想这东西是否会对这可怜的人有用处。"她放下架子，"我自己从来没有沾过一滴，但我

condescendingly. "I never touch a drop myself, but I always carry it with me in case of accidents. And this *is* a sort of accident, isn't it?"

"I should say it was," replied Conway with grimness. He unscrewed the bottle, smelt it, and poured some of the brandy into the man's mouth. "Just the stuff for him. Thanks." After an interval the slightest movement of eyelids was visible. Mallinson suddenly became hysterical. "I can't help it," he cried, laughing wildly. "We all look such a lot of damn fools striking matches over a corpse… And he isn't much of a beauty, is he? Chink, I should say, if he's anything at all."

"Possibly." Conway's voice was level and rather severe. "But he's not a corpse yet. With a bit of luck we may bring him round."

"Luck? It'll be his luck, not ours."

"Don't be too sure. And shut up for the time being, anyhow."

There was enough of the schoolboy still in Mallinson to make him respond to the curt command of a senior, though he was obviously in poor control of himself. Conway, though sorry for him, was more concerned with the immediate problem of the pilot, since he, alone of them all, might be able to give some explanation of their plight. Conway had no desire to discuss the matter further in a merely speculative

总是随身携带，以防意外发生，而现在便是这种意外，不是吗？"

"我想是的，"康维冷酷地回应道。他扭开瓶盖，闻了闻，向那人嘴里倒了一点白兰地。"仅仅是为他填些东西而已，谢谢。"一段间隔过后，那人的眼皮轻轻地动了动。马林逊突然变得歇斯底里。"我忍不住了，"他大叫，狂放地哈哈大笑，"我们所有人就看着这些该死的蠢货，划着火柴围绕着一具死尸……而他不算好看，是吧？'小瘪三'，我应该说，他就是这副样子。"

"可能是，"康维的声音平缓但严厉，"可他并非一具死尸，我们将他带上，可能会有点好运气呢。"

"好运？这会是他的运气，不是我们的。"

"别太过肯定，不管怎么说，闭上嘴待一段时间！"

马林逊身上还有十足的学生气，导致他本身对长者的命令有这天生的盲从性，尽管显而易见，他自控力并不怎么样。虽然，康维对他感到抱歉，可他更关心这飞行员当下的问题，因为他在他们所有人中孤立着，也许能够对他们的状况给出解释。康维没有以单纯推测的方法来进一步讨论这件事的欲望，

way; there had been enough of that during the journey. He was uneasy now beyond his continuing mental curiosity, for he was aware that the whole situation had ceased to be excitingly perilous and was threatening to become a trial of endurance ending in catastrophe. Keeping vigil throughout that gale-tormented night, he faced facts nonetheless frankly because he did not trouble to enunciate them to the others. He guessed that the flight had progressed far beyond the western range of the Himalayas towards the less known heights of the Kuen-Lun. In that event they would by now have reached the loftiest and least hospitable part of the earth's surface, the Tibetan plateau, two miles high even in its lowest valleys, a vast, uninhabited, and largely unexplored region of wind-swept upland. Somewhere they were, in that forlorn country, marooned in far less comfort than on most desert islands. Then abruptly, as if to answer his curiosity by increasing it, a rather awe-inspiring change took place. The moon, which he had thought to be hidden by clouds, swung over the lip of some shadowy eminence and, whilst still not showing itself directly, unveiled the darkness ahead. Conway could see the outline of a long valley, with rounded, sad-looking low hills on either side jet-black against the deep electric blue of

旅途期间已经讨论得足够了。现在他心神不宁，已经再没有心思去查明其中的究竟；因为他意识到整个情况已经不再是令人兴奋的冒险，而预示着将变成一场持久的考验，最终以灾难性的结局结束。这一夜狂风肆虐，康维一直守夜。虽然如此，可他坦诚面对现实，他并未让这一结论去困扰其他人。他猜测这次飞行已经远远越过喜马拉雅山西部山脉，朝向昆仑山那些鲜为人知的高峰进发。以此推论，他们到现在已经抵达地球表面最高也是最荒无人烟的地带，即西藏高原，这里最低的峡谷也有两英里高，这是一大片杳无人迹、完全未被探索的、狂风肆虐的高原区域。他们正置身那片废弃的山野之地。这种陷入孤独无助之境，远远不如被放逐到沙漠孤岛更惬意。突然之间，一种令人振奋的变化发生了，就像要回答他的好奇一样。被藏到云朵后面的月亮又悬挂在有些朦朦胧胧的高地边缘的上空，同时仍然没有显现出来，前方渐渐揭开了黑暗的面纱。康维能够看到那长长的山谷的轮廓，每一侧都是圆的，看上去令人忧伤的低矮山峰，墨黑色烘托着夜幕下那深深的电火花蓝色。但他的双眼无法抵抗地被引领向山谷的前方，因为在那里，它们高耸着形成隘口，在月光的朗照下异常辉煌。他似乎将它视为世界上最可

the night-sky. But it was to the head of the valley that his eyes were led irresistibly, for there, soaring into the gap, and magnificent in the full shimmer of moonlight, appeared what he took to be the loveliest mountain on earth. It was an almost perfect cone of snow, simple in outline as if a child had drawn it, and impossible to classify as to size, height or nearness. It was so radiant, so serenely poised, that he wondered for a moment if it were real at all. Then, while he gazed, a tiny puff clouded the edge of the pyramid, giving life to the vision before the faint rumble of the avalanche confirmed it.

He had an impulse to rouse the others to share the spectacle, but decided after consideration that its effect might not be tranquilizing. Nor was it so, from a commonsense view-point; such virgin splendors merely emphasized the facts of isolation and danger. There was quite a probability that the nearest human settlement was hundreds of miles away. And they had no food; they were unarmed except for one revolver; the aeroplane was damaged and almost fuel-less, even if anyone had known how to fly. They had no clothes suited to the terrific chills and winds; Mallinson's motoring-coat and his own ulster were quite inadequate, and even Miss Brinklow, woolied and mufflered as for a polar expedition

爱的山峰。它几乎是一座完美的冰锥，轮廓很简单，就像一个孩童描绘的，它的高度或者距离都不可能估量。它是如此的熠熠生辉，如此的安详，泰然自若，以至于康维考虑了一会儿，它是否是真实的。然后，当他凝视时，一股轻轻的烟雾遮住了这金字塔一般的山的边缘，在那微弱的雪崩隆隆作响加以证实之前，先证实了这一景象的真实性。

他有一种冲动想叫醒其他人来分享这壮丽的景象。可考虑后认为这样可能会破坏这种静谧。不只是如此，从常识出发，如此的原始的壮观景象仅仅是强调了与世隔绝以及潜在危险等事实。很可能，最近的人类定居者也有百里之远。他们没有食物；他们没有武器，除了一把左轮手枪；即使有人懂得如何驾驶这飞机，它也已经损坏而且几乎没有燃料了。他们没有能抵挡这恐怖的寒冷的衣服，马林逊的摩托服还有他自己的风衣根本不够用，布琳克罗小姐甚至穿上羊毛衣，围上围巾，仿佛是一次极地探险（康维第一眼看到她时，认为这相当滑稽），她明显感觉不到兴奋。他们所有人，除了康维自己，都被

(ridiculous, he had thought, on first beholding her), could not be feeling happy. They were all, too, except himself, affected by the altitude. Even Barnard had sunk into melancholy under the strain. Mallinson was muttering to himself; it was clear what would happen to him if these hardships went on for long. In face of such distressful prospects Conway found himself quite unable to restrain an admiring glance at Miss Brinklow. She was not, he reflected, a normal person, no woman who taught Afghans to sing hymns could be considered so. But she was, after every calamity, still normally abnormal, and he was deeply obliged to her for it. "I hope you're not feeling too bad?" he said sympathetically, when he caught her eye.

"The soldiers during the war had to suffer worse things than this," she replied.

The comparison did not seem to Conway a very valuable one. In point of fact, he had never spent a night in the trenches quite so thoroughly unpleasant, though doubtless many others had. He had concentrated his attention on the pilot, now breathing fitfully and sometimes slightly stirring. Probably Mallinson was right in guessing the man Chinese. He had the typical Mongol nose and cheekbones, despite his successful impersonation of a British flight – lieutenant. Mallinson had called him ugly, but Conway, who had

高海拔所影响，甚至巴纳德在过度紧张之下都陷入抑郁中。马林逊喃喃自语：非常清楚倘若这种苦难持续很长时间，他会怎么样。面对如此凄苦困难重重的前景，康维发现自己根本无法抑制自己对布琳克罗小姐投去崇拜的目光。他细想着，她并非一个普通人，没有一个教阿富汗人唱圣歌的女性会被如此认为！但在每一次磨难以后，她还是具备平凡里的不平凡的特质，因此他对她产生了深深的好感。"我希望你不要感觉太糟糕。"当他捕捉到她的目光时，他同情地说道。

"士兵在战争期间一定遭受了比这更糟糕的情况。"她回应道。

对康维而言，这种比喻对他来说没有任何价值。其实，以前在战壕里，自己从来没有度过一个如此难过的夜晚，毫无疑问，其他很多人都有过这种经历。他将注意力都集中在那个飞行员身上，现在他的呼吸断断续续，偶尔有轻微的抽搐。马林逊猜测这个人可能是中国人。他有着典型的蒙古式的鼻子和颧骨，虽然他成功地假冒了一位英国空军上尉。马林逊说他很丑，但曾经在中国生活过的康维却觉得，他绝对属于看得过去的类型，但是

lived in China, thought him a fairly passable specimen, though now, in the burnished circle of match-flame, his pallid skin and gaping mouth were not pretty.

The night dragged on, as if each minute were something heavy and tangible that had to be pushed to make way for the next. Moonlight faded after a time, and with it that distant specter of the mountain; then the triple mischiefs of darkness, cold, and wind increased until dawn. As though at its signal, the wind dropped, leaving the world in compassionate quietude. Framed in the pale triangle ahead, the mountain showed again, gray at first, then silver, then pink as the earliest sun rays caught the summit. In the lessening gloom the valley itself took shape, revealing a floor of rock and shingle sloping upwards. It was not a friendly picture, but to Conway, as he surveyed, there came a queer perception of fineness in it, of something that had no romantic appeal at all, but a steely, almost an intellectual quality. The white pyramid in the distance compelled the mind's assent as passionlessly as a Euclidean theorem, and when at last the sun rose into a sky of deep delphinium blue, he felt only a little less than comfortable again.

As the air grew warmer the others wakened, and he suggested carrying the pilot into the open, where the sharp dry air

现在，在一圈柴火的光线之下，他那惨白的皮肤以及张开的嘴确实不怎么好看。

夜晚拖拖拉拉地向前行进，似乎每一分钟都有些沉重而且能够触摸；仿佛不得不将推着它为下一分钟让路。过了一会儿，月光逐渐黯淡下去，与远处鬼魂般的群山连在一起；然后是黑暗加倍在作怪，寒冷以及狂风加剧直到黎明。仿佛是信号一般，风逐渐减弱，留给这个世界富于同情的静谧。前面是惨白的三角形框架，山峰再次呈现在眼前。最初是灰色，然后是银色，再然后当太阳最初的光线投射到山峰上，山峰竟呈现出粉色。在逐渐减弱的阴暗里，山谷显露出自己的形状，岩石以及卵石倾斜着，向上凸显出一片地面。这并非一幅柔和的画面；但对康维而言，当他眺望周围时，里面包含着一种奇怪的精细感觉；根本没有什么浪漫主义的吸引力，却只是一种坚硬如钢的、几乎是睿智的特质。在远处，这座白色金字塔迫使你想起它就像欧几里德法则一样没有激情。当太阳最终升起在深蓝色的天空时，他再次感觉到一丝丝的惬意。

当空气逐渐升温时，其他人都醒了。他便建议将飞行员抬到旷地中去。那里猛烈而干燥的空气还有

and the sunlight might help to revive him. This was done, and they began a second and pleasanter vigil. Eventually the man opened his eyes and began to speak convulsively. His four passengers stooped over him, listening intently to sounds that were meaningless except to Conway, who occasionally made answers. After some time the man became weaker, talked with increasing difficulty, and finally died. That was about mid-morning.

Conway then turned to his companions. "I'm sorry to say he told me very little – little, I mean, compared with what we should like to know. Merely that we are in Tibet, which is obvious. He didn't give any coherent account of why he had brought us here, but he seemed to know the locality. He spoke a kind of Chinese that I don't understand very well, but I think he said something about a lamasery near here, along the valley, I gathered, where we could get food and shelter. Shangri-La, he called it. *La* is Tibetan for mountain pass. He was most emphatic that we should go there."

"Which doesn't seem to me any reason at all why we should," said Mallinson. "After all, he was probably off his head. Wasn't he?"

"You know as much about that as I do. But if we don't go to this place, where else

阳光可能会对抢救他有帮助。这个方案得以实施，于是他们开始了第二轮的守夜行动。这个人最终睁开了双眼，然后开始痉挛般地讲话。他的4位乘客都俯下身去，仔细倾听着对他们毫无意义的声音，除了康维能偶尔作出回答。一段时间过后，这人逐渐虚弱，说话也愈发困难，最终去世，当时大约是上午的中间时分。

然后康维转向他的同伴，"我非常遗憾地说，他仅仅告诉我一点点，我的意思是，跟我们想要知道的比，只有一点。只有一点是显而易见的，那就是我们已经置身西藏，至于他为什么将我们带到这里，他并未给出相关的理由，但他似乎清楚位置。他讲的那一种汉语我不怎么能理解，可我认为他说到沿着山谷附近一座喇嘛寺。我猜我们能够去那里找些食物，也能避避风寒。他称呼那里为香格里拉。'拉'在藏语中代表'山中隘道'。他着重强调我们应该去那里。"

"我看我们似乎根本没有理由去那里，"马林逊说道，"毕竟，他也许头脑混乱了，不是吗？"

"你所了解的与我知道的差不多。但如果我们不去那个地方，

are we to go?"

"Anywhere you like, I don't care. All I'm certain of is that this Shangri-La, if it's in that direction, must be a few extra miles from civilization. I should feel happier if we were lessening the distance, not increasing it. Damnation, man, aren't you going to get us back?"

Conway replied patiently: "I don't think you properly understand the position, Mallinson. We're in a part of the world that no one knows very much about, except that it's difficult and dangerous even for a fully equipped expedition. Considering that hundreds of miles of this sort of country probably surround us on all sides, the notion of walking back to Peshawar doesn't strike me as very hopeful."

"I don't think I could possibly manage it," said Miss Brinklow seriously.

Barnard nodded. "It looks as if we're darned lucky, then, if this lamasery *is* just around the corner."

"Comparatively lucky, maybe," agreed Conway. "After all, we've no food, and as you can see for yourselves, the country isn't the kind it would be easy to live on. In a few hours we shall all be famished. And then to-night, if we were to stay here, we should have to face the wind and the cold again. It's not a pleasant prospect. Our only chance, it seems to me, is to find

我们还有其他地方可以去吗？

"去任何想去的地方，我不在乎。我可以肯定的是，这个香格里拉，如果在那个方向上，肯定与文明世界还要有好几里呢。倘若我们是在缩短距离而非拉长的话，我会感觉更开心。真该死，老兄，你不打算带我们回去了吗？"

康维耐心回应道："我认为你并未完全了解我们的位置，马林逊。我们现在置身于世界上没人了解多少的地方，即便是装备齐全的探险，都十分困难和危险。考虑一下，可能有几百里这样的区域正在四面八方包围着我们，我觉得走着回到白沙瓦没有什么希望。"

"我认为我可能无法完成。"布琳克罗认真地说道。

巴纳德点点头，"看起来，如果这喇嘛寺就在附近，那咱们还真是非常走运的。"

"可能相当幸运，"康维赞同道，"毕竟，我们没有食物，而且你们自己也都看到了，这地方并非容易生存之处。几个小时之后，我们便会全部挨饿。然后今晚，如果我们还待在这里，便要再次面对狂风严寒，这并非是我们所期盼的结果。我看，我们唯一的机会便是发现其他人，但除了已经被告知的地

some other human beings, and where else should we begin looking for them except where we've been told they exist?"

"And what if it's a trap?" asked Mallinson, but Barnard supplied an answer. "A nice warm trap," he said, "with a piece of cheese in it, would suit me down to the ground."

They laughed, except Mallinson, who looked distraught and nerve-racked. Finally Conway went on: "I take it, then, that we're all more or less agreed? There's an obvious way along the valley; it doesn't look too steep, though we shall have to take it slowly. In any case, we could do nothing here. We couldn't even bury this man without dynamite. Besides, the lamasery people may be able to supply us with porters for the journey back. We shall need them. I suggest we start at once, so that if we don't locate the place by late afternoon we shall have time to return for another night in the cabin."

"And supposing we *do* locate it?" queried Mallinson, still intransigeant. "Have we any guarantee that we shan't be murdered?"

"None at all. But I think it is a less, and perhaps also a preferable risk to being starved or frozen to death." He added, feeling that such chilly logic might not be entirely suited for the occasion: "As a matter of fact, murder is the very last thing

方，我们还能去哪里呢？"

"如果那是个陷阱怎么办？"马林逊问道。巴纳德给出了答案。"一个绝佳又温馨的陷阱，"他说，"里面还有一片奶酪，这简直太合我的心意了。"

大家哈哈大笑，除了马林逊，他看起来一副心烦意乱、精神紧张的样子。最后，康维继续说："我赞同，那么我们大家都或多或少同意了吧？沿着山谷有条明显的小路，看起来不怎么陡峭，我们要走得慢些。不管怎么说，我们在这里无所事事。我们甚至不能不用炸药便将这个人埋葬。此外，喇嘛寺里的人也许能够为我们提供回程的向导呢。我们会需要他们的，我建议我们立刻启程，这样的话，如果我们到傍晚都无法找到那地方，也能及时返回机舱再待一晚。"

"那倘若我们确实找到了呢？"马林逊依旧毫不妥协地质问道，"谁又能保证我们不被人杀掉呢？"

"没人能。但我觉得这样的风险较小，与被饿死或被冻死相比来说，这可能是一个可取的冒险。"康维感觉如此令人心寒的逻辑可能完全不适合于这种场合，补充道，"其实，人们很少能将谋杀与

one would expect in a Buddhist monastery. It would be rather less likely than being killed in an English cathedral."

"Like Saint Thomas of Canterbury," said Miss Brinklow, nodding an emphatic agreement, but completely spoiling his point. Mallinson shrugged his shoulders and responded with melancholy irritation: "Very well, then, we'll be off to Shangri-La. Wherever and whatever it is, we'll try it. But let's hope it's not half-way up that mountain."

The remark served to fix their glances on the glittering cone towards which the valley pointed. Sheerly magnificent it looked in the full light of day; and then their gaze turned to a stare, for they could see, far away and approaching them down the slope, the figures of men. "Providence!" whispered Miss Brinklow.

一座佛教寺庙联系起来。当然比起在英国大教堂里出现的杀人案件，这里当真是鲜有可能出现。"

"类似坎特伯雷教堂的圣·托马斯。"布琳克罗小姐点头表示强有力的赞同。但她完全误解了康维的意思。马林逊耸耸肩，忧郁又愤怒地回应道："那太好了！我们就前往香格里拉。不管它在什么地方，也不管它是什么，我们会试试的。但咱们还是希望它不要在那座山的半山腰上。"

这句话将大家的目光都锁定到那座熠熠生辉的雪锥，山谷也朝向它展开。在白天充足的光线下，它看起来雄伟壮丽，他们那双凝视出神的眼睛突然瞪大了许多，因为他们能够看到，在远处，一些人影正沿着斜坡下来。"天意啊！"布琳克罗小姐低声细语道。

CHAPTER 3

第三章

PART of Conway was always an onlooker, however active might be the rest. Just now, while waiting for the strangers to come nearer, he refused to be fussed into deciding what he might or mightn't do in any number of possible contingencies. And this was not bravery, or coolness, or any especially sublime confidence in his own power to make decisions on the spur of the moment. It was, if the worst view be taken, a form of indolence, an unwillingness to interrupt his mere spectator's interest in what was happening.

As the figures moved down the valley they revealed themselves to be a party of a dozen or more, carrying with them a hooded chair. In this, a little later, could be discerned a person robed in blue. Conway could not imagine where they were all going, but it certainly seemed providential, as Miss Brinklow had said, that such a detachment should chance to be passing just there and then. As soon as he was within hailing distance he left his own party and walked ahead, though not hurriedly, for he knew that Orientals enjoy the ritual of meeting and like to take their

康维总是一个旁观者，但充满活力可能是他性格的主要方面。就是现在，当他们正等着那些陌生人逐渐靠近时，他拒绝考虑有任何意外可能发生的情况下，他该做什么。这不是勇敢或者冷静，或是在事发之时，自己有当机立断的异常的自信。倘若从最糟糕的角度看，这是一种懒惰，不愿意在发生事情时使自己的利益受到损害。

当那些人影移动下山谷时，可以看出，是一个有十二三人或更多人的团体，抬着一个带帐篷的轿子，片刻之后，乘客们能够辨认出里面有一个身着蓝色长袍的人。康维无法想象他们所有人准备去什么地方；但肯定，似乎就像布琳克罗小组所说的那样，是天意，如此不偏不倚，恰巧就在此时此地和他们碰上了。没到双方走近，康维便丢下同伴，走上前去，但并不匆忙。因为他清楚东方人讲究会面的礼节而且喜欢在上面花时间。当还有几码的距离时，他停住了，并恭恭

time over it. Halting when a few yards off, he bowed with due courtesy. Much to his surprise the robed figure stepped from the chair, came forward with dignified deliberation, and held out his hand. Conway responded, and observed an old or elderly Chinese, gray-haired, clean-shaven, and rather pallidly decorative in a silk embroidered gown. He in his turn appeared to be submitting Conway to the same kind of reckoning. Then, in precise and perhaps too accurate English, he said: "I am from the lamasery of Shangri-La."

Conway bowed again, and after a suitable pause began to explain briefly the circumstances that had brought him and his three companions to such an unfrequented part of the world. At the end of the recital the Chinese made a gesture of understanding. "It is indeed remarkable," he said, and gazed reflectively at the damaged aeroplane. Then he added: "My name is Chang, if you would be so good as to present me to your friends."

Conway managed to smile urbanely. He was rather taken with this latest phenomenon, a Chinese who spoke perfect English and observed the social formalities of Bond Street amidst the wilds of Tibet. He turned to the others, who had by this time caught up and were

敬敬地鞠了一躬。令他大感惊奇的是，这位身着长衫的人物从轿子里迈步下来，以一种威严从容的表情走上前来，然后伸出手。康维回应着，并观察着这位汉族老者或者说是上了些年纪的汉人，头发花白，刮得干干净净的脸被一套丝质刺绣的长衫映衬得相当苍白。现在似乎轮到他向康维表达同样预先准备好的恭敬之情。然后，他以纯正到太过精准的英语说："我来自香格里拉寺。"

康维再次鞠躬致意，在适宜的停顿之后，他开始简略地解释这种情况，将他还有他的3个同伴带到这个世界上人迹罕至之地。在结束时，这个汉族人做出一个表示理解的姿势。"这确实是非同凡响啊，"他说着并对那架破损的飞机凝神思考着，然后补充道，"我姓张，如果你愿意，可以把我介绍给你这些朋友。"

康维竭力笑得彬彬有礼。他被刚才的景象彻底弄晕了——一个汉人讲一口出色的英语，而且遵守邦德大街的社交礼仪，却置身西藏的荒野当中！他转向其他人，这时他们已经都赶上前来，对于刚才的偶遇都表现出不同程度的惊奇。"布

regarding the encounter with varying degrees of astonishment. "Miss Brinklow… Mr. Barnard, who is an American… Mr. Mallinson… and my own name is Conway. We are all glad to see you, though the meeting is almost as puzzling as the fact of our being here at all. Indeed, we were just about to make our way to your lamasery, so it is doubly fortunate. If you could give us directions for the journey – "

"There is no need for that. I shall be delighted to act as your guide."

"But I could not think of putting you to such trouble. It is exceedingly kind of you, but if the distance is not far – "

"It is not far, but it is not easy, either. I shall esteem it an honor to accompany you and your friends."

"But really – "

"I must insist."

Conway thought that the argument, in its context of place and circumstance, was in some danger of becoming ludicrous. "Very well," he responded. "I'm sure we are all most obliged."

Mallinson, who had been somberly enduring these pleasantries, now interposed with something of the shrill acerbity of the barrack-square. "Our stay won't be long," he announced curtly. "We shall pay for anything we have, and we should like to hire some of your men to

琳克罗小姐……巴纳德先生，美国人……马林逊先生……还有，我的名字是康维。我们所有人都很高兴见到您。但这次碰面几乎就像我们到达这里的事情一样完全令人迷惑。的确，我们刚刚正打算前往你们寺，如果您能够为我们的旅行指引方向，那我们更是加倍幸运了。"

"不需要如此客气，我非常高兴成为你们的向导。"

"但我怕这会带给您很大的麻烦，您太善良了，但如果距离不算太远的话……"

"不算远，可也不容易走。若我可以陪同你和你的朋友，这是我的荣幸。"

"可确实——"

"我一定会的。"

康维认为这种关于从地点到环境前后经过的争执有蕴含某种荒唐可笑之嫌。"非常好，"他回应道，"我肯定我们所有人都感激不尽。"

马林逊之前一直抑郁地忍受着这些打趣，现在却带着某种古板刺耳的刻薄插话道："我们不会待得很久的，"他草率地宣布着，"我们会偿付我们使用的任何东西，我们想雇用你们的人帮我们回去。我们希望尽快返回文明世界。"

help us on our journey back. We want to return to civilization as soon as possible."

"And are you so very certain that you are away from it?"

The query, delivered with much suavity, only stung the youth to further sharpness. "I'm quite sure I'm far away from where I want to be, and so are we all. We shall be grateful for temporary shelter, but we shall be more grateful still if you'll provide means for us to return. How long do you suppose the journey to India will take?"

"I really could not say at all."

"Well, I hope we're not going to have any trouble about it. I've had some experience of hiring native porters, and we shall expect you to use your influence to get us a square deal."

Conway felt that most of all this was rather needlessly truculent, and he was just about to intervene when the reply came, still with immense dignity: "I can only assure you, Mr. Mallinson, that you will be honorably treated and that ultimately you will have no regrets."

"*Ultimately*!" Mallinson exclaimed, pouncing on the word, but there was greater ease in avoiding a scene since wine and fruit were now on offer, having been unpacked by the marching party, stocky Tibetans in sheepskins, fur hats, and yak-skin boots. The wine had a pleasant flavor, not unlike a good hock,

"你如此确定你远离文明了吗？"

这种以和蔼可亲的方式表达的质询，只能令这个年轻人更加狂躁。"我非常确定，我已经远离了想去的地方，我们所有人都是这样。对于暂时的避难所，我们感激不尽，但倘若你能为我们提供返回的办法，我们会更为感激的，你觉得前往印度的旅程将会花多长时间？"

"我当真一点儿也说不出来。"

"好吧，我希望我们不会给你带来任何麻烦。我对于雇用当地的搬运工有一些经验，通过您的帮助我们希望得到合理的解决方法。"

康维感到这些话语大部分都是相当不必要的尖刻言辞，他正打算干预一下时，听到了仍然是以非常威严的语气作出的回应，"我只能向你保证，马林逊先生，你将会得到非常体面的款待，最终你不会有任何遗憾的。"

"最终？"马林逊抓住这词大嚷道。但此时酒水和果品被端了上来，更大程度上避免了紧张的局面。这些酒水果品是由行进的团体拿出来的，这些健壮的西藏人身穿羊皮、头戴裘帽、脚蹬牦牛皮靴。这酒有一种令人愉悦的香气，不比

while the fruit included mangoes, perfectly ripened and almost painfully delicious after so many hours of fasting. Mallinson ate and drank with incurious relish; but Conway, relieved of immediate worries and reluctant to cherish distant ones, was wondering how mangoes could be cultivated at such an altitude. He was also interested in the mountain beyond the valley; it was a sensational peak, by any standards, and he was surprised that some traveler had not made much of it in the kind of book that a journey in Tibet invariably elicits. He climbed it in mind as he gazed, choosing a route by *col* and *couloir* until an exclamation from Mallinson drew his attention back to earth; he looked round then and saw the Chinese had been earnestly regarding him. "You were contemplating the mountain, Mr. Conway?" came the enquiry.

"Yes. It's a fine sight. It has a name, I suppose?"

"It is called Karakal."

"I don't think I ever heard of it. Is it very high?"

"Over twenty-eight thousand feet."

"Indeed? I didn't realize there would be anything on that scale outside the Himalayas. Has it been properly surveyed? Whose are the measurements?"

"Whose would you expect, my dear sir? Is there anything incompatible between

上好的葡萄酒差，水果包括芒果都熟得正合适。在这么长时间的禁食之后，这几乎是饕餮美味啊。自讨没趣的马林逊也在大吃大喝。但康维才从刚才的担忧中缓解过来，他很难去触碰离他远的那些水果。他在想这些芒果如何能够在如此高海拔的地方培育，他对山谷外面的那座山也很感兴趣。从任何标准来说，这都是一座非常迷人的山峰。他觉得奇怪，某个旅行家在一类西藏旅行的书中并未对它做多少描绘，却总是引经据典。当他凝视山峰时，在思维里他已经在攀登了，凭借隘口和峡谷选择一条路线……直到马林逊的大喊才将他的注意力拉回现实；他环顾周围，看到那个汉族人正诚挚地望着他。"你凝视这座山呢吧，康维先生？"询问声传来了。

"是的，这是绝佳的景象，我觉得它有名字！"

"它被称为卡拉卡尔。"

"我认为我从来没有听说过，它非常高吗？"

"超过 28000 英尺。"

"当真？我没有意识到除了喜马拉雅山之外还会存在任何如此规模的山峰。它已经被准确地测量过了吗？用谁的测量法？"

"你希望会是谁的呢，我亲爱的先生？在寺院制度和三角法则

monasticism and trigonometry?"

Conway savored the phrase and replied: "Oh, not at all – not at all." Then he laughed politely. He thought it a poorish joke, but one perhaps worth making the most of. Soon after that the journey to Shangri-La was begun.

All morning the climb proceeded, slowly and by easy gradients; but at such height the physical effort was considerable, and none had energy to spare for talk. The Chinese traveled luxuriously in his chair, which might have seemed unchivalrous had it not been absurd to picture Miss Brinklow in such a regal setting. Conway, whom the rarefied air troubled less than the rest, was at pains to catch the occasional chatter of the chair-bearers. He knew a very little Tibetan, just enough to gather that the men were glad to be returning to the lamasery. He could not, even had he wished, have continued to converse with their leader, since the latter, with eyes closed and face half hidden behind curtains, appeared to have the knack of instant and well-timed sleep.

Meanwhile the sun was warm; hunger and thirst had been appeased, if not satisfied; and the air, clean as from another planet, was more precious with every intake. One had to breathe consciously

当中，还存在任何不相容的东西吗？"

康维品味了一下这句话，然后回应道："哦，没有，完全没有。"然后他礼貌地哈哈大笑。他认为这是个不大好的玩笑，但这样的一个玩笑也许值得去开一开。此后不久，前往香格里拉的旅程就开始了。

整个早上，所有人都在轻松的坡度上一直缓慢攀爬；但在如此的高度行走，体力消耗是相当可观的，没有人有多余的力气说话。这汉族人在轿子里，非常舒适地行进着，可又似乎毫无侠义心肠，竟然荒唐到没有将布琳克罗小姐置身到如此豪华的画面当中。比起其他的人，稀薄的空气给康维带来的麻烦更少，但轿夫的偶尔闲谈却让他费神体会。他知道的藏语非常少，仅仅够理解那些人说很高兴返回喇嘛寺。虽然他很希望，但甚至不能与他们的头领继续交谈，因为这个头领一直紧闭着双眼，脸半藏在帘布之后，似乎有能够瞬间睡上一觉的诀窍。

同时，阳光非常温暖；饥饿和口渴即便还存在，也已经被缓解；这儿的空气干净得像来自另一个星球，每一次吸入都觉得更为珍贵，一个人必须有意识地、谨慎地

and deliberately, which, though disconcerting at first, induced after a time an almost ecstatic tranquillity of mind. The whole body moved in a single rhythm of breathing, walking, and thinking; the lungs, no longer discrete and automatic, were disciplined to harmony with mind and limb. Conway, in whom a mystical strain ran in curious consort with skepticism, found himself not unhappily puzzled over the sensation. Once or twice he spoke a cheerful word to Mallinson, but the youth was laboring under the strain of the ascent. Barnard also gasped asthmatically, while Miss Brinklow was engaged in some grim pulmonary warfare which for some reason she made efforts to conceal. "We're nearly at the top," Conway said encouragingly.

"I once ran for a train and felt just like this," she answered.

So also, Conway reflected, there were people who considered cider was just like champagne. It was a matter of palate.

He was surprised to find that beyond his puzzlement he had few misgivings, and none at all on his own behalf. There were moments in life when one opened wide one's soul just as one might open wide one's purse if an evening's entertainment were proving unexpectedly costly but also unexpectedly novel. Conway, on that breathless morning in sight of Karakal,

去呼吸。即使他最初令人心神不宁，一段时间过后又引得你的思想欣喜出神，异常恬静。整个躯体按照呼吸的简单节奏移动着、走着、想着。这个肺，不再是个谨小慎微的自动器官了，而被训练得与思维和肢体和谐统一。康维的内心有一种神秘的紧张感，在他的心底游走。他发觉自己并没有自寻烦恼地因为这惊人的场面而陷入沉思。一两次，他对马林逊说了几句令人振奋的话，但这年轻人却在爬坡的压力下费劲前行。巴纳德也是气喘吁吁，而布琳克罗小姐在与自己的肺进行严酷的斗争，而因为某些原因，她却努力去掩饰。"我们几乎到达山顶了。"康维鼓励地说。

"有一回我追火车，就像是这样的感觉。"她回答道。

如此一来康维也想到，是存在着一些人，认为苹果酒就是香槟，这是个鉴赏力问题！

他很惊奇，发现除了他自己的迷惑以外，他没有什么担忧，对自己的利益也完全没有任何担心。生活里就存在这样的时刻，当一场夜间娱乐惊人的昂贵但却出乎意料地带给你前所未有的新奇时，你就会将自己的灵魂和钱包同时打开。康维，在那个让人喘不过气来的早晨看到卡拉卡尔山时，他内心对这

made just such a willing, relieved, yet not excited response to the offer of new experience. After ten years in various parts of Asia he had attained to a somewhat fastidious valuation of places and happenings; and this he was bound to admit promised unusually.

About a couple of miles along the valley the ascent grew steeper, but by this time the sun was overclouded and a silvery mist obscured the view. Thunder and avalanches resounded from the snow-fields above; the air took chill, and then, with the sudden changefulness of mountain regions, became bitterly cold. A flurry of wind and sleet drove up, drenching the party and adding immeasurably to their discomfort; even Conway felt at one moment that it would be impossible to go much further. But shortly afterwards it seemed that the summit of the ridge had been reached, for the chair-bearers halted to re-adjust their burden. The condition of Barnard and Mallinson, who were both suffering severely, led to continued delay; but the Tibetans were clearly anxious to press on, and made signs that the rest of the journey would be less fatiguing.

After these assurances it was disappointing to see them uncoiling ropes. "Do they mean to hang us already?" Barnard managed to exclaim, with

种全新感觉的提供者表示衷心地感谢，在亚洲不同地方待了10年之后，他已经形成了一种对于不同地域发生的事情进行一番挑剔评价的习惯。但这次，他准备不同以往地承认并接受了。

沿着山谷大约几英里之处，坡度逐渐陡峭，但到那会儿，太阳已被乌云遮住，一抹银色的薄雾使这景色朦朦胧胧。雷声滚滚，雪崩的声音在雪原上方回响着。空气瞬时变得寒冷。然后，随着山区突然不稳定的变化，天气变得特别寒冷。一阵狂风大作，雨夹雪猛落下来，将大家都淋湿了，不知给他们又增添了多少困难和不适，甚至康维都感到这个时候已经不可能进一步向前了。可随后又过了很短的时间，似乎便到达了山脉的顶端。于是轿夫停下来调整着他们的担子。巴纳德和马林逊都受了不少的罪，一直在后面，但非常明显，那些藏族人焦急地赶路，打着手势表明余下的路程将不怎么令人疲惫不堪了。

听到这些保证之后，当看到他们解开绳索时，大家觉得很失望。"他们准备想吊死我们吗？"巴纳德以一种绝望的打诨方式大叫着；

desperate facetiousness; but the guides soon showed that their less sinister intention was merely to link the party together in ordinary mountaineering fashion. When they observed that Conway was familiar with rope-craft, they became much more respectful and allowed him to dispose the party in his own way. He put himself next to Mallinson, with Tibetans ahead and to the rear, and with Barnard and Miss Brinklow and more Tibetans further back still. He was prompt to notice that the men, during their leader's continuing sleep, were inclined to let him deputize. He felt a familiar quickening of authority; if there were to be any difficult business he would give what he knew was his to give – confidence and command. He had been a first-class mountaineer in his time, and was still, no doubt, pretty good. "You've got to look after Barnard," he told Miss Brinklow, half jocularly, half meaning it; and she answered with the coyness of an eagle: "I'll do my best, but you know, I've never been roped before."

But the next stage, though occasionally exciting, was less arduous than he had been prepared for, and a relief from the lung-bursting strain of the ascent. The track consisted of a traverse cut along the flank of a rock wall whose height above them the mist obscured. Perhaps mercifully it also obscured the abyss on

但很快便发现这几个向导没有表现出一丝险恶的意图，仅仅是将大家用登山常用的方式连到一起。当他们发现康维对绑绳子非常熟悉时，感到更加敬佩，便允许他以自己的方式安排大家。康维自己挨着马林逊，并让一些藏族人在最前面和后面，将巴纳德和布琳克罗小姐以及更多的藏族人放到后面的位置，他迅速注意到，这些人在他们的头领继续睡觉期间，愿意让他来代理指挥。他感到一种熟悉的权威感苏醒了；如果出现了任何困难的情况，他将会倾尽自己所能给予的一切——自信以及统领指挥。他曾经是当时一流的登山运动员，现在还是，毋庸置疑，非常出色。"你必须照顾好巴纳德。"他半开玩笑半意味深长地告诉布琳克罗小姐；但她却以一种敏锐和忸怩的方式回答道："我会尽全力，但你清楚，我之前从未被绳子绑过。"

但下一个阶段，尽管偶尔令人振奋，却比他预先准备的要少了些艰难，由于坡度而造成的"让人肺爆"的紧张感也得到了缓解。山路由一条顺着山腰的岩壁横断劈裂而成，在一片云雾之中显得更为神秘。可能是这云雾也仁慈地遮掩着另一侧的万丈深渊，但康维具备一

the other side, though Conway, who had a good eye for heights, would have liked to see where he was. The path was scarcely more than two feet wide in places, and the manner in which the bearers maneuvered the chair at such points drew his admiration almost as strongly as did the nerves of the occupant who could manage to sleep through it all. The Tibetans were reliable enough, but they seemed happier when the path widened and became slightly downhill. Then they began to sing amongst themselves, lilting barbaric tunes that Conway could imagine orchestrated by Massenet for some Tibetan ballet. The rain ceased and the air grew warmer. "Well, it's quite certain we could never have found our way here by ourselves," said Conway intending to be cheerful, but Mallinson did not find the remark very comforting. He was, in fact, acutely terrified, and in more danger of showing it now that the worst was over. "Should we be missing much?" he retorted bitterly. The track went on, more sharply downhill, and at one spot Conway found some edelweiss, the first welcome sign of more hospitable levels. But this, when he announced it, consoled Mallinson even less. "Good God, Conway, d'you fancy you're pottering about the Alps? What sort of hell's kitchen are we making for, that's what I'd like to know? And what's our

双适应高度的锐利双眼，喜欢去看他所在的地方。这条路在某些地方仅仅两英尺宽，而那几位轿夫却可以熟练操纵着轿子前行，对此康维非常崇拜，那位坐轿子的人能够全程熟睡，也令他倍感佩服。这些藏民完全值得依靠，但当小路变宽然后下坡时，他们似乎更为开心。然后他们开始唱起歌来，活泼而粗犷的曲调使康维可以想象出马塞尼特为一些藏族舞剧创作的乐曲。雨停了，空气逐渐变得温暖。"那么，非常肯定的是，我们自己在这里肯定是找不到路的。"康维说着，打算活跃气氛，但马林逊没发现这句评论令人舒服，其实，他已经非常害怕了，现在最糟糕的路段已经结束了，他却更加担心了。"我们会迷路吗？"他尖刻地反击道。山路继续延伸，更加急剧地变下坡。在一个地方，康维发现了雪绒花——这是第一个欢迎的信号。但当他宣布这一发现时，马林逊显得更平静不下来了，"上帝啊，康维，你认为你正在阿尔卑斯山闲逛吗？我很想知道我们究竟打算干什么？当我们抵达时，我们的行动计划是什么？我们准备做些什么？"

plan of action when we get to it? *What are we going to do?*"

Conway said quietly, "If you'd had all the experiences I've had, you'd know that there are times in life when the most comfortable thing is to do nothing at all. Things happen to you and you just let them happen. The war was rather like that. One is fortunate if, as on this occasion, a touch of novelty seasons the unpleasantness."

"You're too confoundedly philosophic for me. That wasn't your mood during the trouble at Baskul."

"Of course not, because then there was a chance that I could alter events by my own actions. But now, for the moment at least, there's no such chance. We're here because we're here, if you want a reason. I've usually found it a soothing one."

"I suppose you realize the appalling job we shall have to get back by the way we've come. We've been slithering along the face of a perpendicular mountain for the last hour – I've been taking notice."

"So have I."

"Have you?" Mallinson coughed excitedly. "I daresay I'm being a nuisance, but I can't help it. I'm suspicious about all this. I feel we're doing far too much what these fellows want us to. They're getting us into a corner."

"Even if they are, the only alternative

康维平静地说道：“如果你拥有像我一样的经历，你便会理解在生活里，有些时候最惬意的事便是根本什么事都不干。事情在你身上发生了，那你便让它发生吧。战争也是如此。就像现在的场合，如果有一丝新奇来调剂这种令人不快之感，那也是一种幸运啊！”

“对我来说，你简直是个烦人的狡辩之人，在巴斯库的那段时间里，你可不是现在的这种心情。”

“当然不是，因为那时我们还有机会按照我们的意志和行动来改变问题，但现在，至少此时此刻没有如此的机遇了。我们在这里是因为我们就在这儿，倘若你需要一个理由，我会去寻找一个令人宽慰的理由。”

“我猜你已经意识到，我们打算原路返回将会是项多么恐怖的工作。我们一直沿着一座陡峭的山峰正面蜿蜒曲折行进了近一个小时——我已经注意到了。”

“我也是。”

“是吗？”马林逊激动地咳嗽着，“我敢说我一直是个令人讨厌的人，但我忍不住要说，我怀疑全部这一切，我感觉我们正在做的事情远远超过了这些家伙想要我们去做的，他们正在将我们带到一个

was to stay out of it and perish."

"I know that's logical, but it doesn't seem to help. I'm afraid I don't find it as easy as you do to accept the situation. I can't forget that two days ago we were in the consulate at Baskul. To think of all that has happened since is a bit overwhelming to me. I'm sorry. I'm overwrought. It makes me realize how lucky I was to miss the war; I suppose I should have got hysterical about things. The whole world seems to have gone completely mad all round me. I must be pretty wild myself to be talking to you like this."

Conway shook his head. "My dear boy, not at all. You're twenty-four years old, and you're somewhere about two and a half miles up in the air: those are reasons enough for anything you may happen to feel at the moment. I think you've come through a trying ordeal extraordinarily well, better than I should at your age."

"But don't *you* feel the madness of it all? The way we flew over those mountains and that awful waiting in the wind and the pilot dying and then meeting these fellows, doesn't it all seem nightmarish and incredible when you look back on it?"

"It does, of course."

"Then I wish I knew how you manage to keep so cool about everything."

"Do you really wish that? I'll tell you if

角落。"

"即使他们是这样，我们唯一的选择也只能是这样，然后等死。"

"我清楚这合乎逻辑，但似乎没有任何帮助。恐怕我不会像你那么容易去接受这种情形。我无法忘记两天之前我们在巴斯库领事馆的情况，想想从那之后所发生的所有一切，我真有点无法接受。我很抱歉，我过度紧张了。这让我意识到我错过战争是多么幸运了；我猜我对待事情有些歇斯底里了，我周围的整个世界似乎彻底变疯了，我这样与你说话肯定非常野蛮。"

康维摇摇头，"我亲爱的小伙子，一点也不。你只有 20 岁，你现在置身于大概两英里半的海拔高度，这足以使你偶尔产生各种情绪和感觉。我觉得你已经格外出色地经历了严酷的考验，比我在你那个年纪时还要更好。"

"但是你没感觉这完全是疯狂的想法吗？我们飞过那些群山，在狂风中痛苦地等待，还有那个飞行员的去世，然后遇到现在这些家伙。当你回顾咱们所经历的一切时，不觉得这像噩梦一般令人难以置信吗？"

"确实，当然如此。"

"那么我希望我能清楚你是如何对每件事保持镇定的。"

"你当真希望那样？如果你

you like, though you'll perhaps think me cynical. It's because so much else that I can look back on seems nightmarish too. This isn't the only mad part of the world, Mallinson. After all, if you *must* think of Baskul, do you remember just before we left how the revolutionaries were torturing their captives to get information? An ordinary washing-mangle, quite effective, of course, but I don't think I ever saw anything more comically dreadful. And do you recollect the last message that came through before we were cut off? It was a circular from a Manchester textile firm asking if we knew of any trade openings in Baskul for the sale of corsets! Isn't that mad enough for you? Believe me, in arriving here the worst that can have happened is that we've exchanged one form of lunacy for another. And as for the War, if you'd been in it you'd have done the same as I did, learned how to funk with a stiff lip."

They were still conversing when a sharp but brief ascent robbed them of breath, inducing in a few paces all their earlier strain. Presently the ground leveled, and they stepped out of the mist into clear, sunny air. Ahead, and only a short distance away, lay the lamasery of Shangri-La.

To Conway, seeing it first, it might have been a vision fluttering out of that solitary

想知道，我就告诉你，尽管你也许会觉得我玩世不恭，因为我还有如此多其他噩梦一般的经历也能让我去回顾。这并非是世界上唯一疯狂的部分。毕竟，马林逊，如果你能想到巴斯库，你还记得就在我们离开之前那些革命者是怎样拷打俘虏以获取情报的吗？通常情况是乱打一气之后再用水冲，这相当有效果。但我不认为我见过任何比这更可笑又可怕的事。你能回忆起在我们被隔离之前传出的最后一个消息吗？那是一个信息循环，来自曼彻斯特一家纺织公司，咨询我们在巴斯库是否知道任何销售紧身胸衣的商业渠道！这对你而言，难道不荒唐吗？相信我，在这里能够发生的最糟糕的情况是我们把一种疯狂的形式和另一种做交换。对战争来说，倘若你置身在那种情况下，你也会和我有相同的举动，学习怎样用一张硬嘴去逃避问题。"

当一段陡峭但又短促的斜坡令他们气喘吁吁时，他们竟然还在交谈着，导致就那么几步便已经与之前所有的路途一样吃力。现在地势逐渐平坦，他们也从迷雾中步入清爽而充满阳光的空气里。前方仅仅很短的距离处，坐落着香格里拉喇嘛寺。

对康维来说，第一眼看见它，它就有一种感觉：那是出自孤寂荒

rhythm in which lack of oxygen had encompassed all his faculties. It was, indeed, a strange and half-incredible sight. A group of colored pavilions clung to the mountainside with none of the grim deliberation of a Rhineland castle, but rather with the chance delicacy of flower-petals impaled upon a crag. It was superb and exquisite. An austere emotion carried the eye upward from milk-blue roofs to the gray rock bastion above, tremendous as the Wetterhorn above Grindelwald. Beyond that, in a dazzling pyramid, soared the snow slopes of Karakal. It might well be, Conway thought, the most terrifying mountainscape in the world, and he imagined the immense stress of snow and glacier against which the rock functioned as a gigantic retaining wall. Someday, perhaps, the whole mountain would split, and a half of Karakal's icy splendor come toppling into the valley. He wondered if the slightness of the risk combined with its fearfulness might even be found agreeably stimulating.

Hardly less an enticement was the downward prospect, for the mountain wall continued to drop, nearly perpendicularly, into a cleft that could only have been the result of some cataclysm in the far past. The floor of the valley, hazily distant, welcomed the eye with greenness;

凉韵律中的悸动景象, 这紧紧围绕着他全部的灵魂, 令他难以呼吸。的确, 这是一种古怪又令人半信半疑的景致。一组色彩纷呈的亭台楼阁依附在山腰。它没有一丝莱茵兰城堡的那种阴暗恐怖和矫揉造作, 但以一种花瓣般意想不到的优雅镶嵌于悬崖之上, 显得华丽精致。一种严肃的感觉将他的目光向上从蓝灰瓦的屋顶带到上面灰色的岩石棱堡, 就像格丽多沃岛上的维特角塔那样蔚为壮观。远处, 在令人眩晕的金字塔上面, 矗立着卡拉卡尔的雪坡。康维认为这可能是世界上最令人胆战心惊的奇特景色了吧! 他还想象着那些仿佛巨人般支撑的岩壁承载着冰山雪川巨大的压力, 想象可能有一天, 整座山将会分崩离析, 卡拉卡尔一半的冰川将会坠入山谷的雄伟场面。他在想如果风险与恐惧联合在一起, 可能会是令人愉悦的刺激感觉。

向下的景致将会更加吸引人。因为山川一直向下延伸, 差不多垂直地形成裂口, 这只能够是很远之前某一次地壳运动的结果。山谷的底部朦胧而遥远, 映入眼帘的是一片翠绿, 将风阻挡在外面, 被主宰的喇嘛寺俯瞰着, 在康维看来, 这

sheltered from winds, and surveyed rather than dominated by the lamasery, it looked to Conway a delightfully favored place, though if it were inhabited its community must be completely isolated by the lofty and sheerly unscalable ranges on the further side. Only to the lamasery did there appear to be any climbable egress at all. Conway experienced, as he gazed, a slight tightening of apprehension; Mallinson's misgivings were not, perhaps, to be wholly disregarded. But the feeling was only momentary, and soon merged in the deeper sensation, half mystical, half visual, of having reached at last some place that was an end, a finality.

He never exactly remembered how he and the others arrived at the lamasery, or with what formalities they were received, unroped, and ushered into the precincts. That thin air had a dream-like texture, matching the porcelain-blue of the sky; with every breath and every glance he took in a deep anesthetizing tranquillity that made him impervious alike to Mallinson's uneasiness, Barnard's witticisms, and Miss Brinklow's portrayal of a lady well prepared for the worst. He vaguely recollected surprise at finding the interior spacious, well warmed, and quite clean; but there was no time to do more than notice these qualities, for the Chinese had left his hooded chair and was already

是个令人愉悦和喜爱的地方。可如果有人居住，那村落肯定被巍峨的以及远方完全不能攀登的山脉所彻底隔绝，只有一条通往喇嘛寺并且完全可以爬过去的隘道。康维凝视着，心中划过一丝紧张的忧虑；可能马林逊的担忧不是完全没有道理的。但这种感觉只是一瞬间的，它很快就被一种更深邃的感觉所吞没：神秘而梦幻——一种终于抵达世界的某个尽头并且是归宿的感觉。

他根本就不能准确记起自己和其他人是如何到达喇嘛寺的，或者他们是通过什么正式手续被接待的，如何被解开绳索，被带进这个寺管区。那稀薄的空气就像梦境的纱网，与瓷青色的天空遥相呼应。伴随着每一次的呼吸，每一次的扫视，他逐渐进入一种深深的仿佛被麻痹了的宁静，令他对类似马林逊的心神不宁、巴纳德的妙语连珠还有布琳克罗小姐为最糟糕的情况做了精心准备的忸怩神情等等都没有丝毫的感觉。他朦朦胧胧地回忆起当时发现里面宽敞而温暖，而且相当干净时的那种惊奇。但他没有时间去更多的留心这些特点，因为那个汉族人已经下了他

leading the way through various antechambers. He was quite affable now. "I must apologize," he said, "for leaving you to yourselves on the way, but the truth is, journeys of that kind don't suit me, and I have to take care of myself. I trust you were not too fatigued?"

"We managed," replied Conway with a wry smile.

"Excellent. And now, if you will come with me, I will show you to your apartments. No doubt you would like baths. Our accommodation is simple, but I hope adequate."

At this point Barnard, who was still affected by shortness of breath, gave vent to an asthmatic chuckle. "Well," he gasped, "I can't say I like your climate yet – the air seems to stick on my chest a bit – but you've certainly got a darned fine view out of your front windows. Do we all have to line up for the bathroom, or is this an American hotel?"

"I think you will find everything quite satisfactory, Mr. Barnard."

Miss Brinklow nodded primly. "I should hope so, indeed."

"And afterwards," continued the Chinese, "I should be greatly honored if you will all join me at dinner."

Conway replied courteously. Only Mallinson had given no sign of his attitude in the face of these unlooked-for

的轿子，准备带他们穿梭于各种各样的厅室。他现在显得那样的和蔼。"我必须道歉，"他说，"我在路上将你们抛在一旁，但实情是，那类的旅行并不适合我，我不得不照顾我自己。我相信你们也没有精疲力竭吧？"

"我们花了很大的力气呢。"康维苦笑着回应。

"太棒了。现在，如果你愿意跟着我，我将带你们去看看你们的套房。毫无疑问，你们会喜欢浴室的。我们的装修非常简单，但我想那样已经足够了。"

此时，巴纳德依然受呼吸困难的影响，发出气喘吁吁的笑声，"好吧，"他喘着气说，"但我还是不能说我喜欢你们这里的气候——空气似乎有点压在我的胸口上——但你们这儿前面的窗外真是有绝佳的风景，我们所有人都需要排队用浴室吗，还有这是美式旅馆么？"

"我认为你会发现每一件事情都会令你相当满意的，巴纳德先生。"

布琳克罗小姐拘谨地点点头："我确实希望如此。"

"那然后呢，"这汉族人继续说道，"倘若你们所有人能与我共进晚餐的话，我会非常荣幸。"

康维谦恭回应道，唯有马林逊的脸上对这意想不到的礼仪没有

amenities. Like Barnard, he had been suffering from the altitude, but now, with an effort, he found breath to exclaim: "And afterwards, also, if you don't mind, we'll make our plans for getting away. The sooner the better, so far as I'm concerned."

什么表情。就像巴纳德，曾因不适应海拔而受了很多苦，但现在，经过努力，他发现已经有气力大喊："那然后呢，倘若你也不介意的话，我们会为回去做一些计划，越快越好，这是我所关心的事。"

CHAPTER 4

第四章

"SO you see," Chang was saying, "we are less barbarian than you expected…"

Conway, later that evening, was not disposed to deny it. He was enjoying that pleasant mingling of physical ease and mental alertness which seemed to him, of all sensations, the most truly civilized. So far, the appointments of Shangri-La had been all that he could have wished, certainly more than he could ever have expected. That a Tibetan monastery should possess a system of central heating was not, perhaps, so very remarkable in an age that supplied even Lhasa with telephones; but that it should combine the mechanics of Western hygiene with so much that was Eastern and traditional, struck him as exceedingly singular. The bath, for instance, in which he had recently luxuriated, had been of a delicate green porcelain, a product, according to inscription, of Akron, Ohio. Yet the native attendant had valeted him in Chinese fashion, cleansing his ears and nostrils, and passing a thin, silk swab under his lower eyelids. He had wondered at the time if and how his three companions were receiving similar attentions.

"这样你们也都看到了，"张说道，"我们不如你们心里想的那么野蛮……"

晚上，康维还不愿意否认这一点。他享受着身体放松和精神警惕相交织的那种愉悦。对他而言，所有的感觉，大部分都是真正的开化和文明。迄今为止，他所能期盼的香格里拉所赋予的全部东西，肯定要比他曾经所能期盼的多得多。那个藏传佛教寺院拥有一套中央供暖系统，这在甚至连拉萨都有电话的时代可能不算特别不同寻常；但它将西方的卫生技术和如此多的东方传统相结合，超出寻常的与众不同让他大为震惊。比如，就在他刚刚尽情享用的那间浴室里，就有一个精致的绿色陶瓷制品，根据商标，这个产品来自俄亥俄艾哥伦。而那些当地的侍者以汉族的方式来伺候他，清洗他的耳朵和鼻孔，在他的下眼睑处用一支细细的丝绸药签来回擦拭。此时此刻，他在想如果他的3个同伴正接受类似的关照的话将会是什么感受呢。

Conway had lived for nearly a decade in China, not wholly in the bigger cities; and he counted it, all things considered, the happiest part of his life. He liked the Chinese, and felt at home with Chinese ways. In particular he liked Chinese cooking, with its subtle undertones of taste; and his first meal at Shangri-La had therefore conveyed a welcome familiarity. He suspected, too, that it might have contained some herb or drug to relieve respiration, for he not only felt a difference himself, but could observe a greater ease among his fellow guests. Chang, he noticed, ate nothing but a small portion of green salad, and took no wine. "You will excuse me," he had explained at the outset, "but my diet is very restricted; I am obliged to take care of myself."

It was the reason he had given before, and Conway wondered by what form of invalidism he was afflicted. Regarding him now more closely, he found it difficult to guess his age; his smallish and somehow undetailed features, together with the moist clay texture of his skin, gave him a look that might either have been that of a young man prematurely old or of an old man remarkably well preserved. He was by no means without attractiveness of a kind; a certain stylized courtesy hung about him in a fragrance too delicate to be detected till one had ceased

康维在中国已经生活了差不多 10 年了，并非全部在大的城镇生活，但他将全部事情都考虑到的话，他觉得这段时光是他生命里最开心的部分。他喜欢中国人，感觉以中国人的方式生活就像在家里；他特别喜爱中国烹饪，喜欢它那微妙又朴素的味道。因此，在香格里拉，他的第一餐饭就向他传达了一种熟悉的欢迎气息，可他也怀疑饭菜中可能含有某种药草或是药剂能够缓解呼吸困难。因为，他自己不是唯一一个感觉有异样的人，他能够发现他的几位同伴都轻松了很多。他注意到张先生什么都没吃，除了一小份蔬菜色拉，也没有喝酒。"你们会原谅我吧，"开餐时他便解释，"但我的饮食是非常严格的，我必须照顾好我自己。"

这是他之前就曾给出的理由，康维在想他是在通过什么样的一种方式来折磨自己。现在康维更为接近他，但他却发现很难猜出他的年纪；他那瘦小的身材以及有些无法说清的容貌，连同他那黏土般质地的湿润皮肤，他的外表——或者是一个早熟的青年男子，或者是一个保养得相当好的老年人。他决不是没有吸引力的那类人；他身上具备某种程式化的谦逊风格，这种优雅太过微妙，以至于直到一个人停止思考时才能察觉得到。他那有刺绣图案的蓝色丝绸长衫带有一贯

to think about it. In his embroidered gown of blue silk, with the usual side-slashed skirt and tight-ankled trousers, all the hue of watercolor skies, he had a cold metallic charm which Conway found pleasing, though he knew it was not everybody's taste.

The atmosphere, in fact, was Chinese rather than specifically Tibetan; and this in itself gave Conway an agreeable sensation of being at home, though again it was one that he could not expect the others to share. The room, too, pleased him; it was admirably proportioned, and sparingly adorned with tapestries and one or two fine pieces of lacquer. Light was from paper lanterns, motionless in the still air. He felt a soothing comfort of mind and body, and his renewed speculations as to some possible drug were hardly apprehensive. Whatever it was, if it existed at all, it had relieved Barnard's breathlessness and Mallinson's truculence; both had dined well, finding satisfaction in eating rather than talk. Conway also had been hungry enough, and was not sorry that etiquette demanded gradualness in approaching matters of importance. He had never cared for hurrying a situation that was itself enjoyable, so that the technique well suited him. Not, indeed, until he had begun a cigarette did he give a gentle lead to his curiosity; he remarked then, addressing Chang: "You seem a very

的侧开下摆，以及脚踝紧裹的裤子，这一整套衣服都是湖水般的天蓝。康维高兴地发现，他具备一种冷静而又生硬的魅力。但他清楚这并不符合每一个人的口味。

其实，这种气氛，与其说是特殊的藏族特点，倒不如说是汉族式的；这环境本身赋予康维一种使人愉悦的回家之感。可他不能期待着其他人能够分享。这个屋子，也很让他惬意，比例精巧，只简单地用绒绣挂毯和一两块精致的漆板装饰着。光线来自于纸质的灯笼，它在恬静的空气里一动不动。他感觉到一阵使精神和肉体宽心的舒适，他的那些关于某种药剂在里面的想法几乎不能被理解。无论是什么东西，如果当真存在的话，巴纳德的气喘病以及马林逊的暴躁早已经缓解了！他俩都吃了很多，比起说话他俩更愿意在吃上找到满足。康维也已经够饿的了，但他并不觉得遗憾，因为礼仪需要在处理重要事务中循序渐进。他从来不在乎在本来很令人享受的情况下匆匆忙忙，因此这种方式对他来说极为合适。不，确实，直到他开始点上一支烟，才和缓地引导他的好奇心，然后他对张评论道："你们似乎是一个非常幸运的群体，对陌生人那么好客。我想你们不会经常招待客人吧。"

fortunate community, and most hospitable to strangers. I don't imagine, though, that you receive them often."

"Seldom indeed," replied the Chinese, with measured stateliness. "It is not a traveled part of the world."

Conway smiled at that. "You put the matter mildly. It looked to me, as I came, the most isolated spot I ever set eyes on. A separate culture might flourish here without contamination from the outside world."

"Contamination, would you say?"

"I use the word in reference to dance bands, cinemas, electric signs, and so on. Your plumbing is quite rightly as modern as you can get it, the only certain boon, to my mind, that the East can take from the West. I often think that the Romans were fortunate; their civilization reached as far as hot baths without touching the fatal knowledge of machinery."

Conway paused. He had been talking with an impromptu fluency which, though not insincere, was chiefly designed to create and control an atmosphere. He was rather good at that sort of thing. Only a willingness to respond to the superfine courtesy of the occasion prevented him from being more openly curious.

Miss Brinklow, however, had no such scruples. "Please," she said, though the word was by no means submissive, "will you tell us about the monastery?"

"确实很少，"汉族人以慎重威严的神色回应道，"这里并非一个经常被人们所光顾的地方。"

康维微微一笑，"你对此事很温和，在我看来，这是我所见过的最偏僻之处了，有一种独特的文化在这里繁荣发展，而免受来自外界的污染。"

"污染，你的意思是？"

"这个词汇是指那些乐队、电影院和电气标志等等。对我而言，你们的抽水马桶已经相当摩登了，只有某种恩惠才能让东方从西方引进它。我经常想罗马人是幸运的，他们的文明可以达到热水浴室的高度而免受那些灾难性机械技术文化的触碰。"

康维停顿了片刻。他始终即兴地滔滔不绝，但不是故弄玄虚，主要是打算去营造并控制一种氛围。他非常擅长这类事情，唯一的愿望是回应一下这种极致谦恭的礼仪，以免令自己的好奇心暴露太过。

但布琳克罗小姐却并无这种顾虑。"麻烦您，"她说，但是词汇决不谦恭，"能给我们讲讲关于这座寺庙的事吗？"

Chang raised his eyebrows in very gentle deprecation of such immediacy. "It will give me the greatest of pleasure, madam, so far as I am able. What exactly do you wish to know?"

"First of all, how many are there of you here, and what nationality do you belong to?" It was clear that her orderly mind was functioning no less professionally than at the Baskul mission-house.

Chang replied: "Those of us in full lamahood number about fifty, and there are a few others, like myself, who have not yet attained to complete initiation. We shall do so in due course, it is to be hoped. Till then we are half-lamas, postulants, you might say. As for our racial origins, there are representatives of a great many nations among us, though it is perhaps natural that Tibetans and Chinese make up the majority."

Miss Brinklow would never shirk a conclusion, even a wrong one. "I see. It's really a native monastery, then. Is your head lama a Tibetan or a Chinese?"

"No."

"Are there any English?"

"Several."

"Dear me, that seems very remarkable." Miss Brinklow paused only for breath before continuing: "And now, tell me what you all believe in."

Conway leaned back with somewhat amused expectancy. He had always found

张扬了扬眉毛，非常温和地对这种直接表示赞成。"这将是我最大的快乐，女士，尽我可能吧。你希望知道些什么呢？"

"首先，你们这里有多少人，你又属于什么民族？"很明显，她那有条理性的思维在运作时与她在巴斯库的修道院时同样专业。

张答道："我们那些人中全职喇嘛大概有50个，有一些其他人，就像我自己，还没有获得完全的入会仪式，我们应该经过充分的课程后便能够入行了，这是被大家所盼望的。直到那时，我们就会是半个喇嘛了，你们可以说这是基本条件。说到我们的种族来源，我们当中有许许多多民族的代表，但这可能是自然的，藏族和汉族占了大多数。"

布琳克罗小姐从不会让一个结论溜掉，哪怕是错误的结论。"我清楚，这是一座本土寺庙，你们的喇嘛主持是藏族人还是汉族人？"

"都不是。"

"这里有英国人吗？"

"有几个。"

"上帝！那非常不同凡响啊。"布琳克罗小姐停顿，片刻，似仅仅是为了呼吸一下以便继续问："现在，告诉我你们所有人都信奉什么？"

康维向后倚着，带着一种觉得

pleasure in observing the impact of opposite mentalities; and Miss Brinklow's girl-guide forthrightness applied to Lamaistic philosophy promised to be entertaining. On the other hand, he did not wish his host to take fright. "That's rather a big question," he said, temporizingly.

But Miss Brinklow was in no mood to temporize. The wine, which had made the others more reposeful, seemed to have given her an extra liveliness. "Of course," she said with a gesture of magnanimity, "I believe in the true religion, but I'm broadminded enough to admit that other people, foreigners, I mean, are quite often sincere in their views. And naturally in a monastery I wouldn't expect to be agreed with."

Her concession evoked a formal bow from Chang. "But why not, madam?" he replied in his precise and flavored English. "Must we hold that because one religion is true, all others are bound to be false?"

"Well, of course, that's rather obvious, isn't it?"

Conway again interposed. "Really, I think we had better not argue. But Miss Brinklow shares my own curiosity about the motive of this unique establishment."

Chang answered rather slowly and in scarcely more than a whisper: "If I were to put it into a very few words, my dear sir, I should say that our prevalent belief is in moderation. We inculcate the virtue of

有点好玩的预感，他总能在观察冲突双方的心智里发现乐趣；布琳克罗小姐女权主义的直率与喇嘛教的哲学相碰撞一定会很有意思。在另一方面，他不希望他的主人受到惊吓。"这是个相当大的问题。"他趁势说道。

但布琳克罗小姐却无视这种见风使舵的行为。让其他人更为安静的酒精赋予了她一种格外的活力。"当然，"她带着一种宽宏大量的姿态说，"我信仰真正的宗教，但我足够心胸开阔去承认其他人。我是指外国人，他们对自己的观点经常表现出忠诚。自然，在一个喇嘛寺里，我不期望被赞同。"

她的让步引来张的一个正式鞠躬。"但，为什么不呢，女士？"他用精准而纯正的英语回应道，"一定是由于我们秉持的宗教是真的，而其他所有宗教都肯定是假的吗？"

"哦，当然了，相当明显，不是吗？"

康维再次插话道："真的，我认为我们最好不要争吵。但布琳克罗小姐分享了我对于建立这样一所独特宗教机构的动机的好奇心。"

张以几乎是嘟囔的方式回答得相当缓慢："如果我概括为非常简短的几句话，我亲爱的先生，我

avoiding excess of all kinds – even including, if you will pardon the paradox, excess of virtue itself. In the valley which you have seen, and in which there are several thousand inhabitants living under the control of our order, we have found that the principle makes for a considerable degree of happiness. We rule with moderate strictness, and in return we are satisfied with moderate obedience. And I think I can claim that our people are moderately sober, moderately chaste, and moderately honest."

Conway smiled. He thought it well expressed, besides which it made some appeal to his own temperament. "I think I understand. And I suppose the fellows who met us this morning belonged to your valley people?"

"Yes. I hope you had no fault to find with them during the journey?"

"Oh, no, none at all. I'm glad they were more than moderately sure-footed, anyhow. You were careful, by the way, to say that the rule of moderation applied to *them* – am I to take it that it does not apply to your priesthood also?"

But at that Chang could only shake his head. "I regret, sir, that you have touched upon a matter which I may not discuss. I can only add that our community has various faiths and usages, but we are most of us moderately heretical about them. I am deeply grieved that at the moment I

应当说，我们普遍的信仰是中庸之道。我们谆谆劝导所有类型的避免过激言行的美德，甚至包括过度的美德，如果你会宽恕这种自相矛盾的观点的话。在你们已经见到的这个山谷里，其中有好几千的居民生活在我们的制约之下。我们已经发现，在相当大的程度上，准则能够带来幸福；我们用中庸的严谨来约束支配，但反过来，我们又满足于中庸的顺从。我觉得我能够宣称：我们的人民是适度地朴素无华，适度地保持贞节，适度地忠诚老实。"

康维微微一笑，他认为表达得非常好，此外这些话令他的表现非常具有吸引力。"我觉得我理解了。我猜想早上来看我们的那些人是你们山谷的居民吧？"

"是的，我希望你们在旅途期间没有发现他们有什么过错吧？"

"哦，没有，完全没有。总之，我非常高兴他们的步伐更为稳定，你非常谨慎，顺便提一下，中庸之道的准则运用于他们，我是不是也应该认为，它并不适用于你的教职呢？"

张对此只能摇头，"我很抱歉，先生，你触及了我不能讨论的事情。我只能再补充一句，我们这个群体具备多种信仰以及习惯，可我们当中的大部分都能适度地对待这些异教徒。我深表遗憾，在这一刻我不能再多说了。"

cannot say more."

"Please don't apologize. I am left with the pleasantest of speculations." Something in his own voice, as well as in his bodily sensations, gave Conway a renewed impression that he had been very slightly doped. Mallinson appeared to have been similarly affected, though he seized the present chance to remark: "All this has been very interesting, but I really think it's time we began to discuss our plans for getting away. We want to return to India as soon as possible. How many porters can we be supplied with?"

The question, so practical and uncompromising, broke through the crust of suavity to find no sure foothold beneath. Only after a longish interval came Chang's reply: "Unfortunately, Mr. Mallinson, I am not the proper person to approach. But in any case, I hardly think the matter could be arranged immediately."

"But something has *got* to be arranged! We've all got our work to return to, and our friends and relatives will be worrying about us. We simply *must* return. We're obliged to you for receiving us like this, but we really can't slack about here doing nothing. If it's at all feasible, we should like to set out not later than to-morrow. I expect there are a good many of your people who would volunteer to escort us – we should make it well worth their while,

"请不要道歉，这已经给我留下了愉悦的思考余地。"在他自己声音里的某种东西，还有他自己身上的感觉，都赋予了康维一种再生的印象，那就是他已经被非常轻微地麻痹了。马林逊似乎也有类似的反应，但他抓住现在的机会评论道："所有这些都非常有意思。可我当真觉得现在是时候开始讨论我们离开这里的计划了。我们想尽快返回印度，您能够为我们提供多少个向导呢？"

这个问题如此实际，没有一丝妥协，戳穿了温和的外表，下面却没有确切的立足点。仅仅是在很长的间隔之后，张的回答才传来："很不幸，马林逊先生，我不是讨论这个问题的合适人选，可不管怎样，我觉得这事很难被立即安排。"

"但一些事情必须得被安排啊！我们所有人回去都有工作要做。我们的朋友亲戚也会为我们担心，我们必须得回去。我们内心对你们这样的款待深表感激，但我们当真不能在这里无所事事，什么都不做。倘若确实可行，我们想明天之前就出发，我期望有很多你们的人愿意做志愿者护送我们——当然我们会让他们觉得那样做是值得的。"

of course."

Mallinson ended nervously, as if he had hoped to be answered before saying so much; but he could extract from Chang no more than a quiet and almost reproachful: "But all this, you know, is scarcely in my province."

"Isn't it? Well, perhaps you can do *something,* at any rate. If you could get us a large-scale map of the country, it would help. It looks as if we shall have a long journey, and that's all the more reason for making an early start. You have maps, I suppose?"

"Yes, we have a great many."

"We'll borrow some of them, then, if you don't mind. We can return them to you afterwards. I suppose you must have communications with the outer world from time to time. And it would be a good idea to send messages ahead, also, to reassure our friends. How far away is the nearest telegraph line?"

Chang's wrinkled face seemed to have acquired a look of infinite patience, but he did not reply.

Mallinson waited a moment and then continued: "Well, where do you send to when you want anything? Anything civilized, I mean." A touch of scaredness began to appear in his eyes and voice. Suddenly he thrust back his chair and stood up. He was pale, and passed his hand wearily across his forehead. "I'm so

马林逊紧张地结束演讲，就像他期望着在说那么多之前便能被回答；但他能够从张那儿获得的只是平和的、几乎有点责备口气的回答："但全部这些，你要清楚，没有一点在我的权限范围之内。"

"不是吗？好吧，无论如何，你也许能够办一些事。如果你能给我们找一张这个区域的地图，这会有帮助的。看起来，我们好像会有很长的旅程，这也是我们要早点启程的原因，你们有地图吧，我猜？"

"是的，我们有很多。"

"那么倘若你不介意的话，我们想借几张，随后便会归还，我猜你们一定偶尔与外界有联系，如果能提前发封信也是个好主意，以便让家人朋友放心。最近的电报局有多远呢？"

张那布满皱纹的脸孔似乎是一副充满无穷耐心的表情，但他没有回答。

马林逊等了一会儿，然后继续说："好吧，你们需要任何东西时，你们想要发信时，都会去哪里呢？我是指任何文明开化的东西。"在他的双眼和声音里都开始出现一丝恐慌。突然，他猛地向后推了一把他的椅子，然后站起身来。他面色惨白，烦躁地用手来回擦着他的

tired," he stammered, glancing round the room. "I don't feel that any of you are really trying to help me. I'm only asking a simple question. It's obvious you must know the answer to it. When you had all these modern baths installed, how did they get here?"

There followed another silence.

"You won't tell me, then? It's part of the mystery of everything else, I suppose. Conway, I must say I think you're damned slack. Why don't *you* get at the truth? I'm all in, for the time being – but – to-morrow, mind – we *must* get away to-morrow – it's essential – "

He would have slid to the floor had not Conway caught him and helped him to a chair. Then he recovered a little, but did not speak.

"To-morrow he will be much better," said Chang gently. "The air here is difficult for the stranger at first, but one soon becomes acclimatized."

Conway felt himself waking from a trance. "Things have been a little trying for him," he commented with rather rueful mildness. He added, more briskly: "I expect we're all feeling it somewhat. I think we'd better adjourn this discussion and go to bed. Barnard, will you look after Mallinson? And I'm sure *you're* in need of sleep too, Miss Brinklow." There had been some signal given, for at that moment a servant appeared. "Yes, we'll get along –

前额。"我真是太烦了，"他结结巴巴地说着，扫视了一下屋子，"我感觉你们当中没有任何人是当真试着在帮我。我仅仅是在问一个简单的问题，显而易见，你一定清楚怎样回答。你何时安装了这些现代化浴室，这些东西又是如何到这儿的？

然后又是一阵沉默。

"那么，你不会告诉我了？我猜这是一切事情的秘密所在。康维，我必须说我觉得你真他妈的懒散，你为什么不面对事实？我只能暂时认了，但明天，记住啊，我们必须要走，这是最基本的。"

如果不是康维抓住他帮他回到椅子上，他就会滑倒在地上。然后他稍微恢复了一下，但没再说任何话。

"明天他会好一些的，"张温和地说道，"这里的空气会让刚来的人觉得不适，可很快便会适应的。"

康维发觉自己从恍惚中逐渐清醒过来，"事情有点令他难受了，"他用相当沮丧而温和的方式评论道。然后更加轻松地补充道，"我期望我们所有人都稍微有些感觉，我认为我们最好终止这次讨论，然后上床休息。巴纳德，你照顾一下马林逊好吧？布琳克罗小姐，我确定你也需要睡一觉了。"就在这时，传来一阵信号，有个侍者出现了。"是的——我们会在一

good night – good night – I shall soon follow." He almost pushed them out of the room, and then, with a scantness of ceremony that was in marked contrast with his earlier manner, turned to his host. Mallinson's reproach had spurred him.

"Now, sir, I don't want to detain you long, so I'd better come to the point. My friend is impetuous, but I don't blame him, he's quite right to make things clear. Our return journey has to be arranged, and we can't do it without help from you or from others in this place. Of course, I realize that leaving to-morrow is impossible, and for my own part I hope to find a minimum stay quite interesting. But that, perhaps, is not the attitude of my companions. So if it's true, as you say, that you can do nothing for us yourself, please put us in touch with someone else who can."

The Chinese answered: "You are wiser than your friends, my dear sir, and therefore you are less impatient. I am glad."

"That's not an answer."

Chang began to laugh, a jerky high-pitched chuckle so obviously forced that Conway recognized in it the polite pretense of seeing an imaginary joke with which the Chinese "saves face" at awkward moments. "I feel sure you have no cause to worry about the matter," came the reply, after an interval. "No doubt in due course we shall be able to give you all

起——晚安——晚安——我随后就会跟来的。"康维几乎是将他们几个推出屋子，然后，以一种很勉强的谦恭神态转向他的主人，和他原先的态度形成强烈对比。马林逊的责备刺激了他。

"现在，先生，我不希望耽搁你太长时间，所以我最好直奔主题。我的朋友有些鲁莽，可我并不责备他，他希望将事情弄明白，这是相当正确的，我们的回程必须被安排一下，而我们没有你或这里的其他人的帮助是无法做到的。当然，我意识到明天启程是不可能的，从我自己的立场来说，我明白短时间的逗留也是有意思的。可这也许并非是我同伴们的态度。那么，如果是真的，就像你说的，你自己也无能为力，那么就请让我们和其他能够帮助我们的人联系上。"

这位汉族人答道："你比你的朋友更明智，我亲爱的先生，因此你没那么急躁，我很高兴。"

"这并不是答案。"

张开始哈哈大笑，一种扯动的强挤出来的笑是如此的明显，使康维认识到中国人在尴尬时刻会"保全脸面"，以彬彬有礼的方式展现出来一种虚伪的笑脸。"我很肯定地感觉到，你们没有理由为此事忧虑，"隔了一段时间之后，传来了回答，"毋庸置疑，到时候我们能够给予你们所需的全部帮助。就像

the help you need. There are difficulties, as you can imagine, but if we all approach the problem sensibly, and without undue haste – "

"I'm not suggesting haste. I'm merely seeking information about porters."

"Well, my dear sir, that raises another point. I very much doubt whether you will easily find men willing to undertake such a journey. They have their homes in the valley, and they don't care for leaving them to make long and arduous trips outside."

"They can be prevailed upon to do so, though, or else why and where were they escorting you this morning?"

"This morning? Oh, that was quite a different matter."

"In what way? Weren't you setting out on a journey when I and my friends chanced to come across you?"

There was no response to this, and presently Conway continued in a quieter voice: "I understand. Then it was *not* a chance meeting. I had wondered all along, in fact. So you came there deliberately to intercept us. That suggests you must have known of our arrival beforehand. And the interesting question is, *How*?"

His words laid a note of stress amidst the exquisite quietude of the scene. The lantern light showed up the face of the Chinese; it was calm and statuesque. Suddenly, with a small gesture of the

你们能够想象到的，是存在一些困难，可我们所有人都要明智地处理问题，而不能过于草率仓促。"

"我不是仓促，我仅仅是想寻找关于向导的信息。"

"好吧，我亲爱的先生，这引发了另外一个问题。我非常怀疑你们是否可以轻易找到一个愿意承担这种长途跋涉的人。他们的家在山谷里，而且他们不喜欢离开家到外面去做长途艰险的行程。"

"但他们能够被说服去这么做啊，否则今天早上他们为什么要将你护送到什么地方？"

"今天早上？哦，那根本是完全不同的问题。"

"以什么方式？当我和我的朋友碰巧遇到你们时，你们不正出发去旅行吗？"

张对此没有回应。康维马上以更加平和的声音继续说："我知道了。那么这并非是一次偶然的碰面。其实，我始终在纳闷。这么说你们是故意去那里拦截我们的。这便暗示了你们一定预先清楚我们会来，有趣的是，你们是怎么知道的？"

他的话在异常寂静的气氛当中注入了一种紧张感。灯笼的光线映衬出那汉族人的面孔，非常镇定又轮廓清晰。突然，伴随一个轻微的手势，张打破了这种紧张局面；

hand, Chang broke the strain; pulling aside a silken tapestry, he undraped a window leading to a balcony. Then, with a touch upon Conway's arm, he led him into the cold crystal air. "You are clever," he said dreamily, "but not entirely correct. For that reason I should counsel you not to worry your friends by these abstract discussions. Believe me, neither you nor they are in any danger at Shangri-La."

"But it isn't danger we're bothering about. It's delay."

"I realize that. And of course there *may* be a certain delay, quite unavoidably."

"If it's only for a short time, and genuinely unavoidable, then naturally we shall have to put up with it as best we can."

"How very sensible, for we desire nothing more than that you and your companions should enjoy your stay here."

"That's all very well, and as I told you, in a personal sense I can't say I shall mind a great deal. It's a new and interesting experience, and in any case, we need some rest."

He was gazing upward to the gleaming pyramid of Karakal. At that moment, in bright moonlight, it seemed as if a hand reached high might just touch it; it was so brittle-clear against the blue immensity beyond.

"To-morrow," said Chang, "you may find it even more interesting. And as for

他将一块丝质挂毯掀到旁边，推开一扇朝向走廊的窗户。然后，他碰了碰康维的胳膊，带着康维进入外面凉爽凛冽的空气中。"你非常聪明，"他做梦似的说道，"可不完全正确，因为这个原因，我应该劝告你不要让这些抽象的讨论令你的朋友们担心；相信我，你和他们几个在香格里拉都不会有任何危险。"

"但令我们困扰的并非什么危险，而是耽误时间。"

"我意识到了，当然，可能有一定的耽搁，这完全无法避免。"

"倘若仅仅是短短的几天，真的无法避免的话，那么自然，我们也不得不尽我们所能容忍一下了。"

"这多么明智啊！因为我们不期待什么，只是盼着您和您的同伴们能享受待在这里的时间。"

"那是再好不过了，就像我告诉你的那样，从我个人立场出发，我不能说我非常介意。这是一种全新而又有趣的经历，况且无论如何，我们需要一些休息。"

他抬头凝视着那金字塔式的卡拉卡尔山的隐约光芒。此刻，在明亮的月光下，它似乎就在手能够触摸得到的高度，它如此鲜明清晰地映衬着远方巨大的蓝色苍穹。

"明天，"张说道，"你们可能会发现这里甚至更有趣，如果你觉

rest, if you are fatigued, there are not many better places in the world."

Indeed, as Conway continued to gaze, a deeper repose overspread him, as if the spectacle were as much for the mind as for the eye. There was hardly any stir of wind, in contrast to the upland gales that had raged the night before; the whole valley, he perceived, was a land-locked harbor, with Karakal brooding over it, lighthouse-fashion. The smile grew as he considered it, for there was actually light on the summit, an ice blue gleam that matched the splendor it reflected. Something prompted him then to enquire the literal interpretation of the name, and Chang's answer came as a whispered echo of his own musing. "Karakal, in the valley patois, means Blue Moon," said the Chinese.

Conway did not pass on his conclusion that the arrival of himself and party at Shangri-La had been in some way expected by its inhabitants. He had had it in mind that he must do so, and he was aware that the matter was important; but when morning came his awareness troubled him so little, in any but a theoretical sense, that he shrank from being the cause of greater concern in others. One part of him insisted that there was something distinctly queer about the place, that the attitude of Chang on the

得疲劳，也可以在这里休息。世界上没有几个比这更好的地方了。"

确实，当康维继续凝望时，一种更深刻的宁静之情蔓延到他的全身，就像这奇异的光景一样充满了他的眼睛和思维。没有一丝风来扰乱，这和前晚肆虐高原的狂风形成强烈对比，他察觉到整个山谷仿佛一个内陆港湾，被卡拉卡尔山以一座灯塔的样子笼罩着。当他思考时，一抹笑容浮现出来，因为这山峰上竟然泛着光芒，那是冰雪蓝色的光晕和它反射的月光在遥相辉映。然后，某种东西企图令他询问这座山名字的字面意义，张的回答仿佛是他自己冥想的低沉回声："卡拉卡尔，在山谷本地语中代表'蓝月亮'。"这位汉族人说道。

康维并未将他的结论泄露出去。即他和他的同伴们来到香格里拉在某种意义上是被这里的居民所预料到的。他将这种结论藏在脑海里，他一定得这么做，他意识到这件事非常重要。但当清晨降临时，他的意识有一点令他困扰，即使是理论上的感觉，他也要避免自己会引发其他人更大的关注。一方面他坚信这里存在一些格外奇怪的东西。另一方面前天晚上张的态度也远远没有使他安心，其实，他们成了囚徒，直到当局决定为他们

previous evening had been far from reassuring, and that the party were virtually prisoners unless and until the authorities chose to do more for them. And it was clearly his duty to compel them to do this. After all, he was a representative of the British Government, if nothing else; it was iniquitous that the inmates of a Tibetan monastery should refuse him any proper request... That, no doubt, was the normal official view that would be taken; and part of Conway was both normal and official. No one could better play the strongman on occasions; during those final difficult days before the evacuation he had behaved in a manner which (he reflected wryly) should earn him nothing less than a knighthood and a Henty school prize novel entitled *With Conway at Baskul*. To have taken on himself the leadership of some scores of mixed civilians, including women and children, to have sheltered them all in a small consulate during a hot-blooded revolution led by antiforeign agitators, and to have bullied and cajoled the revolutionaries into permitting a wholesale evacuation by air, it was not, he felt, a bad achievement. Perhaps by pulling wires and writing interminable reports, he could wangle something out of it in the next New Year Honors. At any rate it had won him Mallinson's fervent admiration. Unfortunately, the youth must now be finding him so much more of a

做些什么。显而易见,迫使当局做些什么是他的责任。毕竟,他是英国政府的一位代表。一个藏传佛教寺院拒绝他任何的合理要求都是不公正的……毋庸置疑,这是一个正统官员应采纳的观点,从康维的立场来说,他既正统又是官员。在很多场合,没有人能够更加彰显强者风范;在撤离前那困难的最后几天当中,他行为举止的方式(他淡然地反应着),能为他写一部起码能够赢得骑士身份、还有亨廷学院奖的小说,并命名为《康维在巴斯库》。在由排外鼓动者领导的狂热革命期间,他挺身而出,领导混杂着不同民族的群众,包括妇女和儿童,他将他们所有人保护进一个小的领事馆当中,还允许那些被恐吓和被蒙骗的革命者通过飞机进行大规模的遣送疏散。他感觉这并非一个糟糕的成绩。可能通过牵线搭桥还有撰写没完没了的报告,他还能够弄到下一年的新年荣誉勋章。无论如何,这为他赢得了马林逊狂热的崇拜。不幸的是,这年轻人现在发现更多的却是失望。当然,这很遗憾,但康维也逐渐习惯于人们喜欢他仅仅是由于他们并不理解他。他并非名副其实地是一个果断、意志坚强、大刀阔斧的帝国建造人。他能给予的仅仅是雕虫小技,时不时被命运和外交部安排去故伎重演,就为了那么一点任何人都能得到的与惠特克这本小人书

disappointment. It was a pity, of course, but Conway had grown used to people liking him only because they misunderstood him. He was not genuinely one of those resolute, strong-jawed, hammer-and-tongs empire builders; the semblance he had given was merely a little one act play, repeated from time to time by arrangement with fate and the foreign office, and for a salary which anyone could turn up in the pages of Whitaker.

The truth was, the puzzle of Shangri-La, and of his own arrival there, was beginning to exercise over him a rather charming fascination. In any case he found it hard to feel any personal misgivings. His official job was always liable to take him into odd parts of the world, and the odder they were, the less, as a rule, he suffered from boredom; why, then, grumble because accident instead of a chit from Whitehall had sent him to this oddest place of all?

He was, in fact, very far from grumbling. When he rose in the morning and saw the soft lapis blue of the sky through his window, he would not have chosen to be elsewhere on earth either in Peshawar or Piccadilly. He was glad to find that on the others, also, a night's repose had had a heartening effect. Barnard was able to joke quite cheerfully about beds, baths, breakfasts, and other hospitable amenities. Miss Brinklow

差不多的薪水。

实情是香格里拉之谜和他自己是如何来到这里的都开始令他伤脑筋，并且这是一种相当吸引人的魔力。但不论如何，他发现他很难感到有任何个人的疑虑。他自己的职务工作总是可能将他带到世界上古怪的地方。作为一种规律，越不古怪，他越感觉厌倦。他又怎会抱怨取代了来自白厅的调令，将他送到这个最为稀奇的地方呢？

其实，他鲜有抱怨。当他清晨起床，通过窗户看到那柔和的青金色的蔚蓝天空时，他都不打算到世界上其他任何地方去，不管是白沙瓦抑或皮卡迪利。他很开心地发现，一夜的休息也对其他几位有振奋的效果。巴纳德能够相当兴奋地对床、浴室、早餐还有其他好客的礼仪开玩笑了。布琳克罗小姐承认，最令人兴奋的是她在为她精心准备的套房里没有找到任何一点

admitted that the most strenuous search of her apartment had failed to reveal any of the drawbacks she had been well prepared for. Even Mallinson had acquired a touch of half-sulky complacency. "I suppose we shan't get away to-day after all," he muttered, "unless somebody looks pretty sharp about it. Those fellows are typically Oriental, you can't get them to do anything quickly and efficiently."

Conway accepted the remark. Mallinson had been out of England just under a year; long enough, no doubt, to justify a generalization which he would probably still repeat when he had been out for twenty. And it was true, of course, in some degree. Yet to Conway it did not appear that the Eastern races were abnormally dilatory, but rather that Englishmen and Americans charged about the world in a state of continual and rather preposterous fever-heat. It was a point of view that he hardly expected any fellow Westerner to share, but he was more faithful to it as he grew older in years and experience. On the other hand, it was true enough that Chang was a subtle quibbler and that there was much justification for Mallinson's impatience. Conway had a slight wish that he could feel impatient too; it would have been so much easier for the boy.

He said: "I think we'd better wait and see what to-day brings. It was perhaps too optimistic to expect them to do anything

毛病。甚至马林逊也是一副阴沉的自鸣得意的表情。"我猜咱们今天不会离开的,"他喃喃自语道,"除非有人对此事看起来异常着急。那些家伙是典型的东方人,你无法令他们高效快捷地去做任何事。"

康维接受这种评论。马林逊离开英国仅仅一年,毋庸置疑,这已经足够让他去判断事物的普遍性。当他离开英国 20 年之后,也许仍然会重复。这千真万确,当然,只是就某种程度而言。但对康维而言,东方人似乎并非反常地拖拉,而英国人和美国人倒是以一种持续的异常荒谬的狂热心态来挑战世界。这个观点,他很难期待任何西方人可以分享,但随着他的年纪逐渐增大,阅历逐渐丰富,他对此更有信心。另一方面,千真万确,张是一个敏锐的狡辩之人,对于马林逊的不耐心也是正常的。康维有一个微小的希望,就是他也能感到不耐烦,这会令那位小伙子轻松一些。

他说:"我觉得我们最好等等看今天会发生什么。昨晚期待他们有任何的行动都是太乐观了。"

last night."

Mallinson looked up sharply. "I suppose you think I made a fool of myself, being so urgent? I couldn't help it; I thought that Chinese fellow was damned fishy, and I do still. Did you succeed in getting any sense out of him after I'd gone to bed?"

"We didn't stay talking long. He was rather vague and noncommittal about most things."

"We shall jolly well have to keep him up to scratch to-day."

"No doubt," agreed Conway, without marked enthusiasm for the prospect. "Meanwhile this is an excellent breakfast." It consisted of pomelo, tea, and chupatties, perfectly prepared and served. Towards the finish of the meal Chang entered and with a little bow began the exchange of politely conventional greetings which, in the English language, sounded just a trifle unwieldy. Conway would have preferred to talk in Chinese, but so far he had not let it be known that he spoke any Eastern tongue; he felt it might be a useful card up his sleeve. He listened gravely to Chang's courtesies, and gave assurances that he had slept well and felt much better. Chang expressed his pleasure at that, and added: "Truly, as your national poet says, 'Sleep knits up the raveled sleeve of care.'"

This display of erudition was not too well received. Mallinson answered with

马林逊严厉地抬头望着，"我觉得你是把我这种焦急当成傻瓜吗？但我忍不住；我认为那个汉族家伙真他妈靠不住，我仍然如此觉得。在我上床休息以后，你从他那里获得任何有意义的东西了吗？"

"我们没谈太长时间。他说的大部分事情都很晦涩，不明朗。"

"我们今天不得不继续和他周旋，我们会乐在其中的。"

"毋庸置疑，"康维表示赞同，可并无预期的热情，"同时，这是顿很棒的早餐。"早餐由精心准备的柚子、茶水以及麦面煎饼组成，服务周到。早餐快结束时，张进来了，微微鞠躬致意后，便开始用听起来有点笨拙的英语礼貌地表达那惯例的问候。康维更愿意以汉语交谈，可迄今为止他都没有被看出来他会说任何的东方语言，他感到这是他自己手里非常有用处的一张牌。他严肃地听着张的礼貌问候，然后向他确认他睡得很好而且感觉好多了。张对此表达了他的愉悦，补充道："确实，就像你们英国一个诗人说的那样：'好眠织补牵心袖'。"

这种博学多识的展示，却并未受到良好的回应。马林逊以一种轻

that touch of scorn which any healthy-minded young Englishman must feel at the mention of poetry. "I suppose you mean Shakespeare, though I don't recognize the quotation. But I know another one that says 'Stand not upon the order of your going, but go at once.' Without being impolite, that's rather what we should all like to do. And I want to hunt round for those porters right away, this morning, if you've no objection."

The Chinese received the ultimatum impassively, replying at length: "I am sorry to tell you that it would be of little use. I fear we have no men available who would be willing to accompany you so far from their homes."

"But good God, man, you don't suppose we're going to take that for an answer, do you?"

"I am sincerely regretful, but I can suggest no other."

"You seem to have figgered it all out since last night," put in Barnard. "You weren't nearly so dead sure of things then."

"I did not wish to disappoint you when you were so tired from your journey. Now, after a refreshing night, I am in hope that you will see matters in a more reasonable light."

"Look here," intervened Conway briskly, "this sort of vagueness and prevarication won't do. You know we

蔑的神态回应到。他觉得任何一个思维健康的英国青年肯定是一提到诗就会有感觉，"我觉得你的意思是指莎士比亚吧，尽管我辨认不出来这句。但我清楚另一句是这样说的，'别站着等待出发的命令，立刻出发。'这并非粗鲁无礼，那的确是我们所有人都应该做的事，而且我想立刻去附近搜寻那些向导，就在今天早上，如果你同意的话。"

这个汉族人对这个最后通谍无动于衷，他拉长声音回应道："我非常遗憾地告诉你，这没有一丝用处，我担心我们找不到人愿意如此远离他们的家来陪伴你们。"

"上帝啊，伙计，但你不会觉得我们会接受这个答案吧，是吧？"

"我由衷地抱歉，但我不能提出其他意见了。"

"你似乎昨晚就已经全部算计好了吧，"巴纳德插话道，"否则，你不会对这些事情如此确定无疑。"

"我不希望在你们由于旅行而精疲力竭时让你们失望。现在，在一夜的恢复之后，我希望你们会发现事情都在更为合理的范围中。"

"看看，"康维尖锐地插话道，"这种含糊推诿不会有任何作用，你清楚我们不可能无限期地待在

can't stay here indefinitely. It's equally obvious that we can't get away by ourselves. What, then, do you propose?"

Chang smiled with a radiance that was clearly for Conway alone. "My dear sir, it is a pleasure to make the suggestion that is in my mind. To your friend's attitude there was no answer, but to the demand of a wise man there is always a response. You may recollect that it was remarked yesterday, again by your friend, I believe, that we are bound to have occasional communication with the outside world. That is quite true. From time to time we require certain things from distant *entrepôts,* and it is our habit to obtain them in due course, by what methods and with what formalities I need not trouble you. The point of importance is that such a consignment is expected to arrive shortly, and as the men who make delivery will afterwards return, it seems to me that you might manage to come to some arrangement with them. Indeed I cannot think of a better plan, and I hope, when they arrive – "

"When *do* they arrive?" interrupted Mallinson bluntly.

"The exact date is, of course, impossible to forecast. You have yourself had the experience of the difficulty of movement in this part of the world. A hundred things may happen to cause uncertainty, hazards of weather – "

这里，同样，显而易见的，我们也不可能自己离开，那么对此你有什么建议啊？"

张露出灿烂的微笑，明显是给康维一个人看的。"我亲爱的先生，给出我头脑中的建议是一件很令人高兴的事。对你朋友的那种态度，没有任何答案，但对于一个聪明人的要求，总会有一个回应的。你可能记得昨天你的朋友再次提及到，我相信我们和外界肯定有偶然的联系，那是千真万确的。偶尔我们需要从很远的地方得到某些东西，我习惯以期货形式获得。至于是何种方式，通过何种手续，我没有必要麻烦你们。最重要的一点是这样的货物都能被预计短期抵达，而当送货人随后返回时，我觉得你们似乎应该设法与他们取得联系做些安排。的确，我不能想出一个更好的方案了，我期待他们的抵达。"

"他们何时抵达？"马林逊粗鲁地插嘴道。

"确切的日期当然不可能预知出来，你们自己已经有过在这个地方活动的困难经历，有100种事情可能会导致不确定性，比如恶劣的天气……"

Conway again intervened. "Let's get this clear. You're suggesting that we should employ as porters the men who are shortly due here with some goods. That's not a bad idea as far as it goes, but we must know a little more about it. First, as you've already been asked, when are these people expected? And second, where will they take us?"

"That is a question you would have to put to them."

"Would they take us to India?"

"It is hardly possible for me to say."

"Well, let's have an answer to the other question. When will they be here? I don't ask for a date, I just want some idea whether it's likely to be next week or next year."

"It might be about a month from now. Probably not more than two months."

"Or three, four, or five months," broke in Mallinson hotly. "And you think we're going to wait here for this convoy or caravan or whatever it is to take us God knows where at some completely vague time in the distant future?"

"I think, sir, the phrase 'distant future' is hardly appropriate. Unless something unforeseen occurs, the period of waiting should not be longer than I have said."

"But *two months*! Two months in this place! It's preposterous! Conway, you surely can't contemplate it! Why, two weeks would be the limit!"

康维再次插话道:"咱们得弄清楚,你是在建议我们应该去雇用那些短期就应当抵达这里的人当作行李搬运工,这只要能实现,就不算一个坏主意。可我们必须再对此多了解一点,第一,就像你已经被问到的,这些送货人预计何时抵达?第二,他们会带我们到哪里?"

"这是一个你们应该去问他们的问题。"

"他们会带我们去印度吗?"

"我几乎不可能回答这个。"

"好吧,那我们回答一下另一个问题,他们何时会到这儿?我没有问具体日期,我只是想有个概念,可能的时间是下星期还是明年。"

"距现在大概还有几个月吧,也许不超过两个月。"

"3 个月、4 个月,或者 5 个月,"马林逊激动地插话,"那你觉得我们会在这里等这个送货队,要么马帮、要么其他什么人带走我们吗?上帝晓得那完全模糊晦涩的遥远未来的时间会在什么地方?"

"我觉得,先生,'遥远的未来'这个词完全不合适。除非一些不能预见的事情发生,否则需要等待的时间应该不会长于我所说的。"

"但两个月!两个月在这里!真是荒谬!康维,你肯定不能指望这个!哎哟,两周已经是极限了!

Chang gathered his gown about him in a little gesture of finality. "I am sorry. I did not wish to offend. The lamasery continues to offer all of you its utmost hospitality for as long as you have the misfortune to remain. I can say no more."

"You don't need to," retorted Mallinson furiously. "And if you think you've got the whip hand over us, you'll soon find you're damn well mistaken! We'll get all the porters we want, don't worry. You can bow and scrape and say what you like – "

Conway laid a restraining hand on his arm. Mallinson in a temper presented a child-like spectacle; he was apt to say anything that came into his head, regardless alike of point and decorum. Conway thought it readily forgivable in one so constituted and circumstanced, but he feared it might affront the more delicate susceptibilities of a Chinese. Fortunately Chang had ushered himself out, with admirable tact, in good time to escape the worst.

张上下整理了一下他的长衫，轻微做了个姿势表示结束。"我很抱歉，我不希望冒犯你们，只要你们的不幸还在持续，喇嘛寺就会继续给你们所有人最热情的款待，我能说的就是这些了。"

"你不需要说什么了，"马林逊暴躁地反驳道，"如果你认为你可以控制我们，你很快就会发现你大错特错了！不要担心，我们会找到我们需要的全部搬运工。你可以鞠躬作揖，然后爱说什么就说什么。"

康维用手拉着他的胳膊想制止他。马林逊在闹小孩脾气，他总是说出在他头脑里出现的任何事情，也不管有没有意义或得不得体。康维认为一个人这样的性格处在这样的环境，是可以被原谅的，可他担心这样可能冒犯了这个汉族人，让他更加多心。幸亏张很知趣地自己退了出去，用一种让人佩服的机智，极为及时地摆脱了糟糕的情况。

CHAPTER 5

第五章

THEY spent the rest of the morning discussing the matter. It was certainly a shock for four persons who in the ordinary course should have been luxuriating in the clubs and mission houses of Peshawar to find themselves faced instead with the prospect of two months in a Tibetan monastery. But it was in the nature of things that the initial shock of their arrival should have left them with slender reserves either of indignation or astonishment; even Mallinson, after his first outburst, subsided into a mood of half-bewildered fatalism. "I'm past arguing about it, Conway," he said, puffing at a cigarette with nervous irritability. "You know how I feel. I've said all along that there's something queer about this business. It's crooked. I'd like to be out of it this minute."

"I don't blame you for that," replied Conway. "Unfortunately, it's not a question of what any of us would like, but of what we've all got to put up with. Frankly, if these people say they won't or can't supply us with the necessary porters, there's nothing for it but to wait till the

整个上午他们都在议论这件事。令他们4个大为震惊的是,大家在正常情况下本该是在白沙瓦豪华喧腾的夜总会和安宁闲适的礼拜堂尽情享受的,现在却面临要在一座喇嘛寺熬上两个月的情境。可事情往往就是这样,他们刚到时的那份震惊本会让他们心中仍存一丝微弱的愤怒或者惊诧;但现在就连马林逊在暴怒之后也平静下来,被一种令人困惑的宿命论情绪所纠缠。"我懒得再谈论这事,康维,"他一面说,一面神经过敏地吸着烟,"你知道我是什么感觉,我一直都说这事有些可疑,现在更加离奇了。我想立刻离开这儿。"

"你这样说我不会责怪你,"康维回答,"不幸的是,这不是我们任何一个人愿不愿意的问题,而是我们全都不得不容忍现状的问题。坦率地说,假如这些人不愿或者不能为我们提供必要的向导,那除了等到后面其他人到达,我们别

other fellows come. I'm sorry to admit that we're so helpless in the matter, but I'm afraid it's the truth."

"You mean we've got to stay here for two months?"

"I don't see what else we can do."

Mallinson flicked his cigarette ash with a gesture of forced nonchalance. "All right, then. Two months it is. And now let's all shout hooray about it."

Conway went on: "I don't see why it should be much worse than two months in any other isolated part of the world. People in our jobs are used to being sent to odd places, I think I can say that of us all. Of course, it's bad for those of us who have friends and relatives. Personally, I'm fortunate in that respect, I can't think of anyone who'll worry over me acutely, and my work, whatever it might have been, can easily be done by somebody else."

He turned to the others as if inviting them to state their own cases. Mallinson proffered no information, but Conway knew roughly how he was situated. He had parents and a girl in England; it made things hard.

Barnard, on the other hand, accepted the position with what Conway had learned to regard as an habitual good humor. "Well, I guess I'm pretty lucky, for that matter, two months in the penitentiary won't kill me. As for the folks in my hometown, they

无他法。我非常遗憾，却不得不承认，我们对此束手无策，但这恐怕是事实。"

"你的意思是我们必须待在这儿两个月？"

"我想不出其他办法。"

马林逊若无其事地弹了一下烟灰，"好吧，就这样，就两个月，现在让咱们为此欢呼吧。"

康维接过话头："我看不出待在这儿两个月会比待在世上任何别的偏僻地方差很多。我们这种工作的人，习惯被派驻到不固定的稀奇古怪的地方，我想可以说我们大家都是这种情况。当然，对于我们当中那些有亲朋好友的人来说，这很糟糕。就我个人而言，我有幸适应了这样的生活，我不用挂念谁在深切地担心着我，还有我的工作，不管以前从事什么行业，我都能比别人更加轻而易举地做好。"

他转向其他几人，像是在邀请他们谈谈自己的情况。马林逊一言不发，可康维大体上知道他处于怎样的境地，英国有他的父母和女友，这让事情有些难办。

另一方面，巴纳德接受了康维试着把这当作习以为常的幽默的这样一种境况。"好吧，在这件事情上，我想我还是相当幸运的，在监狱里待两个月不会使我精疲力竭。至于我家乡的父老乡亲，他们

won't bat an eye. I've always been a bad letter writer."

"You forget that our names will be in the papers," Conway reminded him. "We shall all be posted missing, and people will naturally assume the worst."

Barnard looked startled for the moment; then he replied, with a slight grin: "Oh, yes, that's true, but it don't affect me, I assure you."

Conway was glad it didn't, though the matter remained a little puzzling. He turned to Miss Brinklow, who till then had been remarkably silent; she had not offered any opinion during the interview with Chang. He imagined that she too might have comparatively few personal worries. She said brightly: "As Mr. Barnard says, two months here is nothing to make a fuss about. It's all the same, wherever one is, when one's in the Lord's service. Providence has sent me here. I regard it as a call."

Conway thought the attitude a very convenient one, in the circumstances. "I'm sure," he said encouragingly, "you'll find your mission society pleased with you when you *do* return. You'll be able to give much useful information. We'll all of us have had an experience, for that matter. That should be a small consolation."

The talk then became general. Conway was rather surprised at the ease with

处之泰然，所以我老是写不好信。"

"要记得在信中提到我们的名字，"康维提醒他说，"否则我们会被布告失踪，而人们会自然地朝最坏的方向想。"

此刻，巴纳德大吃一惊，他轻轻地咧了咧嘴，笑着回答："哦，对了，那是必须的，虽然这对我没有什么影响，但我保证办到。"

虽然这句话仍然有些令人困惑，但它并不是特别重要、没有太大关系，这让康维感到很高兴。他转向到一直沉默无言的布琳克罗小姐，与张讨论时她也没有发表任何意见。于是他猜想，相比较而言她个人可能没有太多的烦恼与焦虑。布琳克罗突然轻快地说："就像巴纳德先生所言，在这待两个月没什么可大惊小怪的。受主的庇佑，不论你在哪里都一样，上帝已经把我送到这里，我就把它当做主的召唤。"

康维觉得在这样的环境中，这种的态度是很让人省心的。"我敢肯定，"他令人鼓舞地说，"当你真真切切地回去后，你会发现你的教会社团会为你很高兴，那时你就能够提供给他们许多有价值的信息。经历了这件事，我们大家都会有一番不同寻常的经历；那也将成为一种小小的慰藉。"

此后，他们的谈话变得轻松而

which Barnard and Miss Brinklow had accommodated themselves to the new prospect. He was relieved, however, as well; it left him with only one disgruntled person to deal with. Yet even Mallinson, after the strain of all the arguing, was experiencing a reaction; he was still perturbed, but more willing to look at the brighter side of things. "Heaven knows what we shall find to do with ourselves," he exclaimed, but the mere fact of making such a remark showed that he was trying to reconcile himself.

"The first rule must be to avoid getting on each other's nerves," replied Conway. "Happily, the place seems big enough, and by no means overpopulated. Except for servants, we've only seen one of its inhabitants so far."

Barnard could find another reason for optimism. "We won't starve, at any rate, if our meals up to now are a fair sample. You know, Conway, this place isn't run without plenty of hard cash. Those baths, for instance, they cost real money. And I can't see that anybody earns anything here, unless those chaps in the valley have jobs, and even then, they wouldn't produce enough for export. I'd like to know if they work any minerals."

"The whole place is a confounded mystery," responded Mallinson. "I daresay they've got pots of money hidden away,

广泛起来。令康维相当惊讶的是，巴纳德和布琳克罗小姐居然已经适应了新的环境，他很宽慰。然而，同时还有一个闷闷不乐的马林逊需要对付。但是在这一系列的争辩之后，甚至马林逊也慢慢发生着转变，虽然他仍然不安，但已经愿意看到事情更光明的一面。"天知道我们能拿自己怎么办？"他呼喊道，但他发表这样的言论只不过表示他是在试着缓解自己的情绪而已。

"首要的规定是我们必须要避免相互刺激或烦扰，"康维回应，"令人高兴的是，这地方看来够大，而且决不会人口过剩，除了几个传教士之外，到目前为止，我们才见过一个居民。"

巴纳德还找到另外一个让人乐观的理由，"我们不会挨饿，不管怎样，直到现在，咱们这几顿饭还很像样呢。你知道，康维，没有大量现金这个地方就不能运营了，比如这些浴室，肯定得花钱。还有，我看不出这儿的任何人有收入，除非山谷里的那些家伙有活计；即使如此，他们也不可能生产足够的东西可供出口，我倒想知道他们是不是在开采什么矿物。"

"整个地方就是一个令人迷惑的谜，"马林逊响应说，"我敢说，他们把大量的钱藏了起来，就像耶

like the Jesuits. As for the baths, probably some millionaire supporter presented them. Anyhow, it won't worry me, once I get away. I must say, though, the view is rather good, in its way. Fine winter sport center if it were in the right spot. I wonder if one could get any ski-ing on some of those slopes up yonder?"

Conway gave him a searching and slightly amused glance. "Yesterday, when I found some edelweiss, you reminded me that I wasn't in the Alps. I think it's my turn to say the same thing now. I wouldn't advise you to try any of your Wengen-Scheidegg tricks in this part of the world."

"I don't suppose anybody here has ever seen a ski-jump."

"Or even an ice-hockey match," responded Conway banteringly. "You might try to raise some teams. What about 'Gentlemen v. Lamas'?"

"It would certainly teach them to play the game," Miss Brinklow put in with sparkling seriousness.

Adequate comment upon this might have been difficult, but there was no necessity, since lunch was about to be served and its character and promptness combined to make an agreeable impression. Afterwards, when Chang entered, there was small disposition to continue the squabble. With great

稣会一样。像这些浴缸，很可能是一些拥有百万家资的资助者赠送的。无论如何，一旦我离开这里，这些就不会让我心烦了。尽管如此，我必须承认，从某种程度上看，这儿的景色也是相当漂亮的。如果在适当的地点，这里会是个挺不错的冬季运动中心，我在想，我们能否到远处那些斜坡上去滑雪什么的？"

康维用探究而又逗趣的目光瞥了他一眼，"昨天，当我发现雪绒花的时候，是你提醒了我说我们没在阿尔卑斯山。我想现在该轮到我来说这相同的话了。我可不建议你在世界的这个地方试验文根·斯德基的任何把戏。"

"我估计这里没人见过腾跳式滑雪。"

"冰球赛就更不可能见过了，"康维开玩笑地附和道，"你可以试着组建一个队，'绅士喇嘛队'怎么样？"

"肯定得教他们如何比赛。"布琳克罗小姐神采奕奕而又郑重其事地插了一句。

这件事要得到一个令人满意的解释可能会很困难，但是也没必要了。午餐就要准备好了，菜上得很快，而且都很有特色，令人愉快。到后来，当张进来的时候，大家差点又继续大声争吵，好在言行得体、聪明老练的中国人装出仍然和

tactfulness the Chinese assumed that he was still on good terms with everybody, and the four exiles allowed the assumption to stand. Indeed, when he suggested that they might care to be shown a little more of the lamasery buildings, and that if so, he would be pleased to act as guide, the offer was readily accepted. "Why, surely," said Barnard. "We may as well give the place the once-over while we're here. I reckon it'll be a long time before any of us pay a second visit."

Miss Brinklow struck a more thought-giving note. "When we left Baskul in that aeroplane I'm sure I never dreamed we should ever get to a place like this," she murmured as they all moved off under Chang's escort.

"And we don't know yet why we have," answered Mallinson unforgetfully.

Conway had no race or color prejudice, and it was an affectation for him to pretend, as he sometimes did in clubs and first-class railway carriages, that he set any particular store on the "whiteness" of a lobster-red face under a topee. It saved trouble to let it be so assumed, especially in India, and Conway was a conscientious trouble-saver. But in China it had been less necessary; he had had many Chinese friends, and it had never occurred to him to treat them as inferiors. Hence, in his

每一个人亲密无间的样子，而且这4位背井离乡的游子也允许了这种虚情假意的存在。的确，当他表示4位可能会喜欢多看看喇嘛寺院的建筑，而且如果这样，他将很愿意当作向导时，这个邀请立刻被接受了。"为什么不呢！当然得看看，"巴纳德说，"趁着在这儿，我们可以把这个地方大致地看一看，我觉得我们中的任何一个，短时间内都不会第二次来访。"

布琳克罗小姐突然冒出一句更加耐人寻味的话，"当我们乘坐那架飞机离开巴斯库时，我保证我从来没有幻想过什么时候我们会来到像这样的一个地方。"她嘟囔着。同时，大家在张的陪同下参观寺院。

"我们到现在还搞不懂为什么我们会来到这里。"马林逊没忘加上一句。

康维没有种族或肤色的偏见；而这只是他伪装的故意表现，就像有时在俱乐部和火车的一等车厢里他尤其注意脑门下那张肉红色的脸的"白色成分"一样。这样用心假装也让他省去了很多麻烦，特别是在印度时，而康维也的确是一个小心谨慎避免麻烦的人。但在中国这一套就没有多大必要了，他很多中国朋友，而且他从未想过拿他们当下等人看待。从那时起，在

intercourse with Chang, he was sufficiently unpreoccupied to see in him a mannered old gentleman who might not be entirely trustworthy, but who was certainly of high intelligence. Mallinson, on the other hand, tended to regard him through the bars of an imaginary cage; Miss Brinklow was sharp and sprightly, as with the heathen in his blindness; while Barnard's wise-cracking *bonhomie* was of the kind he would have cultivated with a butler.

Meanwhile the grand tour of Shangri-La was interesting enough to transcend these attitudes. It was not the first monastic institution Conway had inspected, but it was easily the largest and, apart from its situation, the most remarkable. The mere procession through rooms and courtyards was an afternoon's exercise, though he was aware of many apartments passed by, indeed, of whole buildings into which Chang did not offer admission. The party were shown enough, however, to confirm the impressions each one of them had formed already. Barnard was more certain than ever that the lamas were rich; Miss Brinklow discovered abundant evidence that they were immoral. Mallinson, after the first novelty had worn off, found himself no less fatigued than on many sight-seeing excursions at lower altitudes; the lamas,

同张交往时，他就特别留心观察，看出这位老先生虽不是完全值得信赖的，却绝对是有大智慧的博学之人。另一方面，马林逊倾向于通过假想中的条条框框来看待张；布琳克罗小姐是精明活泼的，正如她所具有的那种未开化的盲目；然而，巴纳德睿智与和蔼可亲得像是被某个男管家调教出来似的。

同时，这非同寻常的香格里拉之旅，也足够趣味盎然来颠覆所有这些凡俗之见。这不是康维所造访的第一座寺院机构，可这显而易见是他所见过的最大的一个，不仅如此，它也是最出众、最值得注意的一个。他注意到好多经过的厅堂，甚至还有很多没允许他们进去的整栋的楼房，而就仅仅在房间和庭院之中穿行而过，就得花整整一个下午的时间。经过这么充分的参观，大家都确认了先前已经形成的看法。巴纳德比以前更加肯定喇嘛很富裕，布琳克罗小姐发现了充分的证据说明他们是猥亵的。而马林逊在最初的新鲜感消失之后，只觉得自己比在低海拔地区许多次的短程游览观光更加疲惫不堪，而这些喇嘛恐怕也不像是他心目中的英雄。

he feared, were not likely to be his heroes.

Conway alone submitted to a rich and growing enchantment. It was not so much any individual thing that attracted him as the gradual revelation of elegance, of modest and impeccable taste, of harmony so fragrant that it seemed to gratify the eye without arresting it. Only indeed by a conscious effort did he recall himself from the artist's mood to the connoisseur's, and then he recognized treasures that museums and millionaires alike would have bargained for, exquisite pearl blue Sung ceramics, paintings in tinted inks preserved for more than a thousand years, lacquers in which the cold and lovely detail of fairyland was not so much depicted as orchestrated. A world of incomparable refinements still lingered tremulously in porcelain and varnish, yielding an instant of emotion before its dissolution into purest thought. There was no boastfulness, no striving after effect, no concentrated attack upon the feelings of the beholder. These delicate perfections had an air of having fluttered into existence like petals from a flower. They would have maddened a collector, but Conway did not collect; he lacked both money and the acquisitive instinct. His liking for Chinese art was an affair of the mind; in a world of increasing noise and hugeness, he turned in private to gentle,

唯独康维渐渐折服于这富饶而令人陶醉的圣地。还没有任何一件独特的事物以其逐渐显露的优雅、质朴与无暇的韵致以及充满芳香、让人目不暇接的和谐美景这样深深地吸引过他。的确，只有有意识地努力才能够让他从艺术家的情绪恢复到鉴定家的心态中来。于是他认出了博物馆和百万富翁们都会为之竞相讨价还价的那些珍品：精致的珍珠蓝宋代陶器，珍存了一千多年的水墨画，还有一些绘有淡雅而可爱的仙境的漆器，那细腻入微的笔触自然灵动、形如天成；那些瓷器与釉彩在焕灭为纯粹的思想之前跌宕着瞬息的激情，映射出一个微微颤抖的无可比拟的美妙世界。没有自夸，没有明知结果后的强求，也没有对观赏者情感的集中冲击。这些精致的尽善尽美的珍品散发着一种犹如从鲜花的叶瓣之间飘散出的高雅气息，这一切定会让收藏家疯狂，但康维不善收藏。他既缺乏金钱又没有贪婪的本性；他喜欢中国艺术只是因为一种发自内心的感知，在这个变得日益喧嚣和膨胀的世界里，他转而寄情于这些温和、细致而小巧的物件。当他穿梭在一间间的厅室之时，一幅清晰的图片浮现在他的脑海，那遥远的思绪让他感受到卡拉卡尔山堆琼积玉的宏美映衬着的

precise, and miniature things. And as he passed through room after room, a certain pathos touched him remotely at the thought of Karakal's piled immensity over against such fragile charms.

The lamasery, however, had more to offer than a display of Chinoiserie. One of its features, for instance, was a very delightful library, lofty and spacious, and containing a multitude of books so retiringly housed in bays and alcoves that the whole atmosphere was more of wisdom than of learning, of good manners rather than seriousness. Conway, during a rapid glance at some of the shelves, found much to astonish him; the world's best literature was there, it seemed, as well as a great deal of abstruse and curious stuff that he could not appraise. Volumes in English, French, German, and Russian abounded, and there were vast quantities of Chinese and other Eastern scripts. A section which interested him particularly was devoted to Tibetiana, if it might be so called; he noticed several rarities, among them the *Novo Descubrimento de grao catayo ou dos Regos de Tibet,* by Antonio de Andrada (Lisbon, 1626); Athanasius Kircher's *China* (Antwerp, 1667); Thevenot's *Voyage à la Chine des Pères Grueber et d'Orville;* and Beligatti's *Relazione Inedita di un Viaggio al Tibet.* He was examining the last named when he

脆弱的令人哀婉的魅力。

然而，这喇嘛寺能够展示的不仅仅是中国的艺术珍品。比如，它诸多的特色之一就是那间令人心情非常舒畅的图书室，它高大而宽敞，存放着大量的书籍，如此孤寂而冷落地被收藏在储物间和壁龛之中，整个氛围显示出一种智慧超乎学问、礼仪与德行超乎庄严的境界。康维草草地环视其中的一些书架，他发现太多东西让他大为吃惊，那里居然有世界上经典的文学作品；看起来，似乎还有许多抽象而有趣的东西他无法鉴定。好多卷英文、法文、德文以及俄文版的书籍大量存在，还有许多中文和其他东方文学的书刊。应该说，康维尤其感兴趣的一部分是他所钟爱的有关西藏的书刊，他注意到几部稀有的作品，其中就有由安东尼奥·德·安多拉塔所著的《NoVo Descubrimento de grao catayo ou dos Regos de Tibet》（里斯本，1626年）；艾塞纳修斯·克切的作品《中国》（安特卫普，1667年）；特凡纳特的《Voyage à la Chine des Pères Grueber et d'Orville》和比利加第的《Relazione Inedita di un Viaggio al Tibet》。当康维正在仔细翻阅最后

noticed Chang's eyes fixed on him in suave curiosity. "You are a scholar, perhaps?" came the enquiry.

Conway found it hard to reply. His period of donhood at Oxford gave him some right to assent, but he knew that the word, though the highest of compliments from a Chinese, had yet a faintly priggish sound for English ears, and chiefly out of consideration for his companions he demurred to it. He said: "I enjoy reading, of course, but my work during recent years hasn't supplied many opportunities for the studious life."

"Yet you wish for it?"

"Oh, I wouldn't say all that, but I'm certainly aware of its attractions."

Mallinson, who had picked up a book, interrupted: "Here's something for your studious life, Conway. It's a map of the country."

"We have a collection of several hundreds," said Chang. "They are all open to your inspection, but perhaps I can save you trouble in one respect. You will not find Shangri-La marked on any."

"Curious," Conway made comment. "I wonder why?"

"There is a very good reason, but I am afraid that is all I can say."

Conway smiled, but Mallinson looked peevish again. "Still piling up the mystery," he said. "So far we haven't seen

一部书时，他注意到张正在用世故而好奇的眼神注视着他。"或许，你是个学者？"他询问。

康维觉得难以回答。凭他在牛津任教时期的经历他有权利这样承认。但是，他明白"学者"一词虽然是中国人给予的最高评价，可是在英国人的耳朵里这个称谓却显得骄傲自大、自以为是。而且，最重要的是要考虑他几个同伴的感受，他拒绝了这一称谓。他说："当然，我喜欢阅读，可最近几年的工作中没有提供给我多少搞学术研究的机会。"

"但是你仍有这种愿望？"

"哎，我说不好，不过我的确能感觉到它的吸引力。"

马林逊拿起一部书打断了康维的话："这里有东西让你研究哦，康维，这是一张这个地区的地图。"

"我们收藏了几百张。"张说，"这些地图是供你们查阅的，不过，我可能得提醒你们，省的你们白费心机：你们在任何一张地图上都找不到香格里拉的标记。"

"真奇怪，"康维不解，"我想知道这是为什么？"

"有一个很好的理由，但恐怕我能说的也就这么多了。"

康维笑了笑，可马林逊急躁起来。"他还在夸大其词、故作神秘，"他说，"到现在为止我们看不出有

much that anyone need bother to conceal."

Suddenly Miss Brinklow came to life out of a mute preoccupation. "Aren't you going to show us the lamas at work?" she fluted, in the tone which one felt had intimidated many a Cook's man. One felt, too, that her mind was probably full of hazy visions of native handicrafts, prayer-mat weaving, or something picturesquely primitive that she could talk about when she got home. She had an extraordinary knack of never seeming very much surprised, yet of always seeming very slightly indignant, a combination of fixities which was not in the least disturbed by Chang's response: "I am sorry to say it is impossible. The lamas are never, or perhaps I should say only very rarely, seen by those outside the lamahood."

"I guess we'll have to miss 'em then," agreed Barnard. "But I do think it's a real pity. You've no notion how much I'd like to have shaken the hand of your head-man."

Chang acknowledged the remark with benign seriousness. Miss Brinklow, however, was not yet to be side-tracked. "What do the lamas do?" she continued.

"They devote themselves, madam, to contemplation and to the pursuit of wisdom."

"But that isn't *doing* anything."

任何人要费工夫隐瞒什么嘛。"

突然，布琳克罗小姐从心不在焉的沉默中猛地清醒过来："难道你不带我们看看那些正在修炼的喇嘛吗？"她咄咄逼人的语调让人觉得她是在恐吓一些懦弱的人，又让人觉得她脑子里满满的都是些朦胧的本地手工艺品的幻想，诸如什么编织的跪垫，或者是某些她回家后可以大肆吹嘘的非常生动别致而又原始纯朴的东西。她有一种非同一般的技巧，从不会让自己显出特别惊讶的样子，然而，她又总表现得有些愤愤不平，多种顽固的习惯结合在她身上，就连张的回答都没有让她受到丝毫干扰："很抱歉，这不可能。那些喇嘛绝不——或者我应该说很少——让喇嘛以外的人看到。"

"我想我们必然会错过他们了，"巴纳德表示赞同，"但是我想这真的太可惜了。你根本体会不到我有多想与你们的首领握握手。"

张亲切和蔼而严肃地认可了他的说法。可是布琳克罗小姐还不肯转变话题，"喇嘛都干些什么？"她继续问。

"女士，他们都全心全意地投身于静坐沉思以及对智慧的探求。"

"但这等于没做任何事。"

"Then, madam, they do nothing."

"I thought as much." She found occasion to sum up. "Well, Mr. Chang, it's a pleasure being shown all these things, I'm sure, but you won't convince me that a place like this does any real good. I prefer something more practical."

"Perhaps you would like to take tea?"

Conway wondered at first if this were intended ironically, but it soon appeared not; the afternoon had passed swiftly, and Chang, though frugal in eating, had the typical Chinese fondness for tea-drinking at frequent intervals. Miss Brinklow, too, confessed that visiting art galleries and museums always gave her a touch of headache. The party, therefore, fell in with the suggestion, and followed Chang through several courtyards to a scene of quite sudden and unmatched loveliness. From a colonnade steps descended to a garden, in which a lotus pool lay entrapped, the leaves so closely set that they gave an impression of a floor of moist green tiles. Fringing the pool were posed a brazen menagerie of lions, dragons, and unicorns, each offering a stylized ferocity that emphasized rather than offended the surrounding peace. The whole picture was so perfectly proportioned that the eye was entirely unhastened from one part to another; there was no vying or vanity, and even the

"那么，女士，他们无所事事。"

"我也这样认为，"她看准时机开始总结，"好了，张先生，我确定，参观所有这些东西让我们非常愉快，但是你没有让我相信这样一个地方在做什么实在的好事。我倒更喜欢一些更实际的东西。"

"或许你想要喝茶了？"

康维开始在想这似乎有些讽刺意味，但很快又证明好像不是。一个下午就这样匆匆而过，张先生虽然在吃这方面很节俭，却也有典型的中国人惯有的那种闲暇之余对饮茶之趣的钟爱，而布琳克罗小姐自己也承认参观什么艺术画廊、博物馆之类的总是让她头痛。大伙都赞同这个建议，于是大家跟随张穿过几个庭院。他们突然进入一幅无与伦比的美丽的场景之中：沿着柱廊走来顺阶而下，步入一个花园，一湾诱人的荷花塘静躺在那里，田田的荷叶那样紧密地依偎在一起，让人仿佛置身于青翠欲滴的彩锦地板上。他的边缘装饰着千姿百态的动物铜像，有狮子、龙和独角兽，各自呈现出张牙舞爪的凶猛形象。而这丝毫没有破坏周围的祥和，反而增添了几分宁静。整个如画的景致如此完美地相称，一处处的胜景令人应接不暇；这里没有争斗与虚荣，就连耸立在蓝瓦屋顶上方的美妙绝伦的卡拉卡尔山顶峰

summit of Karakal, peerless above the blue-tiled roofs, seemed to have surrendered within the framework of an exquisite artistry. "Pretty little place," commented Barnard, as Chang led the way into an open pavilion which, to Conway's further delight, contained a harpsichord and a modern grand piano. He found this in some ways the crowning astonishment of a rather astonishing afternoon. Chang answered all his questions with complete candour up to a point; the lamas, he explained, held Western music in high esteem, particularly that of Mozart; they had a collection of all the great European compositions, and some were skilled performers on various instruments.

Barnard was chiefly impressed by the transport problem. "D'you mean to tell me that this pi-anno was brought here by the route we came along yesterday?"

"There is no other."

"Well, that certainly beats everything! Why, with a phonograph and a radio you'd be all fixed complete! Perhaps, though, you aren't yet acquainted with up-to-date music?"

"Oh, yes, we have had reports, but we are advised that the mountains would make wireless reception impossible, and as for a phonograph, the suggestion has already come before the authorities, but

都似乎臣服于这精美雅致优雅的天然画图中。"真是个秀丽俊美又小巧可爱的地方。"巴纳德这样赞叹道。这时张带他们走进一座四面环开的亭子里，让康维更欣喜的是，里面摆放着一台古琴和一台现代的华丽钢琴。康维觉得从某种程度上说，这是整个相当令人惊讶的下午所见到的最让人惊奇的景象。张完全坦率地回答了他所有的问题，归结为一点，张解释说喇嘛们高度推崇西洋音乐，尤其热爱莫扎特的作品；他们收集了全部经典的欧洲乐曲，而且有些喇嘛还能熟练演奏各种乐器。

巴纳德对交通运输问题尤其印象深刻，"你该不会要告诉我，这钢琴也是从我们昨天来的那条路上弄进来的吧！"

"没有别的途径。"

"是吗，这当然什么事都可以解决了！怎么，再加一台留声机和一台收音机你们就什么都全了，尽管你们可能还不了解现代流行音乐。"

"哦，是的。我们已经打过报告了，但是有人建议我们说大山里面不可能接收到无线电波。至于留声机，早就有人已经向权威人士建议过，但他们认为这件事不必太着

they have felt no need to hurry in the matter."

"I'd believe that even if you hadn't told me," Barnard retorted. "I guess that must be the slogan of your society, 'No hurry.'" He laughed loudly and then went on: "Well, to come down to details, suppose in due course your bosses decide that they *do* want a phonograph, what's the procedure? The makers wouldn't deliver here, that's a sure thing. You must have an agent in Pekin or Shanghai or somewhere, and I'll bet everything costs plenty by the time you handle it."

But Chang was no more to be drawn than on a previous occasion. "Your surmises are intelligent, Mr. Barnard, but I fear I cannot discuss them."

So there they were again, Conway reflected, edging the invisible border-line between what might and might not be revealed. He thought he could soon begin to map out that line in imagination, though the impact of a new surprise deferred the matter. For servants were already bringing in the shallow bowls of scented tea, and along with the agile, lithe-limbed Tibetans there had also entered, quite inconspicuously, a girl in Chinese dress. She went directly to the harpsichord and began to play a gavotte by Rameau. The first bewitching twang stirred in Conway a pleasure that was beyond amazement;

急。"

"我相信，即使你没告诉我，"巴纳德反驳道，"我想那一定是你们这个社团组织的标语，'别着急嘛'。"他大笑，然后接着说："好了，来说一些具体的，假设在适当的时候，你的上司们决定他们的确想要一台留声机，那要办理哪些手续？制造商是不会把货运送到这里的，这是必然的事实。你们在北京上海或者别的什么地方一定有代理人，我敢打赌，到你们收到货时，肯定每件东西都得花很多钱。"

可是张再也不像先前的场合一样绘声绘色地讲述了："你的推测还很明智嘛，巴纳德先生，但恐怕我不能再谈论这些事了。"

康维深思，发觉他们又一次处在了那若隐若现、似有似无之间的神秘无形界限的边缘。他想着很快就能通过想象和推断理出头绪，尽管新谜题的影响一再推迟着真相大白。这时，佣人已经把香气沁脾的茶端了进来。这些敏捷而轻便的藏族人进出的同时，一位身穿汉族服饰的女孩也悄无声息地出现在眼前，她径直走过去撩拨琴弦，开始弹奏拉米欧的一首古老的法国加伏特舞曲。这令人心醉的第一声弦音使康维在惊愕之余油然产生一股欣喜之情。那银铃般清脆悦耳的音符洋溢着 18 世纪法兰西的气

those silvery airs of eighteenth-century France seemed to match in elegance the Sung vases and exquisite lacquers and the lotus-pool beyond; the same death-defying fragrance hung about them, lending immortality through an age to which their spirit was alien. Then he noticed the player. She had the long, slender nose, high cheekbones, and egg-shell pallor of the Manchu; her black hair was drawn tightly back and braided; she looked very finished and miniature. Her mouth was like a little pink convolvulus, and she was quite still, except for her long-fingered hands. As soon as the gavotte was ended, she made a little obeisance and went out.

Chang smiled after her and then, with a touch of personal triumph, upon Conway. "You are pleased?" he queried.

"Who is she?" asked Mallinson, before Conway could reply.

"Her name is Lo-Tsen. She has much skill with Western keyboard music. Like myself, she has not yet attained the full initiation."

"I should think not, indeed!" exclaimed Miss Brinklow. "She looks hardly more than a child. So you have women lamas, then?"

"There are no sex distinctions among us."

"Extraordinary business, this lamahood of yours," Mallinson commented loftily,

息；似乎又与文雅的宋代瓷瓶和精致的漆器还有仙境般的莲花塘交相呼应。同样，这沁人心脾的芳香轻柔地弥漫在他们每一个人的身边，好像牵引他们穿越不朽的时空，消融在与现实格格不入的精神世界。后来，康维注意到了演奏者，她有着满族姑娘特有的纤细而略长的鼻子，高高的颧骨和白皙的鹅蛋脸，她乌黑的长发紧紧地梳到脑后编成辫子；她看上去那么精致完美而又乖巧；她的嘴巴就像一朵小小的粉红色牵牛花；她是那样安静，除了那双细指纤纤的玉手。那曲加伏特舞曲一结束，她轻轻地鞠了一躬就离开了。

张微笑着目送姑娘走远，然后带着一丝成功的喜悦靠近康维："满不满意？"他问道。

"她是谁？"没等康维回答，马林逊就抢先问道。

"她叫罗珍，对西洋键盘器乐有很深的造诣。同我一样，她也还没有实现完全进入佛门。"

"我想确实还没有，"布琳克罗小姐叫嚷道，"她看去简直还是个孩子。这么说这里有女喇嘛啦？"

"我们之间没有性别区分。"

"这可太离奇了，你们这种喇嘛僧侣制度。"停顿了一会，马林

after a pause. The rest of the tea-drinking proceeded without conversation; echoes of the harpsichord seemed still in the air, imposing a strange spell. Presently, leading the departure from the pavilion, Chang ventured to hope that the tour had been enjoyable. Conway, replying for the others, seesawed with the customary courtesies. Chang then assured them of his own equal enjoyment, and hoped they would consider the resources of the music room and library wholly at their disposal throughout their stay. Conway, with some sincerity, thanked him again. "But what about the lamas?" he added. "Don't they ever want to use them?"

"They yield place with much gladness to their honored guests."

"Well, that's what I call real handsome," said Barnard. "And what's more, it shows that the lamas do really know we exist. That's a step forward, anyhow, makes me feel much more at home. You've certainly got a swell outfit here, Chang, and that little girl of yours plays the pi-anno very nicely. How old would she be, I wonder?"

"I am afraid I cannot tell you."

Barnard laughed. "You don't give away secrets about a lady's age, is that it?"

"Precisely," answered Chang with a faintly shadowing smile.

逊高傲地议论道。接下来大伙都没再交谈，只是继续静静地品茶。古琴的余音似乎仍在空气中缭绕，仿佛是一种令人难忘的神奇符咒。不久后，张带他们离开了凉亭，他表示希望这次参观愉快而有趣。康维代大家表示了感谢，还礼貌地客套了一番，张也真切地表达了他自己同样的快乐，而且他们在这期间，音乐间和图书室的资源会始终为他们开放，欢迎他们随时使用。康维一再对此表示真挚的感谢。"可是那些喇嘛怎么办？"他又加了一句，"他们从来都不用吗？"

"他们很高兴把地方让给尊敬的客人们使用。"

"好，这就是我所说的真正的慷慨大方，"巴纳德说，"另外，看来喇嘛们都真正知道我们的存在，无论如何，那也更进一步让我感受到在这像在家里一样亲切。张，你们这里肯定有一套一流的团队，你们那位小姑娘钢琴弹得可真出色，我想知道她有多大了。"

"这我恐怕不能告诉你。"

巴纳德笑道："你不能透露女士年龄的秘密，对吗？"

"千真万确。"张答道，脸上微微露出点笑意。

That evening, after dinner, Conway made occasion to leave the others and stroll out into the calm, moon-washed courtyards. Shangri-La was lovely then, touched with the mystery that lies at the core of all loveliness. The air was cold and still; the mighty spire of Karakal looked nearer, much nearer than by daylight. Conway was physically happy, emotionally satisfied, and mentally at ease; but in his intellect, which was not quite the same thing as mind, there was a little stir. He was puzzled. The line of secrecy that he had begun to map out grew sharper, but only to reveal an inscrutable background. The whole amazing series of events that had happened to him and his three chance companions swung now into a sort of focus; he could not yet understand them, but he believed they were somehow to be understood.

Passing along a cloister, he reached the terrace leaning over the valley. The scent of tuberose assailed him, full of delicate associations; in China it was called "the smell of moonlight." He thought whimsically that if moonlight had a sound also, it might well be the Rameau gavotte he had heard so recently; and that set him thinking of the little Manchu. It had not occurred to him to picture women at Shangri-La; one did not associate their presence with the general practice of

那天傍晚，用餐之后，康维趁机避开其他几位，独自溜到了寂静的月光洒落的庭院。那时的香格里拉是那样可爱，深深蕴含在它美好、纯净中的那份神秘让人为之怦然心动。空气是那样清亮而静谧，而卡拉卡尔山巨大的山峰看上去更近了，比白天更加接近。康维感到浑身舒适愉快，心情惬意满足，精神也轻松安逸，而他的思维与心情却不完全一致，他有些激动，也感到困惑；他之前揣测的那丝秘密的线索慢慢变得明朗，但只能揭示那难以理解的背景。这一系列令人惊异的事情碰巧发生在他和3个不期而遇的同伴身上，现在却转变成大家的一个焦点。他还搞不明白这些人是何用意，但他相信总归会真相大白。

通过一道回廊，他来到山谷上方探出的那块小露台。玉兰花的芳香阵阵来袭，饱含着美妙的幻想。在中国，它被叫做"晚香玉"。康维异想天开地寻思着，如果这月色也有声音的话，那应该就是他近来听过的拉米欧的加伏特舞曲。同时，这又让他想起那位满族女孩儿，此前他从未想象过香格里拉会有女性的图像在他心里出现；而人们怎么都不会把她们的出现与一般的修道院生活联想在一起。然

monasticism. Still, he reflected, it might not be a disagreeable innovation; indeed, a female harpsichordist might be an asset to any community that permitted itself to be (in Chang's words) "moderately heretical."

He gazed over the edge into the blue-black emptiness. The drop was phantasmal; perhaps as much as a mile. He wondered if he would be allowed to descend it and inspect the valley civilization that had been talked of. The notion of this strange culture-pocket, hidden amongst unknown ranges, and ruled over by some vague kind of theocracy, interested him as a student of history, apart from the curious though perhaps related secrets of the lamasery.

Suddenly, on a flutter of air, came sounds from far below. Listening intently, he could hear gongs and trumpets and also (though perhaps only in imagination) the massed wail of voices. The sounds faded on a veer of the wind, then returned to fade again. But the hint of life and liveliness in those veiled depths served only to emphasize the austere serenity of Shangri-La. Its forsaken courts and pale pavilions shimmered in repose from which all the fret of existence had ebbed away, leaving a hush as if moments hardly dared to pass. Then, from a window high above the terrace, he caught the rose-gold of

而，他在想，这可能并非是一项令人讨厌的改革，说实在的，就如张先生所言，一个女古琴演奏家在任何一个容许自己适度信奉异端邪说的社会群体中都会是宝贵的人才。

他的目光越过山谷的边缘凝视着那一片深蓝色的空旷天空，这深陷的谷底让人感到那样空灵，其间落差大概有一英里。他在想自己能否被允许走下山谷，去领略一番闲聊中被提及的那些山谷文明。深藏在这些不知名的群山之间，而且被某种不明确的神权政治所控制的奇特文化理念深深地吸引着他，浓厚的兴趣让他像一个历史系的学生一样，更何况这还可能与这喇嘛寺的秘密有关。

突然之间，微风浮动，遥远的山谷下面隐隐约约传来一些声音。认真一听，他可以听到铜锣声、喇叭声，另外还有许多人嚎啕大哭的嘈杂声，当然也可能只是幻觉。随着风的转向，这些声音又渐渐消失；不久又反复地转头飘来，然后再次隐匿在风声之中。然而，这隐秘的深渊中传来的生命与活力的暗示只是渲染了香格里拉的朴素与安宁。月光闪烁下，搁置的庭院和苍寂的凉亭在宁静中安眠，所有生活中的烦恼像潮水般退去，只留下连时光都凝滞的一片静寂。后来，他的视线透过露台高处的一扇

lantern light; was it there that the lamas devoted themselves to contemplation and the pursuit of wisdom, and were those devotions now in progress? The problem seemed one that he could solve merely by entering at the nearest door and exploring through gallery and corridor until the truth were his; but he knew that such freedom was illusory, and that in fact his movements were watched. Two Tibetans had padded across the terrace and were idling near the parapet. Good-humored fellows they looked, shrugging their colored cloaks negligently over naked shoulders. The whisper of gongs and trumpets uprose again, and Conway heard one of the men question his companion. The answer came: "They have buried Talu." Conway, whose knowledge of Tibetan was very slight, hoped they would continue talking; he could not gather much from a single remark. After a pause the questioner, who was inaudible, resumed the conversation, and obtained answers which Conway overheard and loosely understood as follows:

"He died outside."

"He obeyed the high ones of Shangri-La."

"He came through the air over the great mountains with a bird to hold him."

"Strangers he brought, also."

"Talu was not afraid of the outside

窗户，不经意间看到了灯笼发出的玫瑰色的光，那是不是喇嘛们在聚精会神地静坐修行、冥思苦想、探寻学问？他们是不是正在进行虔诚的祈祷呢？看起来只要进入最近的那一扇门，然后透过廊道看一看，这个问题便可解决了，真相就可知了，但他知道这种自由是虚无缥缈的，而且实际上他的行动一直处于被监视之中。两名喇嘛轻手轻脚地从露台上走过，然后在护墙附近无所事事地闲逛着。看上去是两个幽默的家伙，一耸肩就粗心大意地把裸露的肩膀上的彩色披风不小心给脱了。铜锣声和喇叭声又一次响起。康维听见其中一个喇嘛问他的同伴什么，而回答他听清了："他们已经把塔鲁埋葬了。"而康维对藏语知识的了解微不足道，他希望他们可以继续讲下去；单就一句话他无法猜测出多少意思。他们停顿了一会儿之后，刚才说话康维无法听懂的那个提问者重新开始交谈了。康维听到了另一个的回答，也明白了个大概：

"他死在了外面。"

"他是去执行香格里拉首领的命令。"

"他是被一只大鸟驮着翻山越岭回到这里的。"

"他也带回很多异乡人。"

"塔鲁不怕外面的风，也不怕

wind, nor of the outside cold."

"Though he went outside long ago, the valley of Blue Moon remembers him still."

Nothing more was said that Conway could interpret, and after waiting for some time he went back to his own quarters. He had heard enough to turn another key in the locked mystery, and it fitted so well that he wondered he had failed to supply it by his own deductions. It had, of course, crossed his mind, but a certain initial and fantastic unreasonableness about it had been too much for him. Now he perceived that the unreasonableness, however fantastic, was to be swallowed. That flight from Baskul had *not* been the meaningless exploit of a madman. It had been something planned, prepared, and carried out at the instigation of Shangri-La. The dead pilot was known by name to those who lived there; he had been one of them, in some sense; his death was mourned. Everything pointed to a high directing intelligence bent upon its own purposes; there had been, as it were, a single arch of intentions spanning the inexplicable hours and miles. But what was that intention? For what possible reason could four chance passengers in the British government aeroplane be whisked away to these trans-Himalayan solitudes?

Conway was somewhat aghast at the

外面的寒冷。"

"虽然他很久以前就去外面了，可蓝月谷的人都仍然记得他。"

更多的话康维就不能理解了。等了一会儿，他回到了自己的住处。他所听到的足以成为打开这尘封的秘密的又一把钥匙，而且它是如此的合情合理，以至于他怀疑自己的推导是不是存在问题。当然，他脑海中也曾闪过这个念头，可是，最初难以置信的不合理性对他来说无疑是多余的。现在他也意识到了这种不合理性，然而，奇异和荒诞又把它淹没了。从巴斯库飞到这里并不是一个疯子毫无意义的举动。这是一种有计划，有准备的行动，而且是在香格里拉当局首领的教唆下进行的。当地人都知道那个死去的飞行员的名字，从某种意义上来说，他还是他们中的一员，他们为他的死感到哀痛。所有的一切都指向一点：这是一次高明且有目的的指令性行动。连时间和里程的跨度都让人难以理解地按某种意图来被估算；可他们的意图是什么呢？有什么可能的理由可以让这4位不期而遇的乘客乘坐英国政府安排的飞机横穿喜马拉雅山，如此突如其来地被带进这冷僻荒凉之地呢？

康维有点儿被这个问题惊呆

problem, but by no means wholly displeased with it. It challenged him in the only way in which he was readily amenable to challenge – by touching a certain clarity of brain that only demanded a sufficient task. One thing he decided instantly; the cold thrill of discovery must not yet be communicated, neither to his companions, who could not help him, nor to his hosts, who doubtless would not.

了，但绝不会对此完全不满。既然现实已向他发起挑战，他也只能欣然地去经受考验、迎接挑战，用清醒的头脑去感触这一切，这只需要足够的努力。此刻他已下定决心。这冷酷而又让人毛骨悚然的发现绝不能和任何人交流，不能告诉他的同伴，他们帮不了他，更不能让这里的主人知道，他们必定也束手无策。

CHAPTER 6

第六章

"I reckon some folks have to get used to worse places," Barnard remarked towards the close of his first week at Shangri-La, and it was doubtless one of the many lessons to be drawn. By that time the party had settled themselves into something like a daily routine, and with Chang's assistance the boredom was no more acute than on many a planned holiday. They had all become acclimatized to the atmosphere, finding it quite invigorating so long as heavy exertion was avoided. They had learned that the days were warm and the nights cold, that the lamasery was almost completely sheltered from winds, that avalanches on Karakal were most frequent about midday, that the valley grew a good brand of tobacco, that some foods and drinks were more pleasant than others, and that each one of themselves had personal tastes and peculiarities. They had, in fact, discovered as much about each other as four new pupils of a school from which everyone else was mysteriously absent. Chang was tireless in his efforts to make smooth the rough places. He conducted excursions, suggested occupations, recommended

"我认为有些人就必须得去适应更糟糕的环境。"巴纳德在谈论着自己在香格里拉的第一个星期结束时的感受,这必定也是他从中获得的教训之一。到此时,一伙人都被安排妥当,并自然地形成了各自每日惯常的生活规律。在张的帮助下,以前那种每天按部就班、例行度假一样的无聊厌烦的感觉已经不再那样深刻。而且大家都适应了这里的气候和水土;没有了起初的那种殚精竭虑的感觉,大家都觉得心情舒畅,充满活力。他们发现这里白天温暖而夜间较冷,而喇嘛庙几乎能够完全遮蔽住风,而卡拉卡尔山大多在正午发生雪崩。山谷里还生长着一种精良的烟草,这里出产的食物和饮料大都比别的地方的更能深受人们喜爱,当然他们几个每个人都有自己的喜好和怪癖。事实上他们彼此发现他们就像4个新入学的小学生,这个学校的其他人都神秘地缺席。张总是孜孜不倦地尽自己的努力在这个简陋的地方营造和谐有趣的气氛,他组织观光,提议消遣,推荐书籍,在饭桌上出现令人尴尬的停顿时,在每个需要和蔼可亲、需要彬彬有

books, talked with his slow, careful fluency whenever there was an awkward pause at meals, and was on every occasion benign, courteous, and resourceful. The line of demarcation was so marked between information willingly supplied and politely declined that the latter ceased to stir resentment, except fitfully from Mallinson. Conway was content to take note of it, adding another fragment to his constantly accumulating data. Barnard even "jollied" the Chinese after the manner and traditions of a Middle West Rotary convention. "You know, Chang, this is a damned bad hotel. Don't you have any newspapers sent here ever? I'd give all the books in your library for this morning's *Herald-Tribune*." Chang's replies were always serious, though it did not necessarily follow that he took every question seriously. "We have the files of *The Times*, Mr. Barnard, up to a few years ago. But only, I regret to say, the London *Times*."

Conway was glad to find that the valley was not to be "out of bounds," though the difficulties of the descent made unescorted visits impossible. In company with Chang they all spent a whole day inspecting the green floor that was so pleasantly visible from the cliff-edge, and to Conway, at any rate, the trip was of absorbing interest. They traveled in bamboo sedan chairs,

礼、需要足智多谋的场合，无论什么时候，他都用他那迟缓的、小心谨慎而又流畅的话语跟大家调侃、谈心。但所涉及的话题总是划分得很明显，有些他很乐意讲述，有些却委婉地拒绝，这样可以避免因失言而搬弄是非，激起大家的不满的状况，但当然避免不了断断续续发作的马林逊。康维很想记录一些相关内容来为他不断积累的资料再另外增加一些片段。巴纳德甚至以西方中部扶轮社的风俗与传统和那个汉族人开玩笑："你看，张，这是个糟糕透了的破旅馆，难道你从来没有派人送报纸到这里吗？为了借那本今天早上的《先驱者论坛》，我归还了图书室所有的书。"虽然没必要很严肃地对待每个问题，但张的回答总是很认真："巴纳德先生，我们有前几年的《泰晤士报》，但是我很抱歉，其中只有伦敦的《时代》。"

康维欣喜地发现这山谷并非可望而不可即，尽管下山困难重重，无人护送根本就不可能到达。在张的陪同下，他们花了整整一天游览了那一片绿幽幽的山谷，在悬崖峭壁的边缘，可爱秀丽而让人心旷神怡的山谷秀色一览无遗。对康维而言，这无论如何都是一次极其有趣的旅行。他们都坐着竹编的轿

swinging perilously over precipices while their bearers in front and to the rear picked a way nonchalantly down the steep track. It was not a route for the squeamish, but when at last they reached the lower levels of forest and foothill the supreme good fortune of the lamasery was everywhere to be realized. For the valley was nothing less than an enclosed paradise of amazing fertility, in which the vertical difference of a few thousand feet spanned the whole gulf between temperate and tropical. Crops of unusual diversity grew in profusion and contiguity, with not an inch of ground untended. The whole cultivated area stretched for perhaps a dozen miles, varying in width from one to five, and though narrow, it had the luck to take sunlight at the hottest part of the day. The atmosphere, indeed, was pleasantly warm even out of the sun, though the little rivulets that watered the soil were ice-cold from the snows. Conway felt again, as he gazed up at the stupendous mountain wall, that there was a superb and exquisite peril in the scene; but for some chance-placed barrier, the whole valley would clearly have been a lake, nourished continually from the glacial heights around it. Instead of which, a few streams dribbled through to fill reservoirs and irrigate fields and plantations with a disciplined conscientiousness worthy of a sanitary

椅观光，一路在断崖绝壁之中冒险地摇摆晃荡着，而前后的轿夫却漫不经心地颠簸在精选的陡峭山路上。对于过分谨慎的人这根本不算做路。然而当他们最终来到有着茂林密树和山麓小丘的平缓地带时，这喇嘛寺至高无上的宝贵财富就无处不现了。这山谷完全是个肥沃富饶、与世隔绝的乐园。那里垂直高度上千把英尺范围的温度差异就跨越了整个温带和热带地区的温差。这里生长着大量丰富多样的稀有农作物，没有一寸荒废的土地。整个耕作区延伸了大概十几英里，宽度约在1至5英里不等。虽然狭窄，却有幸能够沐浴一天中最温热时段的阳光。即使没有太阳的照射，积雪融化的冰冷溪流浇灌着肥沃的土地，这里的气候也的确十分的温暖宜人。当康维放眼凝视那宏伟雄奇的高山屏障时，他又一次感到这一派盛景之中蕴藏着一种华丽而微妙的凶险；由于刚好有一些天然屏障环绕，整个山谷很显然曾经是个湖，雪山高处的冰川不断地滋养过它。而今取而代之的是几条溪流，淙淙地穿过山谷注入储水库并灌溉着农田和人造林，像受过训练一样各司其职，这真堪称为一项环保工程。整个的设计构思近乎神奇的巧妙，而幸运的是，直到现在，不管是历经地震还是山崩，这个体系的结构框架还是完好无损

engineer. The whole design was almost uncannily fortunate, so long as the structure of the frame remained unmoved by earthquake or landslide.

But even such vaguely future fears could only enhance the total loveliness of the present. Once again Conway was captivated, and by the same qualities of charm and ingenuity that had made his years in China happier than others. The vast encircling *massif* made perfect contrast with the tiny lawns and weedless gardens, the painted tea-houses by the stream, and the frivolously toy-like houses. The inhabitants seemed to him a very successful blend of Chinese and Tibetan; they were cleaner and handsomer than the average of either race, and seemed to have suffered little from the inevitable inbreeding of such a small society. They smiled and laughed as they passed the chaired strangers, and had a friendly word for Chang; they were good-humored and mildly inquisitive, courteous and carefree, busy at innumerable jobs but not in any apparent hurry over them. Altogether Conway thought it one of the pleasantest communities he had ever seen, and even Miss Brinklow, who had been watching for symptoms of pagan degradation, had to admit that everything looked very well "on the surface." She was relieved to find

地保留了下来。

尽管对未来仍然茫然与恐惧，但这种忧虑也只能增加人们对现在一切的珍惜与热爱。康维再次被同样令人迷醉而精巧独特的风格强烈地感染，这已经让他感觉在中国的时光比在别的地方过得要快乐。这广阔的被群山环绕的断层谷地，完美地被小小的草地和没有杂草的花园所映衬，溪水潺潺，油漆过的茶馆如梦中的小憩，玩具似的小屋仿佛将你置身于童话。在他看来，这里的居民非常成功地融合了汉族与藏族文化，但他们一般都比其中任何一个要更加纯洁、更加英俊端庄，而且似乎因团体太小而不可避免的近亲结婚让他们稍稍吃了些苦头。当他们经过被抬在椅子上的这几位陌生人旁边时，都忍俊不禁，有的浅浅一笑，有的哈哈大笑，而且都友好地和张打着招呼。他们性情温和、友善而幽默，对一切充满好奇而喜欢问东问西，讲话谦恭而轻松愉快，忙于数不清的活计但又从不显得神色匆匆、忙忙碌碌。总而言之，康维认定这是他所见过的生活最舒适快乐的群体之一，甚至那位总在窥探异教徒堕落和丢脸迹象的布琳克罗小姐都承认，一切看上去还很不错。看到当

the natives "completely" clothed, even though the women did wear ankle-tight Chinese trousers; and her most imaginative scrutiny of a Buddhist temple revealed only a few items that could be regarded as somewhat doubtfully phallic. Chang explained that the temple had its own lamas, who were under loose control from Shangri-La, though not of the same order. There were also, it appeared, a Taoist and a Confucian temple further along the valley. "The jewel has facets," said the Chinese, "and it is possible that many religions are moderately true."

"I agree with that," said Barnard heartily. "I never did believe in sectarian jealousies. Chang, you're a philosopher, I must remember that remark of yours. 'Many religions are moderately true.' You fellows up on the mountain must be a lot of wise guys to have thought that out. You're right, too, I'm dead certain of it."

"But we," responded Chang dreamily, "are only *moderately* certain."

Miss Brinklow could not be bothered with all that, which seemed to her a sign of mere laziness. In any case she was preoccupied with an idea of her own. "When I get back," she said with tightening lips, "I shall ask my society to send a missionary here. And if they grumble at the expense, I shall just bully them until they agree."

地人全身穿戴整齐，就连妇女们也穿着绑紧裤腿的汉族束脚裤时，她很宽慰。而她尽可能充分发挥自己的想象来仔细观察一座寺庙，结果也不过是发现了一点点某种程度上可以含糊地被当作几分性崇拜的迹象。张解释说这个寺庙有它自己的喇嘛，但处在香格里拉对他们松懈的管理下，他们当然也没有那样的井然有序。很显然，在沿山谷的较远处还有一座道观和一座孔夫子庙。"宝石是多面体的，"那汉族人说，"而且许多宗教都有其适度的真理，这是有可能的。"

"我同意，"巴纳德热情地说，"我从不真正相信宗派妒忌之说。张，你是一个哲学家，我必须记住你说的那句'很多宗教都有其适度的真理'。你们山上那些同伴中也有很多有才之士，一定能够想到这一点。你说得很对，我完全确信。"

"不过，"张梦幻般朦胧地回答，"我们也只是适度的肯定。"

布琳克罗小姐并不为这一切所烦扰，在她看来这只不过是怠惰懒散的标志。无论如何，她总是固执己见。"我回去之后，"她绷紧嘴唇说道，"我要请求我们教会派一个传教士到这儿。如他们嫌花费太大，我就对他们施加压力，直到同意为止。"

That, clearly, was a much healthier spirit, and even Mallinson, little as he sympathized with foreign missions, could not forbear his admiration. "They ought to send *you*," he said. "That is, of course, if you'd like a place like this."

"It's hardly a question of *liking* it," Miss Brinklow retorted. "One wouldn't like it, naturally – how could one? It's a matter of what one feels one ought to do."

"I think," said Conway, "if I were a missionary I'd choose this rather than quite a lot of other places."

"In that case," snapped Miss Brinklow, "there would be no merit in it, obviously."

"But I wasn't thinking of merit."

"More's the pity, then. There's no good in doing a thing because you like doing it. Look at these people here!"

"They all seem very happy."

"*Exactly,*" she answered with a touch of fierceness. She added: "Anyhow, I don't see why I shouldn't make a beginning by studying the language. Can you lend me a book about it, Mr. Chang?"

Chang was at his most mellifluous. "Most certainly, madam, with the greatest of pleasure. And, if I may say so, I think the idea an excellent one."

When they ascended to Shangri-La that evening he treated the matter as one of immediate importance. Miss Brinklow was at first a little daunted by the massive

显然，这是更加健康的一种心态。就连很少怜悯外国传教团的马林逊，都不自禁地有些钦佩。"他们应该派你来，"他说，"当然，那还得看你是不是喜欢这样一个地方。"

"是否喜欢不算问题，"布琳克罗小姐反驳道，"谁也不会喜欢这里，自然——怎么会呢？这是一个人觉得自己应该去做什么的问题。"

"我想，"康维说，"假如我是个传教士的话我宁愿选择这里，而不是其他很多地方。"

"如果那样，"布琳克罗小姐怒气冲冲地打断，"很显然来这里，不会有什么功绩。"

"可是我没有想过什么功绩。"

"那就更可惜了，只凭自己喜欢做什么而去做是没有好处的，你瞧瞧这里的那些人！"

"他们看起来都很幸福。"

"完全正确，"她有些疯狂地回答，"无论如何，我看非得从学习当地语言开始不可。你能借给我一本有关这方面的书吗，张先生？"

张操着优美的、如蜜一般的腔调说："当然可以，女士，我非常乐意。而且，如果我可以这么说的话，我觉得这可是个极其好的主意。"

volume compiled by an industrious nineteenth-century German (she had more probably imagined some slighter work of a "Brush up your Tibetan" type), but with help from the Chinese and encouragement from Conway she made a good beginning and was soon observed to be extracting grim satisfaction from her task.

Conway, too, found much to interest him, apart from the engrossing problem he had set himself. During the warm, sunlit days he made full use of the library and music room, and was confirmed in his impression that the lamas were of quite exceptional culture. Their taste in books was catholic, at any rate; Plato in Greek touched Omar in English; Nietzsche partnered Newton; Thomas More was there, and also Hannah More, Thomas Moore, George Moore, and even Old Moore. Altogether Conway estimated the number of volumes at between twenty and thirty thousand; and it was tempting to speculate upon the method of selection and acquisition. He sought also to discover how recently there had been additions, but he did not come across anything later than a cheap reprint of *Im Western Nichts Neues*. During a subsequent visit, however, Chang told him that there were other books published up to about the middle of 1930 which would doubtless be added to the shelves eventually; they had

当那天傍晚他们又攀登上来回到香格里拉寺之后，张把为他们找书当作最重要的事。布琳克罗小姐开始还被那部由19世纪一个德国人编写的厚实的书籍吓了一跳。她大概能够猜出那是属于微不足道的"藏语速通"那一类的东西。但是在那位汉族先生的帮助和康维的鼓励下，她开了一个很好的头，而且，她很快就从中尝到了甜头。

同样，康维也找到了很多有趣的东西，更不用说他自己想象的那些引人入胜的问题。在温暖而阳光明媚的日子里，他会充分地利用图书室和音乐间，从而更加坚定了他对喇嘛们有相当优秀的文化修养这一想法。他们对书籍的爱好是广泛的，总而言之，不管是古希腊语的柏拉图论，还是英语的奥玛学说；无论是尼采的哲学，或者是牛顿的物理学，还有托马斯·莫尔、汉纳·莫尔、托马斯·穆尔、乔治·摩尔，这里应有尽有，甚至还有奥尔德·摩尔的著作等等。康维估计总共可能在两三万册之间，而且他们遴选和购置这些书籍的手段也很引人深思的。他也曾去探求，试图发现近来的新书怎么增加，但后来也没偶然间找到什么，只是浏览了一本很便宜的《西线无战事》的翻印本。然而，在随后的一次参观中，张告诉他，还有另外

already arrived at the lamasery. "We keep ourselves fairly up-to-date, you see," he commented.

"There are people who would hardly agree with you," replied Conway with a smile. "Quite a lot of things have happened in the world since last year, you know."

"Nothing of importance, my dear sir, that could not have been foreseen in 1920, or that will not be better understood in 1940."

"You're not interested, then, in the latest developments of the world crisis?"

"I shall be very deeply interested – in due course."

"You know, Chang, I believe I'm beginning to understand you. You're geared differently, that's what it is. Time means less to you than it does to most people. If I were in London I wouldn't always be eager to see the latest hour-old newspaper, and you at Shangri-La are no more eager to see a year-old one. Both attitudes seem to me quite sensible. By the way, how long is it since you last had visitors here?"

"That, Mr. Conway, I am unfortunately unable to say."

It was the usual ending to a conversation, and one that Conway found less irritating than the opposite phenomenon from which he had suffered

一些大概 1930 年中期出版发行的书刊最终必定会被增加到书架上，这些书已如期到达喇嘛寺中。"你看，我们都在力求自己与时俱进。"张说道。

"有些人未必会和你意见一致，"康维微笑着说，"你知道，自去年以来，世界上已发生了很多事情。"

"没什么重要的事，亲爱的先生，这在 1920 年时谁也无法预知，到 1940 年世人也未必能更加明白。"

"那么，你对世界范围内危机的最新事态发展也不感兴趣嘛！"

"我会有非常浓厚的兴趣——在恰当的时候。"

"你知道吧，张，我认为我正在开始了解你们。你们的生活方式很不一样，这是事实，比起大多数人，时间似乎对你们意义不大。如果在伦敦，我不会总是热切地想要看最近的几份旧报纸，而在香格里拉的你们除了想看看一年前的旧报纸却不再有更多的渴望。在我看来，这两种态度都非常合乎情理。顺便问一下，自从上一批游客走后，这里多久没有观光者到访了？"

"这个……康维先生，很遗憾，我不能说。"

交谈通常都会这样结束，而康维发现这还不够让人恼怒。相反，

much in his time – the conversation which, try as he would, seemed never to end. He began to like Chang rather more as their meetings multiplied, though it still puzzled him that he met so few of the lamasery personnel; even assuming that the lamas themselves were unapproachable, were there not other postulants besides Chang?

There was, of course, the little Manchu. He saw her sometimes when he visited the music room; but she knew no English, and he was still unwilling to disclose his own Chinese. He could not quite determine whether she played merely for pleasure, or was in some way a student. Her playing, as indeed her whole behavior, was exquisitely formal, and her choice lay always among the more patterned compositions – those of Bach, Corelli, Scarlatti, and occasionally Mozart. She preferred the harpsichord to the piano, but when Conway went to the latter she would listen with grave and almost dutiful appreciation. It was impossible to know what was in her mind; it was difficult even to guess her age. He would have doubted her being over thirty or under thirteen; and yet, in a curious way, such manifest unlikelihoods could neither of them be ruled out as wholly impossible.

Mallinson, who sometimes came to listen to the music for want of anything

有时张会尽他所能百般滔滔不绝，好像永远没完没了，相比之下，这种现象才更让他烦躁不堪。随着会面的增加，他越发欣赏张了。但有些事仍然让他感到困惑茫然，张很少与喇嘛寺的人员见面，就算喇嘛自己傲慢不逊、孤高冷漠，那难道除了张，他们就没有别的圣职志愿者了吗？

有，当然有，就是那个满族小孩儿。他在音乐间里有时会看到她，可她不懂英语，而他还不愿意透露自己会说汉语的事。他不能确定她弹琴只是出于乐趣，还是某种程度上正在学习。她的弹奏，还有整个行为举止的确特别正规，而她总是选择比较有代表性的曲子，如巴赫、卡伦里、史卡拉帝的乐曲，偶尔也有莫扎特的作品。比起钢琴，她更喜欢古琴，但当康维去弹钢琴时，她总会严肃认真地倾听，几乎流露出恭敬而欣赏的神情。谁也不可能知道她心里在想些什么，甚至要猜出她的年龄也很困难。他有时怀疑她 30 多岁了，有时又觉得她不到 13 岁。还有，更加难以理解的是，他们谁都没有办法也不可能断定这种明显不可能的事。

马林逊由于缺乏更好的事情去做，有时也来听听音乐，他发觉

better to do, found her a very baffling proposition. "I can't think what she's doing here," he said to Conway more than once. "This lama business may be all right for an old fellow like Chang, but what's the attraction in it for a girl? How long has she been here, I wonder?"

"I wonder too, but it's one of those things we're not likely to be told."

"Do you suppose she *likes* being here?"

"I'm bound to say she doesn't appear to *dislike* it."

"She doesn't appear to have feelings at all, for that matter. She's like a little ivory doll more than a human being."

"A charming thing to be like, anyhow."

"As far as it goes."

Conway smiled. "And it goes pretty far, Mallinson, when you come to think about it. After all, the ivory doll has manners, good taste in dress, attractive looks, a pretty touch on the harpsichord, and she doesn't move about a room as if she were playing hockey. Western Europe, so far as I recollect it, contains an exceptionally large number of females who lack those virtues."

"You're an awful cynic about women, Conway."

Conway was used to the charge. He had not actually had a great deal to do with the other sex, and during occasional leaves in Indian hill-stations the reputation of cynic

这女孩儿是个难以琢磨、令人困惑的家伙。"我不明白她到这里干什么，"他不止一次地对康维说，"喇嘛这种行当对张那样的老头也许还合适，可对一个小姑娘到底有什么吸引力？我想知道她来这里多久了？"

"我也想知道，可这似乎是我们不便被告知的事。"

"你猜想她喜欢在这里吗？"

"我敢说她看起来不像是不喜欢这里。"

"她看上去好像毫无感情，就此而言，与其说她是人，倒不如说更像个象牙娃娃。"

"不管怎么说，像个迷人的东西。"

"就其自身而言。"

康维笑了笑，"马林逊，要是再冷静地想象一下，事情可远远不止这些。毕竟，这象牙娃娃守规矩，穿衣打扮很有品位，面貌也妩媚动人，对古琴有很深的造诣，而且她不会像打曲棍球似的满屋乱转，依我所掌握的来看，在西欧有极大数量的女性缺乏这种美德。"

"你在对待女性方面也太过于讽刺、挖苦了吧，康维。"

康维已经习惯了这种谴责。实际上他和异性没有太多的接触，偶尔去印度山中避暑休假，就已经开始轻易地遭受愤世嫉俗、玩世不恭

had been as easy to sustain as any other. In truth he had had several delightful friendships with women who would have been pleased to marry him if he had asked them – but he had not asked them. He had once got nearly as far as an announcement in the *Morning Post*, but the girl did not want to live in Pekin and he did not want to live at Tunbridge Wells, mutual reluctances which proved impossible to dislodge. So far as he had had experience of women at all, it had been tentative, intermittent, and somewhat inconclusive. But he was not, after all that, a cynic about them.

He said with a laugh: "I'm thirty-seven – you're twenty-four. That's all it amounts to."

After a pause Mallinson asked suddenly: "Oh, by the way, how old should you say Chang is?"

"Anything," replied Conway lightly, "between forty-nine and a hundred and forty-nine."

Such information, however, was less trustworthy than much else that was available to the new arrivals. The fact that their curiosities were sometimes unsatisfied tended to obscure the really vast quantity of data which Chang was always willing to outpour. There were no secrecies, for instance, about the customs

的名声。事实上，他曾经与女性有过几段愉快美好的友谊，而且只要他要求，她们谁都很高兴嫁给他，可是他没有开口。有一次，他几乎要在《早邮报》上刊出结婚启事了，可那姑娘不想居住在北京，而他也不愿意定居到昙桥井，彼此都很勉强，后来结果是两人都不可能离开原居住地。在他与女性所有的交往中，关系基本是暂时的，时断时续的，而且颇为不确定。终究，他并非真对女性喜挑剔、好挖苦。

他嘲笑说："我 37 岁，你 24 岁，就这么回事。"

停顿了一会儿，马林逊突然问道："哦，顺便问一下，你说张有多少岁呢？"

"随便多少数都行，"康维草率地回道，"在 49 至 149 之间。"

然而，对于几位新访客来说，这些信息比亲自可以得到的情况更不可信。事实上，他们几个的好奇心有时得不到满足，这导致张一直想倾诉的很多事情都变得更加朦胧晦涩、含糊不清。这里没有什么可遮遮掩掩的，比如说，康维对山谷里居民的风俗习惯很感兴趣，

and habits of the valley population, and Conway, who was interested, had talks which might have been worked up into a quite serviceable degree thesis. He was particularly interested, as a student of affairs, in the way the valley population was governed; it appeared, on examination, to be a rather loose and elastic autocracy operated from the lamasery with a benevolence that was almost casual. It was certainly an established success, as every descent into that fertile paradise made more evident. Conway was puzzled as to the ultimate basis of law and order; there appeared to be neither soldiers nor police, yet surely some provision must be made for the incorrigible? Chang replied that crime was very rare, partly because only serious things were considered crimes, and partly because everyone enjoyed a sufficiency of everything he could reasonably desire. In the last resort the personal servants of the lamasery had power to expel an offender from the valley – though this, which was considered an extreme and dreadful punishment, had only very occasionally to be imposed. But the chief factor in the government of Blue Moon, Chang went on to say, was the inculcation of good manners, which made men feel that certain things were "not done," and that they lost caste by doing them. "You English

他有关此的谈论应该可以写成相当实用的学术论文，就像喜欢钻研事态的学生一样，他尤其对山谷居民被管理的模式感兴趣；从调查的情况看，这是一种相当散漫而富有弹性的独裁统治，由喇嘛寺非常仁爱、几乎是漫不经心地实施管理。这当然可谓一种既定的成功，每一次下山到这肥沃富饶的乐园都可以得到进一步的肯定。康维对这里法律和秩序的根本原则是什么感到迷惑，这里看起来既没有士兵，也没有警察，不过针对那些屡教不改、无可救药的人肯定需要制定一些相应的规定和条款。张回答说，犯罪在这里是非常稀少的，一是因为只有严重的事端才被认为是犯罪，二是因为每个人都充分享有他们合情合理所想要的东西，最后还有一个可以凭借的手段，就是喇嘛寺中的任何成员都有把一个不法之徒驱逐出山谷的权利——然而，这已经算是最极端、最令人恐惧的处罚了，只在万不得已的时候人们才这么做。张接着说，但主要的因素在于蓝月亮山谷的首领们总在对居民谆谆教诲，灌输给他们得体的举止、良好的德行，让他们懂得有些事情不应该做，做了就会失去社会地位和做人的尊严。"你们英国人也在灌输同样的思想情感，"张说，"可在你们的公立学校，恐怕就该另当别论了。比如说，我们

inculcate the same feeling," said Chang, "in your public schools, but not, I fear, in regard to the same things. The inhabitants of our valley, for instance, feel that it is 'not done' to be inhospitable to strangers, to dispute acrimoniously, or to strive for priority amongst one another. The idea of enjoying what your English headmasters call the mimic warfare of the playing-field would seem to them entirely barbarous – indeed, a sheerly wanton stimulation of all the lower instincts."

Conway asked if there were never disputes about women.

"Only very rarely, because it would not be considered good manners to take a woman that another man wanted."

"Supposing somebody wanted her so badly that he didn't care a damn whether it was good manners or not?"

"Then, my dear sir, it would be good manners on the part of the other man to let him have her, and also on the part of the woman to be equally agreeable. You would be surprised, Conway, how the application of a little courtesy all round helps to smooth out these problems."

Certainly during visits to the valley Conway found a spirit of goodwill and contentment that pleased him all the more because he knew that of all the arts, that of government has been brought least to perfection. When he made some

这个山谷的居民会觉得'所谓不应该做的事'就是对陌生人冷淡、不恭敬，激烈的争执，与别人争取优先权等。而你们英国校长们运动场上所谓模拟战争的游戏在他们看来整个是残暴的，实在是对低层次本能的一种恶意的、肆无忌惮的、不负责任的刺激。"

康维问这里是否从来没有因女人而引发的争执。

"非常少，因为夺人之爱不会被认为是有礼貌、懂规矩、讲道德的得体行为。"

"假若有人非常强烈地想得到她，他才不管是不是道德呢。"

"那么，我亲爱的先生，如果另外那个男的主动把她让给他，而且女方也同样欣然赞同，才能算是好的德行。康维，这会让你感到吃惊，可大家普遍都谦恭有礼就有助于平息事端、解决问题。"

当然，在参观山谷期间，康维发现了一种亲善友好、知足感恩的风貌，这让他更加欣喜，因为他知道所有的人文科学和政治都达不到这样尽善尽美。他发自内心的赞赏了一番，可张却回答："哎，但

complimentary remark, however, Chang responded: "Ah, but you see, we believe that to govern perfectly it is necessary to avoid governing too much."

"Yet you don't have any democratic machinery – voting, and so on?"

"Oh, no. Our people would be quite shocked by having to declare that one policy was completely right and another completely wrong."

Conway smiled. He found the attitude a curiously sympathetic one.

Meanwhile, Miss Brinklow derived her own kind of satisfaction from a study of Tibetan; meanwhile, also, Mallinson fretted and groused, and Barnard persisted in an equanimity which seemed almost equally remarkable, whether it were real or simulated.

"To tell you the truth," said Mallinson, "the fellow's cheerfulness is just about getting on my nerves. I can understand him trying to keep a stiff lip, but that continual joking of his begins to upset me. He'll be the life and soul of the party if we don't watch him."

Conway too had once or twice wondered at the ease with which the American had managed to settle down. He replied: "Isn't it rather lucky for us he *does* take things so well?"

"Personally, I think it's damned

你应该明白，我们相信一点，就是要治理得好，就需要避免管得太多。"

"可是，你们没有任何民主的机制吗，比如说选举等等？"

"哦，没有，如果必须公开声明某一项政策是完全正确的而另一项则是绝对错误的，这会让我们的人民大吃一惊的。"

康维笑了笑。他觉得这种态度有些稀奇，却表示赞同。

在这期间，布琳克罗小姐通过学习藏文得到了满足与快乐，同时，马林逊又开始焦躁、发牢骚，而巴纳德仍持续着那种看起来几乎与之前同样明显的镇静，不管这是真实的还是假象。

"老实告诉你，"马林逊说，"伙伴们的愉快爽朗只会加剧我的局促不安。我知道他铁齿铜牙，可他频频地开玩笑取乐开始让我心烦意乱。要是我们不加小心，他就会成为我们的生活、我们的灵魂。"

那么一两次，康维也在纳闷美国人怎能这样悠闲轻松的安顿下来。他回答："他能够把事情处理得这么好，这对于我们来说相当幸运了，不是吗？"

"就我个人而言，我觉得这很

peculiar. What do you *know* about him, Conway? I mean who he is, and so on."

"Not much more than you do. I understood he came from Persia and was supposed to have been oil-prospecting. It's his way to take things easily – when the air evacuation was arranged I had quite a job to persuade him to join us at all. He only agreed when I told him that an American passport wouldn't stop a bullet."

"By the way, did you ever see his passport?"

"Probably I did, but I don't remember. Why?"

Mallinson laughed. "I'm afraid you'll think I haven't exactly been minding my own business. Why should I, anyhow? Two months in this place ought to reveal all our secrets, if we have any. Mind you, it was a sheer accident, in the way it happened, and I haven't let slip a word to anyone else, of course. I didn't think I'd tell even you, but now we've got on to the subject I may as well."

"Yes, of course, but I wish you'd let me know what you're talking about."

"Just this. Barnard was traveling on a forged passport and he isn't Barnard at all."

Conway raised his eyebrows with an interest that was very much less than concern. He liked Barnard, so far as the

糟糕、很奇怪，你到底了解他什么，康维？我的意思是他是谁，等等。"

"并不比你了解的多多少，我知道他来自波斯，估计他从事过石油勘探。他用这种方法可以很容易地应对很多事情——在安排飞机撤离之前，我还做了很大的工作说服他跟咱们一起走，直到我告诉他美国护照抵挡不了子弹时他才同意了。"

"顺便问一下，你以前见过他的护照吗？"

"可能我见过，但我记不得了。怎么了？"

马林逊大笑："恐怕你会认为我是多管闲事，无论如何，我怎么会呢？在这个地方待两个月，也应该能够破解我们所有的秘密了吧，假如有的话。你要注意，就事情发展的方式来看，这是一个纯粹的意外。当然，我没有向任何人透露半句，我甚至认为连你也不能告诉，可现在既然已经谈到这个话题，我也许可以说上几句。"

"是的，当然。但是我希望你能让我知道你在说什么。"

"是这么回事，那个巴纳德旅行一直用一张伪造的护照，他根本不是巴纳德。"

康维不无担心又饶有兴趣地皱了皱眉头。他喜欢巴纳德，就因为这个人能激发他的各种情感，但

man stirred him to any emotion at all; but it was quite impossible for him to care intensely who he really was or wasn't. He said: "Well, who do you think he is, then?"

"He's Chalmers Bryant."

"The deuce he is! What makes you think so?"

"He dropped a pocketbook this morning and Chang picked it up and gave it to me, thinking it was mine. I couldn't help seeing it was stuffed with newspaper clippings – some of them fell out as I was handling the thing, and I don't mind admitting that I looked at them. After all, newspaper clippings aren't private, or shouldn't be. They were all about Bryant and the search for him, and one of them had a photograph which was absolutely like Barnard except for a mustache."

"Did you mention your discovery to Barnard himself?"

"No, I just handed him his property without any comment."

"So the whole thing rests on your identification of a newspaper photograph?"

"Well, so far, yes."

"I don't think I'd care to convict anyone on that. Of course you might be right – I don't say he couldn't *possibly* be Bryant. If he were, it would account for a good deal of his contentment at being here – he could hardly have found a better place to

他根本不可能很在意这个人到底是谁或不是谁。于是他说:"好了,那么你认为他是谁呢?"

"他叫查麦斯·伯利雅特。"

"他可真倒霉!真是这样!你怎么知道的?"

"今天早上他掉了一个笔记本,张以为是我的,就捡了起来把它拿给了我。我忍不住翻开看了看,发现里面夹满了剪报,我一拿这本子,里面有些东西就掉了出来。我不介意承认看过这些剪报,毕竟简报不是隐私,或者说不会是隐私。可这些,全是关于伯利雅特以及搜寻他的报道,其中一份上登有一张照片,除了那把小胡子外很明显像巴纳德。"

"你和巴纳德本人提到过你的发现吗?"

"没有。我只是把他的东西交给了他,没发表任何意见。"

"那么整件事都只是基于你识别了一张报纸上的照片而已?"

"嗯,到目前为止,是这样。"

"我想我不愿仅凭这个就判定一个人有罪,当然你可能是对的——我也不是说他没可能是伯利雅特。如果他是,这就可以解释他为何满足于这里的生活——他可能很难再找到比这更好的藏身之

hide."

Mallinson seemed a trifle disappointed by this casual reception of news which he evidently thought highly sensational. "Well, what are you going to do about it?" he asked.

Conway pondered a moment and then answered: "I haven't much of an idea. Probably nothing at all. What *can* one do, in any case?"

"But dash it all, if the man *is* Bryant – "

"My dear Mallinson, if the man were Nero it wouldn't have to matter to us for the time being! Saint or crook, we've got to make what we can of each other's company as long as we're here, and I can't see that we shall help matters by striking any attitudes. If I'd suspected who he was at Baskul, of course, I'd have tried to get in touch with Delhi about him – it would have been merely a public duty. But now I think I can claim to be *off* duty."

"Don't you think that's rather a slack way of looking at it?"

"I don't care if it's slack so long as it's sensible."

"I suppose that means your advice to me is to forget what I've found out?"

"You probably can't do that, but I certainly think we might both of us keep our own counsel about it. Not in consideration for Barnard or Bryant or whoever he is, but to save ourselves the

处了。"

马林逊看起来有些许沮丧，他本认为会引起强烈轰动的重大发现居然只得到这样随便的对待。"那好，对于这，你打算怎么处置？"他问道。

康维仔细考虑了一会儿，然后回答说："我也没有办法，或许什么都不要做，无论如何，谁又能做什么呢？"

"但如果真是伯利雅特，那可就见鬼了。"

"亲爱的马林逊，假如这是尼禄，眼下还不太要紧！不管他是虔诚的圣徒还是暴戾的无赖，只要我们还在这儿，都得倾尽所能搞好关系。我不知道太明显地表露任何态度会对解决问题有什么帮助。如果在巴斯库我就会怀疑他，我当然会试着联系德里去查询他的情况，这也仅仅是一个公民的职责，可现在我觉得我可以要求不承担责任。"

"难道你不觉得这么看这事太疏忽懈怠了吗？"

"我不在乎是不是疏忽懈怠，只要它合情合理。"

"我想你的意思是建议我忘记我发现的事情？"

"你可能做不到，但无疑我们应该对这件事保持审慎，不要去考虑他是巴纳德还是伯利雅特还是别的人，而是要避免离开时我们自己不得不去面对糟糕的尴尬局

deuce of an awkward situation when we get away."

"You mean we ought to let him go?"

"Well, I'll put it a bit differently and say we ought to give somebody else the pleasure of catching him. When you've lived quite sociably with a man for a few months, it seems a little out of place to call for the handcuffs."

"I don't think I agree. The man's nothing but a large-scale thief – I know plenty of people who've lost their money through him."

Conway shrugged his shoulders. He admired the simple black-and-white of Mallinson's code; the public school ethic might be crude, but at least it was downright. If a man broke the law, it was everyone's duty to hand him over to justice – always provided that it was the kind of law one was not allowed to break. And the law pertaining to checks and shares and balance-sheets was decidedly that kind. Bryant had transgressed it, and though Conway had not taken much interest in the case, he had an impression that it was a fairly bad one of its kind. All he knew was that the failure of the giant Bryant group in New York had resulted in losses of about a hundred million dollars – a record crash, even in a world that exuded records. In some way or other (Conway was not a financial expert) Bryant had

面。"

"你是说，我们应该让这件事就这样过去？"

"啊，我的想法有点不同，我是说咱们应该把抓获他的乐趣让给别人。当你亲善和蔼地与一个人相处了几个月之后，却为他叫来一副手铐，这似乎有些不合适。"

"我想我不会同意，这家伙不就是个江洋大盗——我知道很多人是因为他才丢了钱财的。"

康维无奈地耸了耸肩。他欣赏马林逊那种纯粹的黑白分明的处事原则。公立学校的伦理学也许是粗陋的，却至少也是直白的，如果有人触犯了法律，把他送交司法机关接受审判是每个人的责任——这一直是一项不允许违犯的法律。而有关检查、分担责任以及资产负债等等的法规显然属于此类。伯利雅特违反了这一法律，但康维对这一案件没有太大的兴趣，他有一种印象，这是那类犯罪中颇为恶劣的一例。他所知道的是，纽约巨大的伯利雅特集团的经营失败导致近亿美元资金的亏损——一次空前的破产，甚至在世界范围内都有明确的记录。在某些方面（康维并不是金融界的专家），伯利雅特一直在华尔街鬼混，他逃到欧洲，在五六个国家间引渡，却摆脱不了被通缉追

been monkeying on Wall Street, and the result had been a warrant for his arrest, his escape to Europe, and extradition orders against him in half a dozen countries.

Conway said finally: "Well, if you take my tip you'll say nothing about it – not for his sake but for ours. Please yourself, of course, so long as you don't forget the possibility that he mayn't be the fellow at all."

But he was, and the revelation came that evening after dinner. Chang had left them; Miss Brinklow had turned to her Tibetan grammar; the three male exiles faced each other over coffee and cigars. Conversation during the meal would have languished more than once but for the tact and affability of the Chinese; now, in his absence, a rather unhappy silence supervened. Barnard was for once without jokes. It was clear to Conway that it lay beyond Mallinson's power to treat the American as if nothing had happened, and it was equally clear that Barnard was shrewdly aware that something had happened.

Suddenly the American threw away his cigar. "I guess you all know who I am," he said.

Mallinson colored like a girl, but Conway replied in the same quiet key: "Yes, Mallinson and I think we do."

捕的结局。

康维最后说："好了，如果你接受我的告诫，就不要再谈论这件事了——不是为了他的利益，而是因为咱们自己。你自己小心，当然，只要你不会忘记他也许有不是那家伙的可能性。"

但是，他就是伯利雅特，那天晚上晚饭过后真相终于暴露了。那时，张已经离开了他们；布琳克罗小姐也去学习她的藏语语法了；剩下3个离乡背井的汉子边喝咖啡边吸烟地面面相觑。席间的交谈变得毫无生气，不止一次地冷场，只有那个汉族人依然那样老练机智、和蔼可亲。现在他已离席，随后便是令人相当不愉快的沉默。巴纳德第一次没有了玩笑和幽默。康维很清楚，要马林逊像任何事都没有发生一样地对待那美国人也太高估他的能力了；而且他也同样清楚巴纳德已经很机敏地意识到发生了什么事。

美国人突然把雪茄扔了，"我猜你们都已经知道我是谁了。"他说。

马林逊的脸一下变红了，但康维用同样平静而温和的语气回答："是的，马林逊和我都知道了。"

"Darned careless of me to leave those clippings lying about."

"We're all apt to be careless at times."

"Well, you're mighty calm about it, that's something."

There was another silence, broken at length by Miss Brinklow's shrill voice: "I'm sure *I* don't know who you are, Mr. Barnard, though I must say I guessed all along you were traveling *incognito*." They all looked at her enquiringly and she went on: "I remember when Mr. Conway said we should all have our names in the papers, you said it didn't affect you. I thought then that Barnard probably wasn't your real name."

The culprit gave a slow smile as he lit himself another cigar. "Madam," he said eventually, "you're not only a smart detective, but you've hit on a really polite name for my present position, I'm traveling *incognito*. You've said it, and you're dead right. As for you boys, I'm not sorry in a way that you've found me out. So long as none of you had an inkling, we could all have managed, but considering how we're fixed it wouldn't seem very neighborly to play the high hat with you now. You folks have been so darned nice to me that I don't want to make a lot of trouble. It looks as if we were all going to be joined together for better or worse for some little time ahead,

"该死的粗心，我就这样草率地把那些剪报到处乱放。"

"人们难免有时会粗心大意。"

"哦，你们对此非常镇定沉着，这有些名堂。"

又是一阵沉默，最后这沉默被布琳克罗小姐尖锐刺耳的声音打破："我确定我不知道你是谁，巴纳德先生，不过，我必须得说，我猜对了你一直都是在隐姓埋名地旅行的事。"他们几个都用探寻的眼神看着她，布琳克罗小姐继续说："我记得康维说，让我们所有人必须把我们的名字写在纸上时，而你说这无所谓，我当时就想，巴纳德很可能不是你真实的名字。"

这位罪犯一面勉强地挤出一丝微笑，一面又给自己点上一支雪茄，"女士，"他终开口了，"你不仅是一位聪明机警的侦探，而且你刚巧为我目前的境遇想出一个很文雅的解释，我在隐姓埋名地旅行。你说出来了，而且说得绝对正确。至于你们两位小伙子，你们已经把我认了出来，从某种意义上讲，我并不遗憾。如果你们没人看出什么迹象，我还可以想方设法应付过去。但想想我们现在的处境都已成定局，再跟你们吹牛似乎就不太好了。你们大家对我都非常好，以至于我不想惹太多的麻烦。看起来，我们还得团结在一起，共同面

and it's up to us to help one another out as far as we can. As for what happens afterwards, I reckon we can leave that to settle itself."

All this appeared to Conway so eminently reasonable that he gazed at Barnard with considerably greater interest, and even – though it was perhaps odd at such a moment – a touch of genuine appreciation. It was curious to think of that heavy, fleshy, good-humored, rather paternal looking man as the world's hugest swindler. He looked far more the type that, with a little extra education, would have made a popular headmaster of a prep school. Behind his joviality there were signs of recent strains and worries, but that did not mean that the joviality was forced. He obviously was what he looked – a "good fellow" in the world's sense, by nature a lamb and only by profession a shark.

Conway said: "Yes, that's very much the best thing, I'm certain."

Then Barnard laughed. It was as if he possessed even deeper reserves of good humor which he could only now draw upon. "Gosh, but it's mighty queer," he exclaimed, spreading himself in his chair. "The whole darned business, I mean. Right across Europe, and on through Turkey and Persia to that little one-horse burg! Police after me all the time, mind

对以后的日子，不论更加美好还是越发糟糕，我们都要团结直到尽我们所能、彼此互相帮助、找到出路。至于以后会发生什么，我认为我们可以听之任之了。"

在康维听来，这些话都极有道理，他饶有兴趣地注视着巴纳德，这也许有些奇怪——这样的时刻居然他萌发出这样由衷的赏识，想想这位笨重肥胖、幽默感很强，看上去像慈父一样的人居然是一位世界级的重大诈骗犯，这也够让人难以理解的了。他看上去远远不像那种人，受过一些不错的教育，本该成为一个很受欢迎的预备学校校长。在他轻松愉快的言行背后隐隐显露着最近才造成的压力和担忧，但这并不意味着这轻松快活是被迫的、不发自内心的。从广义上说，他表里如一，就天性而言，他是一个羔羊般温顺的人，从职业来说，他则是一个如鲨鱼般贪婪狡猾的诈骗犯。

康维说："是的，这样最好不过，我确定无疑。"

这时巴纳德大笑起来，好像拥有一种深深储备着的仅有此时此刻才发挥得出的幽默感。"老天爷啊，这可太疯狂了，"他呼喊着，一面四肢伸展地坐回椅子，"真是一桩可恶的倒霉事，我的意思是，横穿欧洲，然后经土耳其和波斯最后到达那个简陋的小镇！警察总是

you – they nearly got me in Vienna! It's pretty exciting at first, being chased, but it gets on your nerves after a bit. I got a good rest at Baskul, though – I thought I'd be safe in the midst of a revolution."

"And so you were," said Conway with a slight smile, "except from bullets."

"Yeah, and that's what bothered me at the finish. I can tell you it was a mighty hard choice – whether to stay in Baskul and get plugged, or accept a trip in your Government's aeroplane and find the bracelets waiting at the other end. I wasn't exactly keen to do either."

"I remember you weren't."

Barnard laughed again. "Well, that's how it was, and you can figure it out for yourself that the change of plan which brought me here don't worry me an awful lot. It's a first-class mystery, but, speaking personally, there couldn't have been a better one. It isn't my way to grumble as long as I'm satisfied."

Conway's smile became more definitely cordial. "A very sensible attitude, though I think you rather overdid it. We were all beginning to wonder how you managed to be so contented."

"Well, I *was* contented. This ain't a bad place, when you get used to it. The air's a bit snappy at first, but you can't have everything. And it's nice and quiet for a change. Every fall I go down to Palm

跟着我，听着——在维也纳他们差点逮住我！被人追捕最开始还非常令人兴奋，但是过不了多久你就感到紧张不安，在巴斯库才好好休息了一下，我觉得在革命的剧变中我会安全些。"

"果然如此，"康维微笑着说，"除了子弹以外。"

"是啊，变革快结束了，这枪子又来烦扰我。告诉你吧，这可是非常艰难的抉择——是留在巴斯库挨枪子呢，还是接受一次旅行，乘坐你们英国政府的飞机去接受早已在另一头等待着的那副手铐，这两种情况我的确都不愿意啊。"

"我记得你那时还真是这样。"

巴纳德又大笑起来，"好了，就是这么回事，而且，你自己也可以搞清楚，当初的计划被改变，飞机把我们带到这里之后我并不是特别担忧。这是一个绝顶的秘密，但是，就我个人而言，没有比这更好的事情了。既然已经心满意足了，我还抱怨什么呢，这可不是我的处事方式。"

康维的微笑变得更加肯定而真挚，"这真是一种明智的态度。但我觉得你也的确做得太过了点，我们都开始怀疑，你怎么能做到这样的心安知足。"

"哦，我无忧无虑，习惯之后，这也不是很糟糕嘛，开始我也觉得

Beach for a rest cure, but they don't give you it, those places – you're in the racket just the same. But here I guess I'm having just what the doctor ordered, and it certainly feels grand to me. I'm on a different diet, I can't look at the tape, and my broker can't get me on the telephone."

"I daresay he wishes he could."

"Sure. There'll be a tidy-sized mess to clear up, and I know it."

He said this with such simplicity that Conway could not help responding: "I'm not much of an authority on what people call high finance."

It was a lead, and the American accepted it without the slightest reluctance. "High finance," he said, "is mostly a lot of bunk."

"So I've often suspected."

"Look here, Conway, I'll put it like this. A feller does what he's been doing for years, and what lots of other fellers have been doing, and suddenly the market goes against him. He can't help it, but he braces up and waits for the turn. But somehow the turn don't come as it always used to, and when he's lost ten million dollars or so he reads in some paper that a Swede professor thinks it's the end of the world. Now I ask you, does that sort of thing help markets? Of course, it gives him a bit of a shock, but he still can't help it. And there he is till the cops come – if he waits

严寒刺骨,但不能凡事都十全十美吧。对换环境来说,这可是又美丽又安静。每年秋季我都去棕榈海滨做静息疗养,可他们给不了你那些,那里老处在千篇一律的喧嚣杂乱、花天酒地之中,而在这里我想我得到了医嘱,当然,对我来说这很美妙快乐。我现在有不同于以前的饮食,我看不到磁带录像,我的经纪人也无法通过电话与我保持联系。"

"我敢说他希望能和你联系。"

"当然。有那么一点小小的困乱困境要解决一下,这我知道。"

他说得如此真诚坦率,康维不禁回道:"我可是人们所说的高额融资方面的专家。"

它是一个诱因,美国人接受了,没有藐视、没有不情愿。"高额融资往往有太多的欺骗性。"他说道。

"所以我经常怀疑。"

"听着,康维,我给你打个比方。一个伐木工一直从事很多其他伐木工也从事很多年的行业,可突然市场行情变得很不利,他束手无策,只有打起精神来等待转机,可转机一直没像过去那样到来,当已经损失掉差不多 1000 万美元时,他在某张报上读到一个瑞典教授的论点,认为世界末日就要到了。现在我问你,类似这种事对市场有

for 'em. I didn't."

"You claim it was all just a run of bad luck, then?"

"Well, I certainly had a large packet."

"You also had other people's money," put in Mallinson sharply.

"Yeah, I did. And why? Because they all wanted something for nothing and hadn't the brains to get it for themselves."

"I don't agree. It was because they trusted you and thought their money was safe."

"Well, it wasn't safe. It couldn't be. There isn't safety anywhere, and those who thought there was were like a lot of saps trying to hide under an umbrella in a typhoon."

Conway said pacifyingly: "Well, we'll all admit you couldn't help the typhoon."

"I couldn't even pretend to help it – any more than you could help what happened after we left Baskul. The same thing struck me then as I watched you in the aeroplane keeping dead calm while Mallinson here had the fidgets. You knew you couldn't do anything about it, and you weren't caring two hoots. Just like I felt myself when the crash came."

"That's nonsense!" cried Mallinson. "Anyone can help swindling. It's a matter of playing the game according to the rules."

"Which is a darned difficult thing to do

帮助吗？当然，这让他稍稍有些震惊，可他仍然无能为力，而他一直在那儿，直到警察到来——就好像他正在等待他们，我可不会这么做。"

"然后你就断言这一切都只能怪人一再的运气不佳吗？"

"哎，我确实有一大笔钱。"

"你还占有其他人的钱财。"马林逊猛然严厉地插了一句。

"是的，我的确是这样，但为什么呢？因为他们都想不劳而获，却没有头脑自己去争取。"

"我不同意你的说法。这是因为他们信任你，并相信他们的钱财交付给你会安全无事。"

"哎，不会安全，不可能会安全。任何地方都没有安全性。那些认为有安全性的人，就是一群笨蛋，就像在台风中试图躲在一把伞下一样。"

康维抚慰他说道："哦，我们都承认你不可能可以对付台风。"

"我甚至不能装作去对付它，就像咱们离开巴斯库以后发生事情你也手足无措一样。那时我注意到你在飞机上一直保持着死一般的沉着镇定，而同时马林逊却在那儿坐立不安、烦躁不堪，你清楚你对此无能为力，也满不在乎，正和我遭遇企业破产时自己崩溃的感觉一样。"

"胡说八道！"马林逊吼道，

when the whole game's going to pieces. Besides, there isn't a soul in the world who knows what the rules are. All the professors of Harvard and Yale couldn't tell you 'em."

Mallinson replied rather scornfully: "I'm referring to a few quite simple rules of everyday conduct."

"Then I guess your everyday conduct doesn't include managing trust companies."

Conway made haste to intervene. "We'd better not argue. I don't object in the least to the comparison between your affairs and mine. No doubt we've all been flying blind lately, both literally and in other ways. But we're here now, that's the important thing, and I agree with you that we could easily have had more to grumble about. It's curious, when you come to think about it, that out of four people picked up by chance and kidnaped a thousand miles, three should be able to find some consolation in the business. *You* want a rest-cure and a hiding place; Miss Brinklow feels a call to evangelize the heathen Tibetan."

"Who's the third person you're counting?" Mallinson interrupted.

"Not me, I hope?"

"I was including myself," answered Conway. "And my own reason is perhaps the simplest of all – I just rather like being

"任何人都可以阻止欺骗行为，这只是根据规则来进行游戏的问题。"

"可当整个游戏将要支离破碎的时候，真是件要命的难事。除此以外，世界上也没有哪个人物知道规则究竟具体是什么，所有哈佛和耶鲁的教授也无法告诉你。"

马林逊相当轻蔑地回答："我指的是日常行为中那些极其简单的常规。"

"那么，我猜你指的日常行为并不包括管理信托公司吧。"

康维急忙调停："咱们最好别争吵了。我丝毫不反对把我们两人的事情作比较。毋庸置疑，不久前那次盲目的飞行，的确与我们的初衷背道而驰。然而，我们现在已经在这儿了，这才是重要的。你说的对，我们很容易就能做一些比抱怨更有意义的事，但若你清醒地仔细想想，又觉得稀奇古怪，这4个人偶然彼此结识，一起被飞机劫持到千里之外，其中3位应该能够从中找到一些慰藉。就像人们想静息疗养就需要一个安身之处，布琳克罗小姐感到是主的召唤要她给不信教的藏族人宣讲福音。"

"那谁是你包含在内的第三个人？"马林逊打断他。

"我希望不是我。"

"我包括的是我自己，"康维答道，"而我的理由可能是最简单

here."

Indeed, a short time later, when he took what had come to be his usual solitary evening stroll along the terrace or beside the lotus-pool, he felt an extraordinary sense of physical and mental settlement. It was perfectly true; he just rather liked being at Shangri-La. Its atmosphere soothed while its mystery stimulated, and the total sensation was agreeable. For some days now he had been reaching, gradually and tentatively, a curious conclusion about the lamasery and its inhabitants; his brain was still busy with it, though in a deeper sense he was unperturbed. He was like a mathematician with an abstruse problem – worrying over it, but worrying very calmly and impersonally.

As for Bryant, whom he decided he would still think of and address as Barnard, the question of his exploits and identity faded instantly into the background, save for a single phrase of his – "the whole game's going to pieces." Conway found himself remembering and echoing it with a wider significance than the American had probably intended; he felt it to be true of more than American banking and trust company management. It fitted Baskul and Delhi and London, war making and empire-building, consulates and trade concessions and

不过的了——我只是非常喜欢在这儿。"

确实，不久以后，康维每天晚上一如既往地沿着露台或者在荷花塘边独自漫步，这逐渐成为了他的一种习惯。他感到整个身心涌动着异常的舒适与安宁。他只是非常喜欢生活在香格里拉，这是一种绝对真实的感受。她的气氛越是平静，她的神秘感就越振奋人心，而且整体感觉越是令人愉快。这些天来他逐渐尝试性地对喇嘛寺及其居民形成一种奇妙而古怪的结论，他一直在思考这个问题，但就更深的意义来说，他仍然镇定自若。他就像一个数学家在钻研一道深奥难懂的题目，他为此烦恼，但仍显得很沉着而且不受个人情感的影响。

至于那个伯利雅特，康维决定还是把他当作巴纳德。关于他的功过是非和身份的问题也就逐渐消失在整个背景下，除了他那句独特的"整场游戏都支离破碎了"还不断回荡在康维的脑海中，而且可能要比这个美国人想表达的更加意味深长。他觉得这话远比美国银行业务及信托公司的经营管理更要真实，它也适用于巴斯库、德里、伦敦以及诸如战争策划部、帝国大厦、领事馆、贸易租界和政府大楼内的晚宴等场合；这个冷清的世界上到处弥漫着分崩离析的气息。巴

dinner parties at Government House; there was a reek of dissolution over all that recollected world, and Barnard's cropper had only, perhaps, been better dramatized than his own. The whole game *was* doubtless going to pieces, but fortunately the players were not as a rule put on trial for the pieces they had failed to save. In that respect financiers were unlucky.

But here, at Shangri-La, all was in deep calm. In a moonless sky the stars were lit to the full, and a pale blue sheen lay upon the dome of Karakal. Conway realized then that if by some change of plan the porters from the outside world were to arrive immediately, he would not be completely overjoyed at being spared the interval of waiting. And neither would Barnard, he reflected with an inward smile. It was amusing, really; and then suddenly he knew that he still liked Barnard, or he wouldn't have found it amusing. Somehow the loss of a hundred million dollars was too much to bar a man for; it would have been easier if he had only stolen one's watch. And after all, how *could* anyone lose a hundred millions? Perhaps only in the sense in which a cabinet minister might airily announce that he had been "given India."

And then again he thought of the time when he would leave Shangri-La with the returning porters. He pictured the long,

纳德的失败也许只是比康维自己的落魄要更加戏剧化，这整场游戏无疑是到了支离破碎的地步；幸运的是，这些玩游戏的人们并没有像游戏规则本身那样散乱在那些无法挽回的废墟之上。从这个着眼点上讲，金融家们是不幸的。

可是在这儿，在香格里拉，一切都处在深深的平静之中。没有月色的天空被星星闪闪的光芒照亮，一抹淡蓝色的光辉在卡拉卡尔的顶峰隐约可见。后来康维认识到如果计划有所变动，外面世界的脚夫可能马上就会到来。他不会因为有等待的间隙而过度地狂喜，巴纳德也不会，他露出一丝由衷的微笑。的确很有趣，那一刻他突然意识到自己仍然很喜欢巴纳德。又或许，他还没发觉这种乐趣。从某种意义上讲，一亿美元的损失足够把一个人送上审判台。如果他只是偷别人一块表什么的就容易多了。但是一个人到底怎么会丢失一亿美元呢？或许，只有一个内阁大臣轻率地宣布说他的所有财产已经全部赠予印度，这种情况才成立。

而此刻康维又一次开始幻想和回来的搬运工人一起离开香格里拉的时光。他想象着那漫长、

arduous journey, and that eventual moment of arrival at some planter's bungalow in Sikkim or Baltistan – a moment which ought, he felt, to be deliriously cheerful, but which would probably be slightly disappointing. Then the first hand-shakings and self-introductions; the first drinks on clubhouse verandas; sun-bronzed faces staring at him in barely concealed incredulity. At Delhi, no doubt, interviews with the viceroy and the C.I.C., salaams of turbaned menials; endless reports to be prepared and sent off. Perhaps even a return to England and Whitehall; deck games on the P. & O.; the flaccid palm of an under-secretary; newspaper interviews; hard, mocking, sex-thirsty voices of women – "And is it really true, Mr. Conway, that when you were in Tibet…?" There was no doubt of one thing; he would be able to dine out on his yarn for at least a season. But would he enjoy it? He recalled a sentence penned by Gordon during the last days at Khartoum – "I would sooner live like a Dervish with the Mahdi than go out to dinner every night in London." Conway's aversion was less definite – a mere anticipation that to tell his story in the past tense would bore him a great deal as well as sadden him a little.

Abruptly, in the midst of his reflections, he was aware of Chang's approach. "Sir,"

艰辛的旅程，还有到达锡金或巴基斯坦的某个种植园主的小屋的时刻——那一刻他该会多么疯狂、兴高采烈啊。然而，可能他也会有些许轻微的失望。然后就是第一次的握手和自我介绍；第一次在俱乐部会所的走廊里喝酒；阳光照射下古铜色面孔上那双毫不隐晦的怀疑目光盯着看他。在德里，他必然要与总督和总司令会见；还有戴头巾的仆从们的问安；没完没了的报告需要准备和发送，或许他甚至还要回一趟英国，去一趟白厅；在P&O玩几局纸牌，政务机关部下用他们那松弛软弱的手掌同你握手；接受报社的采访；听那些女人们辛苦而又做作的饥渴式的怪叫——"这到底是真的吗？康维先生，那时你在西藏……"有件事是确凿无疑的，他将能够依靠自己的奇谈怪论在外边混吃混喝至少一个季度。可他喜欢这样吗？他记起戈登的一句格言，是他在喀土穆最后的日子里创作的——"我宁愿像一个苦行僧那样生活，永远与救世主玛赫迪同在，也不愿意在伦敦每天夜里都去外面混饭吃。"康维对这些事情的厌恶还是不那么明确，而仅仅是一种预料。用过去时去讲述他的故事将会有更多烦扰，也会给他带来很多悲伤。

正在深思熟虑中的他突然意识到张在靠近。"先生，"这位汉族

began the Chinese, his slow whisper slightly quickening as he spoke, "I am proud to be the bearer of important news…"

So the porters *had* come before their time, was Conway's first thought; it was odd that he should have been thinking of it so recently. And he felt the pang that he was half prepared for. "Well?" he queried.

Chang's condition was as nearly that of excitement as seemed physically possible for him. "My dear sir, I congratulate you," he continued. "And I am happy to think that I am in some measure responsible – it was after my own strong and repeated recommendations that the High Lama made his decision. He wishes to see you immediately."

Conway's glance was quizzical. "You're being less coherent than usual, Chang. What has happened?"

"The High Lama has sent for you."

"So I gather. But why all the fuss?"

"Because it is extraordinary and unprecedented – even I who urged it did not expect it to happen yet. A fortnight ago you had not arrived, and now you are about to be received by *him!* Never before has it occurred so soon!"

"I'm still rather fogged, you know. I'm to see your High Lama – I realize that all right. But is there anything else?"

"Is it not enough?"

人开始说话，他那缓缓的低语轻轻地加快，"能给你们带来重要消息我很引以为豪。"

果然，这些搬运工人提前到达了，这是康维的第一反应。也奇怪，他近来总是想着这件事。他感到一阵极度的痛苦，虽然他也有些许准备。"哦？"他表示疑问。

张看起来处于异常激动的状态。"亲爱的先生，恭喜你，"他接着说，"想到能够承担几分责任，我很高兴——鉴于我坚决的态度以及反复地竭力推荐，大喇嘛终于做出决定，他希望立刻召见你。"

康维用戏弄和疑问的眼神瞥了一眼，"你今天说话可不像往常那样条理清楚，张，发生什么事了？"

"大喇嘛派我来找你。"

"我想也是这样，可是为什么你会这么大惊小怪？"

"因为这是特别的、史无前例的——连极力促成这件事的我都不敢料想有这种机会，而你现在就要被他召见了！以前从来就没有那么快发生过！"

"我还是相当迷惑，你知道，我要去见你们的大喇嘛——我觉得还好。可是还有什么别的事吗？"

Conway laughed. "Absolutely, I assure you – don't imagine I'm being discourteous. As a matter of fact, something quite different was in my head at first. However, never mind about that now. Of course, I shall be both honored and delighted to meet the gentleman. When is the appointment?"

"Now. I have been sent to bring you to him."

"Isn't it rather late?"

"That is of no consequence. My dear sir, you will understand many things very soon. And may I add my own personal pleasure that this interval – always an awkward one – is now at an end. Believe me, it has been irksome to me to have to refuse you information on so many occasions – extremely irksome. I am joyful in the knowledge that such unpleasantness will never again be necessary."

"You're a queer fellow, Chang," Conway responded. "But let's be going, don't bother to explain anymore. I'm perfectly ready and I appreciate your nice remarks. Lead the way."

"这还不够吗？"

康维笑了，"完全够了，我向你保证——不要把我想象得那么粗鲁无礼。事实上，开始我脑子里有一个与众不同的想法。不过，现在我们不用担心那些了。当然，能够见到这位绅士，我感到万分荣幸与欣喜，我们约定在什么时间呢？"

"现在，我就是被派来带你过去见他的。"

"是不是太晚了呢？"

"没关系。亲爱的先生，你很快就会明白很多事情。我可不可以先表达一下自己高兴的心情，这段时间——总是很尴尬——而现在就要结束了。相信我，在很多时间场合我必须要拒绝告诉你们一些信息，这让我厌倦，极其厌烦。知道这种不愉快的搪塞再也没有必要了，我感到非常欣慰。"

"你真是个古怪的家伙，张，"康维答道，"不过，咱们走吧，别再烦恼了。我有思想准备，而且很欣赏你友好的言辞，请带路吧。"

CHAPTER 7

第七章

CONWAY was quite unruffled, but his demeanor covered an eagerness that grew in intensity as he accompanied Chang across the empty courtyards. If the words of the Chinese meant anything, he was on the threshold of discovery; soon he would know whether his theory, still half formed, were less impossible than it appeared.

Apart from this, it would doubtless be an interesting interview. He had met many peculiar potentates in his time; he took a detached interest in them, and was shrewd as a rule in his assessments. Without self-consciousness he had also the valuable knack of being able to say polite things in languages of which he knew very little indeed. Perhaps, however, he would be chiefly a listener on this occasion. He noticed that Chang was taking him through rooms he had not seen before, all of them rather dim and lovely in lantern light. Then a spiral staircase climbed to a door at which the Chinese knocked, and which was opened by a Tibetan servant with such promptness that Conway suspected he had been stationed behind it. This part of the lamasery, on a higher storey, was no less tastefully embellished

他跟随着张穿过空荡荡的庭院时，康维非常镇定，可是他的行为举止却被一种越来越强烈的渴望所支配。如果这个汉族人的话别有意味，他也正要跨入发现真相的门槛。很快他就会知道他那仍然不完全成形的推测是不是不像各种迹象显示的那样不可能。

且不说这些，这无疑将会是一次很有趣的会见。他曾经见过许多特殊的稀奇古怪的统治者，他对他们抱有一种超然的兴趣，而且他是一个精明机灵的人，能以敏锐准确的尺度不含个人偏见地去评价他们。他也有非常有价值的巧妙手法，用他根本不太懂的各种语言不自觉、无意识地说些寒暄、客套之辞。但是，在这种情况下，他可能将主要是一名听众。他注意到张正带着他穿过一些之前从未见过的房间，在灯笼淡淡的光线下一切都显得朦朦胧胧、非常可爱。然后，他们沿着一个螺旋式的楼梯爬上去走到一扇门前，这汉族人敲了敲门。门很快被一个藏族仆人打开，这动作如此敏捷迅速，让康维怀疑他早就在门后站好了。这是喇嘛寺的较高的部分，装饰得与其他建筑

than the rest, but its most immediately striking feature was a dry, tingling warmth, as if all the windows were tightly closed and some kind of steam-heating plant were working at full pressure. The airlessness increased as he passed on, until at last Chang paused before a door which, if bodily sensation could have been trusted, might well have admitted to a Turkish bath.

"The High Lama," whispered Chang, "will receive you alone." Having opened the door for Conway's entrance, he closed it afterwards so silently that his own departure was almost imperceptible. Conway stood hesitant, breathing an atmosphere that was not only sultry, but full of dusk, so that it was several seconds before he could accustom his eyes to the gloom. Then he slowly built up an impression of a dark-curtained, low-roofed apartment, simply furnished with table and chairs. On one of these sat a small, pale, and wrinkled person, motionlessly shadowed and yielding an effect as of some fading, antique portrait in chiaroscuro. If there were such a thing as presence divorced from actuality, here it was, adorned with a classic dignity that was more an emanation than an attribute. Conway was curious about his own intense perception of all this, and wondered if it were dependable or merely

一样雅致，但这里最直接、最显著的特点是干燥，让人窒息、难受的闷热，就好像所有的窗户都牢固地紧紧关着而且有一种什么蒸气供暖设备在最大程度地运行，随着他向前每迈一步，感觉空气越稀薄，越闷得厉害，直到最后张又停在一扇门前，如果说身体的感觉能力可以信赖，这门可能通向一间土耳其浴室。

"大喇嘛要单独接见你。"张在他耳边低声说。然后他开门让康维进去，随即把门关上，悄无声息地，让人几乎感觉不到他的离开。康维犹豫不决地站在那儿，呼吸着酷热而阴郁幽暗的空气，过了几秒钟，眼睛才习惯于这种阴暗的光线。然后，渐渐意识到：这是一间窗帘紧闭、黑暗低矮的房间，简单地配着一张桌子和几把椅子。其中一把椅子上坐着一个矮小、脸色苍白而布满皱纹的人。在幽暗的光线中，静止不动的身影产生一种梦幻般的效果，仿佛是用明暗对照法绘制的一幅褪了色的年代久远的肖像画。假如真有这样一幅脱出于现实的画展现在眼前，那就是在这儿。一种古典的庄严与尊贵处处弥散，装饰衬托着整个画面。康维很好奇自己对这一切产生的强烈感觉，他甚至怀疑它是否真实，还是只不过是自己对这奢华富丽而朦胧昏暗的暖热氛围产生的反应而

his reaction to the rich, crepuscular warmth; he felt dizzy under the gaze of those ancient eyes, took a few forward paces, and then halted. The occupant of the chair grew now less vague in outline, but scarcely more corporeal; he was a little old man in Chinese dress, its folds and flounces loose against a flat, emaciated frame. "You are Mr. Conway?" he whispered in excellent English.

The voice was pleasantly soothing, and touched with a very gentle melancholy that fell upon Conway with strange beatitude; though once again the skeptic in him was inclined to hold the temperature responsible.

"I am," he answered.

The voice went on. "It is a pleasure to see you, Mr. Conway. I sent for you because I thought we should do well to have a talk together. Please sit down beside me and have no fear. I am an old man and can do no one any harm."

Conway answered: "I feel it a signal honor to be received by you."

"I thank you, my dear Conway – I shall call you that, according to your English fashion. It is, as I said, a moment of great pleasure for me. My sight is poor, but believe me, I am able to see you in my mind, as well as with my eyes. I trust you have been comfortable at Shangri-La since your arrival?"

已；在老年人那双历经沧桑、洞穿世事的眼睛的注视下，他顿时手足无措，感到茫然与困惑。他向前迈了几步然后停下。椅子上的那个人的轮廓不再那么模糊了，但简直看不出它有多少血肉；他是个身着汉族服饰的矮小老人，衣服的皱褶和镶边松松垮垮的，与无精打采而消瘦憔悴的身躯形成了对比。"你就是康维先生？"他用极好的英语低声问道。

他的声音亲切和蔼、温柔甜蜜，且带有一丝轻柔的忧郁，犹如一种奇妙的福音飘进康维的脑海。然而，他内心深处的那丝怀疑再一次倾向于这里温度的原因。

"是的。"他回答。

那声音又继续说："很高兴见到你，康维先生。我派人请你，是因为我认为我们还是谈一谈的好。请坐在我旁边，不要害怕，我是个老头，不会对任何人造成任何伤害。"

康维回答道："我觉得能够被您接见非常荣幸。"

"谢谢，我亲爱的康维——按照你们英国人的方式，我应该这么称呼你。正如我所说，这对于我来说是个非常愉快的时刻。我的视力很糟，但请相信我，我能够用心看到你，眼睛也还能看到一点，我相信你到达香格里拉后过得还算舒适安逸。"

"Extremely so."

"I am glad. Chang has done his best for you, no doubt. It has been a great pleasure to him also. He tells me you have been asking many questions about our community and its affairs?"

"I am certainly interested in them."

"Then if you can spare me a little time, I shall be pleased to give you a brief account of our foundation."

"There is nothing I should appreciate more."

"That is what I had thought – and hoped… But first of all, before our discourse…"

He made the slightest stir of a hand, and immediately, by what technique of summons Conway could not detect, a servant entered to prepare the elegant ritual of tea-drinking. The little egg-shell bowls of almost colorless fluid were placed on a lacquered tray; Conway, who knew the ceremony, was by no means contemptuous of it. The voice resumed: "Our ways are familiar to you, then?"

Obeying an impulse which he could neither analyze nor find desire to control, Conway answered: "I lived in China for some years."

"You did not tell Chang?"

"No."

"Then why am I so honored?"

Conway was rarely at a loss to explain

"非常舒适安逸。"

"那我很高兴。张为你尽了最大的努力，确定无疑。这对他来说也是件很高兴的事。他告诉我，你们一直在问一些关于我们这个团体和有关事宜的问题。"

"我的确很感兴趣。"

"那么，如果你能给我些时间，我会非常高兴向你简略叙述一下我们这个机构的创办。"

"那我再感激不过了。"

"那就是我想过并且希望的……但是首先，在我们谈话之前……"

他轻微地打了个手势，用康维都没来得及觉察的方法传唤了一个仆人进来准备了一套典雅礼节性的茶点。小小蛋壳似的茶碗盛着几乎无色的液体，放在涂漆的托盘上端了上来。康维懂得这些礼仪，他丝毫没有对此轻视。这时，那声音又开始说："我们的风俗习惯对你来说都还熟悉吧，对吗？"

康维心中升腾起一种冲动，他既不愿冷静下来分析研究，又找不到加以抑制的欲望，在这种推动的作用下，康维不禁回答，"我在中国生活了几年。"

"你没有告诉张。"

"没有。"

"那么，我为什么这样荣幸可

his own motives, but on this occasion he could not think of any reason at all. At length he replied: "To be quite candid, I haven't the slightest idea, except that I must have wanted to tell you."

"The best of all reasons, I am sure, between those who are to become friends… Now tell me, is this not a delicate aroma? The teas of China are many and fragrant, but this, which is a special product of our own valley, is in my opinion their equal."

Conway lifted the bowl to his lips and tasted. The savor was slender, elusive, and recondite, a ghostly bouquet that haunted rather than lived on the tongue. He said: "It is very delightful, and also quite new to me."

"Yes, like a great many of our valley herbs, it is both unique and precious. It should be tasted, of course, very slowly – not only in reverence and affection, but to extract the fullest degree of pleasure. This is a famous lesson that we may learn from Kou Kai Tchou, who lived some fifteen centuries ago. He would always hesitate to reach the succulent marrow when he was eating a piece of sugar-cane, for, as he explained – 'I introduce myself gradually into the region of delights.' Have you studied any of the great Chinese classics?"

Conway replied that he was slightly acquainted with a few of them. He knew

康维很少为解释动机而茫然不知所措，可是这一次他却想不到任何理由。最后他答道："坦率地说，除了想一定要告诉你，我并没有一点其他想法。"

"这是最好的理由，我确定，介于这些，我们要成为朋友了……现在，请告诉我，这香味是不是清新淡雅？中国茶品种多样且沁人心脾，但这种茶是我们山谷的特产，在我看来完全可以与其他品种媲美。"

康维把碗端起抵于唇间，品尝了一下。这滋味微妙而难以捉摸、深奥而难以理解，幽灵一般的香味缠绕在舌尖之上。他说："味道很可口，而且对我来说，也很新奇。"

"对，就同我们山谷众多的药草一样，这茶独一无二而又珍贵奇特，你当然应该慢慢地细细品尝——不仅出于礼节和钟爱，而且是要最大程度地品味饮茶之趣。这可是从生活在 1500 年前的顾恺之那里学到的著名训诫。当年他在吃甘蔗时，总是从容不迫地不愿意立刻去咀嚼那多汁的精髓部分，他为此解释说——我在引导着自己逐渐进入美妙的境界。'你有没有研究过伟大的中国古典名著？"

康维回答说他稍微了解其中的一小部分。他知道，按照待客礼

that the allusive conversation would, according to etiquette, continue until the tea-bowls were taken away; but he found it far from irritating, despite his keenness to hear the history of Shangri-La. Doubtless there was a certain amount of Kou Kai Tchou's reluctant sensibility in himself.

At length the signal was given, again mysteriously, the servant padded in and out, and with no more preamble the High Lama of Shangri-La began:

"Probably you are familiar, my dear Conway, with the general outline of Tibetan history. I am informed by Chang that you have made ample use of our library here, and I doubt not that you have studied the scanty but exceedingly interesting annals of these regions. You will be aware, anyhow, that Nestorian Christianity was widespread throughout Asia during the Middle Ages, and that its memory lingered long after its actual decay. In the seventeenth century a Christian revival was impelled directly from Rome through the agency of those heroic Jesuit missionaries whose journeys, if I may permit myself the remark, are so much more interesting to read of than those of St. Paul. Gradually the Church established itself over an immense area, and it is a remarkable fact, not realized by many Europeans to-day, that for

仪，这场处处暗含典故的谈话将一直持续到茶碗被端走为止；然而他发现这远远不至于使他烦躁恼怒，尽管他强烈地渴望听听香格里拉的历史。毋庸置疑，大喇嘛身上有某些顾恺之那种从容不迫的特征。

最终，他又神秘兮兮地打了一个手势，那仆人悄无声息地进来随即又出去了。这回，大喇嘛开门见山地开始讲香格里拉的事：

"亲爱的康维，也许你对藏族历史的概况有所了解。张告诉我，你们这几天大量地利用我们的图书室，我确信你们已经对这些地区贫乏但极其有趣的历史记载进行了研究。不管怎样，你都会了解到聂斯托里派基督教在中世纪时代广为流传，遍布亚洲各地，即使在它实际上逐渐衰败之后，人们对它的怀念仍然持续了很长一段时间。17世纪，通过那些英勇的耶稣会传教士的游历，一场基督教复兴运动直接从罗马发起并推动，如果允许我自己评论的话，他们遍布四海的游历要比从圣·帕尔的书上读到的还有趣得多。基督教会逐步建立在广大的地域，这是件成就显著的事，可直到今天，基督教会在拉萨已经存在了38年这个事实仍然没有被很多欧洲人所了解。然而，它在中国不是始于拉萨，而是于1719

thirty-eight years there existed a Christian mission in Lhasa itself. It was not, however, from Lhasa but from Pekin, in the year 1719, that four Capuchin friars set out in search of any remnants of the Nestorian faith that might still be surviving in the hinterland.

"They traveled southwest for many months, by Lanchow and the Koko-Nor, facing hardships which you will well imagine. Three died on the way, and the fourth was not far from death when by accident he stumbled into the rocky defile that remains to-day the only practical approach to the valley of Blue Moon. There, to his joy and surprise, he found a friendly and prosperous population who made haste to display what I have always regarded as our oldest tradition – that of hospitality to strangers. Quickly he recovered health and began to preach his mission. The people were Buddhists, but willing to hear him, and he had considerable success. There was an ancient lamasery existing then on this same mountain-shelf, but it was in a state of decay both physical and spiritual, and as the Capuchin's harvest increased, he conceived the idea of setting up on the same magnificent site a Christian monastery. Under his surveillance the old buildings were repaired and largely reconstructed, and he himself began to live

年由北京传入的，当时有4名天主教方济各会的化缘修士动身去寻找有可能在穷乡僻壤的蛮夷之地仍然幸存的聂斯托里信仰的残存者。

"他们朝西南方向行进了几个月，到兰州和青海就遭遇了你完全可以想象得到的困难。有3个人在途中丧了命，而第四个濒临死亡时，无意间被绊了一跤，跌进了那条至今仍是唯一能够到达蓝月谷的遍布岩石的山间隧道之中。令他高兴而惊奇的是，在那儿他发现了一群亲切友善，并且生活富足的居民，他们都连忙展示一直被我视为山谷最古老的传统——热情好客、对陌生人殷切款待。很快他就恢复了健康并开始讲经传道。这里的人都是佛教徒，却很愿意听他的宣讲，因而他取得了相当大的、很客观的成功。那时在同一座山梁上还有一座古老的喇嘛寺存在，但已处于物质和精神双重衰败的状态，而随着这位方济会修道士的收获不断增多，他萌发了在同一块宏伟壮丽的风水宝地修建一座基督教修道院的构想，在他的监督下，古老的建筑得到了修缮并进行了很大程度的重建，而他本人从1734年开始在这里生活，当时他53岁。

here in the year 1734, when he was fifty-three years of age.

"Now let me tell you more about this man. His name was Perrault, and he was by birth a Luxembourger. Before devoting himself to Far Eastern missions he had studied at Paris, Bologna, and other universities; he was something of a scholar. There are few existing records of his early life, but it was not in any way unusual for one of his age and profession. He was fond of music and the arts, had a special aptitude for languages, and before he was sure of his vocation he had tasted all the familiar pleasures of the world. Malplaquet was fought when he was a youth, and he knew from personal contact the horrors of war and invasion. He was physically sturdy; during his first years here he labored with his hands like any other man, tilling his own garden, and learning from the inhabitants as well as teaching them. He found gold deposits along the valley, but they did not tempt him; he was more deeply interested in local plants and herbs. He was humble and by no means bigoted. He deprecated polygamy, but he saw no reason to inveigh against the prevalent fondness for the *tangatse* berry, to which were ascribed medicinal properties, but which was chiefly popular because its effects were those of a mild narcotic. Perrault, in fact,

"现在我告诉你更多有关他的事情。他的名字是佩劳尔特，按出生地来说，他是卢森堡人。在投身远东布道团之前他曾就读于巴黎大学、波伦亚大学和其他几所大学，他可谓一个学者，现存的有关他早年生平的记载却几乎没有，但无论如何，对于他那时的年龄和职业的人们而言他并没有什么与众不同之处。他爱好音乐和美术，对语言有特别的天分，在他确立自己的职业之前，他尝遍了世界上所有众所周知的乐趣。在他青少年时期，玛普兰魁特正在打仗，他亲身的体验让他明白了战争和侵略的残酷无情和凄惨恐怖。他身体结实健壮，在他来到山谷的最初几年里他和别人一样凭自己的双手劳动，耕耘自己的菜园，除了向那里的居民学习之外，他也教教他们。他在山谷中发现了多座金矿，但这些并没有打动他，他更加深感兴趣的是当地的植物和药材。他谦虚恭顺而且绝不固执己见、心地狭窄，他否定一夫多妻或一妻多夫制，但找不出任何理由去强烈抗议这里普遍盛行的人们对坦加司果的钟爱，他们把这归因于坦加司果的药用属性，但这种果子那么受欢迎其实主要是因为它温和的麻痹作用。实际上，佩劳尔特本人也变得多少有些

became somewhat of an addict himself; it was his way to accept from native life all that it offered which he found harmless and pleasant, and to give in return the spiritual treasure of the West. He was not an ascetic; he enjoyed the good things of the world, and was careful to teach his converts cooking as well as catechism. I want you to have an impression of a very earnest, busy, learned, simple, and enthusiastic person who, along with his priestly functions, did not disdain to put on a mason's overall and help in the actual building of these very rooms. That was, of course, a work of immense difficulty, and one which nothing but his pride and steadfastness could have overcome. Pride, I say, because it was undoubtedly a dominant motive at the beginning – the pride in his own Faith that made him decide that if Gautama could inspire men to build a temple on the ledge of Shangri-La, Rome was capable of no less.

"But time passed, and it was not unnatural that this motive should yield place gradually to more tranquil ones. Emulation is, after all, a young man's spirit, and Perrault, by the time his monastery was well established, was already full of years. You must bear in mind that he had not, from a strict point of view, been acting very regularly; though some latitude must surely be extended to

上瘾了；他就这样接受了当地生活所给予的所有一切，他发现这是无害的，而且令人很愉快，作为回报，他也把西方的精神财富给了这里的人。他不是个苦行僧，他尽情享受这世上美好的事物。他精心地传授烹调术以及教义问答书给他的皈依者。我想让你有这样一个印象，他是个诚挚、忙碌、博学、善良又充满热情的人，加之他修道士的职能，他不但没有不屑穿上泥瓦匠的工作裤，而且还协助了这些特殊建筑的实际建造。当然，那是一项无比艰巨的工程，只有他的自信和坚定不移的信仰能够克服。我说他自信是因为不容置疑，这工程一开始就是一个非常宏大的首屈一指的设想——他自己信仰中的骄傲和自信促使他下定决心在香格里拉的边缘地带建造一座庙宇。因为他相信释迦牟尼能赋予人灵感，罗马当然也绝对有这个能力。

"然而，时光流逝，这一设想会逐渐让位于一个更切合实际的稳定构想，这也并非不合常理。竞争毕竟是一个年轻人的心态，而等到他的修道院完全建立时，佩劳尔特已经一大把年纪了。严格地讲，他的行为举止并不太有规律。不过对于高高在上的教士，某些宽容度必须得给予伸延，这种优越感和高傲可以放置在用年来衡量，而非用

one whose ecclesiastical superiors are located at a distance measurable in years rather than miles. But the folk of the valley and the monks themselves had no misgivings; they loved and obeyed him, and as years went on, came to venerate him also. At intervals it was his custom to send reports to the Bishop of Pekin; but often they never reached him, and as it was to be presumed that the bearers had succumbed to the perils of the journey, Perrault grew more and more unwilling to hazard their lives, and after about the middle of the century he gave up the practice. Some of his earlier messages, however, must have got through, and a doubt of his activities have been aroused, for in the year 1769 a stranger brought a letter written twelve years before, summoning Perrault to Rome.

"He would have been over seventy had the command been received without delay; as it was, he had turned eighty-nine. The long trek over mountain and plateau was unthinkable; he could never have endured the scouring gales and fierce chills of the wilderness outside. He sent, therefore, a courteous reply explaining the situation, but there is no record that his message ever passed the barrier of the great ranges.

"So Perrault remained at Shangri-La, not exactly in defiance of superior orders, but because it was physically impossible

米来衡量的距离之上。然而，山谷的乡民和修道士们自己却没有担忧和疑虑，他们爱戴并且服从他；时间一年年掠过，他们开始崇敬、膜拜他。在休息时间，他习惯派人送报到北京的主教，却往往没有到达，他也只能推断送信人已经屈服于旅途的艰险，佩劳尔特不愿意再让他们去冒生命的危险，到大概那个世纪的中叶之后，他完全放弃了与主教的联系。不过一些以前的信件可以肯定是寄到了，并由此而引起一场对他行为的怀疑。在 1769 年，一个陌生人带来一封写于 12 年前、召唤佩劳尔特去罗马的信。

"如果这一命令没被耽误而准时收到的话，他那时该是 70 多岁了。而实际上，他已经 89 岁。在大山和高原的长途跋涉是难以想象的。他可能从来都没有忍受过外面荒无人烟处狂风暴虐的吹打和凛冽寒风的侵袭。于是，他寄了一封婉转客气的回信解释了当时的情况，可是，那信到底有没有翻越那重重山脉、跨越那层层屏障就不得而知了。

"所以，佩劳尔特继续留在了香格里拉，确切地说，他并非藐视

for him to fulfill them. In any case he was an old man, and death would probably soon put an end both to him and his irregularity. By this time the institution he had founded had begun to undergo a subtle change. It might be deplorable, but it was not really very astonishing; for it could hardly be expected that one man unaided should uproot permanently the habits and traditions of an epoch. He had no Western colleagues to hold firm when his own grip relaxed; and it had perhaps been a mistake to build on a site that held such older and differing memories. It was asking too much; but was it not asking even more to expect a white-haired veteran, just entering the nineties, to realize the mistake that he had made? Perrault, at any rate, did not then realize it. He was far too old and happy. His followers were devoted even when they forgot his teaching, while the people of the valley held him in such reverent affection that he forgave with ever-increasing ease their lapse into former customs. He was still active, and his faculties had remained exceptionally keen. At the age of ninety-eight he began to study the Buddhist writings that had been left at Shangri-La by its previous occupants, and his intention was then to devote the rest of his life to the composition of a book attacking Buddhism from the standpoint of

上级命令，而是他的身体根本不允许他去执行了。无论如何，他已经是一个老人，死神可能很快就会结束他和他无规律的生活。到那个时候，他所创立的机构就会开始发生难以捉摸的变化，那该会是可悲可叹的，却不会让人十分震惊；因为几乎没有人会预料到一个孤立无援的人能够永久地倾覆一个时代的习惯、风俗和传统。当他的控制力有所松懈的时候，他没有西方同僚给予他坚实稳固的支持，他在考虑，在铭刻着这么古老而不同寻常印记的地方，建造这个修道院可能是一个错误。这要求也太多了吧，然而期望一个马上进入90岁的满头白发饱经风霜的老人去认识自己犯下的错误，这种要求不是更过分吗？不管怎样，佩劳尔特一直没领悟到这种错误。他毕竟年龄太大而且太快乐了。他那些追随者甚至在忘掉他的教诲时，还依旧虔诚、依旧专心致志地甘于献身，同时，山谷里的人们仍然如此恭敬地拥护他，这一切让他以一种与日俱增的悠闲自得心态去宽恕他们又陷入以前的风俗习惯中去。他仍然很积极勤奋，他的身体机能仍然格外敏捷。98岁时，他开始研究那些早先的居住者留在香格里拉的佛教徒所写的著作。那时他想将自己的余生致力于编撰一本立足于正统的观点去抨击佛教故步自封的静

orthodoxy. He actually finished this task (we have his manuscript complete), but the attack was very gentle, for he had by that time reached the round figure of a century – an age at which even the keenest acrimonies are apt to fade.

"Meanwhile, as you may suppose, many of his early disciples had died, and as there were few replacements, the number resident under the rule of the old Capuchin steadily diminished. From over eighty at one time, it dwindled to a score, and then to a mere dozen, most of them very aged themselves. Perrault's life at this time grew to be a very calm and placid waiting for the end. He was far too old for disease and discontent; only the everlasting sleep could claim him now, and he was not afraid. The valley people, out of kindness, supplied food and clothing; his library gave him work. He had become rather frail, but still kept energy to fulfill the major ceremonial of his office; the rest of the tranquil days he spent with his books, his memories, and the mild ecstasies of the narcotic. His mind remained so extraordinarily clear that he even embarked upon a study of certain mystic practices that the Indians call *yoga*, and which are based upon various special methods of breathing. For a man of such an age the enterprise might well have seemed hazardous, and it was certainly

止观点的书。他竟然真的完成了这项工作（我们有他完整的手稿），然而他的抨击是非常和善的，原因是那时他已经达到一个世纪的圆满数字——到这个年纪后连最尖锐的刻薄都是很容易消失的。

"同时，你也许能想象的到，许多他早期的门徒都已死去，而且他只有很少数的几位接班人，而且老方济各会统治下的居民人数都在平稳地不断减少，从前曾有80多人，后来渐渐减少到20个，最后仅仅剩12个人，他们中大部分都已很老了。佩劳尔特的生活这时变得非常的平静，只不过在平和沉着地等待生命的尽头。他已经太老了，没有疾病的折磨和不满足的困扰，现在只有永久的安眠才是他所需要的了，而且他也不害怕。山谷的人们都出于仁慈与善良送来食物和衣服，他的图书室还让他有些事做，他的身体变得十分虚弱，但他仍旧保持精神去主持他办公室的重要事宜。余下的安宁、恬静日子他就在书的陪伴、甜蜜的回忆以及适度的自我麻醉中度过。"他的神智仍旧异常清晰，他甚至开始着手研究一种神秘的被印度人称为'瑜伽'的功夫，这功夫基于各种各样的特殊呼吸法。对于一个这么大年龄的人来说，这种运动看起来好像有一定的冒险性，事实也的确是这样。不久，在那值得纪念的

true that soon afterwards, in that memorable year 1789, news descended to the valley that Perrault was dying at last.

"He lay in this room, my dear Conway, where he could see from the window the white blur that was all his failing eyesight gave him of Karakal; but he could see with his mind also; he could picture the clear and matchless outline that he had first glimpsed half a century before. And there came to him, too, the strange parade of all his many experiences, the years of travel across desert and upland, the great crowds in Western cities, the clang and glitter of Marlborough's troops. His mind had straitened to a snow-white calm; he was ready, willing, and glad to die. He gathered his friends and servants round him and bade them all farewell; then he asked to be left alone awhile. It was during such a solitude, with his body sinking and his mind lifted to beatitude, that he had hoped to give up his soul… but it did not happen so. He lay for many weeks without speech or movement, and then he began to recover. He was a hundred and eight."

The whispering ceased for a moment, and to Conway, stirring slightly, it appeared that the High Lama had been translating, with fluency, out of a remote and private dream. At length he went on:

"Like others who have waited long on the threshold of death, Perrault had been

1789 年，佩劳尔特快要去世的消息传遍了山谷。

"他就躺在这个房间，我亲爱的康维，他透过窗户可以看到一团朦朦胧胧的白色，那就是他那双渐渐衰退的眼睛里的卡拉卡尔山，可是他用心灵也能看到它。他可以生动地描绘出半个世纪以前第一次瞥见他那清晰洁净、无与伦比的轮廓。紧接着，他曾经所有的经历都又神奇地重新浮现在眼前：历年来穿越沙漠和高地的旅行、西方大城市里拥挤的人群，还有铿锵有力又光彩夺目的莫尔伯勒部队。他的神智已经收缩为一片雪白的平静，他已经准备好了，希望而且很乐意去死。他把朋友和佣人们聚集到身边向他们告别，然后要求自己独处片刻。在这样一片孤寂之中，他的身体有一种虚脱感，他的意识也开始消散飘向至上的福地，他希望灵魂解脱……但事情并没有像这样发生。他只是无声无息、纹丝不动地躺了好几个星期，之后他又开始恢复，那时他已经 108 岁了。"

这轻声细语的嘟哝停息了一会儿。康维稍微有些激动，在他看来，这大喇嘛一直都在连绵不绝地讲述着一个久远而又隐秘的梦。终于大喇嘛接着说：

"像在死亡的门槛上等待多时的其他人一样，佩劳尔特被授予

granted a vision of some significance to take back with him into the world; and of this vision more must be said later. Here I will confine myself to his actions and behavior, which were indeed remarkable. For instead of convalescing idly, as might have been expected, he plunged forthwith into rigorous self-discipline somewhat curiously combined with narcotic indulgence. Drug-taking and deep-breathing exercises – it could not have seemed a very death-defying regimen; yet the fact remains that when the last of the old monks died, in 1794, Perrault himself was still living.

"It would almost have brought a smile had there been anyone at Shangri-La with a sufficiently distorted sense of humor. The wrinkled Capuchin, no more decrepit than he had been for a dozen years, persevered in a secret ritual he had evolved, while to the folk of the valley he soon became veiled in mystery, a hermit of uncanny powers who lived alone on that formidable cliff. But there was still a tradition of affection for him, and it came to be regarded as meritorious and luck-bringing to climb to Shangri-La and leave a simple gift, or perform some manual task that was needed there. On all such pilgrims Perrault bestowed his blessing – forgetful, it might be, that they were lost and straying sheep. For 'Te

某种意义上的幻觉和他一起返回人世，至于这些幻觉我后面会再更多讲些。现在我先让自己局限于他的行为举止，这的确很值得注意。他并没有像人们期待的那样闲下来继续恢复健康，反而立刻投入严酷苛刻的自我惩戒修行之中，还颇为奇怪的沉溺于麻醉剂。吃一些麻醉药品然后进行深呼吸练习——这似乎也不可能被视为是向死亡挑战的养生法。可事实就是这样，在1794年最后一个老喇嘛去世之时，佩劳尔特仍然活着。

"这几乎给那时在香格里拉的每一个人都带去一丝充满讽刺意味的微笑。这位皱皱巴巴的方济会教士之后很多年都不再衰老，再加上他逐渐坚持不懈的一直秘密进行一种仪式，于是在山谷中的众乡邻眼中，他很快就蒙上一层神秘的面纱，简直成了一位独居于那令人生畏的悬崖绝壁之上的具有神秘力量的隐士。不过，他还有一套能对他们施加影响的传统手段，那就是让人们把爬上香格里拉并留下一些简单的小礼物或者完成那儿需要的一些体力工作视为有功绩的、能带来好运的行为。对所有的香客，佩劳尔特都赐予上帝的祝福——他们也许是健忘的，那些人都像是迷了路，离了群的绵

Deum Laudamus' and 'Om Mane Padme Hum' were now heard equally in the temples of the valley.

"As the new century approached, the legend grew into a rich and fantastic folk-lore – it was said that Perrault had become a god, that he worked miracles, and that on certain nights he flew to the summit of Karakal to hold a candle to the sky. There is a paleness always on the mountain at full moon; but I need not assure you that neither Perrault or any other man has ever climbed there. I mention it, even though it may seem unnecessary, because there is a mass of unreliable testimony that Perrault did and could do all kinds of impossible things. It was supposed, for instance, that he practiced the art of self-levitation, of which so much appears in accounts of Buddhist mysticism; but the more sober truth is that he made many experiments to that end, but entirely without success. He did, however, discover that the impairment of ordinary senses could be somewhat offset by a development of others; he acquired skill in telepathy which was perhaps remarkable, and though he made no claim to any specific powers of healing, there was a quality in his mere presence that was helpful in certain cases.

"You will wish to know how he spent his time during these unprecedented years.

羊。而山谷的寺院中现在同样都可以听到'特迪罗达穆斯'和'确吗呢叭咪眸'。

"当新的世纪即将到来之际，这一传说慢慢变成了一个丰富而怪诞的民间故事——说是佩劳尔特变成了一个神，他能够创造奇迹，在某些特定的夜晚，会飞到卡拉卡尔的顶峰，手持一支蜡烛照亮天空。在满月明朗的夜空，这座山上总会有苍白的光晕。我不需要向你保证无论佩劳尔特还是别的任何人都未曾攀登到那山顶。虽然好像没有必要，但我已经提到过了，因为有大量的并不可靠的证据说明，佩劳尔特曾做过而且能够做出各种不可能的事情。例如可以想象他会练习腾云驾雾的技能，这在很多佛教的奇妙玄想里都出现过。而更严肃的事实是，他曾做过许多这方面的试验，但都彻底没有成功。然而，他的确发现常规观念的残损可以由其他观念的发展来弥补；他习得了'心灵感应'（传心术）的技术，这也许是相当卓越的，可是他没有强求任何一种特定的有治疗功用的能力，不过，仅仅是他的存在就对周围的人们身上的某些病症有一定的帮助。

"你可能很想知道在这史无前例的岁月里他是怎样消磨时间

His attitude may be summed up by saying that, as he had not died at a normal age, he began to feel that there was no discoverable reason why he either should or should not do so at any definite time in the future. Having already proved himself abnormal, it was as easy to believe that the abnormality might continue as to expect it to end at any moment. And that being so, he began to behave without care for the imminence with which he had been so long preoccupied; he began to live the kind of life that he had always desired, but had so rarely found possible; for he had kept at heart and throughout all vicissitudes the tranquil tastes of a scholar. His memory was astonishing; it appeared to have escaped the trammels of the physical into some upper region of immense clarity; it almost seemed that he could now learn *everything* with far greater ease than during his student days he had been able to learn *anything*. He was soon, of course, brought up against a need for books, but there were a few he had had with him from the first, and they included, you may be interested to hear, an English grammar and dictionary and Florio's translation of Montaigne. With these to work on he contrived to master the intricacies of your language, and we still possess in our library the manuscript of one of his first linguistic exercises – a

的。他的生活态度可以这样概括：由于他没有在正常的年龄去世，面对将来的时间他开始感觉不知所措，时间终于证实自己是个异乎寻常的人，他可以相信这种异常能持续下去，同样也可以料想任何时候都有可能结束。就因为这样，他开始不再那么在意这么长时间来一直全身心投入、为之殚精竭虑的紧迫事件，他总是渴望得到却几乎找不到可能的生活现在也已经开始，他历经整个的世事变迁和人生百态，而内心却一直保持着像人文学者那般平和安宁的境界。他的记忆力让人叹服，他似乎摆脱了身体上的束缚，达到了一种无限澄澈的超然领域，看起来他现在可以学好所有东西，比起学生时代那种'学而无不通'还要轻松容易得多。他很快就培养了自己不依赖书本的习惯，除了几本之前就不离手的工具书他仍在用，你肯定很有兴趣来听，这些工具书包括《英语语法词典》和《佛罗里奥之蒙泰恩译文集》。经过不断努力攻读这些书，他掌握了你们纷繁难懂的英语，我们的图书室仍保存着一份他第一次语言练习的原稿，是蒙泰恩关于《虚化为西藏人》一文的论文——这无疑是一部无与伦比的作品。"

translation of Montaigne's essay on Vanity into Tibetan – surely a unique production."

Conway smiled. "I should be interested to see it sometime, if I might."

"With the greatest of pleasure. It was, you may think, a singularly unpractical accomplishment, but recollect that Perrault had reached a singularly unpractical age. He would have been lonely without some such occupation – at any rate until the fourth year of the nineteenth century, which marks an important event in the history of our foundation. For it was then that a second stranger from Europe arrived in the valley of Blue Moon. He was a young Austrian named Henschell who had soldiered against Napoleon in Italy – a youth of noble birth, high culture, and much charm of manner. The wars had ruined his fortunes, and he had wandered across Russia into Asia with some vague intention of retrieving them. It would be interesting to know how exactly he reached the plateau, but he had no very clear idea himself; indeed, he was as near death when he arrived here as Perrault himself had once been. Again the hospitality of Shangri-La was extended, and the stranger recovered – but there the parallel breaks down. For Perrault had come to preach and proselytize, whereas Henschell took a more immediate interest in the gold deposits. His first ambition was

康维笑道："我很有兴趣什么时候看看，要是可以的话。"

"非常乐意。你想想，这是个格外不切实际的成就，可是想到佩劳尔特也达到了一个格外不切实际的年龄，没有这种消遣的话，他一定会孤单寂寞的——无论如何，一直到 19 世纪的第四个年头，我们这个基金会的历史上才发生了一件重要的大事。那时，第二个来自欧洲的陌生人来到了蓝月亮山谷，他是一个年轻的奥地利人，名叫亨斯齐尔，他曾在意大利当过兵，参加过反对拿破仑的战役——他生为贵族，有很高的文化素养，而且行为举止很有魅力。可战争毁灭了他的命运，他怀着想要挽回一切的朦朦胧胧尚不明确的目的，经过俄罗斯游荡到亚洲。如果能知道他是怎样糊里糊涂而准确无误地摸到这片高原山谷的，那一定会很有趣，可他自己都没有特别清晰的印象。和曾经的佩劳尔特一样，他到达山谷时差不多已经处于死亡的边缘。又一次，热情好客的香格里拉张开了温暖的怀抱，让这位外地人渐渐康复过来——然而这种和谐相处很快就被瓦解了。"佩劳尔特开始着手说教传道并劝诱山民改变信仰，而亨斯齐尔立即对金矿产生了浓厚的兴趣，他最初的野

to enrich himself and return to Europe as soon as possible.

"But he did not return. An odd thing happened – though one that has happened so often since that perhaps we must now agree that it cannot be very odd after all. The valley, with its peacefulness and its utter freedom from worldly cares, tempted him again and again to delay his departure, and one day, having heard the local legend, he climbed to Shangri-La and had his first meeting with Perrault.

"That meeting was, in the truest sense, historic. Perrault, if a little beyond such human passions as friendship or affection, was yet endowed with a rich benignity of mind which touched the youth as water upon a parched soil. I will not try to describe the association that sprang up between the two; the one gave utmost adoration, while the other shared his knowledge, his ecstasies, and the wild dream that had now become the only reality left for him in the world."

There was a pause, and Conway said very quietly, "Pardon the interruption, but that is not quite clear to me."

"I know." The whispered reply was completely sympathetic. "It would be remarkable indeed if it were. It is a matter which I shall be pleased to explain before our talk is over, but for the present, if you will forgive me, I will confine myself to

心是让自己发财致富然后尽快返回欧洲。

"但他没有回去。一件古怪的事情发生了——不过从那以后这样的怪事就频繁发生了，所以恐怕我们现在必须承认，这终究不是一件特别奇怪的事情。这山谷，以它的平静祥和和彻底远离尘世烦恼的自由深刻打动了他，使他一次次延期离开。有一天，在听了当地的传说之后，他爬到香格里拉同佩劳尔特见了第一面。

"精确地说，那是一次具有历史意义的会见。要是说佩劳尔特有那么一点拒人千里、超越世人皆有的、比如友谊和爱情这种感情之外的话，他还是赋予了一份丰富的温和与慈祥，犹如清凉的河水浇灌在干涸的土地上，深深地触动了这位青年。我不想详述他们两个之间突然达成了什么联盟；一个表现出极大的崇拜与倾慕，而另一个则与他分享自己的知识、自己的心醉神迷，还有自己疯狂的梦想，现在这些已经变为他在这个世界上仅留的现实。"

趁停顿的一小会儿，康维轻声说道："很抱歉，我打扰一下，可是这对于我来说不是很清晰明了。"

"我知道。"这低声细语的回答饱含同情，"如果的确如此那该有多了不起啊。这个问题我想放

simpler things. A fact that will interest you is that Henschell began our collections of Chinese art, as well as our library and musical acquisitions. He made a remarkable journey to Pekin and brought back the first consignment in the year 1809. He did not leave the valley again, but it was his ingenuity which devised the complicated system by which the lamasery has ever since been able to obtain anything needful from the outer world."

"I suppose you found it easy to make payment in gold?"

"Yes, we have been fortunate in possessing supplies of a metal which is held in such high esteem in other parts of the world."

"Such high esteem that you must have been very lucky to escape a gold rush."

The High Lama inclined his head in the merest indication of agreement. "That, my dear Conway, was always Henschell's fear. He was careful that none of the porters bringing books and art treasures should ever approach too closely; he made them leave their burdens a day's journey outside, to be fetched afterwards by our valley folk themselves. He even arranged for sentries to keep constant watch on the entrance to the defile. But it soon occurred to him that there was an easier and more final safeguard."

"Yes?" Conway's voice was guardedly

在咱们的谈话结束之前解释,但是现在,如果不介意,我自己只局限于讲一些比较简单的情况。你会对这个真相感兴趣的,亨斯齐尔开始了中国艺术珍品的收藏,还有图书室和音乐间资源的购置。他历经非凡的艰辛旅程去到北京,获得了显著的成就,并于 1809 年带回第一批托运的货物。从此,就再也没有离开过山谷,但是,他智谋过人、匠心独运地设计出一套复杂的购物体系,使喇嘛寺从此能够从外面的世界获得任何需要的物品。"

"我认为你们用黄金来付货款会容易些。"

"没错,拥有这么一种被外界的人如此珍视的金属储备,我们感到很幸运。"

"如此地珍视以至于你们避免了淘金热该是非常幸运的。"

大喇嘛倾了一下身点点头明确地表示着赞同,"亲爱的康维,那一直是亨斯齐尔所担忧的,他很小心,从来没有让那些运送书籍、艺术珍品的搬运脚夫们靠得太近。他让他们把货物留在离山谷一天路程的外面,然后由山谷里的居民们自己取回。他甚至安排了哨兵来持续不断地看守山间隘道的入口。不过很快,他又突然想到一种更简单方便而且更确定、彻底的防卫措施。"

"是吗?"康维的声音透出一

tense.

"You see there was no need to fear invasion by an army. That will never be possible, owing to the nature and distances of the country. The most ever to be expected was the arrival of a few half-lost wanderers who, even if they were armed, would probably be so weakened as to constitute no danger. It was decided, therefore, that henceforward strangers might come as freely as they chose – with but one important proviso.

"And, over a period of years, such strangers did come. Chinese merchants, tempted into the crossing of the plateau, chanced occasionally on this one traverse out of so many others possible to them. Nomad Tibetans, wandering from their tribes, strayed here sometimes like weary animals. All were made welcome, though some reached the shelter of the valley only to die. In the year of Waterloo two English missionaries, traveling overland to Pekin, crossed the ranges by an unnamed pass and had the extraordinary luck to arrive as calmly as if they were paying a call. In 1820 a Greek trader, accompanied by sick and famished servants, was found dying at the topmost ridge of the pass. In 1822 three Spaniards, having heard some vague story of gold, reached here after many wanderings and disappointments. Again, in 1830, there was a larger influx. Two

丝紧张与防备。

"你知道，这里根本没有必要害怕会有军队入侵。考虑这个地方的自然环境和地理位置也绝对不可能。曾经预料中要发生的也只是很少几个半途迷路的流浪汉的到来，他们即使全副武装也很可能极度衰弱，根本构不成危险。因此，可以明确，从今以后陌生人应该可以随心所欲地自由进入这里——除了带上一份重要的附文外，别的什么也别带。

"过了好些年，这样的陌生人真的来了。那些汉族商人，不顾一切地冒险进入高原的横断山区，就偶然地踏上了一条崎岖坎坷的Z形攀登路线，而错过了那么多其他可以走的路。游牧的藏族人与他们的部族走散到处徘徊，有时像疲惫不堪的动物一样迷了路流浪到这里。他们都受到了欢迎与款待，可是有些人到达这遮风避雨的山谷的结果却是死亡。在滑铁卢事件发生的那一年（1815 年），有两个英国传教士横越大陆旅行到北京，然后穿越一个不知名的峡谷关口穿越群山峻岭到达山谷，他们的运气好得着实让人惊奇，他们顺利地到达这里，就好像顺路拜访一样。1820 年，一个希腊商人由一些病恹恹而且饥肠辘辘的仆人陪伴着摸爬到附近，被发现在山脊最顶层的山隘上时都快要死了。在 1822 年，3 个西

Germans, a Russian, an Englishman, and a Swede made the dreaded crossing of the Tian-Shans, impelled by a motive that was to become increasingly common – scientific exploration. By the time of their approach a slight modification had taken place in the attitude of Shangri-La towards its visitors – not only were they welcomed if they chanced to find their way into the valley, but it had become customary to meet them if they ever ventured within a certain radius. All this was for a reason I shall later discuss, but the point is of importance as showing that the lamasery was no longer hospitably indifferent; it had already both a need and a desire for new arrivals. And indeed in the years to follow it happened that more than one party of explorers, glorying in their first distant glimpse of Karakal, encountered messengers bearing a cordial invitation – and one that was rarely declined.

"Meanwhile the lamasery had begun to acquire many of its present characteristics. I must stress the fact that Henschell was exceedingly able and talented, and that the Shangri-La of to-day owes as much to him as to its founder. Yes, quite as much, I often think. For his was the firm yet kindly hand that every institution needs at a certain stage of its development, and his loss would have been altogether irreparable had he not completed more

班牙人听到一些含糊不清的有关黄金的故事，就想方设法来到这里，在山谷到处闲逛了好几天，结果却只有失望和沮丧。再一次是在1830年，这里又拥进了一大伙人，其中有两个德国人，一个俄国人，一个英国人和一个瑞典人。这些人被当时越来越多的普遍的科学探索这种动机所推动，异常艰难并充满畏惧地翻越了天山山脉，到他们已经非常接近时，香格里拉对客人的态度稍微地发生了改变——现在，如果客人侥幸找到进入山谷的路，他们不仅能够受到欢迎，而且要是他们碰巧已经冒险来到一定范围之内的话，就有人前去迎接，这已经成了习俗。而全部这些都为一个理由，这个我们后面再谈。不过，很重要的一点就是，喇嘛寺不再不偏不倚地对每位客人都热情周到的接待。目前，新客人的到来已经成为一种需要和热切地渴盼。的确，在接下来的几年中碰巧有不止一伙的探险者为远距离的瞥见卡拉卡尔山的第一眼而自豪狂喜，并意外地与携带着一封满腔热情的邀请函的信使相遇——一封很少被婉言谢绝的邀请函。

"同时，喇嘛寺开始形成它最近的特色。我必须着重强调亨斯齐尔非常能干而且格外天资聪颖这一点。香格里拉之所以能有今天，不仅要归功于它的缔造者，同样得

than a lifework before he died."

Conway looked up to echo rather than question those final words. "*He died!*"

"Yes. It was very sudden. He was killed. It was in the year of your Indian Mutiny. Just before his death a Chinese artist had sketched him, and I can show you that sketch now – it is in this room."

The slight gesture of the hand was repeated, and once again a servant entered. Conway, as a spectator in a trance, watched the man withdraw a small curtain at the far end of the room and leave a lantern swinging amongst the shadows. Then he heard the whisper inviting him to move, and it was extraordinary how hard it was to do so.

He stumbled to his feet and strode across to the trembling circle of light. The sketch was small, hardly more than a miniature in colored inks, but the artist had contrived to give the flesh-tones a waxwork delicacy of texture. The features were of great beauty, almost girlish in modeling, and Conway found in their winsomeness a curiously personal appeal, even across the barriers of time, death, and artifice. But the strangest thing of all was one that he realized only after his first gasp of admiration: the face was that of a young man.

He stammered as he moved away: "But – you said – this was done just

归功于他。没错，非常应该，我经常这么想。每一个机构在特定的发展阶段都需要他亲切热情的双手来全力稳固，可他所有的损失却是无法弥补的，他没有能完成他毕生的事业就离开了人世。"

康维抬起头来，充满敬仰地喃喃重复着："他死了！"

"是的，这非常的突然。他是被杀死的。就是在你们印第安人叛乱的那一年。在他死之前一位汉族画家给他画过素描，现在我可以让你看看——就在这间屋子里。"

大喇嘛再一次轻轻打了一下手势，一位仆人即刻进来。康维作为旁观者，恍惚之间看到这位仆人把屋子另一头的一小片帘布拉开，然后拿一盏灯笼放在中间，摇摇晃晃地照亮阴影。然后他听见轻声细语的嗓音请他过去，但特别离奇的是，康维觉得自己很费劲才能站起身来。

他猛地一个跟跄，然后阔步走到这摇摇晃晃的光环之中。这幅素描很小，几乎不比彩墨袖珍画大多少，但美术家已经设法用丰富的色调烘托出蜡像般精巧细腻的纹理质感。人物面貌及其俊美，几乎像个少女似的造型，康维感到这俊美之中奇妙地透出很强烈的个人感染力，甚至超越了时间、死亡和技巧的界限。但是，这其中最不可思议的一点是，他从崇拜的屏息凝视

before his death?"

"Yes. It is a very good likeness."

"Then if he died in the year you said – "

"He did."

"And he came here, you told me, in 1803, when he was a youth."

"Yes."

Conway did not answer for a moment; presently, with an effort, he collected himself to say: "And he was killed, you were telling me?"

"Yes. An Englishman shot him. It was a few weeks after the Englishman had arrived at Shangri-La. He was another of those explorers."

"What was the cause of it?"

"There had been a quarrel – about some porters. Henschell had just told him of the important proviso that governs our reception of guests. It was a task of some difficulty, and ever since, despite my own enfeeblement, I have felt constrained to perform it myself."

The High Lama made another and longer pause, with just a hint of enquiry in his silence; when he continued, it was to add: "Perhaps you are wondering, my dear Conway, what that proviso may be?"

Conway answered slowly and in a low voice: "I think I can already guess."

"Can you indeed? And can you guess anything else after this long and curious story of mine?"

之中深深嘘了一口气时才注意到，这是一张年轻人的脸。

他一面退回，一面结结巴巴地说道："可是……你说过……这画像恰好是在他死前之完成的呀？"

"是的，画得非常像。"

"那么他是不是在你说的那一年死的？"

"是的。"

"而你告诉我说，他是在1803年、当他还是个青年的时候来到这里的？"

"没错。"

康维好一会儿没有反应；后来，他努力让自己平静下来、泰然自若地说："他是被杀的，是你告诉我的？"

"对。一个英国人开枪打死了他，那是在这个英国人到达香格里拉几个星期之后发生的，他是那伙探险者中的另外一个。"

"这件事的起因是什么？"

"他们为一些脚夫的事争吵了一番，亨斯齐尔只不过告诉他关于接待外来客人的那项重要的管理条例。这是一项执行起来有些困难的工作。从那以后——不是说我已经衰老了——如果要履行这一条例，连我自己都有些勉强。"

这大喇嘛又一次停顿了很长时间，他的沉默中仅仅透出少许询问的暗示；当他又继续说话时，还特别加了一句："亲爱的康维，或

Conway dizzied in brain as he sought to answer the question; the room was now a whorl of shadows with that ancient benignity at its center. Throughout the narrative he had listened with an intentness that had perhaps shielded him from realizing the fullest implications of it all; now, with the mere attempt at conscious expression, he was flooded over with amazement, and the gathering certainty in his mind was almost stifled as it sprang to words. "It seems impossible," he stammered. "And yet I can't help thinking of it – it's astonishing – and extraordinary – and quite incredible – and yet not *absolutely* beyond my powers of belief – "

"What is, my *son*?"

And Conway answered, shaken with an emotion for which he knew no reason and which he did not seek to conceal: "*That you are still alive, Father Perrault.*"

许你想知道那个条例可能会是什么！"

康维压低声音慢悠悠地回答说："我想我已经能够猜到了。"

"你确定？你能猜到我刚才讲的那个冗长而奇怪的故事背后还有别的什么吗？"

康维在考虑怎样回答这个问题，而脑子里却一片混乱。现在整个屋子都晃动着螺纹似的阴影，而这位慈祥的高龄老人就坐在房间的中央。自始至终，老人的整个讲述他都在聚精会神地听。也许他没有弄明白其中全部的言外之意；此刻，他仅仅试图找到一个有意识的词语来表达，可他却整个被惊讶诧异的感觉淹没。在他的头脑中，不断聚集的确定性几乎让他窒息，最终涌现成话语。"这看起来好像不可能，"他结结巴巴地说，"然而我又情不自禁地思考这些事情——这太惊人——太离奇——而且非常不可思议——但也不是绝对超越了我相信的能力……"

"你是什么意思，我的孩子！"

康维心中澎湃起一种莫无缘由的、使他心烦意乱的激动，而他也不愿意试图去掩饰和隐瞒，他答道："您老还活着，佩劳尔特大爷。"

CHAPTER 8

第八章

THERE had been a pause, imposed by the High Lama's call for further refreshment; Conway did not wonder at it, for the strain of such a long recital must have been considerable. Nor was he himself ungrateful for the respite. He felt that the interval was as desirable from an artistic as from any other point of view, and that the bowls of tea, with their accompaniment of conventionally improvised courtesies, fulfilled the same function as a *cadenza* in music. This reflection brought out (unless it were mere coincidence) an odd example of the High Lama's telepathic powers, for he immediately began to talk about music and to express pleasure that Conway's taste in that direction had not been entirely unsatisfied at Shangri-La. Conway answered with suitable politeness and added that he had been surprised to find the lamasery in possession of such a complete library of European composers. The compliment was acknowledged between slow sips of tea. "Ah, my dear Conway, we are fortunate in that one of our members is a gifted musician – he was, indeed, a pupil of Chopin's – and we

大喇嘛要求歇一会儿以恢复精神，谈话就暂时停了下来。康维对此也并不感到奇怪，毕竟讲了这么长时间肯定是非常费神的。他自己也庆幸能借此休息一会儿。他觉得这暂时的休息无论是从谈话艺术还是从其他任何角度来看，都十分必要，还有这些碗茶和席间人们即兴所讲的客套话，与音乐中休止前婉转的装饰奏有同样的作用。这一情形就是大喇嘛有神奇的"心灵感应"的例证，（除非这只是一种巧合），他立刻开始谈论起音乐，并表示很高兴康维对音乐的品味尚未在香格里拉得到完全的满足。康维礼貌性地回应了几句，他还说，看到这喇嘛寺收藏了如此之完整的欧洲作曲家的作品，他倍感惊讶。大喇嘛啜饮了几口茶，并对康维的赞美表示感谢。"啊，我亲爱的康维，很幸运，在我们当中出现了一位很有天赋的音乐家——他真的是肖邦的学生——我们很高兴地把沙龙全权交给他管理。你一定得见见他。"

have been happy to place in his hands the entire management of our salon. You must certainly meet him."

"I should like to. Chang, by the way, was telling me that your favorite Western composer is Mozart."

"That is so," came the reply. "Mozart has an austere elegance which we find very satisfying. He builds a house which is neither too big nor too little, and he furnishes it in perfect taste."

The exchange of comments continued until the tea-bowls were taken away; by that time Conway was able to remark quite calmly: "So, to resume our earlier discussion, you intend to keep us? That, I take it, is the important and invariable proviso?"

"You have guessed correctly, my son."

"In other words, we are to stay here forever?"

"I should greatly prefer to employ your excellent English idiom and say that we are all of us here 'for good.'"

"What puzzles me is why we four, out of all the rest of the world's inhabitants, should have been chosen."

Relapsing into his earlier and more consequential manner, the High Lama responded: "It is an intricate story, if you would care to hear it. You must know that we have always aimed, as far as possible, to keep our numbers in fairly constant

"我很乐意见见他，对了，张曾经跟我说过，在西方作曲家中您最喜欢的是莫扎特。"

"是这样的，"他回答道，"莫扎特的作品中有一种朴素的典雅，我们很喜欢听。我们的音乐家还建了一所大小适中的房屋，里面的家居摆设也非常有品味。"

直到茶碗撤下，他们之间的评论才停止；这时，康维又能够十分平静地说："那么，你可以继续讲我们之前讨论的话题吗？我想起来了，刚才那个，就是那个又重要又永恒不变的条例。"

"你猜对了，我的孩子。"

"也就是说，我们注定得永远待在这里？"

"我想我很应该用你们经典的英语习语说，我们大家都将'永远地'待在这里。"

"令我百思不得其解的是，世界上有那么多人，为什么偏偏是我们这4个人被选中。"

大喇嘛又恢复了原先的样子，而且态度更加傲慢。他答道："这可是个错综复杂的故事，如果你想听的话。你必须要明白，我们一直致力于尽可能地保持我们的人员数量，并不断地发掘新的成员——

recruitment – since, apart from any other reasons, it is pleasant to have with us people of various ages and representative of different periods. Unfortunately, since the recent European War and the Russian Revolution, travel and exploration in Tibet have been almost completely held up; in fact, our last visitor, a Japanese, arrived in 1912, and was not, to be candid, a very valuable acquisition. You see, my dear Conway, we are not quacks or charlatans; we do not and cannot guarantee success; some of our visitors derive no benefit at all from their stay here; others merely live to what might be called a normally advanced age and then die from some trifling ailment. In general we have found that Tibetans, owing to their being inured to both the altitude and other conditions, are much less sensitive than outside races; they are charming people, and we have admitted many of them, but I doubt if more than a few will pass their hundredth year. The Chinese are a little better, but even among them we have a high percentage of failures. Our best subjects, undoubtedly, are the Nordic and Latin races of Europe; perhaps the Americans would be equally adaptable, and I count it our great good fortune that we have at last, in the person of one of your companions, secured a citizen of that nation. But I must continue with the answer to your question.

因为除去别的理由，光是让我们当中有各种不同年龄和代表不同时期的人就是件很令人高兴的事——可惜的是，自从近来爆发了欧洲战争和俄国革命后，西藏的旅行和探险活动几乎都停滞了；事实上，我们最后一名访客，一个日本人，还是1912年来到这里的，说实在的，他并不是很有价值。你知道，亲爱的康维，我们既非庸医，亦非江湖术士，我们不去担保，也不能担保访客能获得成功；有些我们的访者待在这里却没得到丝毫益处；其他一些人也仅仅只是长寿一些，最后还是死于一些微不足道的小毛病。通常来说，我们发现藏族人由于适应了这里的海拔和其他条件，就没有外来种族那么敏感；他们的人都很招人喜欢，所以我们吸纳了他们中不少人，但是我觉得只会有少数几个人能成功。汉族人稍微好一点，但是即使是在他们中间我们的失败率也很高。我们的理想目标，不可否认，是欧洲的斯堪的纳维亚人和拉丁人种；也许美国人同样也能适应。我把这当成我们的极大幸运，能最终在你的几个同伴中找到那个种族中的一员。但是我必须继续回答你提出的问题。现在的情况是，正如我一直在解释的，我们的成员有近 20 年没有更新了，同时在那期间我们又失去了几位成员，这样问题就出现了。不过几年前，

The position was, as I have been explaining, that for nearly two decades we had welcomed no new-comers, and as there had been several deaths during that period, a problem was beginning to arise. A few years ago, however, one of our number came to the rescue with a novel idea; he was a young fellow, a native of our valley, absolutely trustworthy and in fullest sympathy with our aims; but, like all the valley people, he was denied by nature the chance that comes more fortunately to those from a distance. It was he who suggested that he should leave us, make his way to some surrounding country, and bring us additional colleagues by a method which would have been impossible in an earlier age. It was in many respects a revolutionary proposal, but we gave our consent after due consideration. For we must move with the times, you know, even at Shangri-La."

"You mean that he was sent out deliberately to bring someone back by air?"

"Well, you see, he was an exceedingly gifted and resourceful youth, and we had great confidence in him. It was his own idea, and we allowed him a free hand in carrying it out. All we knew definitely was that the first stage of his plan included a period of tuition at an American flying-school."

我们的一名成员突发奇想提出了一个解决之道,他是个年轻人,在我们山谷中土生土长,十分可靠而且完全同情我们的目标,但是像所有的山谷人那样,他受自然因素的限制没能得到像远方来的那些人一样幸运的机会。就是他提议他要离开我们,设法到周围地区带回新的成员,这种方法在以前看来是绝对不可能的。从许多方面看,这都是一个完全创新的提议,但是我们在经过适当的思考之后还是点头了,因为我们也必须跟时代一起进步,你知道,即使是在香格里拉这样的地方。"

"你是说,他是被故意派出来用飞机带回一些人的?"

"好吧,你看,他是个天资聪颖且足智多谋的年轻人,我们对他很有信心。那是他自己的想法,而我们只是放手让他去付诸实践。我们可以肯定的一件事是,他计划的第一步包括到美国一所飞行学校参加培训。"

"But how could he manage the rest of it? It was only by chance that there happened to be that aeroplane at Baskul –"

"True, my dear Conway – many things are by chance. But it happened, after all, to be just the chance that Talu was looking for. Had he not found it, there might have been another chance in a year or two – or perhaps, of course, none at all. I confess I was surprised when our sentinels gave news of his descent on the plateau. The progress of aviation is rapid, but it had seemed likely to me that much more time would elapse before an average machine could make such a crossing of the mountains."

"It wasn't an average machine. It was a rather special one, made for mountain-flying."

"Again by chance? Our young friend was indeed fortunate. It is a pity that we cannot discuss the matter with him – we were all grieved at his death. You would have liked him, Conway."

Conway nodded slightly; he felt it very possible. He said, after a silence: "But what's the idea behind it all?"

"My son, your way of asking that question gives me infinite pleasure. In the course of a somewhat long experience it has never before been put to me in tones of such calmness. My revelation has been greeted in almost every conceivable

"那他后面的一切是怎么完成的呢？这次只是因为碰巧那架飞机正好在巴斯库……"

"是的，我亲爱的康维——生活中很多事都是巧合，但终究它只是刚好成了塔鲁正在寻找的契机。就算他没有把握这一机会，也会有其他机会在一两年之内出现的——当然，也可能一点机会也没有。我承认当我们的哨兵报告他已经在高原上降落时，我很意外。航空学发展很迅速，可是我一直认为造出这样能飞越山峦的普及型飞机还需要很长的时间。"

"那可不是普通飞机，是一种很特别，专门针对在山区飞行制造的。"

"又是碰巧？我们这位年轻的小伙子真是运气好。很遗憾我们不能和他谈论这点——对他的死我们都感到万分悲痛。你应该会喜欢他的，康维。"

康维轻轻点点头，他认为这很有可能。沉默一阵后，他说："可这些事情背后究竟有什么目的呢？"

"我的孩子，你问这个问题的方式让我十分欣慰。因为这么长时间以来，还从来没有人用这么平静的语气问过我这个问题。我每每道出实情的时候，几乎遇到了一切可

manner – with indignation, distress, fury, disbelief, and hysteria – but never until this night with mere interest. It is, however, an attitude that I most cordially welcome. To-day you are interested; to-morrow you will feel concern; eventually, it may be, I shall claim your devotion."

"That is more than I should care to promise."

"Your very doubt pleases me – it is the basis of profound and significant faith… But let us not argue. You are interested, and that, from you, is much. All I ask in addition is that what I tell you now shall remain, for the present, unknown to your three companions."

Conway was silent.

"The time will come when they will learn, like you, but that moment, for their own sakes, had better not be hastened. I am so certain of your wisdom in this matter that I do not ask for a promise; you will act, I know, as we both think best… Now let me begin by sketching for you a very agreeable picture. You are still, I should say, a youngish man by the world's standards; your life, as people say, lies ahead of you; in the normal course you might expect twenty or thirty years of only slightly and gradually diminishing activity. By no means a cheerless prospect, and I can hardly expect you to see it as I

以想象的态度——有义愤填膺的、悲痛万分的、狂暴的、怀疑的，还有歇斯底里的——然而，在今天晚上之前还从来没有人只是因为感兴趣而问我。但是，这是我最热情欢迎的一种态度，今天你感兴趣；明天你将会关心；最后可能我会要求你献身。"

"这恐怕超出了我能保证的限度。"

"我很高兴你有这样的怀疑态度——这是深远而有意义的信仰的基础——不过，我们还是别争了。你感兴趣，那已经够了。我所要求的只有一点，我现在告诉你的一切，你要对你那 3 个同伴保密。"

康维保持沉默。

"总有那么一天他们也会知道，就像你一样，但为他们好，这一刻最好不要来得太快。我非常相信你的智慧，所以我不要你做出保证；你能做到，我知道，就像我们想的最好的那样……现在，让我为你描绘一幅非常令人愉快的画面。你啊，要我说，从世界上的标准来看你仍然算得上年轻人；你的生活，正如人们所说，就在你的面前。在一般情况下，你可能预计 20 至 30 年的时间自己只是少量逐渐地减少活动。这绝不是一个凄惨的前景，我几乎不指望你会有和我有同样的看法——这会是一段细微而又

do – as a slender, breathless, and far too frantic interlude. The first quarter-century of your life was doubtless lived under the cloud of being too young for things, while the last quarter-century would normally be shadowed by the still darker cloud of being too old for them; and between those two clouds, what small and narrow sunlight illumines a human lifetime! But you, it may be, are destined to be more fortunate, since by the standards of Shangri-La your sunlit years have scarcely yet begun. It will happen, perhaps, that decades hence you will feel no older than you are to-day – you may preserve, as Henschell did, a long and wondrous youth. But that, believe me, is only an early and superficial phase. There will come a time when you will age like others, though far more slowly, and into a condition infinitely nobler; at eighty you may still climb to the pass with a young man's gait, but at twice that age you must not expect the whole marvel to have persisted. We are not workers of miracles; we have made no conquest of death or even of decay. All we have done and can sometimes do is to slacken the *tempo* of this brief interval that is called life. We do this by methods which are as simple here as they are impossible elsewhere; but make no mistake; the end awaits us all.

"Yet it is, nevertheless, a prospect of

令人紧张的插曲。你生命的前 25 年（1/4 世纪），无疑已被年幼无知的阴霾所笼罩，而后 25 年又一般生活在更加黑暗的老朽迂腐的阴影之下；而两者之间，只有多么短促而狭小的一束阳光能照亮一个人的生命啊！但是你可能命中注定要比别人幸运，因为以香格里拉的标准来看，你生命中充满阳光的日子几乎还没有开始。有可能，也许，再过几十年你也不会觉得自己比现在变得更老——你有可能保持，就像亨斯齐尔那样，长久而美好的青春。但是，相信我，那还只是前期而且表象的阶段而已。总会有一天当你和其他人年龄一样时，即使缓慢得多，也会进入一种无限崇高的状态。80 岁时你还能爬上山隘，迈着像年轻人一样的步子，可是到了这个数字两倍的年纪时（160 岁），你就不能指望所有这些奇迹还会延续。我们不能创造奇迹，我们不能战胜死亡，甚至不能战胜衰退。所有我们已经做的和有时能够做到的就是放慢那被称作生命的短暂间隙的速度。我们用的方法在这儿非常简单，在别处却不可能实现。但绝不能出错，因为结局等着我们所有的人。"

"然而，我将为你呈现一个非

much charm that I unfold for you – long tranquillities during which you will observe a sunset as men in the outer world hear the striking of a clock, and with far less care. The years will come and go, and you will pass from fleshly enjoyments into austerer but no less satisfying realms; you may lose the keenness of muscle and appetite, but there will be gain to match your loss; you will achieve calmness and profundity, ripeness and wisdom, and the clear enchantment of memory. And, most precious of all, you will have Time – that rare and lovely gift that your Western countries have lost the more they have pursued it. Think for a moment. You will have time to read – never again will you skim pages to save minutes, or avoid some study lest it prove too engrossing. You have also a taste for music – here, then, are your scores and instruments, with Time, unruffled and unmeasured to give you their richest savor. And you are also, we will say, a man of good fellowship – does it not charm you to think of wise and serene friendships, a long and kindly traffic of the mind from which death may not call you away with his customary hurry? Or, if it is solitude that you prefer, could you not employ our pavilions to enrich the gentleness of lonely thoughts?"

The voice made a pause which Conway did not seek to fill.

常迷人的景象——在观察日落时的感受到长久的安宁，外界的人们则是满不在意地听时针摆动的声音，满不在意这一景色。时光流转，你的感受将从肉体的愉悦转化到朴素的状态，而满足感并不会减少，你可能会失去对肉欲和食欲的渴求，可同样你将会得到同等的东西作为补偿；你将收获冷静和深沉、成熟和智慧，还有魔力能使记忆清晰。而最珍贵的一点是，你将拥有时间——那珍稀而美好的礼物——你们西方国家越是追寻它，就失去得越多。你将会有时间去阅读——再也不用匆匆略读来节省时间，或避免研究一些不是那么吸引人的课题。你会有音乐品味——你在这儿有乐谱和乐器，还有时间，音乐能够不被打扰，并且给你无穷的最多姿多彩的乐趣。还有，我们觉得你人缘不错——这难道没有吸引你考虑一种明智而又宁静的友情，一种长久而友好的心神交流，能让死亡不像他一贯那样匆忙地带走你吗？或者说，如果你更喜欢独居，你能不用我们的亭台去充实独自思索的从容与惬意吗？"

他暂时停了下来，而康维并不想去填补这个间隙。

"You make no comment, my dear Conway. Forgive my eloquence – I belong to an age and a nation that never considered it bad form to be articulate… But perhaps you are thinking of wife, parents, children, left behind in the world? Or maybe ambitions to do this or that? Believe me, though the pang may be keen at first, in a decade from now even its ghost will not haunt you. Though in point of fact, if I read your mind correctly, you have no such griefs."

Conway was startled by the accuracy of the judgment. "That's so," he replied. "I'm unmarried; I have few close friends and no ambitions."

"No ambitions? And how have you contrived to escape those widespread maladies?"

For the first time Conway felt that he was actually taking part in a conversation. He said: "It always seemed to me in my profession that a good deal of what passed for success would be rather disagreeable, apart from needing more effort than I felt called upon to make. I was in the Consular Service – quite a subordinate post, but it suited me well enough."

"Yet your soul was not in it?"

"Neither my soul nor my heart nor more than half my energies. I'm naturally rather lazy."

The wrinkles deepened and twisted till

"你一句评论也不发表,我亲爱的康维。请原谅我辩解太多——我的时代和民族从不把能言善辩当做坏事……你也许正想着妻子、父母和孩子,他们还留在另一个世界?或是你在思考做这些事的抱负?相信我,尽管一开始会很痛苦,但再过 10 年,连它的魂魄都不会来纠缠你。不过,实际上,假如我猜得没错的话,你根本没有考虑过这种悲伤的事。"

康维被这准确的判断吓到了。"是这样的,"他回答道,"我还是单身,我几乎没有密友、也没有抱负。"

"没有抱负?那你是怎么设法摆脱那些四处笼罩的不正之风的呢?"

康维第一次觉得他确实是在进行一场对话。他说:"我总是觉得,在我的职业生涯中,为成功而做过的很多事情都是让人相当厌恶的,除了需要比我所想象的更多的努力之外。我从事领事馆服务工作是一个相当次要的职位,但非常适合我。"

"但你的心根本不在那?"

"我的热情、心思甚至一半干劲都不在那上面。我天生就很懒散。"

大喇嘛脸上的皱纹一直在加

Conway realized that the High Lama was very probably smiling. "Laziness in doing stupid things can be a great virtue," resumed the whisper. "In any case, you will scarcely find us exacting in such a matter. Chang, I believe, explained to you our principle of moderation, and one of the things in which we are always moderate is activity. I myself, for instance, have been able to learn ten languages; the ten might have been twenty had I worked immoderately. But I did not. And it is the same in other directions; you will find us neither profligate nor ascetic. Until we reach an age when care is advisable, we gladly accept the pleasures of the table, while – for the benefit of our younger colleagues – the women of the valley have happily applied the principle of moderation to their own chastity. All things considered, I feel sure you will get used to our ways without much effort. Chang, indeed, was very optimistic – and so, after this meeting, am I. But there is, I admit, an odd quality in you that I have never met in any of our visitors hitherto. It is not quite cynicism, still less bitterness; perhaps it is partly disillusionment, but it is also a clarity of mind that I should not have expected in anyone younger than – say, a century or so. It is, if I had to put a single word to it, passionlessness."

Conway answered: "As good a word as

深而且沟壑纵横，直到康维意识到，他很可能是在笑。"在做傻事时的懒惰可是个很好的美德，"他又开始嘀咕了，"无论如何，你都很难发现我们在对这种事提出要求。我相信张已经给你们讲过我们适度的原则，我们总是适度做的事就是行动。我自己，比方说，曾能学10门语言，如果我不懂节制的话，这10门会变为20门，但是我没有。在其他方面也是一样；你会发现我们既不奢靡也不苦修。直到我们到了一定年纪，需要关心照顾，我们才会很高兴地享受餐桌上的乐趣，而我们的年轻同僚们也会从中受益——因为山谷的女人们很乐意将这适度的标准应用到她们自身的贞洁上。考虑了所有方面之后，我觉得你肯定轻易就能适应我们的方式。张的确很乐观——所以通过这次见面，我也很乐观。但是，我承认你身上有一种奇怪的品质，迄今为止我还没有在其他任何一个来访者身上遇到过。不是那么愤世嫉俗，也没有那么辛酸。也许有一部分理想破灭，但头脑清晰，这是我绝不指望能在任何一个年纪不到100岁的人身上看到的，如果要用一个词来描述的话——就是激情缺失。"

康维回道："真是一语中的啊，

most, no doubt. I don't know whether you classify the people who come here, but if so, you can label me '1914-18.' That makes me, I should think, a unique specimen in your museum of antiquities – the other three who arrived along with me don't enter the category. I used up most of my passions and energies during the years I've mentioned, and though I don't talk much about it, the chief thing I've asked from the world since then is to leave me alone. I find in this place a certain charm and quietness that appeals to me, and no doubt, as you remark, I shall get used to things."

"Is that all, my son?"

"I hope I am keeping well to your own rule of moderation."

"You are clever – as Chang told me, you are very clever. But is there nothing in the prospect I have outlined that tempts you to any stronger feeling?"

Conway was silent for an interval and then replied: "I was deeply impressed by your story of the past, but to be candid, your sketch of the future interests me only in an abstract sense. I can't look so far ahead. I should certainly be sorry if I had to leave Shangri-La to-morrow or next week, or perhaps even next year; but how I shall feel about it if I live to be a hundred isn't a matter to prophesy. I can face it, like any other future, but in order to make

毫无疑问。我不知道你是不是给来这儿的人都分类,如果是,你可以给我贴加上'1914–1918'的标签。我觉得,那样就能使我成为你们古董博物馆中与众不同的典型——另外3个和我一道来的人不属于这一类。在我刚提到的那些年里,我已经用尽了大部分的热情和精力,尽管如此,我很少提起这些,但从那时起,我对于这个世界的主要要求就是不要打扰我。我发现在这里有某种魔力和静谧很吸引我,这毫无疑问,就像你谈及的,我会适应这些事的。"

"就是这些,我的孩子?"

"我希望我能保持好你的适度标准。"

"你很聪明——就像张告诉我的一样——你非常聪明。但在我所描绘的前景中难道没有东西使你产生更强烈的感觉吗?"

康维沉默了一阵,然后说:"你所讲的过去的故事给我留下了非常深刻的印象,可是,坦白地说,你对未来的描绘我也感兴趣,但那只是一种抽象的感觉,我眼光没那么长远。如果我明天或者下周就得离开香格里拉,我肯定会很惋惜,或者甚至可能是明年,可是我该做何感想如果我能否活到100岁不是可以预言的。我能面对这个问题,就跟面对未来其他的事情一样。但

me keen it must have a point. I've sometimes doubted whether life itself has any; and if not, long life must be even more pointless."

"My friend, the traditions of this building, both Buddhist and Christian, are very reassuring."

"Maybe. But I'm afraid I still hanker after some more definite reason for envying the centenarian."

"There *is* a reason, and a very definite one indeed. It is the whole reason for this colony of chance-sought strangers living beyond their years. We do not follow an idle experiment, a mere whimsy. We have a dream and a vision. It is a vision that first appeared to old Perrault when he lay dying in this room in the year 1789. He looked back then on his long life, as I have already told you, and it seemed to him that all the loveliest things were transient and perishable, and that war, lust, and brutality might someday crush them until there were no more left in the world. He remembered sights he had seen with his own eyes, and with his mind he pictured others; he saw the nations strengthening, not in wisdom, but in vulgar passions and the will to destroy; he saw their machine power multiplying until a single-weaponed man might have matched a whole army of the Grand Monarque. And he perceived that when

是要让我对它有渴望，那么它本身就必须有意义。有时候我疑惑生命本身是否有任何意义；如果没有，长久的生命就更无意义了。"

"我的朋友，这座建筑结合了佛教和基督教传统，是非常让人安心的。"

"也许是，但是，我担心我还是需要一些更确切的理由来解释人们对百岁长寿老人的羡慕之情。"

"有一个理由，而且很确切。这也就是这群寻找机会的陌生人生活在他们时代之外的所有原因。我们不盲从无用的试验，那是纯粹的异想天开。我们有一个理想和想象。这一想象最开始出现在 1789 年老佩劳尔特弥留之际躺在这间屋里的时候。他回想了自己漫长的一生，就像我已经跟你讲过的，他发觉似乎所有最可爱的事物都那么短暂而且容易消亡。战争、欲望和兽行可能某天会把他们完全摧毁直到在这个世界一点残余也没有。他还清晰地记得那些他所亲眼目睹的画面，又想到了许多其他的情景；他看到那些国家在不断壮大不是以一种明智的方式，而是凭借着一种粗野的激情和毁灭的目的。他看到机器的力量在不断增加，直到一个装备武器的人就可以与法王路易十四整个军队相抗衡。他也感知到当他们用废墟填满了陆地

they had filled the land and sea with ruin, they would take to the air… Can you say that his vision was untrue?"

"True indeed."

"But that was not all. He foresaw a time when men, exultant in the technique of homicide, would rage so hotly over the world that every precious thing would be in danger, every book and picture and harmony, every treasure garnered through two millenniums, the small, the delicate, the defenseless – all would be lost like the lost books of Livy, or wrecked as the English wrecked the Summer Palace in Pekin."

"I share your opinion of that."

"Of course. But what are the opinions of reasonable men against iron and steel? Believe me, that vision of old Perrault will come true. And that, my son, is why *I* am here, and why *you* are here, and why we may pray to outlive the doom that gathers around on every side."

"To outlive it?"

"There is a chance. It will all come to pass before you are as old as I am."

"And you think that Shangri-La will escape?"

"Perhaps. We may expect no mercy, but we may faintly hope for neglect. Here we shall stay with our books and our music and our meditations, conserving the frail elegancies of a dying age, and seeking

和海洋时，他们就会转向天空……难道你能说他的想象不真实吗？"

"确实很真实。"

"但那还不是全部。他还预感到一个时代，疯狂沉浸在杀人技术中的人类会对这个世界变得狂怒以至于所有珍贵的东西将会处于危险的境地，所有的书籍、画像和一切和谐的事物，2000年来人类留存的宝贵的珍品，那些小巧精美而又脆弱的物品将像李维的著作那样散失殆尽，或者遭到破坏，就像英国人洗劫北京圆明园那样。"

"这方面，我同意你的看法。"

"当然，可是明智的人类是抱着一种什么观点在反对工业文明呢？相信我，老佩劳尔特的想象会变成现实。我的孩子，这就是我会在这里的原因，和你们在这里的原因，也是我们会祈求渡过笼罩在我们周围的厄运的原因。"

"摆脱它？"

"有一个机会，它会在你变得像我这么老之前到来的。"

"你觉得香格里拉可以摆脱？"

"也许，我们不奢望怜悯，可是我们会暗自希望被忽略。在这里我们能阅读、聆听和冥想，去保护一个衰败的时代中脆弱的精华，并寻找那种人们在激情耗尽时需要

such wisdom as men will need when their passions are all spent. We have a heritage to cherish and bequeath. Let us take what pleasure we may until that time comes."

"And then?"

"Then, my son, when the strong have devoured each other, the Christian ethic may at last be fulfilled, and the meek shall inherit the earth."

A shadow of emphasis had touched the whisper, and Conway surrendered to the beauty of it; again he felt the surge of darkness around, but now symbolically, as if the world outside were already brewing for the storm. And then he saw that the High Lama of Shangri-La was actually astir, rising from his chair, standing upright like the half-embodiment of a ghost. In mere politeness Conway made to assist; but suddenly a deeper impulse seized him, and he did what he had never done to any man before; he knelt, and hardly knew why he did.

"I understand you, Father," he said.

He was not perfectly aware of how at last he took his leave; he was in a dream from which he did not emerge till long afterwards. He remembered the night air icy after the heat of those upper rooms, and Chang's presence, a silent serenity, as they crossed the starlit courtyards together. Never had Shangri-La offered more concentrated loveliness to his eyes;

的理智。我们要珍惜遗产并传给后代，让我们去争取那一天到来时的欢乐和幸福。"

"然后呢？"

"然后，我的孩子，当强权们相互残杀的时候，基督教的道德准则也许最终能实现，然后顺从的人们将会传承这一切。"

一阵强调的阴影轻轻地笼罩着这位耳语者，康维沉浸在这美的感觉中；他再一次感觉到周围有一股黑暗的气场，但是现在象征性的，好像外面的世界正酝酿着一场暴风雪。后来他看到这位香格里拉的大喇嘛骚动起来，从椅子上站起来，直挺挺的像一个半现身的鬼魂。康维只是想礼貌性地过去帮个忙；可突然之间一种更强烈的冲动驱使着他，他做了一件之前从未对任何人做过的事情，他跪下了，但不知道原因。

"我明白，圣父。"他说。

他并不十分清楚他最后是怎么离开的；他就像在梦境之中，而这梦是他期盼了很久才出现的。他记得那晚离开楼上房间的暖气后，冰冷的空气凉得刺骨，在他们穿过那星光照耀的庭院时，张毫无声息地出现了。他还从未见过香格里拉如此浓缩的美景；这山谷像是静静地躺在悬崖边缘，整个画面就如明

the valley lay imaged over the edge of the cliff, and the image was of a deep unrippled pool that matched the peace of his own thoughts. For Conway had passed beyond astonishments. The long talk, with its varying phases, had left him empty of all save a satisfaction that was as much of the mind as of the emotions, and as much of the spirit as of either; even his doubts were now no longer harassing, but part of a subtle harmony. Chang did not speak, and neither did he. It was very late, and he was glad that all the others had gone to bed.

镜般的湖面完全契合此时他自己的心绪。康维早已处变不惊。这漫长的对话，涉及这么多话题，这使他脑中一片空白，无论在心智还是情感上他都感到满意，精神状态也很好，甚至于他的疑虑也不再让人心烦，反而构成了一种微妙的和谐。张什么也没说，他也没有。夜已经很深了，他很庆幸别的人都已上床休息了。

CHAPTER 9

第九章

IN the morning he wondered if all that he could call to mind were part of a waking or a sleeping vision.

He was soon reminded. A chorus of questions greeted him when he appeared at breakfast. "You certainly had a long talk with the boss last night," began the American. "We meant to wait up for you, but we got tired. What sort of a guy is he?"

"Did he say anything about the porters?" asked Mallinson eagerly.

"I hope you mentioned to him about having a missionary stationed here," said Miss Brinklow.

The bombardment served to raise in Conway his usual defensive armament. "I'm afraid I'm probably going to disappoint you all," he replied, slipping easily into the mood. "I didn't discuss with him the question of missions; he didn't mention the porters to me at all; and as for his appearance, I can only say that he's a very old man who speaks excellent English and is quite intelligent."

Mallinson cut in with irritation: "The main thing to us is whether he's to be trusted or not. Do you think he means to

早晨，他弄不清记忆中的事情到底是真实的还是在做梦。

很快他就明白了。吃早饭时，他一出现在早餐桌前，迎面就收到一连串问题。"你昨晚肯定和那个头头谈了很久吧，"那美国人开口了，"我们本来打算等你，可是我们太累了。他是哪种类型的人？"

"他有没有提到送货人？"马林逊急切地问道。

"我希望你跟他提了关于在这安置一位传教士的事。"布琳克罗小姐说道。

在接受一阵连珠炮似地提问之后，康维经常会有的防备意识又出现了，"恐怕我会让你们所有人失望了，"他回答着而且很快找到了状态，"我没有跟他讨论传教的问题，他也完全没有向我提到什么送货人，至于他的外貌，我只能说他年纪很大，英语极佳，而且很有智慧。"

马林逊愤怒地打断了他的说话："对我们来说最主要的是他是否值得信赖，你觉得他会让我们失

let us down?"

"He didn't strike me as a dishonorable person."

"Why on earth didn't you worry him about the porters?"

"It didn't occur to me."

Mallinson stared at him incredulously. "I can't understand you, Conway. You were so damned good in that Baskul affair that I can hardly believe you're the same man. You seem to have gone all to pieces."

"I'm sorry."

"No good being sorry. You ought to buck up and look as if you cared what happens."

"You misunderstand me. I meant that I was sorry to have disappointed you."

Conway's voice was curt, an intended mask to his feelings, which were, indeed, so mixed that they could hardly have been guessed by others. He had slightly surprised himself by the ease with which he had prevaricated; it was clear that he intended to observe the High Lama's suggestion and keep the secret. He was also puzzled by the naturalness with which he was accepting a position which his companions would certainly and with some justification think traitorous; as Mallinson had said, it was hardly the sort of thing to be expected of a hero. Conway felt a sudden half-pitying fondness for the

望吗？"

"我觉得他不是那种不讲信誉的人。"

"你到底为什么不跟他提送货人的事呢？"

"忘了。"

马林逊不敢相信似的盯着他，"我真不理解你，康维，在巴斯库的事上你做得那么好，我都不敢相信这跟现在的你是同一个人。你似乎完全变了。"

"对不起。"

"不用抱歉，你应该重新振作，表现出你对发生的事情的关心。"

"你误会了，我是说我很抱歉让你们失望了。"

康维的话很简单，他想掩饰自己的想法，他的思绪很复杂，其他人很难猜中。这么轻易就圆了个谎，他自己也有点被吓到。很明显他打算按照大喇嘛的建议保守秘密；同时他也很困扰，当他接受这个职位后，他的同伴肯定会满口说辞地批评他背信弃义。正如马林逊说过的，这根本不是什么能成为英雄的事情。康维突然对这个年轻人生出了一些怜惜之情；然后他狠下心想那些崇拜英雄的人们总要做好梦想被击碎的准备。马林逊在巴斯库是还只是乳臭未干的小毛孩，十分崇拜这位英俊勇敢的陆军上

youth; then he steeled himself by reflecting that people who hero-worship must be prepared for disillusionments. Mallinson at Baskul had been far too much the new boy adoring the handsome games-captain, and now the games-captain was tottering if not already fallen from the pedestal. There was always something a little pathetic in the smashing of an ideal, however false; and Mallinson's admiration might have been at least a partial solace for the strain of pretending to be what he was not. But pretense was impossible anyway. There was a quality in the air of Shangri-La – perhaps due to its altitude – that forbade one the effort of counterfeit emotion.

He said: "Look here, Mallinson, it's no use harping continually on Baskul. Of course I was different then – it was a completely different situation."

"And a much healthier one in my opinion. At least we knew what we were up against."

"Murder and rape – to be precise. You can call that healthier if you like."

The youth's voice rose in pitch as he retorted: "Well, I *do* call it healthier – in one sense. It's something I'd rather face than all this mystery business." Suddenly he added: "That Chinese girl, for instance – how did she get here? Did the fellow tell you?"

尉，可现在这上尉却几乎地位不保，如果说还没下台的话。当一个完美的偶像毁灭时总会有点可悲，但是他是假的；而马林逊的崇拜至少部分是为了减缓他假装扮演不是本来自己角色的紧张。可是假装是不可能的。香格里拉的空气有一种高贵的特质——也许由于它的海拔太高——不容许人虚情假意。

他说："是这样的，马林逊，一直念叨巴斯库的事一点用也没有。当然我不一样了——但现在的环境也完全不同了。"

"在我看来现在这个环境更加健康，至少，我们知道要反抗的是什么。"

"谋杀还有强奸——准确地说，你可以说那更加健康。"

这个年轻人提高声调反驳道："是，我是说这更健康——从某种意义上来讲。相比较那些神秘兮兮的事情，我更情愿面对这些，"突然他又说到，"比如说那满族姑娘——她是怎么来的？他有没有告诉你？"

"No. Why should he?"

"Well, why shouldn't he? And why shouldn't you ask, if you had any interest in the matter at all? Is it usual to find a young girl living with a lot of monks?"

That way of looking at it was one that had scarcely occurred to Conway before. "This isn't an ordinary monastery," was the best reply he could give after some thought.

"My God, it isn't!"

There was a silence, for the argument had evidently reached a dead-end. To Conway the history of Lo-Tsen seemed rather far from the point; the little Manchu lay so quietly in his mind that he hardly knew she was there. But at the mere mention of her Miss Brinklow had looked up suddenly from the Tibetan grammar which she was studying even over the breakfast table (just as if, thought Conway, with secret meaning, she hadn't all her life for it). Chatter of girls and monks reminded her of those stories of Indian temples that men missionaries told their wives, and that the wives passed on to their unmarried female colleagues. "Of course," she said between tightened lips, "the morals of this place are quite hideous – we might have expected that." She turned to Barnard as if inviting support, but the American only grinned. "I don't suppose you folks'd value my opinion on a matter

"没有。为什么他要说呢？"

"哦，为什么不呢？而你又为什么没有问他，如果你真的在乎这件事的话？难道一个年轻姑娘和那么多僧侣住在一起普遍吗？"

康维之前完全没有想到从这个角度看待这件事。"这不是普通的寺院。"这是他在思考一阵后得出的最好的回答。

"天哪，不是这样！"

大家陷入了一片沉默，因为讨论很明显走入了死胡同。对康维来说，罗珍（满族姑娘）的过去和这也没什么关系；这位满族少女在他脑海中的印象是如此朴素，以至于他几乎都想不起来她的存在。可是在他们一提起满族姑娘，布琳克罗小姐就突然从她沉浸的藏语语法中抬起头，要知道她连早餐时间都在学习（康维还以为她带着不可告人的目的真的在没命地在钻研）。刚才提起的关于女孩和僧侣的事让她想起那些印度寺院中的风流韵事，这些故事先是由男修道士告诉他们的妻子，然后这些妻子们又传给那些未婚的女同伴们。"当然，"她双唇紧闭说道，"这些地方的道德风气骇人听闻——这些我们可能预料得到。"她转向巴纳德似乎是在求助，可这美国人只是咧嘴笑笑。"我不指望你们从道德的高度评价我的观点，"他冷冷地说，

of morals," he remarked dryly. "But I should say myself that quarrels are just as bad. Since we've gotter be here for some time yet, let's keep our tempers and make ourselves comfortable."

Conway thought this good advice, but Mallinson was still unplaced. "I can quite believe you find it more comfortable than Dartmoor," he said meaningly.

"Dartmoor? Oh, that's your big penitentiary? – I get you. Well, yes, I certainly never did envy the folks in them places. And there's another thing too – it don't hurt when you chip me about it. Thick-skinned and tender-hearted, that's my mixture."

Conway glanced at him in appreciation, and at Mallinson with some hint of reproof; but then abruptly he had the feeling that they were all acting on a vast stage, of whose background only he himself was conscious; and such knowledge, so incommunicable, made him suddenly want to be alone. He nodded to them and went out into the courtyard. In sight of Karakal misgivings faded, and qualms about his three companions were lost in an uncanny acceptance of the new world that lay so far beyond their guesses. There came a time, he realized, when the strangeness of everything made it increasingly difficult to realize the strangeness of anything; when one took

"不过我应该表达我的观点，争吵没有什么好处。既然我们不得已要在这里待一段时间了，那咱们就都收收脾气，自己也舒服点吧。"

康维认为这主意不错，但马林逊还是显得不安。"我十分坚信，你会觉得这比达特穆尔更舒服。"他有所指地说道。

"达特穆尔？哦，你们那个大监狱？我懂了。好吧，没错，我当然从未忌妒过别的地方的人。还有另一件事——你用这个嘲讽我根本没有杀伤力，要知道我是集脸皮厚和脾气好于一身的。"

康维欣赏地瞥了他一眼，然后又向马林逊投去略带责备的目光；然而他突然有一种感觉，他们都在一个巨大的舞台上表演，而背景只有他自己清楚；这样的内容他又无法与人交流，这使他突然想一个人待着。他对他们点了点头然后溜到了院子里。一看到卡拉卡尔，他所有的疑虑都渐渐消失；对3位同伴的烦恼也消逝在对这个远超乎他们想象的新世界的不可思议的认可里。有这样一个时刻，他意识到，越是想看清事情的奥秘，这事情就越会令你觉得困难；当一个人只是因为惊讶而觉得事情理所当然时，对他自己而言就像对别人一样乏味。因而，他的个性在香格里拉得

things for granted merely because astonishment would have been as tedious for oneself as for others. Thus far had he progressed at Shangri-La, and he remembered that he had attained a similar though far less pleasant equanimity during his years at the War.

He needed equanimity, if only to accommodate himself to the double life he was compelled to lead. Thenceforward, with his fellow exiles, he lived in a world conditioned by the arrival of porters and a return to India; at all other times the horizon lifted like a curtain; time expanded and space contracted and the name Blue Moon took on a symbolic meaning, as if the future, so delicately plausible, were of a kind that might happen once in a blue moon only. Sometimes he wondered which of his two lives were the more real, but the problem was not pressing; and again he was reminded of the War, for during heavy bombardments he had had the same comforting sensation that he had many lives, only one of which could be claimed by death.

Chang, of course, now talked to him completely without reserve, and they had many conversations about the rule and routine of the lamasery. Conway learned that during his first five years he would live a normal life, without any special

以更进一步的发展，他想起了曾经在战争年代练就一种相似但是远没这么欢乐的镇定。

只要他要去适应那被迫的双重生活，他就需要冷静。同伴都被流放了，从那之后，他就生活在送货人的到达与返回到印度的世界里。在所有其他的时间，地平线就像窗帘一样被拉起，时间在延展、空间在收缩，而蓝月亮也被赋予了象征性的意义，未来，如此精美得似乎可以相信只能是在那一弯蓝月亮中发生得一类。有时候他也想知道他那双重生活中哪一个更为真实，但这一问题也并不紧迫；他又一次想起了战争年代，因为在那炮火狂轰滥炸之中，他也曾有过同样舒适的感觉，觉得自己有很多条命，而只有其中一条会被死神带走。

张现在跟他说话毫无保留，他们谈了很多关于喇嘛寺的规章制度和生活惯例的事。康维得知，在开始的5年中他会过正常的生活，而不受任何方式的影响；按张的说法，这样能"使身体适应这里的海

regimen; this was always done, as Chang said, "to enable the body to accustom itself to the altitude, and also to give time for the dispersal of mental and emotional regrets."

Conway remarked with a smile: "I suppose you're certain, then, that no human affection can outlast a five-year absence?"

"It can, undoubtedly," replied the Chinese, "but only as a fragrance whose melancholy we may enjoy."

After the probationary five years, Chang went on to explain, the process of retarding age would begin, and if successful, might give Conway half a century or so at the apparent age of forty – which was not a bad time of life at which to remain stationary.

"What about yourself?" Conway asked. "How did it work out in your case?"

"Ah, my dear sir, I was lucky enough to arrive when I was quite young – only twenty-two. I was a soldier, though you might not have thought it; I had command of troops operating against brigand tribes in the year 1855. I was making what I should have called a reconnaissance if I had ever returned to my superior officers to tell the tale, but in plain truth I had lost my way in the mountains, and of my men only seven out of over a hundred survived the rigors of the climate. When at last I

拔，也要有一段时间来驱散精神上和情感上的悔意"。

康维笑着说到："我猜你接下来肯定要说，没有一种人类感情能连续断绝 5 年？"

"能够，毫无疑问，"这个汉人答道，"但这只像香水那样，我们享受的是他的悲伤。"

在这 5 年的准备时间过后，张接着解释说，延缓衰老的程序就会开启，如果成功的话，这会使康维在半个世纪后看起来依然像现在这样只有 40 岁——这个能保持静止的时间刚好是生命中的好时段。

"那你呢？"康维问，"你这是什么情况？"

"啊，亲爱的先生，我非常幸运能在很年轻的时候就来到这里——那时我只有 22 岁。你可能想不到，我曾经是个军人；1855 年，我曾指挥部队打土匪。如果我回去向我上级汇报任务了的话，应该说当时我正在进行一次所谓的侦察任务，但是坦白说，我在山里迷了路，而我手下百十来号人中只有 7 个挺过了这寒冷的气候。最后当我被救到香格里拉时已相当虚弱，只是因为年轻力壮才活过来的。"

was rescued and brought to Shangri-La I was so ill that extreme youth and virility alone could have saved me."

"Twenty-two," echoed Conway, performing the calculation. "So you're now ninety-seven?"

"Yes. Very soon, if the lamas give their consent, I shall receive full initiation."

"I see. You have to wait for the round figure?"

"No, we are not restricted by any definite age limit, but a century is generally considered to be an age beyond which the passions and moods of ordinary life are likely to have disappeared."

"I should certainly think so. And what happens afterwards? How long do you expect to carry on?"

"There is reason to hope that I shall enter lamahood with such prospects as Shangri-La has made possible. In years, perhaps another century or more."

Conway nodded. "I don't know whether I ought to congratulate you – you seem to have been granted the best of both worlds, a long and pleasant youth behind you, and an equally long and pleasant old age ahead. When did you begin to grow old in appearance?"

"When I was over seventy. That is often the case, though I think I may still claim to look younger than my years."

"Decidedly. And suppose you were to

"22,"康维说道，一面默算，"那么你现在97岁？"

"对，很快，只要喇嘛同意的话，我就可以完全开始了。"

"我懂了。你在等那个整数？"

"不是，我们在年龄上没有任何绝对的限制，但是，一般看来，过了100岁，凡人的冲动和心绪就已经基本上消失了。"

"我也这么认为。那然后呢？你准备坚持多久？"

"照这样看来，我有理由期望有一天能加入喇嘛这个群体，因为香格里拉使这变为可能。也许是几年，也许是一个世纪，或者更久。"

康维点了点头："我不知道是否该祝贺你——你似乎已经拥有了两个世界的最美好的东西，一段去的长久而愉快的青年时光，和一段即将到来的同样漫长而愉快的晚年。你是什么时候开始在外表上变老的呢？"

"过了70岁，通常是这样的，不过我想我还是可以说我比实际年龄看上去要年轻。"

"肯定嘛。假如说你现在要离

leave the valley now, what would happen?"

"Death, if I remained away for more than a very few days."

"The atmosphere, then, is essential?"

"There is only one valley of Blue Moon, and those who expect to find another are asking too much of nature."

"Well, what would have happened if you had left the valley, say, thirty years ago, during your prolonged youth?"

Chang answered: "Probably I should have died even then. In any case, I should have acquired very quickly the full appearance of my actual age. We had a curious example of that some years ago, though there had been several others before. One of our number had left the valley to look out for a party of travelers who we had heard might be approaching. This man, a Russian, had arrived here originally in the prime of life, and had taken to our ways so well that at nearly eighty he did not look more than half as old. He should have been absent no longer than a week (which would not have mattered), but unfortunately he was taken prisoner by nomad tribes and carried away some distance. We suspected an accident and gave him up for lost. Three months later, however, he returned to us, having made his escape. But he was a very different man. Every year of his age was

开山谷，会发生什么？"

"死，如果我离开超过一两天的话。"

"空气是决定性因素么？"

"世界上只有唯一一个蓝月亮山谷，那些指望能找到第二个的人对自然要求太多了。"

"那，如果你在 30 年前离开山谷又会怎样呢，在你还处在长期的青春中时？"

张答道："也许那时我就已经死了。无论如何，我很快就会变得与我的实际年龄一样老。几年之前我们就曾有过一个奇怪的例子，以前也有过另外几次。我们的一个人离开山谷去寻找听说正在朝这里行进的一队旅行者。这个俄国人很早就来到了这里，对我们这一套方法适应得很好，以至于将近 80 岁时看起来还不到 40 岁。本来他出去不该超过一个星期（这没有什么关系），但很不幸他被游牧部落关起来带到了很远的地方。我们推测出了什么差错，以为就这样他就丢了，也就放弃了。然而 3 个月之后，他又回来了，成功逃了出来。但他成了个不一样的人，光阴在他的脸上和动作上都留下了痕迹，不久他就死了，像一个老人一样。"

in his face and behavior, and he died shortly afterwards, as an old man dies."

Conway made no remark for some time. They were talking in the library, and during most of the narrative he had been gazing through a window towards the pass that led to the outer world; a little wisp of cloud had drifted across the ridge. "A rather grim story, Chang," he commented at length. "It gives one the feeling that Time is like some balked monster, waiting outside the valley to pounce on the slackers who have managed to evade him longer than they should."

"*Slackers*?" queried Chang. His knowledge of English was extremely good, but sometimes a colloquialism proved unfamiliar.

"'Slacker,'" explained Conway, "is a slang word meaning a lazy fellow, a good-for-nothing. I wasn't, of course, using it seriously."

Chang bowed his thanks for the information. He took a keen interest in languages and liked to weigh a new word philosophically. "It is significant," he said after a pause, "that the English regard slackness as a vice. We, on the other hand, should vastly prefer it to tension. Is there not too much tension in the world at present, and might it not be better if more people were slackers?"

"I'm inclined to agree with you,"

很长一段时间，康维都没有说话。他们在图书室中交谈着，而在听张叙述的大部分时间里，他都透过窗户朝那条通向外界的隧道眺望；一小团白云横曳在山岭之上。"一个相当残忍恐怖的故事，张，"他最后说，"这让人觉得时间就像一个畏缩不前的魔鬼，等候在山谷的外面准备扑向那些逃避它过久的懒汉们。"

"懒汉？"张表示怀疑。他的英语知识极其出色，可偶尔对某个口语不太熟悉。

"懒汉，"康维解释道，"是一个俚语词汇，代表一个懒惰、毫无用处的家伙。当然了，我没有很认真地在用它。"

张点头对这个小知识表示感谢。他在语言方面有兴趣，而且喜欢从哲学角度权衡一个新词。"这有很深的意味啊，"他停顿一下之后说道，"英国人将懒惰视为一种恶习，但我们却相反，相对于紧张，我们普遍更喜欢慵懒。在这个世界上，难道人们没有过于紧张吗，倘若更多的人是懒汉难道不是更好吗？"

"我倾向于同意你的看法。"

Conway answered with solemn amusement.

During the course of a week or so after the interview with the High Lama, Conway met several others of his future colleagues. Chang was neither eager nor reluctant to make the introductions, and Conway sensed a new and, to him, rather attractive atmosphere in which urgency did not clamor nor postponement disappoint. "Indeed," as Chang explained, "some of the lamas may not meet you for a considerable time – perhaps years – but you must not be surprised at that. They are prepared to make your acquaintance when it may so happen, and their avoidance of hurry does not imply any degree of unwillingness." Conway, who had often had similar feelings when calling on new arrivals at foreign consulates, thought it a very intelligible attitude.

The meetings he did have, however, were quite successful, and conversation with men thrice his age held none of the social embarrassments that might have obtruded in London or Delhi. His first encounter was with a genial German named Meister, who had entered the lamasery during the 'eighties, as the survivor of an exploring party. He spoke English well, though with an accent. A day or two later a second introduction took

大约在与大喇嘛会面的那周期间，康维见了另外几个他未来的同僚。张既不急迫也不勉强地做着引荐，而康维意识到一种崭新的，对他而言相当有吸引力的氛围，在这种氛围里紧急的事既不令人大声喧哗，也没有拖延的失望。"确实，"张解释道，"有一些喇嘛可能在相当长的时间里都不会见你——也许很多年——但你对此千万不必惊奇。当会面应该要发生时，他们会准备好和你相识，他们想避免急急忙忙的会面，这不意味着任何程度的不情愿。"每当康维去外国大使馆拜见新到任的官员时，经常会有相似的感觉，他觉得这是一种非常能被理解的态度。

但他确实有过一些会晤，而且相当成功，那是和他年纪3倍的人交谈，没有一丝在伦敦和德里可能出现的那种强加于人的社交尴尬。他的第一次会面，是与一个亲切的德国人，名叫梅斯特，曾经在80年代期间作为一个探险队的幸存者进入了喇嘛寺。他英文讲得很好，虽然带点口音。一两天之后他又便发生了第二次引见，康维很享受他与大喇嘛特别提及的那个艾

place, and Conway enjoyed his first talk with the man whom the High Lama had particularly mentioned – Alphonse Briac, a wiry, small-statured Frenchman who did not look especially old, though he announced himself as a pupil of Chopin. Conway thought that both he and the German would prove agreeable company. Already he was subconsciously analyzing, and after a few further meetings he reached one or two general conclusions; he perceived that though the lamas he met had individual differences, they all possessed that quality for which agelessness was not an outstandingly good name, but the only one he could think of. Moreover, they were all endowed with a calm intelligence which pleasantly overflowed into measured and well-balanced opinions. Conway could give an exact response to that kind of approach, and he was aware that they realized it and were gratified. He found them quite as easy to get on with as any other group of cultured people he might have met, though there was often a sense of oddity in hearing reminiscences so distant and apparently so casual. One white-haired and benevolent-looking person, for instance, asked Conway, after a little conversation, if he were interested in the Brontës. Conway said he was, to some extent, and the other replied: "You

福斯·布里亚克之间的第一次交谈，他是个瘦长结实、身材矮小的法国人，看起来没有特别老，尽管他将自己宣称为肖邦的学生。康维认为他和那个德国人两个人都将会是很好相处的伙伴。他已经在下意识地分析了，然后在几次更深入的会面之后，他得出了一到两个普遍的结论，他觉察到虽然他所见过的这些喇嘛存在个体的差异；但他们全部拥有一个特质，就是觉得"长生不老"并非一个非常好的称呼，可这是他能够想到的唯一一个词。此外，他们都被赋予一种镇定的智慧，精妙绝伦地充斥在慎重而很均衡的观点之中。康维对于这种手法能够做出非常精确的反应，他意识到，他们都认识到这个问题并觉得很满意。他也发现他们就像有文化的人形成的任何其他团体一样，相当容易相处，虽然在聆听他回忆往事时，常常有一种古怪之感，是如此的冷淡，而且显而易见的漫不经心。举个例子，一个满头银发，模样慈眉善目的老人，在简短的交谈之后询问康维是否对柏拉图学说感兴趣。康维说在某种程度上是的，而老人回应道："你清楚，在 40 年代期间，当我在约克郡西区做一个副牧师时，我曾经造访过海沃斯，并在牧师住宅区住着。从到那里开始，我便对整个柏拉图课题作了一个研究——的确，

see, when I was a curate in the West Riding during the 'forties, I once visited Haworth and stayed at the Parsonage. Since coming here I've made a study of the whole Brontë problem – indeed, I'm writing a book on the subject. Perhaps you might care to go over it with me sometime?"

Conway responded cordially, and afterwards, when he and Chang were left together, commented on the vividness with which the lamas appeared to recollect their pre-Tibetan lives. Chang answered that it was all part of the training. "You see, my dear sir, one of the first steps toward the clarifying of the mind is to obtain a panorama of one's own past, and that, like any other view, is more accurate in perspective. When you have been among us long enough you will find your old life slipping gradually into focus as through a telescope when the lens is adjusted. Everything will stand out still and clear, duly proportioned and with its correct significance. Your new acquaintance, for instance, discerns that the really big moment of his entire life occurred when he was a young man visiting a house in which there lived an old parson and his three daughters."

"So I suppose I shall have to set to work to remember my own big moments?"

"It will not be an effort. They will come

我正在写一本关于这个话题的书，也许找个时候，你会愿意和我一起浏览一下？"

康维诚挚地回应。然后，他与张一起离开，评论着那些喇嘛回忆的他们入藏前的生活的生动画面。张回答那是修炼过程的所有部分。"你知道，我亲爱的先生，通往灵魂澄净的首要步骤之一，便是对自己的过去有一个全面的反省，就像对其他任何远景的展望，要力求准确和清晰。当你在我们当中待了足够长的时间后，你会发现你的晚年生活会逐渐潜移默化到一个焦点上，仿佛一台透镜被调准了的望远镜一般，每一件事情都会静止而清晰地凸显出来，并会依照它的正确含意适当地均衡分配。举个例子，你的新相识便很清楚意识到，他整个一生真正的重要时刻便是当在他还是一个年轻人时去拜访一个庄园，里面住着一个老者和他的 3 个女儿。"

"那么我觉得我应该开始回忆一下我自己的重要时刻了？"

"这不会有多费劲啊。它们会

to you."

"I don't know that I shall give them much of a welcome," answered Conway moodily.

But whatever the past might yield, he was discovering happiness in the present. When he sat reading in the library, or playing Mozart in the music room, he often felt the invasion of a deep spiritual emotion, as if Shangri-La were indeed a living essence, distilled from the magic of the ages and miraculously preserved against time and death. His talk with the High Lama recurred memorably at such moments; he sensed a calm intelligence brooding gently over every diversion, giving a thousand whispered reassurances to ear and eye. Thus he would listen while Lo-Tsen marshaled some intricate fugue rhythm, and wonder what lay behind the faint impersonal smile that stirred her lips into the likeness of an opening flower. She talked very little, even though she now knew that Conway could speak her language; to Mallinson, who liked to visit the music room sometimes, she was almost dumb. But Conway discerned a charm that was perfectly expressed by her silences.

Once he asked Chang her history, and learned that she came of royal Manchu stock. "She was betrothed to a prince of

出现在你脑海里的。"

"我不清楚我应当如何欢迎它们，"康维忧郁地回答道。

但不管过去收获了什么，他现在正在探索幸福。当他坐在图书室里，或者在音乐间弹奏莫扎特的乐曲时，他经常感觉到一种深邃的灵魂情感在入侵，仿佛香格里拉确实是生活的精髓，它被从岁月的魔力中提取出来，并奇迹般地保存下来以抵抗时间和死亡。他与大喇嘛的谈话在这样的时刻便记忆犹新地再现出来，思绪每一次轻轻地转换，他都感觉到一种镇定的智慧，对耳朵和眼睛给予 1000 次低声安慰。因此，当罗珍拨弄出一些难以理解的赋格曲韵律时，他会侧耳倾听，并猜想在那一丝微弱的不带个人情感的微笑背后隐藏的是什么，这种笑容牵动着她的小嘴仿佛变成了一朵盛开的鲜花。她很少讲话，即使她现在清楚康维会讲她的语言；而对偶尔也喜欢到音乐间的马林逊，她差不多就是个哑巴。但康维却觉察出一种迷人的魅力就是通过她的一言不发而完美地表达出来的。

有一次他向张询问她的来历，得知她出身满族皇族血统。"她被许配给一个土耳其王子，当她的轿

Turkestan, and was traveling to Kashgar to meet him when her carriers lost their way in the mountains. The whole party would doubtless have perished but for the customary meeting with our emissaries."

"When did this happen?"

"In 1884. She was eighteen."

"Eighteen *then*?"

Chang bowed. "Yes, we are succeeding very well with her, as you may judge for yourself. Her progress has been consistently excellent."

"How did she take things when she first came?"

"She was, perhaps, a little more than averagely reluctant to accept the situation – she made no protest, but we were aware that she was troubled for a time. It was, of course, an unusual occurrence – to intercept a young girl on the way to her wedding… We were all particularly anxious that she should be happy here." Chang smiled blandly. "I am afraid the excitement of love does not make for an easy surrender, though the first five years proved ample for their purpose."

"She was deeply attached, I suppose, to the man she was to have married?"

"Hardly that, my dear sir, since she had never seen him. It was the old custom, you know. The excitement of her affections was entirely impersonal."

Conway nodded, and thought a little

夫们在山里迷路时，她正在前往喀什与王子见面的路上，如果没有照例碰到我们的使者的话，毫无疑问，整个一队人马就毁灭了。"

"这事发生在什么时候？"

"1884 年，那时她才 18 岁。"

"那时 18 岁？"

张点头道："是的，我们在她身上进行得非常成功，你可以自行评判，她的进展一向非常好。"

"当她初来时，她如何适应呢？"

"她啊，接受起这个这种局面也许比一般人稍有一点困难和勉强——她没有任何抗议，可我们意识到她困扰了一段时间。当然，这是一件不寻常的事儿，在前往自己婚礼的路上，中途截取了这位年轻姑娘……我们所有人都特别焦急，她在这里应该过得很开心。"张温和地微微一笑，"我担心爱情的兴奋不会令她轻易屈服，尽管最初的 5 年对于他们的目的而言，被证明是足够的。"

"我猜，她被她准备要嫁的那个人所深深吸引？"

"应该不是那样，亲爱的先生，她从没见过那个王子。你清楚，这是一个古老的习俗，她对爱欲的兴奋之情完全是人人皆有的啊。"

康维点点头，稍有柔情般地想

tenderly of Lo-Tsen. He pictured her as she might have been half a century before, statuesque in her decorated chair as the carriers toiled over the plateau, her eyes searching the wind-swept horizons that must have seemed so harsh after the gardens and lotus-pools of the East. "Poor child!" he said, thinking of such elegance held captive over the years. Knowledge of her past increased rather than lessened his content with her stillness and silence; she was like a lovely cold vase, unadorned save by an escaping ray.

He was also content, though less ecstatically, when Briac talked to him of Chopin, and played the familiar melodies with much brilliance. It appeared that the Frenchman knew several Chopin compositions that had never been published, and as he had written them down, Conway devoted pleasant hours to memorizing them himself. He found a certain piquancy in the reflection that neither Cortot nor Pachmann had been so fortunate. Nor were Briac's recollections at an end; his memory continually refreshed him with some little scrap of tune that the composer had thrown off or improvised on some occasion; he took them all down on paper as they came into his head, and some were very delightful fragments. "Briac," Chang explained, "has not long been initiated, so you must make

起罗珍,他描绘着她在半世纪之前,庄重而优美地坐在她那被装饰一新的轿子里面的画面,当轿夫们艰苦地跋涉,穿过高原,她双眼寻找着狂风扫过的地平线。在看惯了那东方的花园和荷花池塘之后,似乎一定会觉得如此粗糙。"可怜的姑娘!"他说道,想着如此凄凉的场面会使自己着迷很多年。对她过往的了解增加而并非削减了他对她那恬静和沉默的满意之情;她就像一只可爱又冰冷的花瓶,未经修饰,却保留住了行将流逝的光华。

当布里亚克对他谈起肖邦,然后演奏起那熟悉的旋律时,他也觉得很满意,尽管不是那么心醉神迷。似乎这位法国人清楚好几首肖邦从未被发表过的作品,当他将它们写下来时,康维用了好几个愉快的钟头来自行记忆。想到卡托特和帕克曼都不能如此幸运时,他感觉到一种理所应当的痛快。布里亚克的回忆也没有结束,他的记忆持续不断提醒他,作曲家曲调中有一些小片断被删除了或者是在某些场合被即兴创作的;当这些音符蹦到他脑海中时,他便将它们全部在纸上记下来。某些片断是非常令人愉快的。"布里亚克,"张解释道,"他正式入门还并不太久,倘若他谈起很多关于肖邦的事情,你一定要予以允许,年轻一些的喇嘛很自然地被过往的事所迷住;这是要正视未

allowances if he talks a great deal about Chopin. The younger lamas are naturally preoccupied with the past; it is a necessary step to envisaging the future."

"Which is, I take it, the job of the older ones?"

"Yes. The High Lama, for instance, spends almost his entire life in clairvoyant meditation."

Conway pondered a moment and then said: "By the way, when do you suppose I shall see him again?"

"Doubtless at the end of the first five years, my dear sir."

But in that confident prophecy Chang was wrong, for less than a month after his arrival at Shangri-La Conway received a second summons to that torrid upper room. Chang had told him that the High Lama never left his apartments, and that their heated atmosphere was necessary for his bodily existence; and Conway, being thus prepared, found the change less disconcerting than before. Indeed, he breathed easily as soon as he had made his bow and been granted the faintest answering liveliness of the sunken eyes. He felt kinship with the mind beyond them, and though he knew that this second interview following so soon upon the first was an unprecedented honor, he was not in the least nervous or weighed down with solemnity. Age was to him no more an

来的必要步骤。"

"那我应该将什么视为上了年纪的喇嘛的工作呢？"

"哦，举个例子，大喇嘛几乎花费他全部的生命用于洞察和冥想。"

康维琢磨了片刻，然后说："顺便问一句，你觉得何时我会再见到他？"

"毫无疑问，就在这最初的 5 年结束时，我亲爱的先生。"

但张那信心满满的预言是错的，在康维抵达香格里拉不到一个月的时间里，便接到了第二次召见，前往那个非常炎热的上屋之中。张曾经告诉过他，大喇嘛从来不曾离开他的住所，那里面温热的氛围对他的身体十分必要。而这次，康维有了准备，觉得自己有了改变，不像之前那么惶恐不安了。的确，当他鞠躬并被那深陷的双眼中的活跃之情给予最微弱的回应时，他马上便呼吸自如了。他发现他与这双眼睛背后的思想很是相似，虽然他清楚第一次见面之后，如此快的出现第二次召见是一种空前的荣幸。但他没有丝毫的紧张或被严肃所压下去，对他来说，年纪比起头衔或者肤色，只是一个令人困扰的因素；他从来没有感觉到

obsessing factor than rank or color; he had never felt debarred from liking people because they were too young or too old. He held the High Lama in most cordial respect, but he did not see why their social relations should be anything less than urbane.

They exchanged the usual courtesies, and Conway answered many polite questions. He said he was finding the life very agreeable and had already made friendships.

"And you have kept our secrets from your three companions?"

"Yes, up to now. It has proved awkward for me at times, but probably less so than if I had told them."

"Just as I surmised; you have acted as you thought best. And the awkwardness, after all, is only temporary. Chang tells me he thinks that two of them will give little trouble."

"I daresay that is so."

"And the third?"

Conway replied: "Mallinson is an excitable youth – he's pretty keen to get back."

"You like him?"

"Yes, I like him very much."

At this point the tea-bowls were brought in, and talk became less serious between sips of the scented liquid. It was an apt convention, enabling the verbal

因为他们太年轻或太老而不许喜欢某个人，他以最为虔诚的尊敬对待大喇嘛，但他不清楚他们的社会关系为什么如此的彬彬有礼。

他们照例互相客套寒暄了一番。康维也回答了许多礼貌性的问题。他说他发现这种生活非常惬意而且已经交了一些朋友。

"你还对你的3个同伴保守着我们的秘密吧？"

"是的，直到现在。很多次，它令我非常尴尬，但如果我告诉他们，事情可能更麻烦。"

"就像我猜测的那样，你已经按照你想到的最佳情况去行动了，而尴尬毕竟仅仅是暂时的。张告诉我说他认为他们当中有两个人会带来一些小麻烦。"

"我敢说确实如此。"

"那么第三个呢？"

康维回应道："马林逊是个易激动的青年，他非常盼望回去。

"你喜欢他吗？"

"是的，我非常喜欢他。"

就在此时，茶碗被端了进来。在啜饮这香茗时，谈话变得不那么严肃了。这是一种恰当的习俗，能让洋溢着的言辞语句也获得一种

flow to acquire a touch of that almost frivolous fragrance, and Conway was responsive. When the High Lama asked him whether Shangri-La was not unique in his experience, and if the Western world could offer anything in the least like it, he answered with a smile: "Well, yes – to be quite frank, it reminds me very slightly of Oxford, where I used to lecture. The scenery there is not so good, but the subjects of study are often just as impractical, and though even the oldest of the dons is not quite so old, they appear to age in a somewhat similar way."

"You have a sense of humor, my dear Conway," replied the High Lama, "for which we shall all be grateful during the years to come."

几乎是最细微的芳香。当大喇嘛问到在他的经历中，香格里拉是否并非独特，西方世界是否也能够提供类似的任何东西时，他面带微笑回答道："哦！是的，相当坦白地说，它让我非常怀念牛津大学，我过去在那里讲课。那里的风景不是这么好，但研究的课题也经常不怎么实际，虽然就连那些年纪最大的学监都不是那么老，而且他们似乎是以有点类似这里的方式来计算年纪。"

"你具有一种幽默感，亲爱的康维，"大喇嘛回应道，"对此，我们所有人在未来的岁月都要心存感激。"

CHAPTER 10

第十章

"EXTRAORDINARY," Chang said, when he heard that Conway had seen the High Lama again. And from one so reluctant to employ superlatives, the word was significant. It had never happened before, he emphasized, since the routine of the lamasery became established; never had the High Lama desired a second meeting until the five years' probation had effected a purge of all the exile's likely emotions. "Because, you see, it is a great strain on him to talk to the average new-comer. The mere presence of human passions is an unwelcome and, at his age, an almost unendurable unpleasantness. Not that I doubt his entire wisdom in the matter. It teaches us, I believe, a lesson of great value – that even the fixed rules of our community are only moderately fixed. But it is extraordinary, all the same."

To Conway, of course, it was no more extraordinary than anything else, and after he had visited the High Lama on a third and fourth occasion, he began to feel that it was not very extraordinary at all. There seemed, indeed, something almost preordained in the ease with which their two minds approached each other; it was

当张听说康维再次看到了大喇嘛时，他感叹道："非比寻常。"从一个很难说出夸奖话语之人的嘴里说出来，可见此话意义重大。他强调道，自从喇嘛寺的规章制度建立开始，从未发生过这种情况；除非5年的考验期内能达到对陌生人全部可能情感的净化之前，大喇嘛从不强烈要求第二次会面。"你清楚，因为和普通新到者的谈话，对大喇嘛来说有巨大的负担。人性情感的单纯宣泄对大喇嘛那个年纪来说，是不被接受的，那几乎是令人无法容忍的不快。我不是在此事上怀疑大喇嘛的全部智慧，我相信，它给我们上了关于重大价值的一课，甚至我们这个群体，固定下来的制度规范也仅仅是适度被固定而已，但这依然非比寻常。"

当然，对康维而言，任何其他事情也都没有比这个更非比寻常的了。随后，他第三次，第四次拜访了大喇嘛，他开始觉得这根本没有特别非比寻常的。确实，似乎有些事情几乎轻易就被预先注定了，他们两个人的思想彼此贴近；就好像康维全部隐秘的紧张感都放松

as if in Conway all secret tensions were relaxed, giving him, when he came away, a sumptuous tranquillity. At times he had the sensation of being completely bewitched by the mastery of that central intelligence, and then, over the little pale blue tea-bowls, the celebration would contract into a liveliness so gentle and miniature that he had an impression of a theorem dissolving limpidly into a sonnet.

Their talks ranged far and fearlessly; entire philosophies were unfolded; the long avenues of history surrendered themselves for inspection and were given new plausibility. To Conway it was an entrancing experience, but he did not suspend the critical attitude, and once, when he had argued a point, the High Lama replied: "My son, you are young in years, but I perceive that your wisdom has the ripeness of age. Surely some unusual thing has happened to you?"

Conway smiled. "No more unusual than has happened to many others of my generation."

"I have never met your like before."

Conway answered after an interval: "There's not a great deal of mystery about it. That part of me which seems old to you was worn out by intense and premature experience. My years from nineteen to twenty-two were a supreme education, no doubt, but rather exhausting."

了。当他离开时，这赋予了他一种异常平静的心情。好几次，他都有一种被大喇嘛的不凡才智所彻底折服的感觉；然后，望着那些淡蓝色小茶碗，这种仪式变得更为生动，它们是如此的柔和又微小，以至于他产生了一种将法则清晰地融为一首十四行诗的印象。

他们的谈话范围相当广泛，也无所顾忌。整个哲学全部呈现；这长长的历史隧道让他们自行审视，并被给予了新的合理性。对康维来说，这是一次入门的经历，可他同时保留批判的态度。一次，当他对一个观点争论不休时。大喇嘛回应道："我的孩子，你在年纪上还很年轻，但我洞悉到你的智慧具有上了年纪的成熟，你身上肯定发生过某些不寻常的事吧？"

康维微微一笑："同很多我同年代的人相比，并没有更多的不同寻常之事发生。"

"我从没见过你之前的样子。"

一段间隔后，康维回答道："这并没有很神秘，对你来说，我看起来似乎很老成，这是因为我的精力过早地就被发生在自己身上的事儿所耗尽了。毋庸置疑，我的 19 岁到 23 岁是高等教育阶段，这可

"You were very unhappy at the War?"

"Not particularly so. I was excited and suicidal and scared and reckless and sometimes in a tearing rage – like a few million others, in fact. I got mad-drunk and killed and lechered in great style. It was the self-abuse of all one's emotions, and one came through it, if one did at all, with a sense of almighty boredom and fretfulness. That's what made the years afterwards so difficult. Don't think I'm posing myself too tragically – I've had pretty fair luck since, on the whole. But it's been rather like being in a school where there's a bad headmaster – plenty of fun to be got if you feel like it, but nerve-racking off and on, and not really very satisfactory. I think I found that out rather more than most people."

"And your education thus continued?"

Conway gave a shrug. "Perhaps the exhaustion of the passions is the beginning of wisdom, if you care to alter the proverb."

"That also, my son, is the doctrine of Shangri-La."

"I know. It makes me feel quite at home."

He had spoken no less than the truth. As the days and weeks passed he began to feel an ache of contentment uniting mind and body; like Perrault and Henschell and

"相当令人精疲力竭。"

"战争期间你非常不幸吧？"

"不是特别不幸。我非常兴奋、有自杀倾向，我被吓坏了，鲁莽轻率，偶尔撕心裂肺又暴怒异常。其实，和千千万万的其他人一样，我会疯疯癫癫，酩酊大醉，然后去杀人，肆意纵欲；这是一个人全部情感中的一种自暴自弃，如果一个人做了这一切，那么他也会留下一种极其无聊和焦躁难安的心态，而且一直给以后的生活投下了阴影。不要认为我伪装得太过悲惨，大体上，从那以后，我还是有相当不错的运气的。但完全就像到了一所学校里，学校有个很糟糕的校长，如果你想的话，你还是能获得很多的乐趣，但断断续续总有伤脑筋的事，因此不是令人很满意。我觉得我比大部分人要明白很多。"

"你的学业还会继续吗？"

康维耸耸肩，说："也许激情的耗尽就是智慧的开始，如果你希望更改这句谚语的话。"

"我的孩子，那也是香格里拉的训导。"

"我晓得，它让我感觉相当自在。"

他说得正是真理。随着时间的流逝，他开始感到一种让灵魂和身体整体都满足的渴望：就像佩劳尔特、亨斯齐尔和其他人一样，他正

the others, he was falling under the spell. Blue Moon had taken him, and there was no escape. The mountains gleamed around in a hedge of inaccessible purity, from which his eyes fell dazzled to the green depths of the valley; the whole picture was incomparable, and when he heard the harpsichord's silver monotony across the lotus-pool, he felt that it threaded the perfect pattern of sight and sound.

He was, and he knew it, very quietly in love with the little Manchu. His love demanded nothing, not even reply; it was a tribute of the mind, to which his senses added only a flavor. She stood for him as a symbol of all that was delicate and fragile; her stylized courtesies and the touch of her fingers on the keyboard yielded a completely satisfying intimacy. Sometimes he would address her in a way that might, if she cared, have led to less formal conversation; but her replies never broke through the exquisite privacy of her thoughts, and in a sense he did not wish them to. He had suddenly come to realize a single facet of the promised jewel; he had Time, Time for everything that he wished to happen, such Time that desire itself was quenched in the certainty of fulfillment. A year, a decade hence, there would still be Time. The vision grew on him, and he was happy with it.

Then, at intervals, he stepped into the

沉浸在一种咒符之下，蓝月亮已经征服了他，他无法挣脱开来。群山在一种无法接近的纯净保护中，闪烁着光芒。他的目光沉浸在绿油油的深邃山谷以及那炫目的光彩中，整个画片无与伦比。当他听到从荷花池对面传来的古琴那清亮而单调的声音时，他感到它将景色和声音完美贯穿于一个整体。

他清楚他已经不动声色地爱上了那个满族小姑娘。他的爱不需要什么理由，甚至不需要回应；这是灵魂的奉献，仅能为他的情感世界添上一丝回味。她对他来说，代表着一种符号，是一切精致和柔弱的象征，是她那程式化的谦恭有礼，是她那纤纤玉指在琴键上的触碰所产生的一种完全令人满意的亲密感。偶尔他会用一种不太正式的交谈方式向她表白，如果她注意到的话；但她的回应从来没有打破她内心的微妙隐秘。在某种意义上，康维也不希望事情所有突破。他突然意识到得到这颗很有希望的宝石的单一因素——他有时间，他所希望发生的每一件事情都需要时间。这样的时间会在得到满足的过程中渐渐归于平淡。从此，不管1年或者10年，时间还是有的，这种幻境隐现于他的心底，他为此觉得很幸福。

然后，他不时会步入另一种生

other life to encounter Mallinson's impatience, Barnard's heartiness, and Miss Brinklow's robust intention. He felt he would be glad when they all knew as much as he; and, like Chang, he could imagine that neither the American nor the missionary would prove difficult cases. He was even amused when Barnard once said: "You know, Conway, I'm not sure that this wouldn't be a nice little place to settle down in. I thought at first I'd miss the newspapers and the movies, but I guess one can get used to anything."

"I guess one can," agreed Conway.

He learned afterwards that Chang had taken Barnard down to the valley, at his own request, to enjoy everything in the way of a "night out" that the resources of the locality could provide. Mallinson, when he heard of this, was rather scornful. "Getting tight, I suppose," he remarked to Conway, and to Barnard himself he commented: "Of course it's none of my business, but you'll want to keep yourself pretty fit for the journey, you know. The porters are due in a fortnight's time, and from what I gather, the return trip won't be exactly a joy ride."

Barnard nodded equably. "I never figgered it would," he answered. "And as for keeping fit, I guess I'm fitter than I've been for years. I get exercise daily, I don't have any worries, and the speakeasies

活中，面对马林逊的急躁、巴纳德的热心和布琳克罗小姐固执己见。他感到如果他们所有人都和他知道的一样多，那该多好。就好像张那样，他能想象得出，无论是美国人还是那个修女都会是个难题。巴纳德曾经说了一句话，他甚至笑了出来："你清楚，康维，我不确定这是否是适合定居的绝佳的地方；首先我认为我再没有了报纸和电影，但我认为一个人是能够习惯任何东西的。"

"我猜想那样是可能的。"康维赞同道。

随后，他得知张曾带巴纳德下到山谷里去，按照他自己的要求，以一个"夜猫子"的方式去享受这个地方能够提供的每一种资源。当马林逊听到这件事时，他相当藐视。"我觉得他越来越过分，"他对康维评论道，然后对巴纳德本人，他说道，"当然，这不关我的事，但为了旅程，你要保持健康，你清楚。那些送货人在两星期后应该到这里，从我推断的情况而言，返回的旅程绝对不像乘车般的好玩。"

巴纳德平静地点点头，"我从来不曾想过它会如此。"他回答道，"至于保持健康，我觉得我比前几年健康多了。我每天锻炼，没有任何担心，这个山谷下面的地下酒家

down in the valley don't let you go too far. Moderation, y'know – the motto of the firm."

"Yes, I've no doubt you've been managing to have a moderately good time," said Mallinson acidly.

"Certainly I have. This establishment caters for all tastes – some people like little Chink gels who play the pi-anno, isn't that so? You can't blame anybody for what they fancy."

Conway was not at all put out, but Mallinson flushed like a schoolboy. "You can send them to jail, though, when they fancy other people's property," he snapped, stung to fury that set a raw edge to his wits.

"Sure, if you can catch 'em." The American grinned affably. "And that leads me to something I may as well tell you folks right away, now we're on the subject. I've decided to give those porters a miss. They come here pretty regular, and I'll wait for the next trip, or maybe the next but one. That is, if the monks'll take my word that I'm still good for my hotel expenses."

"You mean you're not coming with us?"

"That's it. I've decided to stop over for a while. It's all very fine for you – you'll have the band playing when *you* get home, but all the welcome I'll get is from a row

不会让你走得太远的。中庸之道，你清楚，这个团体的座右铭。"

"没错，我并不怀疑你一直在设法过一种适度的愉快生活。"马林逊不悦地说道。

"我当然是如此。这里的设施适合各种口味，某些人便喜欢上弹奏钢琴的那个中国人了，不是如此吗？你不能因为别人想象到的东西去责怪任何人嘛。"

康维根本开不了口，但马林逊仿佛小学生一般满脸通红，"但他们觊觎其他人的财产时，你可以送他们去监狱。"他厉声吼着，怒火中烧，几乎失去了理智。

"当然，倘若你能抓到他们。"这美国人和蔼地咧开嘴笑了，"这让我觉得应该立刻告诉你们这些家伙们一些事，现在我们回到正题，我决定先避过那些送货人。他们来这里是相当有规律的，我会等到下次或者可能再下一次才走。这个嘛，如果喇嘛们会采纳我的意见，我的住店费依然很充足。"

"你的意思是你不想和我们一起走？"

"是那样，我决定留下来再待一段时间。这对你们都非常不错啊，当你们回家时，会有乐队演奏音乐，而迎接我的只是一队警察，

of cops. And the more I think about it, the more it don't seem good enough."

"In other words, you're just afraid to face the music?"

"Well, I never did like music, anyhow."

Mallinson said with cold scorn: "I suppose it's your own affair. Nobody can prevent you from stopping here all your life if you feel inclined." Nevertheless he looked round with a flash of appeal. "It's not what everybody would choose to do, but ideas differ. What do you say, Conway?"

"I agree. Ideas do differ."

Mallinson turned to Miss Brinklow, who suddenly put down her book and remarked: "As a matter of fact, I think I shall stay too."

"*What?*" they all cried together.

She continued, with a bright smile that seemed more an attachment to her face than an illumination of it: "You see, I've been thinking over the way things happened to bring us all here, and there's only one conclusion I can come to. There's a mysterious power working behind the scenes. Don't you think so, Mr. Conway?"

Conway might have found it hard to reply, but Miss Brinklow went on in a gathering hurry: "Who am I to question the dictates of Providence? I was sent here for a purpose, and I shall stay."

我想得越多，越觉得似乎不太好。"

"换句话，你仅仅是害怕面对音乐？"

"好吧，总之，我从来就不喜欢音乐。"

马林逊以冷漠的嘲笑口气说道："我觉得这是你自己的事，没有人能够阻止你一辈子待在这里，倘若你觉得心甘情愿的话。"然而他环顾四周，闪现出一种依依不舍的神情，"并非每一个人都要这么去做，但大家想法各异嘛，你说呢，康维？"

"我同意，各人想法确实不同。"

马林逊转向布琳克罗小姐，她突然将手中的书放了下来，评论道："其实，我觉得我也想留下来。"

"什么？"所有人一同惊呼。

她继续说，面带一种明快的微笑，而似乎这并非发自肺腑："你们清楚，我一直在思考这里所发生的事情，我们被带到这里，我能得出的唯一结论便是：一种神秘的力量在幕后操纵，你不这么认为吗，康维先生？"

康维觉得很难回应，但布琳克罗小姐以一种越发着急的神情继续说："我是什么人啊，要去质疑上天的旨意！我是有目的地被派到这里来的，因此我应当待在这里。"

"Do you mean you're hoping to start a mission here?" Mallinson asked.

"Not only hoping, but fully intending. I know just how to deal with these people – I shall get my own way, never fear. There's no real grit in any of them."

"And you intend to introduce some?"

"Yes, I do, Mr. Mallinson. I'm strongly opposed to that idea of moderation that we hear so much about. You can call it broadmindedness if you like, but in my opinion it leads to the worst kind of laxity. The whole trouble with the people here is their so-called broadmindedness, and I intend to fight it with all my powers."

"And they're so broad-minded that they're going to let you?" said Conway, smiling.

"Or else she's so strong-minded that they can't stop her," put in Barnard. He added with a chuckle: "It's just what I said – this establishment caters for all tastes."

"Possibly, if you happen to *like* prison," Mallinson snapped.

"Well, there's two ways of looking even at that. My goodness, if you think of all the folks in the world who'd give all they've got to be out of the racket and in a place like this, only they can't *get* out! Are we in the prison or are *they*?"

"A comforting speculation for a monkey in a cage," retorted Mallinson; he

"你的意思是，你盼望着在这里创建一个修道院？"马林逊问道。

"不只是希望，而是充满预期。我清楚如何与这些人相处，我有自己的方式，我永远不会害怕，他们都不是真正的铁石心肠。"

"你想要推荐一些人吗？"

"没错，我会的，马林逊先生。我强烈反对我们要听如此之多的中庸思想，如果你喜欢的话，你能够称其为'宽宏大量'，可依我看来，它会导致最糟糕的松弛状态。这里人们的整体问题便是他们那所谓的'宽宏大量'，我打算用我的全部力量与它作斗争。"

"他们是如此宽宏大量，至于会让你这么做吗？"康维说道，微微一笑。

"或者说她是如此的有主见，以至于他们无法阻止她。"巴纳德插话道，他咯咯笑着补充道，"这就是我说的，这里适合所有人的口味。"

"有可能，倘若你碰巧喜欢监狱的话。"马林逊快速说。

"那么，看待这个问题恰好有两种方式。天哪，如果你想到这世上所有那些将他们拥有的一切都拿出来被敲诈，然后还要待在一个类似这样地方的人们，只有他们才无法逃出去！究竟是我们在监狱里还是他们啊？"

was still furious.

Afterwards he spoke to Conway alone. "That man still gets on my nerves," he said, pacing the courtyard. "I'm not sorry we shan't have him with us when we go back. You may think me touchy, but being chipped about that Chinese girl didn't appeal to my sense of humor."

Conway took Mallinson's arm. It was becoming increasingly clear to him that he was very fond of the youth, and that their recent weeks in company had deepened the feeling, despite jarring moods. He answered: "I rather took it that I was being ragged about her, not you."

"No, I think he intended it for me. He knows I'm interested in her. I am, Conway. I can't make out why she's here, and whether she really likes being here. My God, if I spoke her language as you do, I'd soon have it out with her."

"I wonder if you would. She doesn't say a great deal to anyone, you know."

"It puzzles me that you don't badger her with all sorts of questions."

"I don't know that I care for badgering people."

He wished he could have said more, and then suddenly the sense of pity and irony floated over him in a filmy haze; this youth, so eager and ardent, would take things very hardly. "I shouldn't worry

"一种瓮中之鳖的自我安慰。"马林逊反驳道,他依然很愤怒。

然后,马林逊单独来和康维聊天。"那家伙依然令我心烦意乱,"他说道,在庭院里踱着步,"返回时,没有他和我们一起,我不觉得遗憾。你可能觉得我暴躁易怒,但对那个满族姑娘的挖苦讽刺无法激发我的幽默感。"

康维抓住马林逊的胳膊。对他来说,他越发清晰地觉得,他非常喜欢这个年轻人,他们最近几周在一起,已经加深了这感觉,尽管他们之间也有误会的时候。他回答道:"我确实觉得是我为她心神不宁,而不是你。"

"不,我觉得他是在说我。他清楚我对她感兴趣,康维,我确实如此。我搞不懂她为什么在这儿,以及她是否真的喜欢一直待在这里。我的上帝,如果我像你似的,会讲她的语言,我会立刻便去找她弄清楚。"

"我在想你是否可以,她对任何人都不会说很多,你清楚。"

"这令我很困惑,关于所有的这些各种各样的问题,你并不会去强迫她。"

"我不愿意强迫别人。"

他希望他多说些,但随后,一种怜悯和讽刺感突然朦胧地涌上心头,这年轻人,如此急迫又热情

about Lo-Tsen if I were you," he added. "She's happy enough."

The decision of Barnard and Miss Brinklow to remain behind seemed to Conway all to the good, though it threw Mallinson and himself into an apparently opposite camp for the time being. It was an extraordinary situation, and he had no definite plans for tackling it.

Fortunately there was no apparent need to tackle it at all. Until the two months were past, nothing much could happen; and afterwards there would be a crisis no less acute for his having tried to prepare himself for it. For this and other reasons he was disinclined to worry over the inevitable, though he did once say: "You know, Chang, I'm bothered about young Mallinson. I'm afraid he'll take things very badly when he finds out."

Chang nodded with some sympathy. "Yes, it will not be easy to persuade him of his good fortune. But the difficulty is, after all, only a temporary one. In twenty years from now our friend will be quite reconciled."

Conway felt that this was looking at the matter almost too philosophically. "I'm wondering," he said, "just how the truth's going to be broached to him. He's counting the days to the arrival of the porters, and if they don't come – "

洋溢，将事情看得非常认真。"倘若我是你，便不会为罗珍担心，"他补充道，"她足够幸福了。"

对康维来说，巴纳德和布琳克罗小姐打算留下来的决定很不错，尽管目前这让自己和马林逊明显处于对立的阵营，这种局面不同寻常。他还没有一个明确的方法去处理。

所幸他根本没有必要去处理它，两个月过去了，什么也没有发生。然后，他会有一个依然很敏感的危机，为此他已经做了准备。有这样那样的理由让他不愿意去担心这个不可避免的结果。但他确实曾经说过："你清楚，张。我烦恼的就是这个年轻的马林逊，恐怕当他弄清楚后，他会做一些非常麻烦的事情。"

张同情地点点头，"是的，说服他接受自己的好运气，并不那么容易。但毕竟困难仅仅是暂时的，从现在开始 20 年之后，我们的这位朋友会相当顺从的。"

康维感到这种看待事情的方式几乎太过哲学化，"我在琢磨"，他说，"到底怎样将真相告诉他。他在数送货人到达的日期。如果他们不来的话……"

"But they *will* come."

"Oh? I rather imagined that all your talk about them was just a pleasant fable to let us down lightly."

"By no means. Although we have no bigotry on the point, it is our custom at Shangri-La to be moderately truthful, and I can assure you that my statements about the porters were almost correct. At any rate, we are expecting the men at or about the time I said."

"Then you'll find it hard to stop Mallinson from joining them."

"But we should never attempt to do so. He will merely discover – no doubt by personal experiment – that the porters are reluctantly unable to take anyone back with them."

"I see. So that's the method? And what do you expect to happen afterwards?"

"Then, my dear sir, after a period of disappointment, he will – since he is young and optimistic – begin to hope that the next convoy of porters, due in nine or ten months' time will prove more amenable to his suggestions. And this is a hope which, if we are wise, we shall not at first discourage."

Conway said sharply: "I'm not so sure that he'll do that at all. I should think he's far more likely to try an escape on his own."

"*Escape*? Is that *really* the word that

"但他们会来啊。"

"哦？我完全觉得，你说的关于他们的一切就是让我们放轻松的一个有趣的童话罢了。"

"决非如此。虽然在这点上，我们并不顽固，而且我们在香格里拉的习惯是适度的真实，但我可以向你保证，我对于送货人情况的陈述几乎都是准确的。总之，我们可以期盼那些人会在我说的那个时间左右到来。"

"你会发现你很难阻止马林逊加入他们离开了。"

"但我们从来没有打算那样做，毋庸置疑，通过自行实验，他只是会发现这些送货人根本无法带任何人一起返回。"

"我懂了，如此一来，这便是办法喽？你期待会发生什么？"

"然后，我亲爱的先生，在一段时间的失望之后，因为他年轻而且很乐观，他会开始希望下一批送货人。预计在 9 到 10 个月之内，就会证明，他会顺从的，明智的办法是暂时先不要泼他冷水。"

康维尖刻地说："我一点也不这么肯定，他会这么做，但我觉得他更有可能想方设法自行逃跑。"

"逃走？你当真要使用这个

should be used? After all, the pass is open to anyone at any time. We have no jailers, save those that Nature herself has provided."

Conway smiled. "Well, you must admit that she's done her job pretty well. But I don't suppose you rely on her in every case, all the same. What about the various exploring parties that have arrived here? Was the pass always equally open to *them* when they wanted to get away?"

It was Chang's turn now to smile. "Special circumstances, my dear sir, have sometimes required special consideration."

"Excellent. So you only allow people the chance of escape when you know they'd be fools to take it? Even so, I expect some of them do."

"Well, it has happened very occasionally, but as a rule the absentees are glad to return after the experience of a single night on the plateau."

"Without shelter and proper clothing? If so, I can quite understand that your mild methods are as effective as stern ones. But what about the less usual cases that don't return?"

"You have yourself answered the question," replied Chang. "They do *not* return." But he made haste to add: "I can assure you, however, that there are few indeed who have been so unfortunate, and

词吗？毕竟，那条隧道在任何时间对任何人开放。我们没人看守，用不着那些人，因为大自然本身便是看守。"

康维微微一笑："好吧，你必须承认大自然将她的工作完成得非常出色，但我并不认为你在每一种情况下都可以依靠她，曾经抵达这里的各种探险队如何了呢？当他们想要离开时，那条隧道也一直同样对他们开放吗？"

此时轮到张微微一笑了，"我亲爱的先生，特殊的情况偶尔需要特殊的考虑呢。"

"精辟。当你得知有些傻瓜要逃走时，你们允许他们有逃走的机会吗？即便是这样，我还是预计他们中的一些人会这么做。"

"哦，这种情况经常发生，可就像一种惯例，逃跑者在经历了在高原上独自过的一夜之后，都很乐于回来。"

"既没有避身处，也没有合适的衣服？如果是这样，我相当理解，你们这种温和的方法与严苛的方法具有相同的效果了。而少数那些没有返回的又怎样呢？"

"你已经自行回答了这个问题。"张回应道，"他们确实没有回来。"但他急忙补充道，"我能够保证，这种如此不幸的人的确非常少，而且我相信，你的朋友不会那

I trust your friend will not be rash enough to increase the number."

Conway did not find these responses entirely reassuring, and Mallinson's future remained a preoccupation. He wished it were possible for the youth to return by consent, and this would not be unprecedented, for there was the recent case of Talu, the airman. Chang admitted that the authorities were fully empowered to do anything that they considered wise. "But *should* we be wise, my dear sir, in trusting our future entirely to your friend's feeling of gratitude?"

Conway felt that the question was pertinent, for Mallinson's attitude left little doubt as to what he would do as soon as he reached India. It was his favorite theme, and he had often enlarged upon it.

But all that, of course, was in the mundane world that was gradually being pushed out of his mind by the rich, pervasive world of Shangri-La. Except when he thought about Mallinson, he was extraordinarily content; the slowly revealed fabric of this new environment continued to astonish him by its intricate suitability to his own needs and tastes.

Once he said to Chang: "By the way, how do you people here fit love into your scheme of things? I suppose it does sometimes happen that those who come here develop attachments?"

么草率，去增加这个数字。"

康维发现这些回答并没有令他完全安心，马林逊的未来还是当务之急。他盼望着有可能的话，这个年轻人会回心转意留在这里，况且这也不是没有先例。就以最近塔鲁这个飞行员为例。张承认当权者有充分的权力去做他们认为明智的任何事情。"但我们应该明智些，亲爱的先生，让我们去相信我们的未来完全取决于你朋友的感激之情吧？"

康维感到这个问题很中肯，因为就马林逊的态度而言，他不得不让人怀疑他一到印度会去做些什么。这是他最喜欢的事，并且他热爱夸张事实。

当然，这个世俗世界中的所有杂念都逐渐被香格里拉这丰富而有渗透力的世界所涤荡。除了当他想到马林逊时，他都格外地满意；这个崭新的环境所慢慢展现的构造正根据他的需要和口味改变着，这一点让他吃惊不已。

一次他对张说："随便问一下，你们是如何处理爱情的呢？我觉得这种情况确实偶尔会发生，就是来到这里的人会发展出彼此的爱慕吧？"

"Quite often," replied Chang with a broad smile. "The lamas, of course, are immune, and so are most of us when we reach the riper years, but until then we are as other men, except that I think we can claim to behave more reasonably. And this gives me the opportunity, Mr. Conway, of assuring you that the hospitality of Shangri-La is of a comprehensive kind. Your friend Mr. Barnard has already availed himself of it."

Conway returned the smile. "Thanks," he answered dryly. "I've no doubt he has, but my own inclinations are not – at the moment – so assertive. It was the emotional more than the physical aspect that I was curious about."

"You find it easy to separate the two? Is it possible that you are falling in love with Lo-Tsen?"

Conway was somewhat taken aback, though he hoped he did not show it. "What makes you ask that?"

"Because, my dear sir, it would be quite suitable if you were to do so – always, of course, in moderation. Lo-Tsen would not respond with any degree of passion – that is more than you could expect – but the experience would be very delightful, I assure you. And I speak with some authority, for I was in love with her myself when I was much younger."

"Were you indeed? And did she respond

"非常经常，"张面带一种宽厚的微笑回应道，"当然了，喇嘛们是免疫的，就像我们大部分人到了更成熟的年纪时一样，直到那时我们和其他人无异，只是我们能更理智地行动。这倒给了我一个机会，康维先生，向你保证香格里拉是很包容的地方，你的朋友巴纳德便已经自行体验过了。"

康维用微笑回应。"谢谢，"他冷淡地回答道，"我毫不怀疑他已经体验过了。可此刻，我自己的倾向我倒不是如此确定。比起肉体方面我更关心的是感情。"

"你觉得有什么原因很容易便能将两个人分开吗？你很可能是爱上罗珍了吧？"

康维有点大吃一惊，但他希望不要表现出来。"你怎么会这样问？"

"因为，我亲爱的先生，倘若你这么做的话，总是适度的话，那当然会相当恰当，虽然罗珍不会对任何程度的感情予以回应，比你能够预计到的程度更深，但这种经历会非常令人愉悦，我向你保证。我以肯定的口气和你说这些，因为当我还年轻时，我也爱上过她。"

"你当真如此吗？她回应了

then?"

"Only by the most charming appreciation of the compliment I paid her, and by a friendship which has grown more precious with the years."

"In other words, she didn't respond?"

"If you prefer it so." Chang added, a little sententiously: "It has always been her way to spare her lovers the moment of satiety that goes with all absolute attainment."

Conway laughed. "That's all very well in your case, and perhaps mine too – but what about the attitude of a hot-blooded young fellow like Mallinson?"

"My dear sir, it would be the best possible thing that could happen! Not for the first time, I assure you, would Lo-Tsen comfort the sorrowful exile when he learns that there is to be no return."

"*Comfort?*"

"Yes, though you must not misunderstand my use of the term. Lo-Tsen gives no caresses, except such as touch the stricken heart from her very presence. What does your Shakespeare say of Cleopatra? – 'She makes hungry where she most satisfies.' A popular type, doubtless, among the passion-driven races, but such a woman, I assure you, would be altogether out of place at Shangri-La. Lo-Tsen, if I might amend the quotation, *removes* hunger where she *least*

吗？"

"只有对我称赞她的最为迷人的感激之情，以及随着岁月逐渐培养的越发珍贵的友谊。"

"换言之，她没有回应？"

"如果你愿意这么说的话，"张稍微简洁地补充道，"这一直是她的方式，就是给她的情人们提供满足的时刻，即在未达成与实现目的间的游走状态。"

康维哈哈大笑："你的情况已经非常不错了，可能我也会如此，但她对类似马林逊这样一个热血青年的态度又会是什么样的呢？"

"我亲爱的先生，那会是能够发生的可能之事中最好的情况了！这不是第一次了，我向你保证，当他得知不能回去时，罗珍会去安慰这个可怜的小伙子的。"

"安慰？"

"是的，但你一定不能理解我对这个词的使用。罗珍不会给予他什么安抚，除了类似那种使人伤心的触动的感觉。你们的莎士比亚对那个埃及艳后克莉奥潘多拉如何评论的？'她在哪里制造饥渴，便最满足哪里'，毫无疑问，在爱情的拉力赛中，这是一种普遍的方式，可这样的女人，我向你保证，总而言之，会在香格里拉之外的地方出现。而罗珍，倘若我改良一句语录，就是'她最小程度满足了哪

satisfies. It is a more delicate and lasting accomplishment."

"And one, I assume, which she has much skill in performing?"

"Oh, decidedly – we have had many examples of it. It is her way to calm the throb of desire to a murmur that is no less pleasant when left unanswered."

"In that sense, then, you could regard her as a part of the training equipment of the establishment?"

"*You* could regard her as that, if you wished," replied Chang with deprecating blandness. "But it would be more graceful, and just as true, to liken her to the rainbow reflected in a glass bowl or to the dewdrops on the blossoms of the fruit tree."

"I entirely agree with you, Chang. That would be *much* more graceful." Conway enjoyed the measured yet agile repartees which his good-humored ragging of the Chinese very often elicited.

But the next time he was alone with the little Manchu he felt that Chang's remarks had had a great deal of shrewdness in them. There was a fragrance about her that communicated itself to his own emotions, kindling the embers to a glow that did not burn, but merely warmed. And suddenly then he realized that Shangri-La and Lo-Tsen were quite perfect, and that he did not wish for more than to stir a faint

里，哪里便会驱走饥渴'。这是一种更为精妙、持续更久的成就。"

"那么，我可以假设一点就是她在表演方面有很多技巧喽？"

"哦，绝对的，我们有许多例子。她可以将那些蠢蠢欲动的欲望安慰得服服帖帖，虽然没有作答但人们依然感到愉悦。"

"那么，从这个意义上，你们将她视为你们这个组织里负责培训的一分子？"

"如果您非要这么想，我也没办法。"张一改往日不温不火的态度回应道，"但更为优雅地说，正如实情一样，还是将她比作玻璃碗上折射出的彩虹或者果树鲜花上的露珠更好一些。"

"我完全赞同，张，那会更加优雅。"康维享受着这种从容不迫但却巧舌如簧的狡辩，他具有那种中国人经常能够看到的幽默。

但是等下次他与那个满族小姑娘单独在一起时，他觉得在张评论中蕴含着很多的哲理。在她身上有一种芳香会传进他的情感里，激起火焰发出光芒，虽然不是熊熊燃烧，但是很温暖。然后，他突然意识到香格里拉和罗珍都相当完美，他不希望再有什么来干扰这份寂静。多年来，他的情感一直像被这个世界刺激的一根神经；而现在所

and eventual response in all that stillness. For years his passions had been like a nerve that the world jarred on; now at last the aching was soothed, and he could yield himself to love that was neither a torment nor a bore. As he passed by the lotus-pool at night he sometimes pictured her in his arms, but the sense of time washed over the vision, calming him to an infinite and tender reluctance.

He did not think he had ever been so happy, even in the years of his life before the great barrier of the war. He liked the serene world that Shangri-La offered him, pacified rather than dominated by its single tremendous idea. He liked the prevalent mood in which feelings were sheathed in thoughts, and thoughts softened into felicity by their transference into language. Conway, whom experience had taught that rudeness is by no means a guarantee of good faith, was even less inclined to regard a well-turned phrase as a proof of insincerity. He liked the mannered, leisurely atmosphere in which talk was an accomplishment, not a mere habit. And he liked to realize that the idlest things could now be freed from the curse of time-wasting, and the frailest dreams receive the welcome of the mind. Shangri-La was always tranquil, yet always a hive of unpursuing occupations; the lamas lived as if indeed they had time

有的痛苦终于都被缓解了，他不再使自己屈服于不管是否是一种痛苦还是一种烦恼的爱情。当他在夜晚经过荷花池塘时，他偶尔会幻想罗珍就在他的臂弯中，可时间感冲淡了这种幻觉，平静之后，他便感到一种无限而又温柔的眷恋。

他觉得自己未曾如此幸福，甚至在战争带来的巨大障碍之前，也没有如此的感觉。他喜欢香格里拉所赋予了那种平静的世界，令他得到了净化，而并非用它那单一的思想主宰他；他喜欢这种平和的心境，感情被隐藏在思想中，而思想则通过它们转化成婉转而得体的语言。康维的经历让他明白了粗鲁和无礼决不得到忠诚和信用，甚至他不能将一个措辞巧妙的词语视为伪善的表现；他也喜欢这种有礼貌却轻松的氛围，在这种氛围下，谈话是一种成就，而不仅仅是一种习惯。他意识到现在让人最悠然自得的便是从浪费时间的咒骂中解脱出来，即使最易碎的梦境也令人心旷神怡。香格里拉总是那样的宁静，但却总有一堆干不完的事情；那些喇嘛们生活着，仿佛手上确实有充裕的时间，时间几乎轻如鸿毛。康维没有见过他们中的其他人，可他逐渐意识到，他们从事的

on their hands, but time that was scarcely a feather-weight. Conway met no more of them, but he came gradually to realize the extent and variety of their employments; besides their knowledge of languages, some, it appeared, took to the full seas of learning in a manner that would have yielded big surprises to the Western world. Many were engaged in writing manuscript books of various kinds; one (Chang said) had made valuable researches into pure mathematics; another was coordinating Gibbon and Spengler into a vast thesis on the history of European civilization. But this kind of thing was not for them all, nor for any of them always; there were many tideless channels in which they dived in mere waywardness, retrieving, like Briac, fragments of old tunes, or like the English ex-curate, a new theory about *Wuthering Heights*. And there were even fainter impracticalities than these. Once, when Conway made some remark in this connection, the High Lama replied with a story of a Chinese artist in the third century B.C. who, having spent many years in carving dragons, birds, and horses upon a cherrystone, offered his finished work to a royal prince. The prince could see nothing in it at first except a mere stone, but the artist bade him "have a wall built, and make a window in it, and observe the stone through the window in

职业广泛且具有多样性；除了他们对语言的知识以外，一些人似乎喜欢无止境的学习，这种态度会使西方世界产生巨大的震动。许多人都从事抄写各类典籍的手稿的工作；张曾说过有一个人还对纯数学做了很有价值的研究，还有一个正在整理吉本和斯潘格勒的资料，以形成一部涉及宽泛的关于欧洲文明历史的论文。可这些不是针对他们所有人的，也不是说他们总是在从事这种事，还有很多事情可以使他们沉溺其中。就像布里亚克在收集一些古老曲调的片断，那个英国的副牧师在研究一种关于《呼啸山庄》的新理论，甚至还有比这更奇怪且不切实际的东西。一次，在他对这种联系做了一些评论之后，大喇嘛用一个公元前3世纪的中国艺术家的故事回应他。那位艺术家花了很多年在石头上雕龙呀，鸟呀，马呀等等，然后将他完成的作品呈献给一位皇室王子，可这位王子最初看不出任何东西，只以为是一些石头，但艺术家告诉他"建一道墙，在上面开一扇窗，通过从窗子投射进来的黎明的曙光来观察这些石头。"王子照做了，发现这些石头确实非常漂亮。"我亲爱的康维，这难道不是一个很动人的故事吗，你不觉得它教给我们非常宝贵的经验吗？"

the glory of the dawn." The prince did so, and then perceived that the stone was indeed very beautiful. "Is not that a charming story, my dear Conway, and do you not think it teaches a very valuable lesson?"

Conway agreed; he found it pleasant to realize that the serene purpose of Shangri-La could embrace an infinitude of odd and apparently trivial employments, for he had always had a taste for such things himself. In fact, when he regarded his past, he saw it strewn with images of tasks too vagrant or too taxing ever to have been accomplished; but now they were all possible, even in a mood of idleness. It was delightful to contemplate, and he was not disposed to sneer when Barnard confided in him that he too envisaged an interesting future at Shangri-La.

It seemed that Barnard's excursions to the valley, which had been growing more frequent of late, were not entirely devoted to drink and women. "You see, Conway, I'm telling you this because you're different from Mallinson – he's got his knife into me, as probably you've gathered. But I feel you'll be better at understanding the position. It's a funny thing – you British officials are so darned stiff and starchy at first, but you're the sort a fellow can put his trust in, when all's

康维表示同意，他很愉悦地意识到，香格里拉的宁静意境包含着一种能从事古怪琐事的无限空间，他自己总是对这样的事情有一种喜好。其实，当他回顾过去时，他看到的满是那些太过漂泊不定，或者过于繁重而永远无法被完成的任务；但此时，它们全部都是可行的，甚至在一种慵懒的情绪下，沉思冥想都令人愉悦。当巴纳德对他倾诉着他对香格里拉那种过度想象的有趣形象时，他也不想表现出嘲笑。

似乎最近，巴纳德到山谷的远足愈发频繁了，不完全是贡献给了美酒和女人。"你知道，康维，我告诉你这个，是因为你与马林逊不同，就像你也许看出来的那样，他总是戳我的痛处，但我感觉你能更好地理解这种处境。这是个好笑的事，你们这些英国官员最初都是如此的刻板和拘谨，但当一切都说到做到时，你就是一个值得信赖的家伙。"

said and done."

"I wouldn't be too sure," replied Conway, smiling. "And anyhow, Mallinson's just as much a British official as I am."

"Yes, but he's a mere boy. He don't look at things reasonably. You and me are men of the world – we take things as we find them. This joint here, for instance – we still can't understand all the ins and outs of it, and why we've been landed here, but then, isn't that the usual way of things? Do we know why we're in the world at all, for that matter?"

"Perhaps some of us don't, but what's all this leading up to?"

Barnard dropped his voice to a rather husky whisper. "Gold, my lad," he answered with a certain ecstasy. "Just that, and nothing less. There's tons of it – literally – in the valley. I was a mining engineer in my young days and I haven't forgotten what a reef looks like. Believe me, it's as rich as the Rand, and ten times easier to get at. I guess you thought I was on the loose whenever I went down there in my little armchair. Not a bit of it. I knew what I was doing. I'd figgered it out all along, you know, that these guys here couldn't get all their stuff sent in from outside without paying mighty high for it, and what else could they pay with except gold or silver or diamonds or something?

"我不太肯定，"康维回应道，微微一笑，"总之，马林逊就和我差不多，都是英国官员嘛。"

"没错，但他只是个孩子，他看待事情不怎么理智，而你和我都是成年人了。我们可以对待事物见机行事。举个例子，这次来到这里，我们还是不能理解事情全部的细节：为什么我们被降落到这里，这不是事情的寻常方式吧？就这点来说，我们究竟知道我们为什么要来到这个世界了吗？"

"也许我们当中的一些人不清楚，但所有这些又会引发什么呢？"

巴纳德压低了声音，沙哑的低声细语："金子，伙计。"他以一种明确的狂喜之情回答道："就是这个，没别的，精确地说，山谷里有成吨的金子，我年轻时是个矿业工程师，我不曾忘记矿脉是什么样子，相信我，这里就像南非一样富有，而且开采它们容易 10 倍。无论何时我坐着我的小轿子下到那里时，我猜你都会觉得我是放荡形骸去了，但一点也不是，我知道我在干什么。我已经推测出来，你清楚，这里的这些人们不可能从外面弄来所有的生活用品而为此不付高额的代价，除了黄金、白银或者宝石或是什么别的东西，他们还能

Only logic, after all. And when I began to scout round, it didn't take me long to discover the whole bag of tricks."

"You found it out on your own?" asked Conway.

"Well, I won't say that, but I made my guess, and then I put the matter to Chang – straight, mind you, as man to man. And believe me, Conway, that Chink's not as bad a fellow as we might have thought."

"Personally, I never thought him a bad fellow at all."

"Of course, I know you always took to him, so you won't be surprised at the way we got on together. We certainly did hit it famously. He showed me all over the workings, and it may interest you to know that I've got the full permission of the authorities to prospect in the valley as much as I like and make a comprehensive report. What d'you think of that, my lad? They seemed quite glad to have the services of an expert, especially when I said I could probably give 'em tips on how to increase output."

"I can see you're going to be altogether at home here," said Conway.

"Well, I must say I've found a job, and that's something. And you never know how a thing'll turn out in the end. Maybe the folks at home won't be so keen to jail me when they know I can show 'em the

用什么来支付？毕竟，这仅仅是推测，当我开始四处搜寻时，没费多长时间，我便发现了全部花招。"

"你自己就能发现它们？"康维问道。

"哦，我可没这么说，但我做了猜测，然后我将此事告诉了张，是坦率地说的，听着，是面对面的。相信我，康维，这个中国佬不像我们曾经想的是个坏家伙。"

"个人而言，我根本就不认为他是个坏人。"

"当然，我清楚你总是求助于他，所以你对我们能融洽相处的这种方式并不惊奇。我们肯定会一鸣惊人的。张给我展示了全部的工地，可能你有兴趣了解的就是，我已经获得了当局的全部许可，去按照我喜欢的方式勘探这个山谷。然后写一份全面的报告。你是怎么想的，伙计？他们似乎相当高兴，有我这样一位专家的服务，特别是当我能够给他们提供如何提高产出量的小窍门时。"

"我能够看出来，你完全准备在这里安家了。"康维说道。

"没错，我必须说我已经找到了一份工作，太了不起了。你永远不知道一件事发展到最后，结局会如何。可能当家乡的人们清楚我给他们指引通往新金矿的道路时，

way to a new gold mine. The only difficulty is – would they take my word about it?"

"They might. It's extraordinary what people *will* believe."

Barnard nodded with enthusiasm. "Glad you get the point, Conway. And that's where you and I can make a deal. We'll go fifty-fifty in everything of course. All you've gotter do is to put your name to my report – British Consul, you know, and all that. It'll carry weight."

Conway laughed. "We'll have to see about it. Make your report first."

It amused him to contemplate a possibility so unlikely to happen, and at the same time he was glad that Barnard had found something that yielded such immediate comfort.

So also was the High Lama, whom Conway began to see more and more frequently. He often visited him in the late evening and stayed for many hours, long after the servants had taken away the last bowls of tea and had been dismissed for the night. The High Lama never failed to ask him about the progress and welfare of his three companions, and once he enquired particularly as to the kind of careers that their arrival at Shangri-La had so inevitably interrupted.

Conway answered reflectively:

便不会这么盼着我去坐牢了，唯一的难点就是，他们会相信我的话吗？"

"他们会的，人们会相信非同一般的东西。"

巴纳德充满激情地点点头，"很高兴你能理解这一点，康维。这便是你和我能够做一笔交易的地方了。在每一件事情上，我们都可以五五分成，而你要去做的就是将你的大名写进我的报告——英国领事，你知道，那样的话它会更有分量的。"

康维哈哈大笑："我们必须再商量一下，你先写你的报告吧。"

这令他很开心，计划已久的一种可能性就如此不太可能地发生了，同时他开心也是因为巴纳德找到了一些能够产生这种满足感的事情。

大喇嘛也是如此，康维开始越来越频繁地会见他。他通常在晚上很晚的时候去拜访他，然后待上好几个小时，直到仆人们将最后的茶碗都拿走后，他才离开去休息。大喇嘛从来没有忘记询问他关于他那3个同伴的进展以及是否安好。一次，他特别询问道，他们抵达香格里拉后，个人的职业生涯是不可避免地被中断了。

康维沉思着回答道："马林逊

"Mallinson might have done quite well in his own line – he's energetic and has ambitions. The two others –" He shrugged his shoulders. "As a matter of fact, it happens to suit them both to stay here – for a while, at any rate."

He noticed a flicker of light at the curtained window; there had been mutterings of thunder as he crossed the courtyard on his way to the now familiar room. No sound could be heard, and the heavy tapestries subdued the lightning into mere sparks of pallor.

"Yes," came the reply, "we have done our best to make both of them feel at home. Miss Brinklow wishes to convert us, and Mr. Barnard would also like to convert us – into a limited liability company. Harmless projects – they will pass the time quite pleasantly for them. But your young friend, to whom neither gold nor religion can offer solace, how about *him*?"

"Yes, he's going to be the problem."

"I am afraid he is going to be *your* problem."

"Why mine?"

There was no immediate answer, for the tea-bowls were introduced at that moment, and with their appearance the High Lama rallied a faint and desiccated hospitality. "Karakal sends us storms at this time of the year," he remarked, feathering the

应该在他自己的行业里干得相当出色，他精力旺盛并且很有野心，而其他两位——"他耸了耸肩，"其实，他们两个人碰巧适合留在这里，无论如何，他们都会待上一段时间。"

他注意到通过挂着帘子的窗户有一道闪电划过，当他沿途穿过庭院来到现在熟悉的房间时，便传来了一阵阵沉闷的雷声。现在什么声音都听不见了，而沉重的挂毯将闪电减弱为仅仅一些苍白的火花。

"没错，"一声回应传来，"我们已经尽了全力，令他们两个人都觉得很自在。布琳克罗小姐希望改变我们，而巴纳德先生也想要改变我们，将这里变成一个股份有限公司。毫无恶意的方案，他们能以此相当愉悦地打发时间，但你那位年轻的朋友，黄金和宗教都不能对他提供安慰，他该怎么办？"

"没错，他将会是个问题。"

"恐怕他将会是你的问题。"

"为什么是我的呢？"

大喇嘛并未立即作答，因为在此刻茶碗被端了进来，对于它们的出现，大喇嘛打起精神，露出一丝微弱又干瘪的笑意。"卡拉卡尔在每年的这个时候都给我们送来暴风雨，"他评论道并依照宗教仪式

conversation according to ritual. "The people of Blue Moon believe they are caused by demons raging in the great space beyond the pass. The 'outside,' they call it – perhaps you are aware that in their patois the word is used for the entire rest of the world. Of course they know nothing of such countries as France or England or even India – they imagine the dread altiplano stretching, as it almost does, illimitably. To them, so snug at their warm and windless levels, it appears unthinkable that anyone inside the valley should ever wish to leave it; indeed, they picture all unfortunate 'outsiders' as passionately desiring to enter. It is just a question of viewpoint, is it not?"

Conway was reminded of Barnard's somewhat similar remarks, and quoted them. "How very sensible!" was the High Lama's comment. "And he is our first American, too – we are truly fortunate."

Conway found it piquant to reflect that the lamasery's fortune was to have acquired a man for whom the police of a dozen countries were actively searching; and he would have liked to share the piquancy but for feeling that Barnard had better be left to tell his own story in due course. He said: "Doubtless he's quite right, and there are many people in the world nowadays who would be glad enough to be here."

渲染着这次交谈，"蓝月谷的人们相信它们是被关口那面、在巨大空间里异常暴怒的恶魔所引起的。'外面'，他们这么称呼，也许你能意识到在他们的方言里，这个词被用来代表山谷以外的整个世界。当然，他们不清楚类似法国、或者英国，甚至印度这样的国家。他们想象着那恐怖的高原延伸着，差不多就像那样无限延伸。对他们来说，那温暖和平静是如此的舒适，如果山谷里面的任何人希望离开它，那似乎是不可思议的。确实，他们构想着所有不幸的'外来人'如此热切地渴望进入山谷中来。这是一个观点的问题，不是吗？"

这让康维回忆起巴纳德说过的有点相似的评论，于是他援引它们。"实在太明智了！"大喇嘛评论道，"他也是我们这里的第一个美国人，我们当真幸运。"

康维觉得有点讽刺意味：喇嘛寺的幸运，就是因为获得了一个被很多国家的警察全力搜寻的人。他想要分享这种讽刺的幽默，可又觉得最好还是留给巴纳德在适当时自己讲述他的故事吧。他说道："毫无疑问，他来这里相当正确，而且在这个世界上还有很多人都巴不得来这里呢。"

"Too many, my dear Conway. We are a single lifeboat riding the seas in a gale; we can take a few chance survivors, but if all the shipwrecked were to reach us and clamber aboard we should go down ourselves… But let us not think of it just now. I hear that you have been associating with our excellent Briac. A delightful fellow countryman of mine, though I do not share his opinion that Chopin is the greatest of all composers. For myself, as you know, I prefer Mozart…"

Not till the tea bowls were removed and the servant had been finally dismissed did Conway venture to recall the unanswered question. "We were discussing Mallinson, and you said he was going to be *my* problem. Why mine, particularly?"

Then the High Lama replied very simply: "Because, my son, I am going to die."

It seemed an extraordinary statement, and for a time Conway was speechless after it. Eventually the High Lama continued: "You are surprised? But surely, my friend, we are all mortal – even at Shangri-La. And it is possible that I may still have a few moments left to me – or even, for that matter, a few years. All I announce is the simple truth that already I see the end. It is charming of you to appear so concerned, and I will not pretend that there is not a touch of

"实在太多了，我亲爱的康维，我们是在狂风中航行的唯一一艘救生艇。我们能够偶然接纳一些幸存者。但倘若全部遭遇海难的人都来到我们这里，爬上甲板，那我们自己都会沉下去的…但我们现在不要考虑这个。我听说你已经与我们那杰出的布里亚克相处甚欢了。他是一个令人愉快的家伙，是我的同乡，尽管我不赞同他关于肖邦的观点，他觉得肖邦是最伟大的作曲家，但你清楚，我更喜欢莫扎特。"

直到茶碗被端走，仆人们最终离开了，康维才敢再问起刚才没被回答的问题，"我们刚才谈论马林逊，你说他将会是我的难题，为什么偏偏是我的呢？"

大喇嘛非常简单地回应道："因为，我的孩子，我就快死了。"

这太意外了，这句话以后，康维有一段时间都说不出话来。最终，大喇嘛继续说："你很惊奇吧？但确实，我的朋友，我们所有人都是要死的，即便是在香格里拉。很可能我还剩下一些时间，或者甚至是，就那一点而论，有几年的时间，我所表明的全部就是一个简单的真理，即我已经看到了终点。你表现出如此关切真令人高兴，即便是在我这个年纪，也不会伪装得想到死亡却没有一丝愁闷的触动。所幸

wistfulness, even at my age, in contemplating death. Fortunately little is left of me that can die physically, and as for the rest, all our religions display a pleasant unanimity of optimism. I am quite content, but I must accustom myself to a strange sensation during the hours that remain – I must realize that I have time for only one thing more. Can you imagine what that is?"

Conway was silent.

"It concerns you, my son."

"You do me a great honor."

"I have in mind to do much more than that."

Conway bowed slightly, but did not speak, and the High Lama, after waiting awhile, resumed: "You know, perhaps, that the frequency of these talks has been unusual here. But it is our tradition, if I may permit myself the paradox, that we are never slaves to tradition. We have no rigidities, no inexorable rules. We do as we think fit, guided a little by the example of the past, but still more by our present wisdom, and by our clairvoyance of the future. And thus it is that I am encouraged to do this final thing."

Conway was still silent.

"I place in your hands, my son, the heritage and destiny of Shangri-La."

At last the tension broke, and Conway felt beyond it the power of a bland and

的是，我没有什么好牵挂的，可以按自然法则死亡。至于其他，我们全部的信仰呈现出的就是一种愉悦统一的乐观主义精神，我相当满足，但在剩下的这些时间里，我必须让自己适应一种奇怪的感觉，我必须意识到我只有再做一件事的时间。你能想到它是什么吗？"

康维一言不发。

"这涉及到你，孩子。"

"你给了我莫大的荣幸。"

"我想做的比这个要多很多呢。"

康维轻轻地点点头，但没有说话。等了片刻之后，大喇嘛继续说道："你也许清楚，在这里这种频繁的交谈并不寻常。但这是我们的传统，如果我能允许我自己自相矛盾的话。我们永远不是传统的奴隶。我们没有顽固不化，也没有一成不变的规矩，我们做我们觉得合理的事，以过去的例子做一点指引，但更多的还是通过我们现有的智慧，通过我们对未来的洞察。因此，我被鼓舞着，要做这最后一件事。"

康维还是一言不发。

"我要将香格里拉的继承权以及命运交到你的手上，我的孩子。"

最终，紧张被打破了。康维觉

benign persuasion; the echoes swam into silence, till all that was left was his own heartbeat, pounding like a gong. And then, intercepting the rhythm, came the words:

"I have waited for you, my son, for quite a long time. I have sat in this room and seen the faces of new-comers, I have looked into their eyes and heard their voices, and always in hope that someday I might find you. My colleagues have grown old and wise, but you who are still young in years are as wise already. My friend, it is not an arduous task that I bequeath, for our order knows only silken bonds. To be gentle and patient, to care for the riches of the mind, to preside in wisdom and secrecy while the storm rages without – it will all be very pleasantly simple for you, and you will doubtless find great happiness."

Again Conway sought to reply, but could not, till at length a vivid lightning-flash paled the shadows and stirred him to exclaim: "The storm… this storm you talked of…"

"It will be such a one, my son, as the world has not seen before. There will be no safety by arms, no help from authority, no answer in science. It will rage till every flower of culture is trampled, and all human things are leveled in a vast chaos. Such was my vision when Napoleon was still a name unknown; and I see it now,

得在这话的背后有一种温和的力量以及和蔼的说服力；声音的回响游荡在寂静中，剩下的全是康维自己的心跳，就像一只铜锣在猛敲。然后，说话声响起，打乱了这一节奏：

"我的孩子，我等待你已经有相当长的一段时间了。我坐在这间屋子里，看到了很多新来的人的面孔，我看着他们的双眼，聆听他们的声音，总是希望有一天我能找到你。我的同僚们虽然睿智但也逐渐上了年纪，而你，年轻却已经很睿智了。我的朋友，我遗留给你的，并不是一个险峻的任务。因为我们的制度只晓得情谊，你要温和、有耐心，要留心去丰富头脑，当暴风雨肆意妄为时，要智慧而秘密地应对。所有这一切对你来说，将会非常轻松简单，毫无疑问，你会发现巨大的幸福。"

康维再次想找到一个答案，但却无法找出来，直到最终一道清晰的闪电划过，使黑暗变得惨白，令他激动地大喊："风暴，你所说的风暴是……"

"我的孩子，它将会是一场前所未见的风暴，到那时，人们通过武力不可能获得安全，权威那里得不到帮助，科学范围里没有答案。它将肆意妄为，直到每一朵文明的花朵都被践踏，全部人类的事物都将处于巨大的混乱状态。当拿破仑

more clearly with each hour. Do you say I am mistaken?"

Conway answered: "No, I think you may be right. A similar crash came once before, and then there were the Dark Ages lasting five hundred years."

"The parallel is not quite exact. For those Dark Ages were not really so very dark – they were full of flickering lanterns, and even if the light had gone out of Europe altogether, there were other rays, literally from China to Peru, at which it could have been rekindled. But the Dark Ages that are to come will cover the whole world in a single pall; there will be neither escape nor sanctuary, save such as are too secret to be found or too humble to be noticed. And Shangri-La may hope to be both of these. The airman bearing loads of death to the great cities will not pass our way, and if by chance he should, he may not consider us worth a bomb."

"And you think all this will come in my time?"

"I believe that you will live through the storm. And after, through the long age of desolation, you may still live, growing older and wiser and more patient. You will conserve the fragrance of our history and add to it the touch of your own mind. You will welcome the stranger, and teach him the rule of age and wisdom; and one of these strangers, it may be, will succeed

还是个无名小卒时，我的预见便是如此；现在，我看着它，每过一小时这个预见便更为清晰。你认为我是错的吗？"

康维回答道："不，我认为你可能是对的，类似的灾难之前曾经出现过，然后黑暗便持续了 100 年。"

"这种对比不太确切。因为那些黑暗时代并非当真如此黑暗，它们充满着忽隐忽现的光亮，即使光亮在整个欧洲的光明都消失了，还有其他光明，差不多从中国一直到秘鲁，将会被重新点燃。但即将到来的黑暗时代将会以一个单一的幕布笼罩着全世界，人们既不能逃脱，也无法避难，而在类似那些太隐秘以至于无法找到，或是太卑微而无人注意之处，才能得以保全。但愿香格里拉能够两者兼具。而那些肩负着生死重任的飞行员飞往大城市时不会经过我们这里，即便他偶尔经过，也不会认为我们值得轰炸。"

"你觉得所有这些都会在我的时代降临？"

"我相信你会经受住这场风暴，然后，经过长时间的荒芜，你可能依然活着，年纪越大越睿智、越有耐心。你会保持我们历史的芬芳，并将你自己的思维能力添加进去。你会欢迎陌生人，传授他们长寿和智慧的秘诀；当你自己非常老

you when you are yourself very old. Beyond that, my vision weakens, but I see, at a great distance, a new world stirring in the ruins, stirring clumsily but in hopefulness, seeking its lost and legendary treasures. And they will all be here, my son, hidden behind the mountains in the valley of Blue Moon, preserved as by miracle for a new Renaissance…"

The speaking finished, and Conway saw the face before him full of a remote and drenching beauty; then the glow faded and there was nothing left but a mask, dark-shadowed, and crumbling like old wood. It was quite motionless, and the eyes were closed. He watched for a while, and presently, as part of a dream, it came to him that the High Lama was dead.

It seemed necessary to rivet the situation to some kind of actuality, lest it become too strange to be believed in; and with instinctive mechanism of hand and eye, Conway glanced at his wrist-watch. It was a quarter-past midnight. Suddenly, when he crossed the room to the door, it occurred to him that he did not in the least know how or whence to summon help. The Tibetans, he knew, had all been sent away for the night, and he had no idea where to find Chang or anyone else. He stood uncertainly on the threshold of the

的时候，其中一个陌生人可能会继承你的事业。虽然我的预见逐渐变弱，但是我能看到极其长的一段时间之后，一个新的世界会在废墟上崛起，虽然缓慢，但却充满希望，寻求着它失去的东西以及传奇般的宝藏。我的孩子，它们全都在这里啊，藏于这个蓝月谷的群山之后，为了一个崭新的文艺复兴而奇迹般地保存在这里……"

谈话结束了，康维看到他面前的那张脸充满了一种遥远的、洋溢着的美好，然后光泽渐渐褪去，什么都没有留下，只有一张阴影模样的面具，枯萎得仿佛朽木，他完全一动不动，双眼紧闭着。他望着他好长一会儿……不久，就像梦的一部分，他意识到大喇嘛已经圆寂了。

他似乎有必要将这种处境好好地回味一番，因为它变得太奇怪，以至于难以置信。在手和眼的本能机制下，康维瞥了一眼他的手表，现在是零点一刻。当他穿过房间来到门口时，他突然想到他丝毫不清楚怎么或者从哪里去寻求帮助。他清楚，那些藏族人已经全部去睡觉了，他也完全不清楚去哪里找张或者其他人。他站在黑暗走廊的门槛上，拿不定主意；通过窗户他能够看到天空非常晴朗，群山仍然熠熠生辉，仿佛一幅银色的壁画

dark corridor; through a window he could see that the sky was clear, though the mountains still blazed in lightning like a silver fresco. And then, in the midst of the still encompassing dream, he felt himself master of Shangri-La. These were his beloved things, all around him, the things of that inner mind in which he lived increasingly, away from the fret of the world. His eyes strayed into the shadows and were caught by golden pin-points sparkling in rich, undulating lacquers; and the scent of tuberose, so faint that it expired on the very brink of sensation, lured him from room to room. At last he stumbled into the courtyards and by the fringe of the pool; a full moon sailed behind Karakal. It was twenty minutes to two.

Later, he was aware that Mallinson was near him, holding his arm and leading him away in a great hurry. He did not gather what it was all about, but he could hear that the boy was chattering excitedly.

似的，然后，康维仍然在梦境的包围中，他感觉到自己就是香格里拉的主人。这些他所深爱的东西，全部围绕着他，他愈发赖以生存的灵魂里的东西，已经远离了尘世的困扰。他的双眼迷离着进入一片黑影中，然后又被华美般呈波浪状的漆器上闪烁着的针点状的金光所捕捉。晚香玉的香气是如此的微弱，若有若无，总是在嗅觉的边缘，引诱他从一个屋子到另一个屋子，最终，他蹒跚着进入了庭院，来到池塘的边缘；一轮满月正在卡拉卡尔山后自由升起。现在已是 1 点 40 分了。

然后，他意识到马林逊就在他的旁边，正抓住他的胳膊，非常急迫地要拉他走。他没有弄清楚这一切都是怎么回事，但他能听到这小子正兴奋地在说着什么。

CHAPTER 11

第十一章

THEY reached the balconied room where they had meals, Mallinson still clutching his arm and half-dragging him along. "Come on, Conway, we've till dawn to pack what we can and get away. Great news, man – I wonder what old Barnard and Miss Brinklow will think in the morning when they find us gone… Still, it's their own choice to stay, and we'll probably get on far better without them… The porters are about five miles beyond the pass – they came yesterday with loads of books and things… to-morrow they begin the journey back… It just shows how these fellows here intended to let us down – they never told us – we should have been stranded here for God knows how much longer… I say, what's the matter? Are you ill?"

Conway had sunk into a chair, and was leaning forward with elbows on the table. He passed his hand across his eyes. "Ill? No. I don't think so. Just – rather – tired."

"Probably the storm. Where were you all the while? I'd been waiting for you for hours."

"I – I was visiting the High Lama."

"Oh, *him!* Well, *that's* for the last time, anyhow, thank God."

他们来到这间带有阳台的房间，这是他们用餐的地方。马林逊还是紧紧抓着康维的胳膊，半拖着他向前。"来吧，康维，我们在黎明之前尽可能收拾东西，然后离开。这可是重大的新闻，伙计——我在想，早上老巴纳德以及布琳克罗小姐发现咱俩走了，会想些什么……尽管如此，他们依然选择留下来，没有他们，我们也许能够干得更好……那些脚夫大约在距隘口5英里的地方，他们昨天来的，携带着许多书和一些东西……明天他们便要启程返回了……这说明这里的这些家伙是多么希望将我们留下来——他们从来没有告诉过我们——上帝晓得我们还会被困在这里多长时间……我说，有什么事吗？你生病了吗？"

康维一屁股坐到椅子中，身体向前倾，肘部抵在桌上，他用手揉着眼睛，"生病？没有，我觉得不是，就是……精疲力竭。"

"也许是由于那场暴风雨？当时你究竟在什么地方？我一直等了你好几个小时了。"

"我……我正拜访大喇嘛。"

"哦，他呀！那么，这是最后一次喽，不管怎么说，谢天谢地。"

"Yes, Mallinson, for the last time."

Something in Conway's voice, and still more in his succeeding silence, roused the youth to irascibility. "Well, I wish you wouldn't sound so deuced leisurely about it – we've got to get a considerable move on, you know."

Conway stiffened for the effort of emerging into keener consciousness. "I'm sorry," he said. Partly to test his nerve and the reality of his sensations he lit a cigarette. He found that both hands and lips were unsteady. "I'm afraid I don't quite follow… you say the porters…"

"Yes, the porters, man – do pull yourself together."

"You're thinking of going out to them?"

"*Thinking* of it? I'm damn well certain – they're only just over the ridge. And we've got to start immediately."

"*Immediately?*"

"Yes, yes – why not?"

Conway made a second attempt to transfer himself from one world into the other. He said at length, having partly succeeded: "I suppose you realize that it mayn't be quite as simple as it sounds?"

Mallinson was lacing a pair of knee-high Tibetan mountain-boots as he answered jerkily: "I realize everything, but it's something we've got to do, and we shall do it, with luck, if we don't delay."

"I don't see how –"

"Oh, Lord, Conway, must you fight shy

"是的，马林逊，最后一次。"

在康维的声音里有某种东西，而且在他那随后的沉默里反而更多了，将这小伙子激怒了，"好了，我希望关于这件事，你不要再有任何的迟疑……你知道，我们应该开始行动了。"

过度地沉浸在更强烈的意识中使康维变得僵硬起来。"我非常抱歉，"他说道，为了考验他的神经以及感官的真实性，他点上一支烟。他发现双手和嘴唇哆哆嗦嗦，"恐怕我并未完全弄明白……你说那些脚夫……"

"没错，是脚夫，伙计……你要控制住你自己啊。"

"你在考虑出去找他们？"

"考虑？我是相当确定……他们就在翻过山的那侧，我们准备立刻启程。"

"立刻？"

"是的，是的，为什么不呢？"

康维再次企图让自己的思维从一个世界转移到另一个世界里，部分承接着上面的话，他最终说道："我觉得你应当意识到，那完全不像它听起来那样简单。"

当马林逊急促地回答时，他正在给一双高度及膝的藏族登山靴系鞋带："我意识到每一件事了，但我们必须去做，如果我们不耽搁又够幸运的话，我们应该能够做到。"

"我不清楚如何……"

of everything? Haven't you any guts left in you at all?"

The appeal, half passionate and half-derisive, helped Conway to collect himself. "Whether I have or haven't isn't the point, but if you want me to explain myself, I will. It's a question of a few rather important details. Suppose you *do* get beyond the pass and find the porters there, how do you know they'll take you with them? What inducement can you offer? Hasn't it struck you that they mayn't be quite so willing as you'd like them to be? You can't just present yourself and demand to be escorted. It all needs arrangements, negotiations beforehand –"

"Or anything else to cause a delay," exclaimed Mallinson bitterly. "God, what a fellow you are! Fortunately I haven't you to rely on for arranging things. Because they *have* been arranged – the porters have been paid in advance, and they've agreed to take us. And here are clothes and equipment for the journey, all ready. So your last excuse disappears. Come on, let's *do* something."

"But – I don't understand…"

"I don't suppose you do, but it doesn't matter."

"Who's been making all these plans?"

Mallinson answered brusquely: "Lo-Tsen, if you're really keen to know. She's with the porters now. She's waiting."

"哦，上帝，康维，你一定要这么畏惧吗？难不成你身上剩余的勇气丝毫没有了？"

这半愤怒半讥讽的控诉，让康维回过神来，"我是否有勇气这不重要，可倘若你让我解释一下的话，我会解释。这是个有许多相当重要的细节的问题。假设你确实能通过隘口，在那里找到那些脚夫，那你如何知道他们会带你一起走？你有什么办法说服他们？难不成你没想到他们可能不会像你所希望他们的那样，愿意带你走？你不能只是自己出现在那里，然后要求被带走，这全都需要预先安排和谈判。"

"或者其他任何情况也会导致延误，"马林逊恶狠狠地大嚷，"上帝，你是个什么东西！幸亏我不需要靠你来安排这些事，因为事情已经被安排好了——脚夫事先已经付了钱，他们也同意带我们走，还有，这是旅途需要的衣服和装备，全都准备好了。因此，你那最后一条借口也不存在了。来吧，我们做点什么吧。"

"但……我不理解……"

"我知道你不会理解，可这没有关系。"

"谁制订了全部这些计划？"

马林逊鲁莽地回答道："如果你当真渴望知道的话，是罗珍。她现在正与脚夫在一起，她正等我们呢。"

"*Waiting?*"

"Yes. She's coming with us. I assume you've no objection?"

At the mention of Lo-Tsen the two worlds touched and fused suddenly in Conway's mind. He cried sharply, almost contemptuously: "That's nonsense. It's impossible."

Mallinson was equally on edge. "Why is it impossible?"

"Because… well, it is. There are all sorts of reasons. Take my word for it; it won't do. It's incredible enough that she should be out there now – I'm astonished at what you say has happened – but the idea of her going any further is just preposterous."

"I don't see that it's preposterous at all. It's as natural for her to want to leave here as for me."

"But she doesn't want to leave. That's where you make the mistake."

Mallinson smiled tensely. "You think you know a good deal more about her than I do, I dare say," he remarked. "But perhaps you don't, for all that."

"What do you mean?"

"There are other ways of getting to understand people without learning heaps of languages."

"For heaven's sake, what *are* you driving at?" Then Conway added more quietly: "This is absurd. We mustn't

"等？"

"是的，她与我们一起走。我想你没有反对意见吧？"

一提及"罗珍"两个字，康维内心深处，两个世界便相互接触并突然融合了。他几乎轻蔑地厉声大叫："一派胡言，这不可能。"

马林逊同样急切，"为什么不可能？"

"好吧，因为……这存在各种类型的理由。相信我，不可能的，她现在会离开这里，简直太令人难以置信了…我对你所说的已经发生的事大为震惊……但她会离开这里半步的想法本身就是非常荒谬的。"

"我完全看不出来这种想法很荒谬。对她来说，想要离开这里的想法与我一样，非常自然。"

"可她不想离开，这便是你犯错误的地方。"

马林逊紧张地微微一笑，"我敢说，你觉得对于她，你比我要了解的多很多，"他评论道，"可虽然如此，也许你并未真正了解她。"

"你什么意思？"

"在没有学习多种语言的情况下，也可以有另外的方式去理解别人嘛。"

"看在上帝的分上，你究竟用意何在？"康维更加镇定地补充，"这太荒谬了。我们不能再争执下

wrangle. Tell me, Mallinson, what's it all about? I still don't understand."

"Then why are you making such an almighty fuss?"

"Tell me the truth, *please* tell me the truth."

"Well, it's simple enough. A kid of her age shut up here with a lot of queer old men – naturally she'll get away if she's given a chance. She hasn't had one up to now."

"Don't you think you may be imagining her position in the light of your own? As I've always told you, she's perfectly happy."

"Then why did she say she'd come?"

"She said that? How could she? She doesn't speak English."

"I asked her – in Tibetan – Miss Brinklow worked out the words. It wasn't a very fluent conversation, but it was quite enough to – to lead to an understanding." Mallinson flushed a little. "Damn it, Conway, don't stare at me like that – anyone would think I'd been poaching on *your* preserves."

Conway answered: "No one would think so at all, I hope, but the remark tells me more than you were perhaps intending me to know. I can only say that I'm very sorry."

"And why the devil should you be?"

Conway let the cigarette fall from his fingers. He felt tired, bothered, and full of

去了，告诉我，马林逊，这一切究竟是怎么回事？我仍然不能理解。"

"那为什么你如此乱作一团？"

"告诉我真相，请告诉我真相吧。"

"好吧，足够简单。一个与她年纪相仿的小伙子突然出现，而这里都是一群古怪的老头子——自然而然，如果她有机会，她会逃走，只是直到现在她都没有机会而已。"

"你不觉得你可能只是在以你的见解去想象她的处境吗？就像我总是告诉你的那样，她非常开心。"

"那么她为什么说想走呢？"

"她说这句话了吗？她如何能说呢？她不会讲英语。"

"我用藏语问她的……布琳克罗小姐能够拼出几个词。对话并非非常顺畅……但足够了……能够理解。"马林逊有点脸红，"该死的，康维，不要这样瞪着我，任何人都会觉得我已经侵入了你的领地。"

康维回答道：我希望"根本没有人会如此认为，但这些话告诉我的也许比你打算让我知道的东西更多。我只能说，我非常抱歉。"

"该死，为什么你会这样呢？"

康维任凭那支香烟从指间滑

deep conflicting tenderness that he would rather not have had aroused. He said gently: "I wish we weren't always at such cross-purposes. Lo-Tsen is very charming, I know, but why should we quarrel about it?"

"*Charming?*" Mallinson echoed the word with scorn. "She's a good bit more than that. You mustn't think everybody's as cold-blooded about these things as you are yourself. Admiring her as if she were an exhibit in a museum may be your idea of what she deserves, but mine's more practical, and when I see someone I like in a rotten position I try and *do* something."

"But surely there's such a thing as being too impetuous? Where do you think she'll go to if she does leave?"

"I suppose she must have friends in China or somewhere. Anyhow, she'll be better off than here."

"How can you possibly be so sure of that?"

"Well, I'll see that she's looked after myself, if nobody else will. After all, if you're rescuing people from something quite hellish, you don't usually stop to enquire if they've anywhere else to go to."

"And you think Shangri-La is hellish?"

"Definitely, I do. There's something dark and evil about it. The whole business has been like that, from the beginning – the way we were brought here, without reason at all, by some madman – and the

落。他觉得精疲力竭、心烦意乱，充满着矛盾。他宁愿这些根本不曾发生。他轻柔地说道，"我希望我们不要总是意见相左。我清楚罗珍非常吸引人，但为什么我们要为此争吵呢？"

"吸引人？"马林逊以不屑的神情重复这个词，"她远远不止是吸引人，你千万不要觉得每个人对这类事情都像你自己似的冷若冰霜。仿佛她是博物馆的一件展品来崇拜她，这可能是你认为她应得的想法，但我的想法更实际，当我发现我爱上一个人到不能自拔的地步时，我会试着做些什么。"

"但这的确有点太过冲动吧？你认为如果她真的离开这里，她将会去什么地方呢？"

"我觉得在中国或其他地方，她一定有朋友。不管怎么说，她将会比在这儿更好。"

"你怎么会这么有把握呢？

"好吧，倘若没有其他人愿意，我会让她跟随我。毕竟，倘若你从一个凶恶的地方将人们救出来，如果他们有其他任何地方能去，你通常也不会停下来去询问的。"

"你觉得香格里拉非常凶恶？"

"一点也没错，我是这么认为的。这里存在着某种黑暗和邪恶的东西。整件事从一开始便像这样——我们被某个疯了的人，在

way we've been detained since, on one excuse or another. But the most frightful thing of all – to me – is the effect it's had on you."

"On *me*?"

"Yes, on you. You've just mooned about as if nothing mattered and you were content to stay here forever. Why, you even admitted you liked the place… Conway, what *has* happened to you? Can't you manage to be your real self again? We got on so well together at Baskul – you were absolutely different in those days."

"My *dear* boy!"

Conway reached his hand towards Mallinson's, and the answering grip was hot and eagerly affectionate. Mallinson went on: "I don't suppose you realize it, but I've been terribly alone these last few weeks. Nobody seemed to be caring a damn about the only thing that was really important – Barnard and Miss Brinklow had reasons of a kind, but it was pretty awful when I found *you* against me."

"I'm sorry."

"You keep on saying that, but it doesn't help."

Conway replied on sudden impulse: "Then let me help, if I can, by telling you something. When you've heard it, you'll understand, I hope, a great deal of what now seems very curious and difficult. At any rate, you'll realize why Lo-Tsen can't possibly go back with you."

完全没有理由的情况下，带到这里…自从那以后，便以一种或另一种借口将我们扣留在此。而所有事情中最为恐怖的就是……它已经对你造成了影响。"

"对我？"

"没错，对你。你已经对此失了神，好像没什么东西是重要的，而你心满意足地永远待在这儿。为什么，你甚至承认你喜欢这个地方……康维，你究竟发生了什么事？难不成你都不能认清自己了么？在巴斯库，我们在一起相处得多么好——在那些日子，你绝对和现在不同。"

"我亲爱的小伙子！"

康维向马林逊伸出了他的双手，马林逊紧紧握住了，回应他的是热烈又急切的真挚感情，"我觉得你没有意识到，但过去的几周以来，我一直非常孤独。似乎没有人对于唯一一件真正重要的事有丝毫的关心——巴纳德以及布琳克罗小姐也就罢了，但当我发现你都反对我时，真是太恐怖了。"

"我非常抱歉。"

"你一直这么说，但不管用。"

康维在突然涌现的冲动下回应道："那么，如果我可以，让我告诉你一些事情来帮助你吧。当你听完后，我希望你会理解。现在有非常多似乎极其稀奇而又棘手的情形，总之，你会意识到，为什么罗珍不可能与你一同回去。"

"I don't think anything would make me see that. And do cut it as short as you can, because we really haven't time to spare."

Conway then gave, as briefly as he could, the whole story of Shangri-La, as told him by the High Lama, and as amplified by the conversation both with the latter and with Chang. It was the last thing he had ever intended to do, but he felt that in the circumstances it was justified and even necessary; it was true enough that Mallinson *was* his problem, to solve as he thought fit. He narrated rapidly and easily, and in doing so came again under the spell of that strange, timeless world; its beauty overwhelmed him as he spoke of it, and more than once he felt himself reading from a page of memory, so clearly had ideas and phrases impressed themselves. Only one thing he withheld – and that to spare himself an emotion he could not yet grapple with – the fact of the High Lama's death that night and of his own succession.

When he approached the end he felt comforted; he was glad to have got it over, and it was the only solution, after all. He looked up calmly when he had finished, confident that he had done well.

But Mallinson merely tapped his fingers on the table-top and said, after a long wait: "I really don't know what to say, Conway… except that you must be completely mad…"

"没有任何东西能让我看出来她不会走的原因，而且你要尽可能说得简短，因为我们当真没有什么时间可去浪费了。"

然后，康维尽可能简要地讲出关于香格里拉的整个故事，就像他被大喇嘛告知的那样，还对大喇嘛与张的谈话加以详述。这是他打算去做的最后一件事，但他感到在这种环境里，这很合理，甚至非常有必要，马林逊是他的大难题，这是绝对千真万确的了，以至于他要按照他觉得恰当的方式去解决。他快速而自如地陈述着，而这样做却又让他再次置身于那个奇异而永恒的世界的魔咒之下；当他讲述时，香格里拉的美令他无法抵挡。他不止一次觉得自己是在阅读一页记忆，这些念头还有语句本身令人如此清晰地深刻铭记，只有一件事他守口如瓶，就是他自己省去的、至今都不能与之抗衡的一种感情——就是那晚大喇嘛的去世以及他自己的接任这一事实。

当他接近结尾时，他感到很惬意；他觉得终于挨过去了，非常高兴。毕竟，这是唯一的解决办法。当他说完后，他冷静地抬起头来，自信他做得非常好。

但在漫长的等待之后，马林逊只是用他的手指敲着桌面："我真不清楚要说什么，康维……除非你完全疯了……"

There followed a long silence, during which the two men stared at each other in far different moods – Conway withdrawn and disappointed, Mallinson in hot, fidgeting discomfort. "So you think I'm mad?" said Conway at length.

Mallinson broke into a nervous laugh. "Well, I should damn well say so, after a tale like that. I mean… well, really… such utter nonsense… it seems to me rather beyond arguing about."

Conway looked and sounded immensely astonished. "You think it's nonsense?"

"Well… how else can I look at it? I'm sorry, Conway – it's a pretty strong statement – but I don't see how any sane person could be in any doubt about it."

"So you still hold that we were brought here by blind accident – by some lunatic who made careful plans to run off with an aeroplane and fly it a thousand miles just for the fun of the thing?"

Conway offered a cigarette, and the other took it. The pause was one for which they both seemed grateful. Mallinson answered eventually: "Look here, it's no good arguing the thing point by point. As a matter of fact, your theory that the people here sent someone vaguely into the world to decoy strangers, and that this fellow deliberately learned flying and bided his time until it happened that a suitable machine was due to leave Baskul with

随后是长久的寂静，在此期间，这两个人便在大相径庭的心境中，凝视着彼此——康维觉得孤立无援，而且很失望，而马林逊则置身于狂热、坐立不安的局促当中，"那么，你觉得我疯了？"最终，康维说道。

马林逊爆发出一阵神经兮兮的哈哈大笑，"好吧！在类似这样的奇闻之后，我他妈真的只能这么说！我的意思是……哦，真的…完全是胡言乱语……我似乎都完全不用对此争辩了。"

康维望着他，听着这大惊失色的言语："你觉得这是一派胡言？"

"好吧……我还能如何呢？我非常遗憾，康维，这是非常惟妙惟肖的论述——但我无法看出来任何一个头脑清醒的人怎么就能够对此没有丝毫怀疑呢。"

"那么你仍然觉得我们是被一次盲目的意外事故带到这里的？是某个疯子制订了周密的计划，以便劫持一架飞机逃跑，然后飞行 1000 英里，就是为了开这个大玩笑吗？"

康维递过去一支烟，另一个接了过去。这时，片刻的停顿似乎是他俩都很感激的。马林逊最终回答道："看看，一点点地争执这件事没有丝毫好处。实际上，你的理论就是，这里的人稀里糊涂地将某些人派到世界各地，去诱骗一些陌生人，因此那家伙有意去学习飞行，

four passengers… well, I won't say that it's literally impossible, though it does seem to me ridiculously far-fetched. If it stood by itself, it might just be worth considering, but when you tack it on to all sorts of other things that are *absolutely* impossible – all this about the lamas being hundreds of years old, and having discovered a sort of elixir of youth, or whatever you'd call it… well, it just makes me wonder what kind of microbe has bitten you, that's all."

Conway smiled. "Yes, I dare say you find it hard to believe. Perhaps I did myself at first – I scarcely remember. Of course it *is* an extraordinary story, but I should think your own eyes have had enough evidence that this is an extraordinary place. Think of all that we've actually seen, both of us – a lost valley in the midst of unexplored mountains, a monastery with a library of European books – "

"Oh, yes, and a central heating plant, and modern plumbing, and afternoon tea, and everything else – it's all very marvelous, I know."

"Well, then, what do you make of it?"

"Damn little, I admit. It's a complete mystery. But that's no reason for accepting tales that are physically impossible. Believing in hot baths because you've had them is different from believing in people hundreds of years old just because they've

等待时机，直到碰巧有架合适的飞机预计要与4个乘客一起离开巴斯库……那么，我不是说这完全不可能。尽管对我而言，它似乎荒唐可笑又有些牵强。倘若这是事实，那也许还值得思忖的，但当你硬将它附加于其他绝对不可能的各种类型的事上时——所有关于百岁年纪的喇嘛发现一种永葆青春的长生不老药，或者你所说的无论什么东西……那么，这就令我感到惊奇，你吃错药了，就这么回事。"

康维微微一笑："没错，我知道你会很难相信。也许我自己最初也是这样——我几乎记不起来了。当然，这是一个不同寻常的故事，但我觉得你自己的双眼会发现关于这个非比寻常之地的足够证据。想想我们实际亲眼看到的所有东西，咱们两个人——在未被探索的群山当中有一个迷失的山谷，有一座喇嘛寺，其中还带有一个收藏欧洲书籍的图书馆……"

"哦，是的，还有一套中央供暖设备，现代化的抽水马桶，下午茶，以及其他的每一件事——我知道，这些全都非常令人惊奇。"

"哦，那么你对此了解多少？"

"非常少，我承认。它完全是一个谜。但不存在什么理由让我去接受一种按自然法则来说并不可能的故事。你肯定相信有热水浴室，因为你使用过它们；这不同于

told you they are." He laughed again, still uneasily. "Look here, Conway, it's got on your nerves, this place, and I really don't wonder at it. Pack up your things and let's quit. We'll finish this argument a month or two hence after a jolly little dinner at Maiden's."

Conway answered quietly: "I've no desire to go back to that life at all."

"What life?"

"The life you're thinking of… dinners… dances… polo… and all that…"

"But I never said anything about dances and polo! Anyhow, what's wrong with them? D'you mean that you're not coming with me? You're going to stay here like the other two? Then at least you shan't stop *me* from clearing out of it!" Mallinson threw down his cigarette and sprang towards the door with eyes blazing. "You're off your head!" he cried wildly. "You're mad, Conway, that's what's the matter with you! I know you're always calm, and I'm always excited, but I'm sane, at any rate, and you're not! They warned me about it before I joined you at Baskul, and I thought they were wrong, but now I can see they weren't –"

"What did they warn you of?"

"They said you'd been blown up in the War, and you'd been queer at times ever since. I'm not reproaching you – I know it was nothing you could help – and Heaven knows I hate talking like this… Oh, I'll

相信一个人有几百岁的年纪，仅仅是由于他们告诉你的便是如此。"马林逊再次哈哈大笑，但仍然并不轻松，"看这里，这个地方把你的勇气带走了。我并不惊奇。收拾好你的东西，然后我们就走。一两个月之后当我们在梅登餐馆里兴高采烈的小吃一顿之后，我们就会结束这种争执。"

康维平静地答道："我完全没有欲望要回到那样的生活中去。"

"什么生活？"

"你正在想的那种生活……晚宴……舞会……马球……所有这些……"

"但我从来没有说任何关于跳舞和马球的事情啊，不管怎么说，这些有什么问题？你的意思是，你不打算和我一起走？你准备像其他两个人一样待在这里？那么，至少你不应该阻拦我彻底离开这里！马林逊扔掉他的香烟，突然猛地冲向门口，双眼冒着火光："你失去理性了！"他疯狂地大喊道，"你疯了，康维，这是你自己的问题！我清楚你总是很镇定，而我总是很激动，但我现在头脑清醒，至少，你现在神智不正常！在巴斯库我加入你那边之前便有人提醒过我，我当时认为他们是错的，但现在，我能够看出来他们没错…"

"他们当时提醒你什么了？"

"他们说你是在战争里塑造出来的人，而且自从那时开始，你

go. It's all frightful and sickening, but I must go. I gave my word."

"To Lo-Tsen?"

"Yes, if you want to know."

Conway got up and held out his hand. "Good-by, Mallinson."

"For the last time, you're not coming?"

"I can't."

"Good-by, then."

They shook hands, and Mallinson left.

Conway sat alone in the lantern-light. It seemed to him, in a phrase engraved on memory, that all the loveliest things were transient and perishable, that the two worlds were finally beyond reconciliation, and that one of them hung, as always, by a thread. After he had pondered for some time he looked at his watch; it was ten minutes to three.

He was still at the table, smoking the last of his cigarettes, when Mallinson returned. The youth entered with some commotion, and on seeing him, stood back in the shadows as if to gather his wits. He was silent, and Conway began, after waiting a moment: "Hullo, what's happened? Why are you back?"

The complete naturalness of the question fetched Mallinson forward; he pulled off his heavy sheepskins and sat down. His face was ashen and his whole body trembled. "I hadn't the nerve," he cried, half sobbing. "That place where we

便时不时地很古怪，我不是在责备你，我清楚你也没有办法，但天晓得我多痛恨类似这样的谈话…哦！我会走的，不管路途多么令人恐怖和厌倦，但我必须要走，我已做出我的承诺。"

"为了罗珍？"

"没错，倘若你想知道。"

康维站起身来，伸出手，"再见，马林逊！"

"最后一次，你不走吗？"

"我不能走。"

"那么，再见了！"

他们握了握手，马林逊离开了。

康维独自一人坐在灯光下。对他而言，似乎有一句警言妙语铭刻进记忆里：所有最美好的东西都是短暂而脆弱的，而两个世界最终无法协调统一，其中一个一直以来就那样被一根线悬在半空。在他思忖了一段时间之后，他看了看手表，现在是凌晨2点50分。

他还是坐在桌子旁边，吸着最后一支烟。这时马林逊回来了。这个年轻人以某种焦躁不安的神情走了进来，一看见康维，就站回到阴影里，好像是在调整他的情绪。他沉默不语，在等了一段时间之后，康维说道："喂，发生了什么事，你为什么回来了？"

这个问题将马林逊引上前来；他脱掉他那厚重的羊皮外套，然后坐了下来。他脸色惨白，他的整个

were all roped – you remember? I got as far as that… I couldn't manage it. I've no head for heights, and in moonlight it looked fearful. Silly, isn't it?" He broke down completely and was hysterical until Conway pacified him. Then he added: "They needn't worry, these fellows here – nobody will ever threaten them by land. But, my God, I'd give a good deal to fly over with a load of bombs!"

"Why would you like to do that, Mallinson?"

"Because the place wants smashing up, whatever it is. It's unhealthy and unclean – and for that matter, if your impossible yarn were true, it would be more hateful still! A lot of wizened old men crouching here like spiders for anyone who comes near… it's filthy… who'd want to live to an age like that, anyhow? And as for your precious High Lama, if he's half as old as you say he is, it's time someone put him out of his misery… Oh, why *won't* you come away with me, Conway? I hate imploring you for my own sake, but damn it all, I'm young and we've been pretty good friends together – does my whole life mean nothing to you compared with the lies of these awful creatures? And Lo-Tsen, too – *she's* young – doesn't *she* count at all?"

"Lo-Tsen is not young," said Conway.

Mallinson looked up and began to titter hysterically. "Oh, no, not young – not young at all, of course. She looks about

身体颤抖着。"我没有勇气,"他哭着说道,半呜咽着,"在那个我们所有人都被绑上绳索的地方……你记得吗?我已经到了那里……但我没有任何办法。我对于高山峻岭没有办法,而且在月光下它们看起来非常恐怖。我很傻,不是吗?"他完全被击败了,有些歇斯底里,康维只能抚慰他。然后马林逊补充道:"他们不用担心,这些家伙在这儿,没有人在陆地上会威胁到他们,但我的上帝,我哪天会用满载着炸弹的飞机狠狠打击他们。"

"你为什么这样做,马林逊?"

"因为这里需要土崩瓦解,无论它是什么。它不健康,不干净,并且由于这件事情,倘若你那不可能的奇谈是真的,那它会更令人痛恨!这么多枯萎消瘦的老头蜷缩在这里,蜘蛛一般等待着任何一个靠近的人……太肮脏了……不管怎么说,谁想活到这样的年纪?你那高贵的大喇嘛,倘若他有你说的他的年纪的一半,那也是时候送他摆脱他的痛苦了。哦,你为什么不愿意与我一起离开,康维?因为我的原因,我痛恨去恳求你,但更加见鬼的是,我还很年轻,我们在一起始终是非常亲密的朋友——比起那些可怕之人的谎言,我的整个生命对你而言,不名一文吗?还有罗珍,她也很年轻,难道她完全没有价值吗?"

"罗珍并不年轻。"康维说。

seventeen, but I suppose you'll tell me she's really a well-preserved ninety."

"Mallinson, she came here in 1884."

"You're raving, man!"

"Her beauty, Mallinson, like all other beauty in the world, lies at the mercy of those who do not know how to value it. It is a fragile thing that can only live where fragile things are loved. Take it away from this valley and you will see it fade like an echo."

Mallinson laughed harshly, as if his own thoughts gave him confidence. "I'm not afraid of that. It's here that she's only an echo, if she's one anywhere at all." He added after a pause: "Not that this sort of talk gets us anywhere. We'd better cut out all the poetic stuff and come down to realities. Conway, I want to help you – it's all the sheerest nonsense, I know, but I'll argue it out if it'll do you any good. I'll pretend it's something possible that you've told me, and that it really does need examining. Now tell me, seriously, what evidence have you for this story of yours?"

Conway was silent.

"Merely that someone spun you a fantastic rigmarole. Even from a thoroughly reliable person whom you'd known all your life, you wouldn't accept that sort of thing without proof. And what proofs have you in this case? None at all, so far as I can see. Has Lo-Tsen ever told

马林逊抬起头，歇斯底里地傻笑道："哦，不，不年轻……一点也不……当然，她看起来大概 17 岁，你会告诉我，她是一个保养得很好的 90 岁高龄的人。"

"马林逊，她 1884 年便来了。"

"伙计，你在说疯话吧。"

"马林逊，她的美与世上其他的美无异，存在于那些不知道如何评估它的人们的仁慈和怜悯中。它很脆弱，仅仅能够生存在被爱护的地方。倘若将它从山谷里带出去，你便会看到它仿佛回声一般慢慢消失。"

马林逊粗俗地哈哈大笑，好像他的想法给了他信心。"我不担心这个。倘若她在任何地方根本就是一个回声的话，那么在这里她也只能是个回声。"他停顿后补充道，"这类谈话不会将我们带到任何地方。咱们最好停止全部诗情画意的东西，回到现实中来。康维，我想帮你，我清楚，这一切纯属一派胡言，但我要说服你，只要这会对你有好处。我会假装认为你曾经告诉我的一些事情是真的，但还是需要仔细查证。现在，你认真告诉我，关于你的这个故事，你有什么证据吗？"

康维沉默不语。

"仅仅是有人对你编了个荒诞不经的谎话，即使出自一个完全可靠、而且你这一辈子都对他很理解的人之口，你也不能在没有证据

you her history?"

"No, but –"

"Then why believe it from someone else? And all this longevity business – can you point to a single outside fact in support of it?"

Conway thought a moment and then mentioned the unknown Chopin works that Briac had played.

"Well, that's a matter that means nothing to me – I'm not a musician. But even if they're genuine, isn't it possible that he could have got hold of them in some way without his story being true?"

"Quite possible, no doubt."

"And then this method that you say exists – of preserving youth and so on. What is it? You say it's a sort of drug – well, I want to know *what* drug? Have you ever seen it or tried it? Did anyone ever give you any positive facts about the thing at all?"

"Not in detail, I admit."

"And you never asked for details? It didn't strike you that such a story needed any confirmation at all? You just swallowed it whole?" Pressing his advantage, he continued: "How much do you actually know of this place, apart from what you've been told? You've seen a few old men – that's all it amounts to. Apart from that, we can only say that the place is well fitted up, and seems to be run on rather highbrow lines. How and why it

的情况下便接受这类事嘛。对这桩事，你有什么证据？迄今为止，我能够看出来，完全没有。罗珍曾经告诉过你她的故事吗？"

"没有，但……"

"那么，你为什么要相信从其他人那里得到的消息？就说长生不老这件事吧——你能指出一个单一的外界的实例来支撑它吗？"

康维想了片刻，然后提及了布里亚克曾经弹奏过的那些不为人知的肖邦作品。

"这是一件对我而言毫无意义的事情——我并非一个音乐家。但即使它们是真实的，难道如果他以某种方式得到它们，而他的故事不是真的，这不可能吗？"

"非常有可能，毋庸置疑。"

"然后你所说的存在着永葆青春还有等等的这个方法，它是什么？你说是一类药，那么，我想弄清是什么药？你曾经看到过还是尝试过？对这件事，有任何人曾经给过你任何实例吗？"

"不怎么详细，我承认。"

"你从不询问细节吗？它没令你想到这完全需要一些证实吗？你就全部囫囵吞枣了？"坚持着他的优势，他继续说道："事实上，你对这里究竟知道多少，除了你被告诉的那些？你是看到了一些老人，这是总计的全部。除此之外，我们只能说这地方装备得非常精良，而且似乎在文化修养相当高

came into existence we've no idea, and why they want to keep us here, if they do, is equally a mystery, but surely all that's hardly an excuse for believing any old legend that comes along! After all, man, you're a critical sort of person – you'd hesitate to believe all you were told even in an English monastery – I really can't see why you should jump at everything just because you're in Tibet!"

Conway nodded. Even in the midst of far keener perceptions he could not restrain approval of a point well made. "That's an acute remark, Mallinson. I suppose the truth is that when it comes to believing things without actual evidence, we all incline to what we find most attractive."

"Well, I'm dashed if I can see anything attractive about living till you're half-dead. Give me a short life and a gay one, for choice. And this stuff about a future war – it all sounds pretty thin to me. How does anyone know when the next war's going to be or what it'll be like? Weren't all the prophets wrong about the last war?" He added, when Conway did not reply: "Anyhow, I don't believe in saying things are inevitable. And even if they were, there's no need to get into a funk about them. Heaven knows I'd most likely be scared stiff if I had to fight in a war, but I'd rather face up to it than bury myself here."

的轨迹上被经营着，但它如何以及为什么存在，我们一无所知，而且为什么他们想将我们一直留在这里——倘若他们确实想——也同样是个谜，但肯定，所有这些都难以成为去相信任何一个随之而来的古老传说的借口！毕竟，伙计，你举足轻重，你犹犹豫豫以至于在一个讲英语的寺庙里去相信你被告知的一切，我真是弄不明白你为何对每一件事都欣然接受，仅仅是由于你置身西藏？！"

康维点点头，即使心里很明白，他也无法忍住去赞同一个精辟的观点，"这是一个非常敏锐的评论，马林逊。我觉得真理便是在毫无实际证据的条件下相信事物，我们全都倾向于我们所发现的东西是最具吸引力的。"

"那么，倘若在你半死不活之前，我能够看到关于生存的任何具有吸引力的东西，算我见鬼了。如果让我做选择，给我短暂而又快乐的一生就好。那些关于未来战争的东西对我而言，听起来非常空洞。一个人怎么会晓得下场战争何时爆发，或者将会是如何呢？所有关于上一场战争的预言不都是错的吗？"康维没有作答，马林逊补充道："总之，我都不会相信所谓事情是必然的说法。而且即使真是必然的，我们也没有必要为此乱作一团。天知道，倘若我不得不参加战斗，我最可能被吓死，但比起在这里

Conway smiled. "Mallinson, you have a superb knack of misunderstanding me. When we were at Baskul you thought I was a hero – now you take me for a coward. In point of fact, I'm neither – though of course it doesn't matter. When you get back to India you can tell people, if you like, that I decided to stay in a Tibetan monastery because I was afraid there'd be another war. It isn't my reason at all, but I've no doubt it'll be believed by the people who already think me mad."

Mallinson answered rather sadly: "It's silly, you know, to talk like that. Whatever happens, I'd never say a word against you. You can count on that. I don't understand you – I admit that – but – but – I wish I did. Oh, I wish I did. Conway, can't I possibly help you? Isn't there anything I can say or do?"

There was a long silence after that, which Conway broke at last by saying: "There's just a question I'd like to ask – if you'll forgive me for being terribly personal."

"Yes?"

"Are you in love with Lo-Tsen?"

The youth's pallor changed quickly to a flush. "I dare say I am. I know you'll say it's absurd and unthinkable, and probably it is, but I can't help my feelings."

"I don't think it's absurd at all."

The argument seemed to have sailed into a harbor after many buffetings, and

埋没我自己，我更愿意面对战争。"

康维微微一笑："马林逊，你真有绝招来误解我。当我们在巴斯库时，你觉得我是个英雄，但此时你将我视为一个懦夫。实际上，我两者都不是，当然了，尽管这并没什么关系。如果你愿意，当你返回印度时，你可以告诉人们我决定留在一个西藏寺庙中，因为我担心另一场战争将会发生。可那根本不是我的理由，但我丝毫不怀疑，那些觉得我疯了的人们会这种相信说法。"

马林逊相当悲伤地回答道："那太愚蠢了，你知道，像那样说你。无论发生什么，我永远不会说伤害你的话，你完全要相信这点。我不能理解你，我承认。但，但我希望我能。哦，我希望我能。康维，我不能帮你吗？没有任何事情是我能说或者能做的吗？"

随后便是一片长久的寂静，最终康维开口打破了沉默："只有一个问题我希望问问你——你会宽恕我这种非常无礼的行为吧？"

"可以。"

"你是爱上罗珍了吗？"

那个年轻人惨白的脸迅速变为一片绯红，"我敢说我是的。我清楚你会说这是荒诞不经又不可思议的，也许真是如此，但我无法抑制我的感情呀，"

"我根本没觉得这荒诞不经。"

Conway added: "I can't help *my* feelings either. You and that girl happen to be the two people in the world I care most about… though you may think it odd of me." Abruptly he got up and paced the room. "We've said all we *can* say, haven't we?"

"Yes, I suppose we have." But Mallinson went on, in a sudden rush of eagerness. "Oh, what stupid nonsense it all is – about her not being young! And foul and horrible nonsense, too. Conway, you *can't* believe it! It's just too ridiculous. How can it really mean anything?"

"How can you really know that she's young?"

Mallinson half-turned away, his face lit with a grave shyness. "Because I *do* know… Perhaps you'll think less of me for it… but *I* do know. I'm afraid you never properly understood her, Conway. She was cold on the surface, but that was the result of living here – it had frozen all the warmth. But the warmth was there."

"To be unfrozen?"

"Yes… that would be one way of putting it."

"And she's *young,* Mallinson – you are so *sure* of that?"

Mallinson answered softly: "God, yes – she's just a girl. I was terribly sorry for her, and we were both attracted, I suppose. I don't see that it's anything to be ashamed of. In fact in a place like this I should

这种争论在来回颠簸后似乎渐渐驶进了港湾。康维补充道:"我也无法抑制我的感情呀!而你和那个女孩碰巧是世界上我最为在意的两个人,尽管你可能觉得我非常古怪。"突然间,他站起身来在屋子里踱步,"我们已经说了我们能说的一切了,不是吗?"

"没错,我认为是这样。"马林逊以一种突然涌现的急切之情继续说,"哦,所有这些都是愚蠢的废话,关于她不再年轻的说法,也是愚蠢又恐怖的胡言乱语。康维,你不能相信啊!这太荒唐可笑了。它如何能够真的代表任何东西呢?"

"你又如何当真清楚她还年轻呢?"

马林逊半扭过身,脸上呈现出一种羞怯之态:"因为我确实清楚……也许对此你想的比我少…但我确实清楚…恐怕你从来不曾适度地理解她,康维,她表面冷若冰霜,但那是在这里生活的结果,这里将全部的热情冰冻了。但她的热情还在。"

"她的热情将要解冻了吗?"

"没错,可以这么说。"

"她还很年轻,马林逊,你对此这么确定?"

马林逊温柔地回答道:"上帝,没错,她就是个小女孩。我为她深感遗憾,我认为我们两个人彼此吸引。我不觉得这有任何值得害羞的地方。其实,在类似这样一个地方

think it's about the decentest thing that's ever happened…"

Conway went to the balcony and gazed at the dazzling plume of Karakal; the moon was riding high in a waveless ocean. It came to him that a dream had dissolved, like all too lovely things, at the first touch of reality; that the whole world's future, weighed in the balance against youth and love, would be light as air. And he knew, too, that his mind dwelt in a world of its own, Shangri-La in microcosm, and that this world also was in peril. For even as he nerved himself, he saw the corridors of his imagination twist and strain under impact; the pavilions were toppling; all was about to be in ruins. He was only partly unhappy, but he was infinitely and rather sadly perplexed. He did not know whether he had been mad and was now sane, or had been sane for a time and now mad again.

When he turned, there was a difference in him; his voice was keener, almost brusque, and his face twitched a little; he looked much more the Conway who had been a hero at Baskul. Clenched for action, he faced Mallinson with a sudden new alertness. "Do you think you could manage that tricky bit with a rope if I were with you?" he asked.

Mallinson sprang forward. "*Conway!*" he cried chokingly. "You mean you'll *come?* You've made up your mind at

我觉得这大概是曾经发生过的最正当不过的事……"

康维来到阳台上,凝视着熠熠生辉的卡拉卡尔山的雾霭,月亮高高地升起在一片风平浪静的海洋上。他突然感到一个美梦已经慢慢消散,仿佛所有太过可爱的东西第一次触及现实时便会消失一样,整个世界的未来将会用青春以及爱的天平来衡量,它将会轻如空气。而他也清楚,在自己的世界里驻扎的他那灵魂已经成为香格里拉的缩影,而这个世界也置身危险当中。因为正当他令自己鼓起勇气时,他看到他那想象的通路在猛烈的冲击下已经变得扭曲不堪,那些亭台楼阁已经摇摇欲坠,所有这一切都会幻化为一片废墟。他只是有几分不开心,可他觉得自己正忧伤地不知所措。他不知道他是否已经疯了,还是头脑清醒;要不就是已经清醒了一段时间,而现在再次疯了。

当他转过身后,他便不一样了;他的声音更为尖厉,几乎就是粗鲁;他的脸有点扭曲,他看起来远远胜于在巴斯库曾经是个英雄的康维。为了付诸行动,他咬紧牙关,以一种突然出现的全新的机警神情面对着马林逊。"倘若我和你一起走,你觉得你能设法略施小计,弄根绳子来吗?"他问道。

马林逊迅速跳了起来。"康维!"他哽咽着大喊道,"你的意思

last?"

They left as soon as Conway had prepared himself for the journey. It was surprisingly simple to leave – a departure rather than an escape; there were no incidents as they crossed the bars of moonlight and shadow in the courtyards. One might have thought there was no one there at all, Conway reflected; and immediately the idea of such emptiness became an emptiness in himself; while all the time, though he hardly heard him, Mallinson was chattering about the journey. How strange that their long argument should have ended thus in action, that this secret sanctuary should be forsaken by one who had found in it such happiness! For indeed, less than an hour later, they halted breathlessly at a curve of the track and saw the last of Shangri-La. Deep below them the valley of Blue Moon was like a cloud, and to Conway the scattered roofs had a look of floating after him through the haze. Now, at that moment, it was farewell. Mallinson, whom the steep ascent had kept silent for a time, gasped out: "Good man, we're doing fine – carry on!"

Conway smiled, but did not reply; he was already preparing the rope for the knife-edge traverse. It was true, as the youth had said, that he had made up his mind; but it was only what was left of his

是你会走吗？你最终下定决心了？"

当康维一为旅程准备好，他们便离开。这次离开是出奇地简单，与其说逃跑，倒不如说是离开；当他们穿过月光中的横木障碍物以及院落中的阴影时，没有任何意外发生。平常人可能会认为这里根本没有任何人，康维仔细思考着，但这样的空虚感立刻就变成了内心的一片空白。同时，马林逊始终都在对于旅程絮絮叨叨，尽管他很难听进去。他们那长长的争论在行动中就这样结束了，这是多么奇怪啊，这座神秘的圣殿应该被它如此愉悦的发现者所抛弃！的确，不到一小时之后，他们在一条通路的拐角处气喘吁吁地停了下来，最后看了看香格里拉。他们下面那深邃的蓝月谷仿佛一朵浮云，对康维而言，那些星罗棋布的屋顶，穿过一片朦胧，呈现出一幅漂浮般的模样追随着他。现在，在这个时刻，是该告别了！而马林逊被陡峭的上坡路弄得沉默了好长一段时间，大口喘着气说道："好伙计，我们干得不错，继续！"

康维微微一笑，但没有回答；他已经在为翻过刀削一样的横断山崖而准备绳索。这是真的，就像那个小伙子所说的那样，他已经下定了决心，但这仅仅是他那内心中

mind. That small and active fragment now dominated; the rest comprised an absence hardly to be endured. He was a wanderer between two worlds and must ever wander; but for the present, in a deepening inward void, all he felt was that he liked Mallinson and must help him; he was doomed, like millions, to flee from wisdom and be a hero.

Mallinson was nervous at the precipice, but Conway got him over in traditional mountaineering fashion, and when the trial was past, they leaned together over Mallinson's cigarettes. "Conway, I must say it's damned good of you… Perhaps you guess how I feel… I can't tell you how glad I am…"

"I wouldn't try, then, if I were you."

After a long pause, and before they resumed the journey, Mallinson added: "But I *am* glad – not only for my own sake, but for yours as well… It's fine that you can realize now that all that stuff was sheer nonsense… it's just wonderful to see you your real self again…"

"Not at all," responded Conway, with a wryness that was for his own private comforting.

Towards dawn they crossed the divide, unchallenged by sentinels, even if there were any; though it occurred to Conway that the route, in the true spirit, might only be moderately well watched. Presently they reached the plateau, picked clean as a

所剩下的东西；那渺小而又活跃的片段现在主宰着他，而其余的则构成了难以忍受的空虚。他是在两个世界当中的游荡者，必须永远游荡下去；但现在，在一种逐渐加深的内在空虚里，他能感觉到的全部便是他喜欢马林逊，而且必须得帮助他；就像成千上万的人一样，他命中注定要逃离智慧而去成为一个英雄。

马林逊对于攀登悬崖非常紧张，但康维用传统的登山方法帮他翻了过去，当最严酷的部分过去时，他们倚靠在一起，吸着马林逊的香烟，"康维，我必须说你真是太好了！可能你能猜出我什么感觉，我无法告诉你我有多高兴……"

"倘若我是你，那么我便不会去尝试。"

长长地停顿过后，在他们重新上路之前，马林逊补充道："但我很开心，不仅为我自己，也是为了你，现在你能够意识到全部的那些东西纯属一派胡言，这真是太棒了，能够看到你重新成为真实的你，简直太不同凡响了！"

"一点也不。"康维回应道，用一种出于他个人安慰的扭曲表情。

直到黎明，他们翻越了山岭，即使那里有任何岗哨，他们也顺利通过。尽管对康维来说，这条路在真实的情况下，只能被适度地看

bone by roaring winds, and after a gradual descent the encampment of porters came in sight. Then all was as Mallinson had foretold; they found the men ready for them, sturdy fellows in furs and sheepskins, crouching under the gale and eager to begin the journey to Tatsien-Fu – eleven hundred miles eastward on the China border.

"He's coming with us!" Mallinson cried excitedly when they met Lo-Tsen. He forgot that she knew no English; but Conway translated.

It seemed to him that the little Manchu had never looked so radiant. She gave him a most charming smile, but her eyes were all for the boy.

守着。不久，他们便抵达了高地，被呼啸的大风吹得像一根干净的骨头，在一个缓和的下坡之后，脚夫的营地已进入眼帘。然后所有的情况都像先前说的那样，他们发现那些人已经为他们准备好了，这些身着裘皮还有羊皮、身材强壮的家伙们，在寒风中蜷缩着，都渴望着开始前往向东 1100 英里之外在中国边境线上的稻城府（四川省稻城县）的旅程了。

"他与我们一起走！"当他们看到罗珍时，马林逊便兴奋地大叫道。他忘了她不懂英语；但康维翻译了一下。

对他而言，这满族小姑娘似乎从来不曾看起来如此容光焕发。她给予他最为迷人的笑容，但她的眼里全是都是马林逊那小伙子。

EPILOGUE

尾声

IT was in Delhi that I met Rutherford again. We had been guests at a Viceregal dinner-party, but distance and ceremonial kept us apart until the turbaned flunkeys handed us our hats afterwards. "Come back to my hotel and have a drink," he invited.

We shared a cab along the arid miles between the Lutyens still-life and the warm, palpitating motion picture of Old Delhi. I knew from the newspapers that he had just returned from Kashgar. His was one of those well-groomed reputations that get the most out of everything; any unusual holiday acquires the character of an exploration, and though the explorer takes care to do nothing really original, the public does not know this, and he capitalizes the full value of a hasty impression. It had not seemed to me, for instance, that Rutherford's journey, as reported in the press, had been particularly epoch-making; the buried cities of Khotan were old stuff, if anyone remembered Stein and Sven Hedin. I knew Rutherford well enough to chaff him about this, and he laughed. "Yes, the truth would have made a better story," he admitted

在德里我再次碰见了卢瑟福。我们都是总督晚宴的客人。但座次和一些礼节，一直将我俩分隔开，直到随后戴头巾的侍从将礼帽递给我们时，我俩才凑到一起。"到我的旅馆去喝一杯吧。"他邀请我。

我们一同搭出租车在鲁丁恩斯镇的一片恬静以及老德里城区那温暖又令人心悸的动态图画中，沉闷地沿途经过了数英里。我从报纸上得知他刚刚从喀什返回，他是那种对待个人声誉非常小心的人，将每一件事情都处理得最为妥当；任何一次不同寻常的假期总是需要一种探险的特质，尽管这位探险者对于本来的度假要去做什么完全不在意，公众对此也不清楚，然后他便充分利用这种匆忙印象的价值。举个例子，卢瑟福的这次旅行，就像媒体报道的那样，具有特殊的划时代意义；被埋没的霍尔丹古城已经是陈年旧物了，倘若有任何人还记得苏丹以及西文·海定的话。我对卢瑟福相当了解，以至于拿此和他开玩笑。然后他哈哈大笑："是的，事实的真相应该是去编一个更好的故事。"他隐隐约约地承认了

cryptically.

We went to his hotel room and drank whisky. "So you *did* search for Conway?" I suggested when the moment seemed propitious.

"Search is much too strong a word," he answered. "You can't search a country half as big as Europe for one man. All I can say is that I have visited places where I was prepared to come across him or to get news of him. His last message, you remember, was that he had left Bangkok for the northwest. There were traces of him up-country for a little way, and my own opinion is that he probably made for the tribal districts on the Chinese border. I don't think he'd have cared to enter Burma, where he might have run up against British officials. Anyhow, the definite trail, you may say, peters out somewhere in Upper Siam, but of course I never expected to follow it that far."

"You thought it might be easier to look for the valley of Blue Moon?"

"Well, it did seem as if it might be a more fixed proposition. I suppose you glanced at that manuscript of mine?"

"Much more than glanced at it. I should have returned it, by the way, but you left no address."

Rutherford nodded. "I wonder what you made of it?"

"I thought it very remarkable –

这点。

我们进入他的房间，喝了些威士忌。"如此说来，你去寻找康维了？"当机会合适时，我暗示他。

"寻找是个过于强烈的字眼，"他回答道，"你无法在一个与半个欧洲差不多大的国家里去找到一个人，我能说的就是，我拜访了我打算会碰到他，或者能得到关于他消息的所有地方。他最后的消息，你记得吧，就是他已经离开曼谷前往西北方向了。有一点关于他的迹象表明他去了北方的国家。而我自己的观点是，他也许设法前往中国边境上的那些少数民族地区了。我觉得他不喜欢进入缅甸，在那里他可能会遇到一些英国官员，总之，在泰国北部的某个地方，他的踪迹逐渐消失了。当然，我从来不期盼着要追踪到如此远的地方去。"

"你认为也许发现蓝月亮谷会更容易一些吗？"

"那么，这似乎会是个更为确定的问题了，我猜想你已经浏览过我的那份手稿了？"

"何止浏览，我原本应当已经寄回给你了，但你没留下任何地址。"

卢瑟福点点头，"我在猜你会怎么评论？"

"我认为这非常不同寻常，有

assuming, of course, that it's all quite genuinely based on what Conway told you."

"I give you my solemn word for that. I invented nothing at all – indeed, there's even less of my own language in it than you might think. I've got a good memory, and Conway always had a way of describing things. Don't forget that we had about twenty-four hours of practically continuous talk."

"Well, as I said, it's all very remarkable."

He leaned back and smiled. "If that's all you're going to say, I can see I shall have to speak for myself. I suppose you consider me a rather credulous person. I don't really think I am. People make mistakes in life through believing too much, but they have a damned dull time if they believe too little. I was certainly taken with Conway's story – in more ways than one – and that was why I felt interested enough to put as many tabs on it as I could – apart from the chance of running up against the man himself."

He went on, after lighting a cigar. "It meant a good deal of odd journeying, but I like that sort of thing, and my publishers can't object to a travel book once in a while. Altogether I must have done some thousands of miles – Baskul, Bangkok, Chung-Kiang, Kashgar – I visited them

点桀骜不驯。当然，这完全是相当真实地基于康维告诉你的那些东西的评价。"

"我可以庄严地宣誓，我完全没有臆造什么——真的，其中我自己的语言甚至比你能够想到的还要少，我记忆力很不错，而康维描述事情也总有自己的方式。不要忘记，事实上，我们有一场大概 24 小时的连续谈话。"

"那么，就像我所说的，这稿子真的是非常不同寻常。"

他向后倚着，微微一笑，"倘若这便是你准备说的一切，那我觉得我必须为自己说几句。我猜你觉得我是一个相当容易轻信别人的人，但我真的觉得我不是。在生活中，人们由于相信太多而犯错误，但如果他们相信的太少，他们便会过着相当单调的日子。我肯定以更多的方式，相信康维的故事，这便是我为什么感到这么有兴趣，以至于会尽可能将它以尽量多的细节呈现出来，先不说是否有机会偶然遇到他本人了。"

他点上一支烟之后，继续说到："它意味着许许多多古怪的旅行，可我喜欢这类东西。而且我的出版商偶尔也会出一本游记。总而言之，我一定已经周游了好几千英里，巴斯库、曼谷、重庆、喀什，所有的地方我都去过了，那个神秘

all, and somewhere inside the area between them the mystery lies. But it's a pretty big area, you know, and all my investigations didn't touch more than the fringe of it – or of the mystery either, for that matter. Indeed, if you want the actual downright facts about Conway's adventures, so far as I've been able to verify them, all I can tell you is that he left Baskul on the twentieth of May and arrived in Chung-Kiang on the fifth of October. And the last we know of him is that he left Bangkok again on the third of February. All the rest is probability, possibility, guesswork, myth, legend, whatever you like to call it."

"So you didn't find anything in Tibet?"

"My dear fellow, I never got into Tibet at all. The people up at Government House wouldn't hear of it; it's as much as they'll do to sanction an Everest expedition, and when I said I thought of wandering about the Kuen-Luns on my own, they looked at me rather as if I'd suggested writing a life of Gandhi. As a matter of fact, they knew more than I did. Strolling about Tibet isn't a one-man job; it needs an expedition properly fitted out and run by someone who knows at least a word or two of the language. I remember when Conway was telling me his story I kept wondering why there was all that fuss about waiting for porters – why didn't

之处便位于它们当中区域里的某个地方。但你清楚，这是个相当大的区域。对于此事，我全部的调查都不曾触及比它的边缘更多的地方，要不就是连那个谜的边缘都不曾触及。的确，如果你想要关于康维冒险经历的完全真实的材料，迄今为止，我能够证实的部分，我全部能够告诉你：他在去年 5 月 20 日离开巴斯库，在 10 月 5 日抵达重庆，而最后我们了解到他的情况就是在今年 2 月 3 日他再次离开曼谷。其余的全部就是或许、可能、猜测、神话、传奇，你喜欢怎么称呼都可以。"

"你在西藏没发现任何东西？"

"我亲爱的朋友，我从来没有去过西藏。那些高坐在政府部门交椅上的人们不理睬我的请求。这就与让他们去批准到埃菲尔士峰探险差不多。当我说我想独自去昆仑山地区游览一番时，他们望着我就仿佛我打算去夺取甘地的生命一般。其实，他们知道的比我多，在西藏跋山涉水不是一个人的工作，那需要一支适当装备的探险队，还要由一个最少了解一两门当地语言的向导带领。我记得当康维正在给我讲述他的故事时，我一直在想为什么所有这些小题大做的人要等脚夫呢，为什么他们不简单地自

they simply walk off? I wasn't very long in discovering. The government people were quite right – all the passports in the world couldn't have got me over the Kuen-Luns. I actually went as far as seeing them in the distance, on a very clear day – perhaps fifty miles off. Not many Europeans can claim even that."

"Are they so very forbidding?"

"They looked just like a white frieze on the horizon, that was all. At Yarkand and Kashgar I questioned everyone I met about them, but it was extraordinary how little I could discover. I should think they must be the least-explored range in the world. I had the luck to meet an American traveler who had once tried to cross them, but he'd been unable to find a pass. There *are* passes, he said, but they're terrifically high and unmapped. I asked him if he thought it possible for a valley to exist of the kind Conway described, and he said he wouldn't call it impossible, but he thought it not very likely – on geological grounds, at any rate. Then I asked if he had ever heard of a cone-shaped mountain almost as high as the highest of the Himalayas, and his answer to that was rather intriguing. There was a legend, he said, about such a mountain, but he thought himself there could be no foundation for it. There were even rumors, he added, about mountains actually higher than

己走？没用太长时间，我便发现了。那些政府官员是相当正确的，世界上所有的护照都不能让我进入昆仑山地区。事实上，我已经到了能够在远处看到这列山脉的地方了，那是一个非常晴朗的白天，也许是在 50 英里以外的地方。有多少欧洲人能得到我这样的机会？"

"那些山峰真的是如此让人难以亲近吗？"

"它们看起来就像地平线上耸起的白色绒毛而已，关于它们，我在雅坎德和喀什问了我遇见的每一个人，但非同寻常的是，我没能发现一点儿线索，我觉得它们肯定是世界上最人迹罕至的山脉了。我有幸遇见一位曾经尝试要翻越这些山脉的美国旅行家，但他没能找到一个关口，他说这里确实有一些关口，可它们都非常高，地图上并未标注，我问他是否认为有可能存在一个类似康维所描述的那样的一个山谷。他说也许有可能，可他觉得在地质结构上又不太可能。然后我又问他是否曾经听说过一座与喜马拉雅山的最高峰一样高的锥形山峰，他对此问题的回答也相当有迷惑性。他说的确存在一个关于这座山的传说，可他自己觉得那没有什么根据可言；甚至存在一些谣传，他补充道，谣传说有座山其实比埃菲尔主峰（珠穆朗玛）还

Everest, but he didn't himself give credit to them. 'I doubt if any peak in the Kuen-Luns is more than twenty-five thousand feet, if that,' he said. But he admitted that they had never been properly surveyed.

"Then I asked him what he knew about Tibetan lamaseries – he'd been in the country several times – and he gave me just the usual accounts that one can read in all the books. They weren't beautiful places, he assured me, and the monks in them were generally corrupt and dirty. 'Do they live long?' I asked, and he said, yes, they often did, if they didn't die of some filthy disease. Then I went boldly to the point and asked if he'd ever heard legends of extreme longevity among the lamas. 'Heaps of them,' he answered: 'it's one of the stock yarns you hear everywhere, but you can't verify them. You're told that some foul-looking creature has been walled up in a cell for a hundred years, and he certainly looks as if he might have been, but of course you can't demand his birth certificate.' I asked him if he thought they had any occult or medicinal way of prolonging life or preserving youth, and he said they were supposed to have a great deal of very curious knowledge about such things, but he suspected that if you came to look into it, it was rather like the Indian rope trick – always something that

要高，可他自己并不相信这些谣传。'我怀疑在喀拉昆仑山区一带是否会有山峰高于2500英尺。'他说。可他承认它们从来不曾被准确测量过。

"然后我问他知道些什么关于藏族喇嘛寺的——他去过那里很多次了，但他给我说的就是那些我们能够从所有书籍里读到的寻常东西。他对我保证那些喇嘛寺不是多漂亮的地方，其中的僧侣们通常都很腐化又肮脏。'他们能活很久吗？'我问道。他说是的，他们经常活得很久，如果他们并非死于某些污秽的疾病的话。然后我大着胆子转到一个问题上，问他是不是曾经听过在喇嘛当中有长生不老的传说。'有很多，'他回答道，'它是一类你可以在每一个地方都听到的普通奇谈，可你不能证实它们。你被告知某个愚蠢模样的家伙被塞进一个密室里长达100年，他肯定看起来就像他之前的样子，但当然，你不能去索要他的出生证件了。'我问他是否觉得他们有任何超自然的能量，或者能延长生命或者永葆青春的药物手段，他猜测说他们对于这类事情会有很多非常奇特的知识，可他怀疑如果你去仔细观察，它可能就只是类似印度人玩的那种绳线把戏而已，总是有其他人曾经看到的一些东西，但他说

somebody else had seen. He did say, however, that the lamas appeared to have odd powers of bodily control. 'I've watched them,' he said, 'sitting by the edge of a frozen lake, stark naked, with a temperature below zero and in a tearing wind, while their servants break the ice and wrap sheets round them that have been dipped in the water. They do this a dozen times or more, and the lamas dry the sheets on their own bodies. Keeping warm by will-power, so one imagines, though that's a poor sort of explanation.'"

Rutherford helped himself to more drink. "But of course, as my American friend admitted, all that had nothing much to do with longevity. It merely showed that the lamas had somber tastes in self-discipline... So there we were, and probably you'll agree with me that all the evidence, so far, was less than you'd hang a dog on."

I said it was certainly inconclusive, and asked if the names "Karakal" and "Shangri-La" had meant anything to the American.

"Not a thing – I tried him with them. After I'd gone on questioning him for a time, he said: 'Frankly, I'm not keen on monasteries – indeed, I once told a fellow I met in Tibet that if I went out of my way at all, it would be to avoid them, not pay them a visit.' That chance remark of his

喇嘛似乎具备一种控制躯体的奇异能量。'我看见过他们,'他说,'他们赤身裸体地坐在冰冻的湖边,在零度以下的气温中,置身于刺骨的寒风里。同时,他们的仆人破开冰面,用在水里浸过的单被裹在他们身上,他们十几次或更多次地做这件事,喇嘛用自己的身体将被单烘干,凭借意志力来保持温暖,所以你可以想象了吧,尽管这是一种很牵强的解释。'"

卢瑟福给自己添了更多的酒,"但当然,就像我这位美国朋友已经承认的那样,所有一切和长寿没有太多的关系,它只是表明喇嘛在自我修炼时有一些令人郁闷的品味而已……所以说了这么多,可能你会同意,我所有的这些证据迄今为止还是不怎么能够说明问题。"

我说这肯定是尚未有定论的,并询问道"卡拉卡尔"和"香格里拉"这两个名称对美国人而言,是否有任何意义。

"完全没有——我试着问过他这两个名字,有一次,当我一直问他这个问题后。他说:'坦白讲,我对寺庙僧院之类的并不热衷,的确,我曾经告诉过我在西藏碰到的一个家伙,倘若能不碰见那些寺庙,我肯定会避开,更不去拜访它

gave me a curious idea, and I asked him when this meeting in Tibet had taken place. 'Oh, a long time ago,' he answered, 'before the War – in nineteen-eleven, I think it was.' I badgered him for further details, and he gave them, as well as he could remember. It seemed that he'd been traveling then for some American geographical society, with several colleagues, porters, and so on – in fact, a pukka expedition. Somewhere near the Kuen-Luns he met this other man, a Chinese who was being carried in a chair by native bearers. The fellow turned out to speak English quite well, and strongly recommended them to visit a certain lamasery in the neighborhood – he even offered to be the guide there. The American said they hadn't time and weren't interested, and that was that." Rutherford went on, after an interval: "I don't suggest that it means a great deal. When a man tries to remember a casual incident that happened twenty years ago, you can't build *too* much on it. But it offers an attractive speculation."

"Yes, though if a well-equipped expedition had accepted the invitation, I don't see how they could have been detained at the lamasery against their will."

"Oh, quite. And perhaps it wasn't Shangri-La at all."

们。'他的一席话碰巧使我产生了一个古怪的念头，我问他在西藏这次碰面是何时发生的。'哦，很久之前'，他回答道，'在战前，我觉得应该是在 1911 年……'我迫使他说进一步的细节，然后他就将他能够记起来的部分和盘托出，似乎那时他一直与一些同事还有脚夫为一些美国地理社团做旅行考察——其实，那完全是一次探险远足。在昆仑山附近的某个地方他碰到了另一个人，是个汉族人，他一直坐在由当地轿夫抬着的轿子里，结果这家伙英语竟然说得相当不错，然后他极力推荐他们去拜访在附近的某个喇嘛寺，他甚至提出要亲自作为向导带他们过去。那美国人说他们没有时间，而且也不感兴趣，就是这么回事。"隔了一段时间之后，卢瑟福继续说，"我不是说这具有很重大的意义，当一个人试着对 20 年前发生的一个偶然事件回忆时，你不能在其基础上拓展得太多，可它毕竟还是提供了一个相当吸引人的揣测。"

"是的，但倘若一个装备精良的探险队接受了邀请，我也无法看出来他们如何能够在违背他们意愿的情况下，被困在那个喇嘛寺中。"

"哦，完全正确。而且也许它根本就不是香格里拉。"

We thought it over, but it seemed too hazy for argument, and I went on to ask if there had been any discoveries at Baskul.

"Baskul was hopeless, and Peshawar was worse. Nobody could tell me anything, except that the kidnaping of the aeroplane did undoubtedly take place. They weren't keen even to admit that – it's an episode they're not proud of."

"And nothing was heard of the plane afterwards?"

"Not a word or a rumor, or of its four passengers either. I verified, however, that it was capable of climbing high enough to cross the ranges. I also tried to trace that fellow Barnard, but I found his past history so mysterious that I wouldn't be at all surprised if he really were Chalmers Bryant, as Conway said. After all, Bryant's complete disappearance in the midst of the big hue and cry was rather amazing."

"Did you try to find anything about the actual kidnaper?"

"I did. But again it was hopeless. The Air Force man whom the fellow had knocked out and impersonated had since been killed, so one promising line of enquiry was closed. I even wrote to a friend of mine in America who runs an aviation school, asking if he had had any Tibetan pupils lately, but his reply was prompt and disappointing. He said he couldn't differentiate Tibetans from

我们思前想后，但还是似乎太过模糊，以至于我们无法去争执。然后我继续询问在巴斯库地区是否有任何线索。

"巴斯库是毫无希望的，白沙瓦就更糟糕了，没有一个人能够告诉我任何情况，除了那次劫持飞机的事毋庸置疑地发生了以外，他们甚至不愿意承认那件事，这并非让他们自豪。"

"后来便没有听到那架飞机的任何消息了吗？"

"一个字都没有，或者谣言，或者关于那4名乘客，全都没有。但我证实了那飞机确实能飞得足够高，越过那些山脉，我也尝试着跟踪巴纳德，但我发现他的过往是如此神秘，以至于倘若他果真如康维所言，是查麦斯·伯利雅特的话，我完全不惊讶。毕竟，伯利雅特在那一片大喊大叫声中的彻底消失，也相当令人惊奇。"

"你试着去找关于那个劫机犯的任何情况了吗？"

"我试了，但还是没有什么希望。那个被劫机犯击倒、毫无知觉的飞行员后来也死了。于是，一条很有希望的询问线索也断了。我甚至给我在美国经营一家航空学校的一位朋友写了封信，问他最近是否有任何西藏的学员，但他的回答非常迅速也很令人失望。他说他无法从中国人里辨认出藏族人，而且

Chinese, and he had had about fifty of the latter – all training to fight the Japs. Not much chance there, you see. But I did make one rather quaint discovery – and which I could have made just as easily without leaving London. There was a German professor at Jena about the middle of the last century who took to globe-trotting and visited Tibet in 1887. He never came back, and there was some story about him having been drowned in fording a river. His name was Friedrich Meister."

"Good heavens – one of the names Conway mentioned!"

"Yes – though it may only have been coincidence. It doesn't prove the whole story, by any means, because the Jena fellow was born in 1845. Nothing very exciting about that."

"But it's odd," I said.

"Oh, yes, it's odd enough."

"Did you succeed in tracing any of the others?"

"No. It's a pity I hadn't a longer list to work on. I couldn't find any record of a pupil of Chopin's called Briac, though of course that doesn't prove that there wasn't one. Conway was pretty sparing with his names, when you come to think about it – out of fifty-odd lamas supposed to be on the premises he only gave us one or two. Perrault and Henschell, by the way,

他曾经教过大约 50 个中国人，全部是为抗击日本人而来进行培训的，你看，那里也没什么机会。但我的确有一个相当离奇而有趣的发现，而且我非常轻松，不用出伦敦便能发现。大约上世纪中期，有一个德国耶拿的教授进行了一次环球徒步旅行，然后在 1887 年拜访了西藏，他再也没有回来过。当时有关于他在涉水时溺水而亡的传言。他的名字叫弗伦德利克·梅斯特。"

"谢天谢地，这是一个康维提及过的名字。"

"没错，但可能仅仅是一种巧合而已，它无法证明整个故事的真实性，无论如何，因为那个耶拿人生在 1845 年，所以也没有什么非常令人兴奋的。"

"但这也很奇怪啊！"我说。

"哦，是的，足够奇怪了。"

"你成功追踪了其他的任何人吗？"

"没有，我没有一个更长的名单去研究，这是一个遗憾。虽然我无法找到那位名叫布里亚克的肖邦的学生的任何记录。当然也不能证明就不存在这个人。康维仅仅就提了这几个人的名字，你思考一下，假定前提是五十多个喇嘛，他仅仅对我们提了一两个。顺便说一下，佩劳尔特还有亭斯齐尔，他们

proved equally impossible to trace."

"How about Mallinson?" I asked. "Did you try to find out what happened to him? And that girl – the Chinese girl?"

"My dear fellow, of course I did. The awkward part was, as you perhaps gathered from the manuscript, that Conway's story ended at the moment of leaving the valley with the porters. After that he either couldn't or wouldn't tell what happened – perhaps he might have done, mind you, if there'd been more time. I feel that we can guess at some sort of tragedy. The hardships of the journey would be perfectly appalling, apart from the risk of brigandage or even treachery among their own escorting party. Probably we shall never know exactly what did occur, but it seems tolerably certain that Mallinson never reached China. I made all sorts of enquiries, you know. First of all I tried to trace details of books, et cetera, sent in large consignments across the Tibetan frontier, but at all the likely places, such as Shanghai and Pekin, I drew complete blanks. That, of course, doesn't count for much, since the lamas would doubtless see that their methods of importation were kept secret. Then I tried at Tatsien-Fu. It's a weird place, a sort of world's-end market town, deuced difficult to get at, where the Chinese coolies from Yunnan transfer their loads of tea to the

被证明是完全不可能去调查的。"

"马林逊又如何呢？"我问道，"你试着去弄清他又发生了什么事了吗？而那个姑娘呢，那个中国女孩？"

"我亲爱的伙计，我当然试过了，令人尴尬的部分就是，也许就像你从书稿里得出的结论那样，康维的故事在他们与那些脚夫一同离开山谷那一刻便结束了，从那以后他既不能，也不愿意告诉我发生了什么——如果有更多的时间，他可能会这么做的。我感觉我们能够猜到某些这类的悲剧。旅行的艰难是非常骇人听闻的，除去强盗抢劫的危险，甚至陪同他们的一伙人自己也会背信弃义。我们可能永远无法确切弄清出现了什么情况。但似乎有一点还算过得去，即马林逊从来不曾抵达中国。你清楚我做了全面的寻访调查，首先我竭尽全力地追溯了书籍以及其他的细节，然后寄了大量的委托信到西藏边境以及类似上海、北京之类的所有可能之地。但我完全没得到任何消息。当然，那也起不到多少作用，因为，毋庸置疑，那些喇嘛知道他们运输物品的途径是保密的。然后，我试着到了稻城府。那是一个不可思议之地，仿佛世界尽头中的一类集镇，非常难以到达。来自云南的汉族脚夫们在这里将他们运载的茶叶转给藏族人。关于这点，你能够

Tibetans. You can read about it in my new book when it comes out. Europeans don't often get as far. I found the people quite civil and courteous, but there was absolutely no record of Conway's party arriving at all."

"So how Conway himself reached Chung-Kiang is still unexplained?"

"The only conclusion is that he wandered there, just as he might have wandered anywhere else. Anyhow, we're back in the realm of hard facts when we get to Chung-Kiang, that's something. The nuns at the mission hospital were genuine enough, and so, for that matter, was Sieveking's excitement on the ship when Conway played that pseudo-Chopin." Rutherford paused and then added reflectively: "It's really an exercise in the balancing of probabilities, and I must say the scales don't bump very emphatically either way. Of course if you don't accept Conway's story, it means that you doubt either his veracity or his sanity – one may as well be frank."

He paused again, as if inviting a comment, and I said: "As you know, I never saw him after the War, but people said he was a good deal changed by it."

Rutherford answered: "Yes, and he was, there's no denying the fact. You can't subject a mere boy to three years of intense physical and emotional stress

在我的新书出版时读到。欧洲人不经常到这么遥远的地方去。我发现那里的人们相当文明、有礼貌，可这里完全没有康维一群人曾经到过的迹象。"

"那么，康维自己如何到的重庆依然无法解释？"

"唯一的结论便是他流落到了那里。就类似他可能流落到别的任何地方一样。总之，当我们抵达重庆时，又置身于这些难事困扰的局面当中。因此，在教会医院的那些修女们也足够真诚了。"那么，关于那件事，就是在船上，当康维弹奏肖邦的练习曲时清上近素的兴奋之情，"卢瑟福停顿下来，然后沉思着补充道，"这当真是一个平衡各种可能性的练习，而且，我必须说平衡不会非常明显地偏向任何一方。当然倘若你不接受康维的故事，那就代表着你要么怀疑他的诚实，要么怀疑他的神智，一个人可能也是坦诚的。"

他再次停顿下来，好像是邀我来评论。于是我说道："就像你清楚的那样，战后我再也没看到他，可有人说他被战争改变了很多。"

卢瑟福回答道："是的，他改变了很多，这不能否认，你不能令只不过还是一个孩子的人在承受3年强烈的身体以及精神的压力后

without tearing something to tatters. People would say, I suppose, that he came through without a scratch. But the scratches were there – on the inside."

We talked for a little time about the war and its effects on various people, and at length he went on: "But there's just one more point that I must mention – and perhaps in some ways the oddest of all. It came out during my enquiries at the mission. They all did their best for me there, as you can guess, but they couldn't recollect much, especially as they'd been so busy with a fever epidemic at the time. One of the questions I put was about the manner Conway had reached the hospital first of all – whether he had presented himself alone, or had been found ill and been taken there by someone else. They couldn't exactly remember – after all, it was a long while back – but suddenly, when I was on the point of giving up the cross-examination, one of the nuns remarked quite casually, 'I think the doctor said he was brought here by a woman.' That was all she could tell me, and as the doctor himself had left the mission, there was no confirmation to be had on the spot.

"But having got so far, I wasn't in any mood to give up. It appeared that the doctor had gone to a bigger hospital in Shanghai, so I took the trouble to get his

而不去将一些东西撕成碎片。我觉得，人们会说他都没受什么伤便挨过来了，但他的创伤在那里……在内心深处。"

我们就战争及其对不同人的影响又聊了一会儿，最后他继续说："但我必须仅仅再提一点，并且也许要以某些最古怪的方式来说。我在教会做询问调查期间得到了这一点。就像你能够猜测的那样，他们那里的所有人为我竭尽全力，但他们无法回忆起多少，特别是他们在那会儿正非常忙碌地处理一位患伤寒的病人。首先，我提出的问题之一便是关于康维抵达医院的方式，他是否是自己一个人来的，或者是被其他的什么人发现他病了，然后被送到医院来的？可是，他们都无法确切地回忆起来，毕竟已经过去很长时间了，但突然，当我准备交互讯问时，其中一个修女非常随意地说了一句：'我觉得医生曾经说过他是被一个女的带到医院来的。'这是她能告诉我的全部，而因为那个医生已经离开了教会医院，可以在那里也没有得到进一步的证实。

"但已经走了如此之远，我不想放弃！似乎这个医生前往了上海一家更大的医院，于是我克服困难得到了他的地址，然后便去上海拜

address and call on him there. It was just after the Jap air-raiding, and things were pretty grim. I'd met the man before during my first visit to Chung-Kiang, and he was very polite, though terribly overworked – yes, terribly's the word, for, believe me, the air-raids on London by the Germans were just nothing to what the Japs did to the native parts of Shanghai. Oh, yes, he said instantly, he remembered the case of the Englishman who had lost his memory. Was it true he had been brought to the mission hospital by a woman? I asked. Oh, yes, certainly, by a woman, a Chinese woman. Did he remember anything about her? Nothing, he answered, except that she had been ill of the fever herself, and had died almost immediately… Just then there was an interruption – a batch of wounded were carried in and packed on stretchers in the corridors – the wards were all full – and I didn't care to go on taking up the man's time, especially as the thudding of the guns at Woosung was a reminder that he would still have plenty to do. When he came back to me, looking quite cheerful even amidst such ghastliness, I just asked him one final question, and I daresay you can guess what it was. 'About that Chinese woman,' I said. 'Was she young?'"

Rutherford flicked his cigar as if the narration had excited him quite as much as

访他。那是在日军的空袭刚过去之后，整个城市都是一片狼藉。我之前在第一次到重庆去期间，与这个人见过面，尽管他相当忙碌，但依然非常礼貌地见了我。没错，话又说回来，相信我，德军对伦敦的空袭与日本人对上海本土部分的所作所为相比根本就不算什么。哦，没错，他立刻便说他记得那个已经丧失了记忆的英国人；'你被一个妇女带到教会医院来是真的吗？'我问。'哦，是的，当然，被一个女人带来的，一个汉族妇女。''对于那个女人，你记得任何情况吗？''记不得了，'他回答道，'只记得她自己也患有伤寒病，而且几乎是马上便死了……'然后我们便被打断了，有一大堆伤员被抬了进来，然后将走廊里的担架挤得满满当当，病房全都满了，我也不想继续占用那位医生的时间，特别是吴淞那儿震耳欲聋的枪声像是提醒着他仍然有很多的事要去做。当他又回到我这里时，他看起来相当振奋，即使是在如此惊恐的气氛当中。我仅仅问了他最后一个问题，我敢说你能够猜出来是什么。'关于那个汉族女人，我说，她年轻吗？'"

卢瑟福弹了弹烟头，这个故事令他兴奋的程度与他所希望的故

he hoped it had me. Continuing, he said: "The little fellow looked at me solemnly for a moment, and then answered in that funny clipped English that the educated Chinese have – 'Oh, no, she was most old – most old of anyone I have ever seen.'"

We sat for a long time in silence, and then talked again of Conway as I remembered him, boyish and gifted and full of charm, and of the war that had altered him, and of so many mysteries of time and age and of the mind, and of the little Manchu who had been "most old," and of the strange ultimate dream of Blue Moon.

"Do you think he will ever find it?" I asked.

事令我兴奋的程度完全差不多。他继续说道:"那个身材矮小的家伙很严肃地望了我一会儿,然后以一种受过良好教育的中国人所具有的流利又清晰地英语回答道——'哦,不,她很老了,比我曾经见过的任何人都老。'"

我们在一片沉寂中坐了很长时间。后来,我们再次聊起康维,如同我记忆里他的模样,一脸稚气、才华横溢又充满魅力。然后又聊到那场改变了他的战争,还有关于时间、年龄以及思维的诸多神秘之事。还有那位变得年老的满族小姑娘以及那奇异又无法企及的蓝月亮之梦。

"你觉得他会找到香格里拉吗?"我问道。

(完)

中英对照全译本系列书目表

英国文学卷

《简爱》

《傲慢与偏见》

《理智与情感》

《爱玛》

《金银岛》

《呼啸山庄》

《双城记》

《雾都孤儿》

《柳林风声》

《鲁滨逊漂流记》

《一九八四 动物庄园》

《爱伦·坡短篇小说选》

《福尔摩斯经典探案集 血字的研究 四签名》

《福尔摩斯经典探案集 巴斯克维尔的猎犬 恐怖谷》

《福尔摩斯经典探案集 福尔摩斯历险记》

《福尔摩斯经典探案集 福尔摩斯回忆录》

《福尔摩斯经典探案集 福尔摩斯归来记》

《福尔摩斯经典探案集 最后的致意》

《福尔摩斯经典探案集 福尔摩斯新探案集》

《德伯家的苔丝》

《培根散文集》

《格列佛游记》

《道林·格雷的画像》

《消失的地平线》

美国文学卷

《红字》

《小妇人》

《伟大的盖茨比》

《瓦尔登湖》

《房龙地理》

《纯真年代》

《秘密花园》

《嘉莉妹妹》

《人类的故事》

《老人与海》

《太阳照常升起》

《乞力马扎罗的雪 海明威短篇小说选》

《哈克贝利·费恩历险记》

《马克·吐温短篇小说选集》

《汤姆·索亚历险记》

《欧·亨利短篇小说选集》

《本杰明·富兰克林自传》

《杰克·伦敦小说选 野性的呼唤 海狼》

《小公主》

《永别了，武器》

《丧钟为谁而鸣》

《包法利夫人》

《海底两万里》

《木偶奇遇记》

《爱的教育》

《地心游记》

《八十天环游地球》

《少年维特之烦恼》

《名人传》

《变色龙 契诃夫短篇小说选》

其他文学卷

《绿山墙的安妮》

《尼尔斯骑鹅旅行记》

《尼尔斯骑鹅旅行记：续集》

《泰戈尔诗歌集 新月集&飞鸟集》

欧洲文学卷

《茶花女》

《高老头》

《欧也妮·葛朗台》